FOLLOW POLLY'S LANE

A NOVEL

To Joan:
you can't
unscramble
an egg.

YVONNE VAN LANKVELD

Follow Polly's Lane
Copyright © 2025 by Yvonne Van Lankveld

All rights reserved. No part of this publication may be reproduced, distributed, or transmitted in any form or by any means, including photocopying, recording, or other electronic or mechanical methods, without the prior written permission of the author, except in the case of brief quotations embodied in critical reviews and certain other non-commercial uses permitted by copyright law.

Cover image of Lake Erie and the Point Abino lighthouse courtesy of Brad Wood Photography, Port Colborne, Ontario

Tellwell Talent
www.tellwell.ca

ISBN
978-1-83418-521-7 (Hardcover)
978-1-83418-520-0 (Paperback)
978-1-83418-522-4 (eBook)

The same boiling point that softens the potato hardens the egg.
It's about what you're made of, not the circumstances.

Author Unknown

This novel is dedicated to the incredible health care providers I have had the honour of working with, who understood the intrinsic and extrinsic needs of the heart, and gave until there was nothing left. While none are represented here, many are deeply rooted in my memory, some long after they were gone.

All of the characters and settings within this novel are a work of fiction, as is Polly's Lane and New Abino, however, Point Abino and its historic lighthouse is real. Much of the Niagara River meanders from Lake Erie to Lake Ontario, dividing Canada and the United States. Like Polly's Lane, tiny roadways run off main roads and end at either lake. While most belong to the local municipalities, a few private roads are still maintained at the collective discretion of their owners.

Other Works

The Road to Alright (2019, 2nd edit. 2022)

The Park Street Secrets (2022, 2nd edit., 2023)

PROLOGUE

The Development of Polly's Lane

Polly's Lane is a private dead-end road built one hundred years ago, and located fifteen minutes from New Abino, a small hamlet near Point Abino, Ontario, Canada. It is half a kilometre, or a quarter mile long and provides access to three grand but dilapidated seasonal manors that face Lake Erie. The two homes closest to the main road sit on one-acre lots. The last and oldest, a three-acre estate, ends where a protected forest begins, with deer, fox and small rodents roaming freely. Polly's Lane was officially titled and the properties numbered Lot 1, 2, and 3 (with green reflective signs) only after emergency vehicles, responding to a party brawl, couldn't find it.

Originally from New York, the Polly family built first on what is now known as Lot 3, at the dead-end of the gravel lane. Patrick Polly, the only known descendant with a current phone number, lost interest in the tired manor about the same time his third wife divorced him.

The Hope family immigrated to Atlanta, Georgia, from Canada decades ago when Frederick, the family patriarch, earned his first million. The Hopes returned to spend summers on Polly's Lane until their other vacation homes became more inviting. Sadly, their Lot 2 property fell into disrepair.

Scott Reese from New York was the least wealthy, but most committed to preventing his aging manse on Lot 1 from resembling those of his neighbours. Situated closest to the main road, its many previous owners left a hodgepodge of unfinished upgrades and, after squabbling with his contractor over staggering costs, he did the same.

A very distant relative of the Polly family, known to everyone as Cousin Al, remained in the area after a revolving summer romance ended. He lovingly maintained these properties well into his seventies, until the Polly's Lane people couldn't, or wouldn't, pay his paltry salary.

Each lakefront property has a two-bedroom bunkie, situated close to the lane. Historically, the bunkies accommodated seasonal help, overflow guests, or were used for storage. While the main homes, landscaping and docks have been neglected for years, their bunkies still house tenants.

THE RESIDENTS OF POLLY'S LANE

Nurse Sonnet O'Brien rented the Reese bunkie four years ago after Stan, her husband, left her the year before. A friend of a friend of a co-worker connected them - Scott Reese was as eager to rent it out as Sonnet was to hide there from Stan. Her initial plan, when she could afford better, was to return to Niagara Falls, but the longer she stayed, the more the lake consoled her, especially after a gruelling shift. It also reminded her of her Irish childhood, where the salty sea and a few tin cans kept Sonnet and her two brothers occupied for hours.

Fletcher Hope moved into the Hope bunkie after he was deported from the United States when the president made good on his campaign promise and sent convicted criminals who were not citizens back to their country of origin. Two burly federal immigration officers delivered him back to Canada; with nowhere to go, the Hopes parked him in the bunkie and supported him until things got sorted out. That was two years ago.

Reba Adler, almost fifty, had her son Digger when she was fifteen and relocated to Ontario from Nova Scotia, mostly to forget their past. Cousin Al met Reba at the New Abino diner where she worked and connected her to Patrick Polly two years ago; he gladly rented out his bunkie. It was a win-win arrangement.

After Fletcher left his dinner on his property's decomposing dock, a stray dog discovered it. A lab mix, minus collar and tags, became a regular consumer of handouts on the lane. He eventually learned to respond to three names: Rufus (popular with saints and singers), Tucker, and Useless. Over time, he became the lane's self-appointed security detail.

NOVEMBER 1ˢᵀ

Sonnet O'Brien
(on the hospital's long-term care unit)
3:15 PM

Sonnet plopped her bony, sixty-year-old bottom down on the black vinyl chair in her supervisor's office. The skin behind her face mask was soaked from sweat. She pushed her fist gently into her breastbone, hoping the T-shirt beneath her scrubs would absorb the moisture pooling there. She had hustled to finish her tasks before her day shift ended and hand off her patient load to the afternoon staff, determined not to be late for the meeting with her supervisor. Still, the chair behind the tiny desk across from her remained vacant, even though Sonnet arrived on time. Instead of the physical and mental demands of her day easing away, she grew more agitated, unsure why this meeting had been called.

Sonnet transferred to chronic care from the cancer floor three months ago; she had witnessed too many young lives, on the cusp of independence, die there. Death in long-term care was more predictable. All old people died. It completed their circle of life, and she knew death long before she became a nurse.

Balancing an open laptop in the palm of her hand, Roberta rushed into her small office, followed closely by her director. Sonnet gave the director her chair while Candace, Sonnet's union representative, lingered outside, then entered last. Squeezing four people into this converted storage closet was like setting a hot oven on broil. Union involvement usually meant trouble, and Sonnet had no idea what kind of trouble she was in. She looked at Candace, who shrugged her shoulders and, by the confused exchange of frowns, neither knew what today's agenda was.

"Can I have a word with Sonnet?" Candace asked.

"Sure," snipped Roberta, "but please be quick." Candace and Roberta knew the exact wording that entitled staff to union representation. Roberta had no choice but to let them talk. She was a follow-the-rules supervisor, with no flexibility in bending them. Sonnet trailed Candace into a slightly larger supply room.

"Any idea of what this is about?" asked Candace.

"None."

"When was the meeting called?"

"Two days ago."

"You should have told me," Candace bristled, furiously scratching her scalp.

"I didn't think it was important."

"It's important when both your supervisor and director are present."

"I didn't know the director was attending."

"So, there's nothing even remotely concerning to you?"

"Nothing. I come to work. I do my job. I give the best care I can. Sometimes I stay late and sit with those who have no family. I go home, return on my next shift, and repeat." Sonnet's shoulders sagged from the weight of her explanation.

"And do you submit for overtime if you stay late?"

"You and I both know that doesn't happen without pre-approval."

"Huh. Well, let's go see what's got these two bosses all fired up today."

Not suspecting something serious was amiss until now, Sonnet followed Candace back to the sweltering cubicle. Roberta straightened her posture and tugged at her lab coat while Candace shut the door. Both supervisor and director remained seated in the cramped space, twisting awkwardly to look up at Sonnet and Candace.

"Sonnet, thanks for coming in," Roberta started. "We'll get right to the point. I asked to meet with you because I'm concerned about the inordinate amount of time that you're spending on the unit after your shift ends."

Sonnet's jaw went slack.

"Are you fu—, are you kidding me?" Candace blurted out.

The director glared at the union rep, who glared at Roberta, who pursed her lips into a thin line.

Sonnet remained silent, uninterested in Roberta and Candace volleying quotes from the Respectful Code of Conduct policy.

"Excuse me, but I have to use the washroom," Sonnet said quietly, opening the door.

"This won't take long," Roberta said.

"I'm sorry, but I need to use the washroom," she repeated, desperately short of breath.

"Are you denying her the right to use the washroom?" Candace hissed.

Sonnet stood up, unable to grasp the words swirling around her, and left as the remaining women exchanged accusations.

Sonnet walked down the cluttered hallway, passing the patient rooms she had floated in and out of today and many workdays in the last three months. She heard Mr. Cutler call her name as she walked by his door. Most patients, or at least those with minds still attached to a memory, knew she always responded when they called. Some had reasons with a good cause; others just wanted to feel a warm hand on theirs or share a story she'd already heard before. Sonnet hesitated, then returned to Mr. Cutler.

"Honey, you look so tired today," he sighed. His wiry eyebrow hairs made him look scruffier than usual.

"It's been a long day." She took his right hand and squeezed it gently, noticing him wince, then rubbing his left eye with his free hand. Leaning in, she spotted a wayward eyebrow hair extending into his eyelashes. "Does your eye feel scratchy?"

He nodded. "Like something's in it."

"I think I can fix that." She walked back to the supply room and returned, opening a sterilized suture removal kit containing tweezers and scissors. "Would you mind if I trimmed your eyebrows a little bit?"

"Sure ... the last time someone prettied them up was just before I went dancing," he chuckled and patted his stumps, legs lost to diabetic complications.

Mr. Cutler remained still and listened to his nurse hum softly while trimming his eyebrows. Sonnet tried to block out the meeting she'd just abandoned, calmly progressing to clip away stray ear and nose hairs. Healthcare aides shaved his beard when they had time, but time and energy were scarce. Sonnet slid her stethoscope off her neck, inserted her earpieces and rotated the flat base around his chest. She knew his arrhythmias well; the extra minute they shared was more important to both.

"There you go. Now you can go dancing," she said, pulling her soaked mask down long enough to force a smile. His clean linen and disinfectant scent told her his bottom didn't need changing.

Sonnet returned the scissor kit and continued down the hall, heading away from her meeting and toward the exit sign. She was almost at the door when Candace caught up with her.

"Where are you going?" she barked.

"To my locker."

"What for? You left ten minutes ago to use the washroom."

Sonnet ignored her and kept walking.

"Sonnet! Stop!"

"Why?"

Candace's eyes grew wide with frustration over Sonnet's unexplained behaviour. "Where did you go?"

"A patient needed me."

"You've already finished your shift. What's the matter with you? You're making the rest of us look bad for hanging around."

Sonnet swallowed her answer, rather than voicing it, as the union rep followed her downstairs to the locker room. It stunk like a hockey bag camouflaged with cologne and fabric softener. Still waiting for an explanation, Candace watched Sonnet empty her locker into two fabric shopping bags, throw her worn sneakers in the garbage bin and slide her feet into a slightly newer pair.

"What the hell are you doing?"

Sonnet exhaled heavily, hoisted the shopping bags over her good shoulder and left her locker open; someone else would occupy it soon and need the laminated instructions for the safe use of personal protective equipment taped to its door. Candace slumped down onto the wooden bench in the middle of the room.

"Sonnet. Look at me. What's wrong with you?"

Sonnet peeled off her soiled mask, flushed cheeks and blank stare failing to register with Candace.

"Whatever Roberta's issue is with you, we can file a grievance. But you have to stop playing the martyr."

Sonnet shut her eyes tightly and rubbed the itchy skin around them so hard that it burned, deeply offended by Candace's comment. Martyrs sacrificed life itself for the sake of freedom. Sonnet made many sacrifices, but she was not a martyr. Still, it was easier to avoid speaking than defend herself. Nurses were leaving their profession in droves. Some fled during the pandemic, while others stayed until they felt less remorse for abandoning their peers. Now Sonnet had hit that proverbial wall, realizing she could no longer be a good nurse. She had given and given, and there was no more left in her to give. She felt a sharp stab in her gut, radiating right and around her back, blaming it on having only enough time to eat two bites of her sandwich.

Leaving Candace sitting on the bench, Sonnet hurried through an underground tunnel, exiting to the hospital's outdoor parking lot. Winter was creeping up. Approaching her car, Sonnet was reminded that her worn tires needed replacing. But not today, her only goal was to get herself home. As her old white SUV came to life, she let it idle, then shifted into drive.

Swiping her employee pass card across the scanner until the parking lot gate lifted, she exited and merged into the traffic on the street. Her phone rang. She glanced at the lit screen displaying the hospital's number, then returned it unanswered to the side pocket of her scrubs. It didn't matter. She wasn't coming back.

It rang twice more during her half-hour drive home to New Abino. She navigated her car around the ruts and washed-out edges of Polly's Lane until she pulled into what remained of a gravel driveway to the right of her bunkie, beside Fletcher's place. Sonnet knew little about him other than that he was privileged and rotting away from doing nothing. She also found that when Fletcher swam in the lake during summer, his visual myriads of hero and villain tattoos repulsed her.

Like his, her little place needed painting, among other things, none of which the tenants or owners had any desire to do.

She unlocked her bunkie door, slid her heavy purse off her shoulder and dropped it on the kitchen table. She shed her coat and shoes, opened the fridge and gulped the last bit of orange juice from its carton. She put the container in the sink and shuffled to the living room, layered with months of clutter and dust. Easing down onto her shabby, floral sofa, she massaged her aching feet, then stretched out and propped two lumpy pillows under her head. She silenced her phone, ringing yet again. Too tired to check if her door was locked, she buried herself under her old duvet and immediately fell asleep.

Fletcher Hope
(Lot 2: middle bunkie)
4:30 PM

Ten minutes earlier, Fletcher checked his phone screen when he heard Sonnet's car roll into her driveway, located to the left of his bunkie. She was late getting home and rarely slammed her car door like she did today.

Even though Fletcher Hope didn't choose his surname, it couldn't have represented him better. Born into a family full of hopes and dreams, somehow his never came to fruition. Before moving to the lane and after his stint in jail for a stupid mistake, he lived in a world of debauched behaviours. How he kept his jobs for as long as he did was even beyond his own reasoning. With each one he lost, his mother always persuaded Frederick, his father, to support him until somehow, and somewhere, he managed to land another. With Fletcher's familial influence, he had many chances others would not have been offered, but his misguided intelligence always bombed the opportunity.

While Fletcher's family still lived in Canada, he attended a notable college in the United States on a football scholarship. When a knee injury sidelined him during his last year, he limped through the last quarter of his football and academic career. A failure to graduate would negatively impact not only the school's prestigious reputation of producing high-calibre athletes, but his father's substantial donations as well. Football and the Hope family's financial holdings were Fletcher's most influential social currency. He was not an elite athlete, and players on competing teams knew it. Yet, he was well-liked by his teammates, coaches and sports medicine professionals who babysat him through low-risk practices and cleared him to play in the final game. This culminated in his final injury, ironically not during the game, but from being at the bottom of a victory pile-up of his teammates.

Fletcher squeaked through final exams with only a passing grade and many repeats of the narcotic that he depended on. Living pain-free made life easy. Sometimes he consumed too many pills and beer, went where he shouldn't go, and in the company he shouldn't keep. Weekends led to weeks of excess, promiscuous sex, and all kinds of happenings. Prescriptions and poor judgment caught up with him years later when police identified him on some old and unrelated old security footage. He was fired from his job and incarcerated. His sentence included addiction treatment in an upscale facility, funded by his father. Once discharged from rehab, he was deported back to Canada.

When Fletcher returned to Polly's Lane two years ago, he learned that being alone wasn't so bad, at least most of the time. Memories of family summers weathered with the manor's cedar shakes. Already needing extensive repairs, it became uninhabitable after Fletcher forgot to shut the water off when the lake froze, causing the pipes to burst. He simply moved to the bunkie and, other than the manor reminding him of his mistake, Fletcher was quite content. A monthly allowance included fuel for his crotch-rocket motorcycle, usable only in good weather. He laid low in the cold months, fixated on his screens. A beautiful girl from the Korean take-out restaurant often delivered meals, provisions and herself for the night. Online shopping met all his other needs, and he adjusted nicely to it.

Fletcher generally ignored his neighbours despite their proximity. He learned their names and habits by peeking through their windows when they were gone. He snooped through their mail when it was delivered to the three dilapidated boxes labelled *1, 2* and *3*; barely upright and supporting each other, they marked the sloped entrance to Polly's Lane from the main road.

Reba Adler, and Digger
(Lot 3: the end of the lane)
5:30 PM

Reba was a damn good server at the New Abino Diner, better known as the Winer Diner because of its owner, Ziggy Winerowski. Reba and Ziggy didn't particularly care for each other, but he needed Reba as much as she needed the work. She loved the familiar faces, the smell of coffee and all-day breakfasts, just like at her grandmother's house. Black and white checkered floor tiles clashed with colourful vintage metal-edged Formica tables. Mismatched chairs and dishes blended beautifully with the mismatched diners.

Reba called the regular guys 'honey' and gifted lusty looks to those whose eyes danced with the excitement they had lost at home. She took orders accurately and conveyed them to the kitchen staff. She handled food safely and calculated the correct change from a secret pocket in her frilly apron. She rarely spread gossip, which kept the regulars coming back. She ignored the luring invites of transient men and never took them personally. She was also perceptive, knowing what her regulars wanted to eat before they did. She knew who stopped at two cups of coffee and worried about the drinkers heading home. She gently curfewed them after a few beers, reminding them to get home before supper was on the table, or they'd all be in trouble. That's why everyone loved Reba.

Reba's mother didn't fancy her mother's name, Rebecca, but like Nana Becca, Reba was oblivious to her captivating beauty. Her skin was fair, her eyes bright green, and at forty-nine, her hair was still a luxurious copper. Reba's name meant "fourth born." She was indeed the fourth, demanding more of her mother's attention as a child back in Nova Scotia than her five brothers combined. Restless and bucking her share of chores, she also created enough chaos at her rural school that her teachers passed her along to the next grade to avoid having her in their classroom twice.

Reba also exasperated her father, so when she turned fourteen, he found her a job at the grocery store when summer came and prayed for calm, with Reba occupied during the day. Her quick wit and emerald eyes caught the attention of everyone in the store, especially the boys who worked there.

Gilbert, better known as Gil, was no exception. At sixteen, he already had a year of experience behind him. He was organized, charming and efficient at rotating the produce to minimize waste. He was more responsible than the other teens, helped his single mother pay the bills and, like Reba, was often sent home at day's end with stale-dated food to feed the family. He arrived before sunrise on his boss's days off to unload deliveries at the back entrance, but while one teenager was responsible, two often meant trouble.

Gil was as handsome as he was horny. A distinct advantage of unlocking the back door was being alone for an hour before the others clocked in. Reba discovered that when her father dropped her off early one day. To the pair, it was like exploring school before it opened. Their first idle moments were spent sharing a shelf-stocking stool in the candy aisle. On their second encounter, Gil planted a kiss on Reba's full lips at some point between the bakery and frozen food deliveries. Kissing led to touching, which led to having sex against the lumpy sacks of potatoes at the back of the warehouse. By summer's end, their withdrawal method of birth control proved ineffective, and Reba was pregnant. She lasted in school until Christmas, when rumours that Reba was "knocked up" were visually confirmed.

Gil refused to take responsibility for fatherhood for many reasons, both good and bad. He didn't have the financial means to support a new family and help his single mother. He needed to maintain his marks and athletic prowess to earn the university scholarship he was being groomed for. And, because the other stock-boys bragged about enjoying an occasional 'quickie' with Reba, they all absolved themselves of getting Reba pregnant.

Minimizing humiliation, Reba's parents hustled her off to live with Nana Becca in a nearby seaside community. Little Digby, nicknamed Digger, entered their world, complicated by a low birth weight, shortly after Reba turned fifteen.

Penny, an empathic public health nurse with experience in teen pregnancies and their associated risks, came loaded with wisdom and maternal instincts to offer Reba at Digby's well-baby visits. It was Penny who listened to Reba's recount of the terrifying birth and the hospital staff insinuating that she was adding to the burdened social welfare system. Penny also noted that as Digger grew, his developmental milestones lagged behind the normal timelines. When she gently shared her observations with Reba, the naïve teen vowed she'd never conceive again, let alone create another Digger. The uncertainty of their combined future terrified her.

Penny scheduled visits with Reba at the end of the day to allow for extra time. They talked about postpartum depression, new motherhood and, most importantly, birth control. She listened patiently to Reba's limited knowledge about making babies and how it was God's will to conceive and give every blessed child a good life. With these chats, Reba realized why her parents had six children, regardless of the economic consequences, and that her and Digger's chances of returning to her cramped family's home were slim to none.

Penny continued to visit Reba long after her well-baby program obligations ended. She kept Reba supplied with contraceptives and reassurance that what her family didn't know wouldn't hurt them. Once Digger started sleeping through the night, Reba found work as a server at a fish-and-chip place, which conveniently opened at dinnertime. This left Nana Becca feeding little Digger his supper and bedtime bottle. Because Nana and the baby's bedtime was about the same, this arrangement suited everyone, especially Reba. Penny scaled back her visits but remained a phone call away, so when Reba picked up chlamydia from a chance encounter with the short-order cook, Penny took her to the nurse practitioner at the sexual health clinic, who interpreted the lab results and reminded Reba that the best peckers always came wrapped. She was restocked with a fine assortment of condoms and advice from these women, whom she affectionately called her 'other mothers.' Even though it happened long ago, those smart, confident mentors never made her feel she was anything less.

Today, Reba picked Digger up from his job at New Abino Groceries & More after her shift at the diner, but for whatever reason, forgot to give Ziggy, both the diner owner and only cook, Mr. Bennett's standard 'burger, no onions and fries' order. This happened rarely, but it did, and twice within three weeks. Or, at least, twice that she was reminded.

Digger squeezed his tall, masculine frame into their cramped blue Toyota and, as Reba ground the stick shift into drive, Digger sensed something was amiss.

"You okay, Mom?"

"I'm good. You okay, Digger?"

"I'm good too."

"Okay, then." But both, restless and fearing dread, knew that all was not right.

The fifteen-minute commute home to their bunkie at the lane's dead-end was mostly quiet. Digger hoped his mother wouldn't miss the overgrown entrance off the main road like she did last week. It was already dark when Reba slowed the car to a crawl and carefully turned into the lane. Cousin Al had long stopped coming around to trim the trees encroaching on the narrow road. Maybe Reba would ask him the next time he ate breakfast at the diner if he'd lend her his chainsaw in exchange for a few meals. It wasn't something Digger could do because noise and vibration overwhelmed him or, worse, might cause him to have a seizure. His only episode, prompted by flashing strobe lighting at a carnival when he was thirteen, was one too many. That and the follow-up medical appointments still haunted both mother and son.

Reba's immediate challenge was to inch forward between the tree limbs and avoid the potholes eroding what remained of the lane's asphalt. Instinctively, she and Digger moved their heads in unison as if to dodge the branches. They also raised their shoulders, even though it did nothing to prevent the car from bottoming out.

They passed Sonnet's darkened bunkie. Her car was home, and this was unusual. They drove a few hundred feet more, heads dodging and shoulders shrugging as they crawled past the amber glow of lights, not only in Fletcher's bunkie but the same rooms in the big manor that he'd left on three nights ago. The road wasn't as rough between

Fletcher's bunkie and theirs, but the overgrowth there was the densest. On cue, Reba stopped the car; Digger got out and shut his door, then hoisted a tree limb high enough for her to pass. Digger walked the last fifty feet, allowing Reba to squeeze her car into the clearing with just enough space to park and open one door. She popped open the trunk, and Digger hoisted out an old blue milk crate loaded with their dinner.

Once inside, Reba removed the containers and portioned their meal onto plates. Tonight's Winer Diner feature was Digger's favourite—meatloaf and mashed potatoes. His contribution from the grocery store's hot deli was Asian stir-fried veggies, something Ziggy never made. Most of the meatloaf landed on Digger's plate; Reba preferred more veggies. She added five little packets of ketchup that Digger habitually used to criss-cross red lines on his potatoes. Dinner was hot, delicious, and consumed while watching the news on TV. Reba then washed the dishes, Digger dried them, and put them away in time for both to return to their armchairs for *Wheel of Fortune*. He loved to watch contestants spin the wheel as much as he loved trying to solve the puzzles.

Digger and Reba Adler came as a package deal, so if you didn't want one, you weren't entitled to the other. Because Digger was rarely accepted for who and what he was, male mentors were scarce. For that reason, Reba avoided long-term relationships. With all his little quirks, as she called them, he grew up with her being his only advocate and cheerleader.

Like his maternal ancestry, Digger had fair skin, emerald eyes and thick waves of copper hair. He looked nothing like his father. Reba called Gil a 'good for nothing son of a bitch' more often than she called him by name, so there was little incentive for Digger to ask about him or, worse, attempt to contact him.

To the Adlers, Ontario was a world away from Nova Scotia. Sometimes, they were gifted small amounts of cash from family. There were occasional phone calls and, very rarely, visits, for which the usual motive was for relatives to see Niagara Falls. Reba and Digger were the sideshows. Calls from Nova Scotia were preceded by, "Hello, Digger, how's the job going," and then, "Is your mother home?" Even when his mother answered, once whoever was calling got beyond the niceties, who died and who was in trouble, it always ended with, "Love you and talk soon." After the novelty of the phone wore off, Digger left the business of communication to his mother.

Besides protecting Digger, Reba tried to maintain a cheerful home. Following a small dose of the daily news, they watched travel, comedies and game shows. She often said, "Nobody needs to be miserable unless they deserve it," and according to Reba, neither Adler did.

Digger was named Digby because Reba hoped he'd be strong like an old Norseman. While growing up, he struggled with his mind, yet his appearance was that of a normal boy. Even after Penny, the nurse, planted the seed that he was unique, it took Reba time to process the signs. He didn't speak until age four. Reba's mother said the same thing about her, but with so many brothers, there was always someone else to do the talking for her.

When Digger started school, his challenges grew. He struggled with naming things, colours, and shapes. He mixed up sounds and the order of the alphabet. She grew frustrated by his inability to manage zippers, tie his shoes or hold a pencil straight. When Reba and his teacher had a standoff over Digger's jagged printing, his teacher all but ignored him for the rest of the year.

The following year, it became clear to Reba that Digger was unable, as opposed to unwilling, to learn to read and write. With limited resources at Digger's rural school, he was relegated to the library for the last hour of most days. A young mother volunteered to work with him while her own little ones played nearby. They shared healthy snacks with him, but his biggest reward was their kindness and respect.

Digger's masculine features grew to represent his name, and as his body matured, so did the obstacles he faced. Entering high school, he was assigned to a regular class. Students converging from a half-dozen elementary schools were funnelled into one high school, so statistically, five of six hormonal teens had no idea who he was or what made him different. He shot up to a lean height of over six feet by Thanksgiving, making him a prime recruit for the basketball team. "Coach" knew everything about shooting three-pointers, practice drills and keeping the boys sequestered from the girls in gym class, but knew nothing about Digger. When Reba was contacted about him trying out for the team, she insisted that Coach come to her house alone, so they could have a little chat.

Coach wasn't sure what Reba had in mind, but he arrived freshly showered and ready for whatever the becoming Reba was willing to offer. She sat him down at her small kitchen table, dressed in her snug, red-and-white work uniform. Coach found that very appealing, and based on past experiences, it didn't take Reba long to realize his agenda differed from hers. She bent forward, allowing him a little look at what he wouldn't get to fondle, and recited the speech she rehearsed in her head long before he and his charm arrived.

Reba explained Digger's "invisible disability" to Coach, who had never trained a student like him before.

"Digger has many personality traits that do him well."

"Like what? Can you name a few?" Coach half-listened, half-confused, but totally in awe of her cleavage and emerald eyes. She named some of Digger's characteristics and then explained her circumstances.

"I work hard to pay the bills and support him. He eats more than a horse."

"Well, I can't help you with that."

"I know that, but because I work, I can't always get him to where he needs to be, that is, if you still want him to play."

"That part we can help you with."

"So, you can guarantee to get him to and from practice and games on the days I can't?"

"We sure can."

"Safely?" In his mind, Coach sized up his recruit's sprouting stature, envisioning a winning season.

"Of course."

So, near the end of the meeting, she moved closer and gave Coach a scented whiff and a long peek, followed by a stern warning. If he treated Digger with respect, defended him for who and what he was, and, oh, one more thing, protected him from the bullies she knew he would face, she was agreeable to Digger trying out. Both parties recognized this as a tall order, and Reba suggested he take a long weekend to think about it. As she showed him the door, Reba gently patted Coach on the backside, leaving him thoroughly befuddled about what was yet to come, not only with Digger but with his mother as well.

When Digger was made, or rather, was placed on the basketball team, he was the tallest teen in the school. An arrangement was already made for him to skip class to attend practice, and as usual, his teachers were more than happy to let him go. Working with Digger soon overwhelmed Coach, but Reba's warning not to cast her son aside stuck. With a measure of guilt, Coach enlisted the help of his assistant coach, affectionately known as AC. AC was a tenured teacher and the school's guidance counsellor. After observing Digger struggle through simple drills, AC felt certain that Digger could play a modified guard position. If Coach lowered his expectations and planted Digger near the net, Digger could adapt to that role of catching passes from his teammates and shooting the ball through the hoop.

In the 1994 movie *Forrest Gump*, the lead character's incredible running ability on his football team was not hindered by his disorder, but then, Digger was not Forrest Gump. He was not on the autism spectrum, as Forrest was, and AC sensed that. But unlike Forrest, Digger's disability was never formally identified. AC's job as a guidance counsellor was to help students sort through their academic and social challenges, a role AC took very seriously. When Coach handed Digger off to him, it compelled AC to help him beyond the game of basketball.

When AC asked to meet with Reba and Digger on the gym bleachers after practice, Reba braced for another insult. She sat straight up beside Digger, ready to shield him. AC's middle girth was round and soft under his well-worn T-shirt, damp with old sweat and spaghetti splatter from lunch. His black sneakers matched his shorts, complete with frayed edges.

It took a few sentences to allow Reba to let her guard down and believe that AC did not have the same self-serving intention as Coach. Reba watched Digger as Digger watched AC, who appeared to be genuinely drawn to him.

As AC slowly and simply explained his reason for the meeting, neither Digger nor his mother felt threatened. AC spoke about his observations as Reba nervously picked at the clumps of discarded gum under her seat. He believed Digger was intelligent, and hearing this comment, Reba furrowed her brow and leaned in; the words "Digger" and "intelligent" had never been married into the same sentence. She moved closer to Digger while AC, sitting two bleachers lower, looked up to face them. Excluding his physical stature, most people looked down on Digger and Reba, by association, as his single parent.

AC also suggested something Reba already knew. Digger's educators took the path of least resistance by moving him up the academic line because few took the time to know Digger and his learning capabilities. He explained that finding out how Digger's brain worked may help him and those close to him.

AC asked if the term "dyslexia" meant anything to Reba or Digger. Neither had heard it before. It didn't frighten Digger, mainly because Reba wasn't afraid, but AC's next statement did. He said Digger could be examined by a neuropsychologist, another foreign word to the Adlers. The sides of Reba's head started to prickle as she struggled to listen. AC explained that the school had access to an expert who could do some testing with Digger. AC immediately read the panic on their faces and paused, recognizing it from other families. When Digger's shoulders relaxed and the lines on Reba's forehead loosened, he continued. He said Digger *and* Reba were the most important people in this picture, much more important than basketball. AC was merely the vehicle to get Digger some help, but only if they thought it had value. Simply worded, consent wouldn't happen unless they both understood his offer. Either could change their mind at any time, no questions asked. AC's eyes met Reba's—she saw his honesty. There was no hidden agenda.

AC explained what a neuropsychologist did and what the tests were. No needles, no machines, no pain, and no money involved. Reba's role involved providing a detailed history, including Digger's developmental milestones. For Digger, his task was like doing homework with someone beside him, except without the worry of a pass or fail. Reba watched the muscles in her son's neck relax as AC said that some questions would frustrate him, and it was okay to feel that way. Digger's answers would be interpreted by the neuropsychologist, whose assessment would be used to develop a learning plan that everyone could understand.

Reba's shoulders rolled and relaxed as she watched AC intently. He reminded her of Penny, the nurse who invested more of herself than necessary; Reba sensed that AC may do the same. Penny cared, and maybe AC did too. He didn't want an answer today or even tomorrow, but if and when they both agreed, he would meet with them again to answer any questions if they chose to proceed. AC stood up first, straightening crumpled papers on his old clipboard. Digger and Reba followed him down the bleacher seats and across the worn gym floor.

"Where would we have to go to do this stuff?" Digger asked.

"Nowhere. She, ah, Dr. Hiller comes here," AC said quietly, massaging a scarred knee.

"Oh."

"Might not be for a while, so you have lots of time to think."

"Will you be there?"

AC looked down, then up at Digger, who stared at his shoes in anticipation of a negative response. AC fondled the keys attached to his clipboard.

"If you want me to be there, Digger, I will be there. And, if you're having a moment when you're frustrated, you can twirl one of these," he said, pulling out a red and an orange fidget spinner from his pocket. He handed both to Digger. Both gadgets were warm in his hands, and neither appeared new. "You can keep one. I spin this instead of yelling during a stressful game." Digger carefully eyed both, then chose the orange spinner. AC demonstrated how the movable part of the little gadget spun so easily, and his student followed.

"I like you even more now," Digger said, smiling. Reba's eyes went blurry, even though she stopped crying years ago.

It was a few months before Digger was tested because of the scarcity of specialists, and the even longer wait-list to see the young and brilliant Dr. Hiller. True to AC's promises, she came to the school, and the assessment consumed two exhausting afternoons. Dr. Hiller checked Digger's hearing with a little tuning fork, both grinning when she told him it was better than hers. She then asked him to read some letters to check his vision, which didn't go so well. Not because he couldn't see them, but because he couldn't read them. She tried new charts, one with images of chickens and sailboats, then another where Digger described how a hand was positioned. When Dr. Hiller smiled and said his answers were perfect, he beamed, and Reba stopped holding her breath. If Digger needed hearing aids or glasses held on with a strap around his head for playing basketball, the Adlers would face a whole new level of humiliation, regardless of the money Reba didn't have to pay for them.

Digger did the "homework" part that AC so accurately described, while Reba completed pages and pages of questions about her, Gil, and Digger. By the second day, they were both done thinking about anything more than having supper and watching the sun go down.

It was a long month before the Adlers learned that Digger was neurodivergent, which meant his brain worked in unique ways. Reba repeated the word to herself a few times, letting each syllable roll off her tongue. AC met with the Adlers to sort out how to move forward, now knowing Digger's strengths and challenges. AC and the specialist suggested that if everyone important to the Adlers knew this, things would grow easier; there was no reason to distrust them. AC offered to share the pertinent details with Digger's teachers and Coach, with the Adlers' consent. Their job was to tell Joe, Digger's boss, and the Adlers would do that together.

Some unpredictable things happened after this. In the weeks following, Reba started having flashbacks of the trouble she got into when she was young. While observing Digger from a distance, she also couldn't do some of the "homework" Digger failed at during his assessment. She interpreted this as the reason she hated school. Suddenly, it made sense that what she was labelled, like being lazy and stupid, was not true, or her fault. *Well, maybe just a little,* she thought. Suddenly, guilt flooded her when she realized Gil was no longer the only scapegoat for their son's troubles and Reba's grief.

Of the people who were educated about Digger, some made the effort to apply what they learned, but were outnumbered by those who chose not to change their opinion of him, or his mother. Even though the Adlers had a brighter outlook for their future, summer brought a much-needed break from worrying about it.

When the new school year resumed, Digger was given more support. To implement the specialist's recommendations, Digger was excused from a few regular classes and assigned a peer support, hand-picked by AC and his teachers. This scholarly student, named Denise, had no special training except for career aspirations of becoming a special-education teacher. Volunteering with high-needs students also boosted her university admission chances. Digger would get help, Denise would follow her dreams, and AC would add one more student to his roster of success stories. It was a win-win-win situation.

Digger and Denise met on Mondays and Fridays in a little study room in the library. Denise kept the door shut; Digger faced away from the window to minimize distraction from his lesson plan. She learned his abilities, knew his rituals, and tolerated the days he forgot to brush his teeth.

Denise was the opposite of the girls on the cheerleading squad. She wore horn-rimmed glasses, had questionable hygiene, took medication for her skin and had dark, wiry hair, some of which grew in places that it shouldn't. Despite these things, her self-esteem was solid, boosted by her parents' positive outlook on life.

The pair, student and mentor, were nicknamed 'D'n'D', with various interpretations, depending on which clique of students mocked them. These included 'Dirty and Dirt-Poor' and 'Dumb and Dumber', despite both being brighter than those labelling them. Digger was oblivious to the names, and Denise felt obligated to keep it that way. She closed the blinds in the little study room to block out the pests on the other side. This added privacy allowed Denise to occasionally run her fingers over the pencil-thin scars on his knuckles, created by ruler smacks in grade school.

Digger appeared calm while she stroked his fingers; the next week, she held his hand. On the third Friday, she offered to drive him home after school in her father's new pickup truck. Digger, lured by the vehicle's advanced technology, agreed, but when Denise stopped and parked in a small clearing overlooking St. Mary's River, Digger grew anxious. Denise insisted all was well, and they would just sit back and watch the river go by. Digger became claustrophobic when she tried to snuggle closer. Feeling even more confined than he did in the little room in the library, he left her in the truck and walked the one-hour trek home.

Reba arrived home with dinner before Digger, alarmed that he wasn't there. Nana Becca, fraught with worry, alternated between pacing the floor and rocking her chair with enough force to move it halfway across the room. Reba called the school, which was closed by then. She checked the basketball schedule and the calendar, both of which were clear. So, Nana Becca rocked in her chair and let Reba take over the pacing until Digger walked through the door.

Reba didn't know whether to yell at Digger or hug him, so she hugged him first. She took ten deep breaths and by that time was calm enough to make sense of what she said.

"And how was your day?" she blurted out before realizing the trio was equally agitated.

"Not the best."

"Neither was mine nor Nana's. Care to explain why?"

"Not really."

"Digger, what happened?"

"Nothing."

"Did something happen?"

"Nothing happened."

"Usually when you say 'nothing,' it's something. Did something happen at school? Is that why you're late?"

"No."

"Well, it's gotta be something. Now, let's hear it."

While Digger described how Denise drove him to the river in her father's truck, everyone's dinner got cold. By the time Reba squeezed every hand-holding and intimate detail out of Digger, topped up by his long walk home, she was so livid that dinner, cold or warmed up, wasn't on her radar. Digger understood fear, but not her reasons why. When she hugged him three times that night, he asked why she hugged him two more times than she usually did. She told him she was so happy that he was safe at home and that nothing happened. Digger wasn't quite sure why she thought "nothing" happened, but he felt much better after he ate both his meal and hers. Nana Becca never left her rocking chair, alternating mouthfuls of dinner with shaking her head from side to side.

Reba went to bed that night with more flashbacks, this time recalling the days of her misspent youth, including her sexual encounters with Gil and the other boys. In those days, it was easier to give in than to say no, especially since most of her hook-ups pleasured both participants. No one hurt Reba more than Gil when he abandoned her at the very age that their son was then, yet it was so different with Digger, who needed more protecting than she did at fourteen.

The weekend followed Digger's ride to St. Mary's River, and by Monday, Reba had her intentions organized. She drove to the school in the afternoon, just before Digger's session with Denise. Reba found AC in the gym, getting ready for practice, and asked him for a few minutes of his time. Physically seeking out AC in the school, and outside of the business of basketball, was a first.

"This shouldn't take too long," she explained, still in her navy-and-white uniform, complete with a frilly apron, flushed and slightly out of breath. Coach, who saw Reba for the second time in that uniform, even though he was on the other side of the gym, also became a little breathless.

"Is there anything I need to know ahead of time?" AC asked.

"Nope. Just keep your eyes and ears wide open."

"Where are we going?"

"You'll see soon enough. Follow me." They walked into the library together, Reba moving purposefully and AC limping on his sore knee to keep up. They first observed three nosy students hovering outside Digger and Denise's little study room.

"Get lost," Reba hissed to them, loud enough for other giggling students to hear and quickly disperse. The teenagers made faces, then disappeared at the sight of AC's stern expression.

Reba went to open the study room door.

"Shit."

She pointed to the doorknob, and AC looked closer. It was covered in lubricant. He handed her a soiled sweatband from his damp pocket. She wiped what she could off her hand, then the door and opened it wide to find Denise and Digger sitting beside each other with their backs to the shuttered window. Denise, flushed from arousal, jumped up out of her seat and re-adjusted her skirt.

"Denise, please leave," AC ordered between clenched teeth. She reached to gather her possessions, but AC said, "Stop. Everything stays on the table." Denise opened her mouth to protest. "You're best not to speak. Go straight to the principal's office."

AC remained where he stood behind a seated Digger and Reba beside him, fumbling as he gathered up Denise's possessions. He wiped more lubricant off the door handle, then led the Adlers to the principal's office, where he kindly and accurately set the stage and reason for the gathering.

Of all the things that Reba was grateful for in the last week, maybe even the previous year, it was that three days ago, she calmed down enough to reassure Digger that he had done nothing wrong. So, in the presence of AC and the principal, she patiently encouraged Digger to explain every inappropriate action, in her mind, that Denise took. Every date, time, and minute of what Denise said and did, including the ride to the river. Reba came prepared with her own 'evidence' to ensure that Denise never touched her son again.

AC opened the door and instructed Denise to come in and defend herself. The meeting, unfortunately, regressed, as most prior school-related meetings about Digger did. Digger, still processing what was happening, said almost nothing in Denise's presence. Reba interjected on Digger's behalf by fishing out a yellow, lined notepad from her purse, where she had methodically hand-written everything she could solicit from Digger's memory. This surprised everyone, especially Digger, who became distraught. He shook his head repeatedly and wrung his hands until they turned red, finally interrupting the momentum of her dialogue.

"Mom!"

"Digger, everything I wrote here is exactly what you told me."

"But I didn't think you would tell everybody."

"This is important, Digger, and you did nothing wrong."

"Yes, I did." His remark caught everyone's attention, including a red-faced Denise, who slouched in her seat and glared at Digger. "Denise said our learning was a secret, and now five people know!" He counted each person, but would not make eye contact.

The accusations and conflict escalated, yet Denise took no responsibility for her behaviour. She put the onus on Digger, whose face showed only torment. Exasperated, he looked at Reba to defend him as she always had before, and she did. Again. She stood up and slapped both palms hard against the principal's desk.

"If you knew anything about Digger, except how he shoots baskets and scores, you'd know that he never, ever lies. He doesn't even know how to lie!"

"Every kid lies." The principal's stinging remark added more fuel to the fire in the room. Reba was livid, leering at him. Spit sprayed out of her mouth as she shouted.

"For God's sake! You don't get it, do you? It's not something people like Digger do, unlike this tramp sitting here, who breathes lies. She even deserves an 'A Plus' for it!"

Denise responded by wailing. Digger stood up and began pacing in an office that was not designed for pacing. He activated the orange gadget in his hand, spinning it as quickly as it would go. AC opened the principal's door; Digger left to walk the halls, leaving the others to sort things out.

The stand-off among the remaining four continued. Denise stuck to lying as much as Reba was glued to the truth; the women volleyed accusations across the desk until the principal finally intervened.

"Enough. I'll need some time to think this through."

Denise left first and, before closing the door, the adults overheard her taunt Digger as she passed him.

"It's my word against yours," she scoffed, clicking her ballet flats as she hurried down the hall.

"Digger, just keep walking and don't talk to anybody. I'll be out soon," Reba cautioned and closed the door just in time to catch the principal whispering to AC that Denise's parents owned the only pharmacy in town. Reba knew that – she filled her prescriptions there.

"What do her fancy parents have to do with my son?"

AC looked apologetically at Reba, wishing he'd never been a part of this. The principal ignored her comment.

"Mrs. Adler, thank you for coming in."

"I'm not leavin' just yet."

"I'll need to think this situation through."

"Please. Don't mess with me."

"We're not, but Digger, and you being his mother, can't always hide behind his problem."

"Blessed Jesus and son of Mary, Digger is not even fifteen, and she's what, eighteen? He couldn't even understand that she was teaching him to pleasure her."

The principal took a sip of his coffee to camouflage a smirk. AC lowered his head and closed his eyes, disgusted at the man he also reported to.

"Now, Mrs. Adler."

"Don't you 'Mrs. Adler' me. She was taking advantage of him."

"Perhaps not, but we'll get back to you after we investigate this further." He remained seated, hands on his chair's armrests.

"You're wrong! If that's not taking advantage of my son, I hope you rot in Hell!"

"We'll get back to you soon." When the principal stood up and motioned her to the door, Reba knew she had lost another battle. She gathered herself and her belongings, pointing to the yellow notes she left for him on his desk.

"Evidence," she said.

"That won't be necessary," the principal responded, sliding the yellow papers back to her.

AC followed Reba to the door.

"I'm so sorry this has happened. I sensed Digger was out of sorts, and I asked him about it a few times, but he would never say why."

"No, he wouldn't. He promised to keep her secret. He never breaks his word."

"I wish I would've taken more time with him."

Reba didn't know how to respond, and didn't. She walked to the end of the hall where Digger stood, then followed him to his locker. He scooped out his rancid basketball uniform and a dead lunch, rolled them together into a ball and shoved them into his knapsack. He shuffled behind Reba to her old SUV, their commute silent, and it wasn't until they were almost back to Nana Becca's house that Reba realized she was supposed to work today. For the first time in her life, she was late for work, yet relieved that once she finally got there, her shift was busy enough to block out her afternoon.

The next day and the day after that, and all the way until Friday, it rained. Reba gave Digger the option of going to school. Digger only missed school when he was ill, which was rare. Reba felt his sadness, and Digger saw hers. They both decided that it was best if Digger stayed home for the remainder of that week. On Friday, neither was surprised when AC stopped by, and Reba knew the answer before AC relayed the principal's decision. Sitting around the kitchen table, he gave them ample time to absorb each sentence.

Denise would no longer be tutoring Digger, nor would Reba allow that to happen. AC, to paraphrase the principal's words as gently as he could muster, referenced the curious innocence of youth, then said neither would be suspended from school. The word "suspension" resounded through Reba's head like a hundred cowbells clanging all at once. She thanked AC as best as she knew how for his care and concern, and for delivering the news. AC stood up and, putting his soiled sneakers back on at the door, said he had no vote in the decision. He then asked Digger if he would like to continue playing basketball. Digger looked at Reba, who, unblinking, stared back at him.

Digger shook his head. AC zipped his jacket up and shook Digger's hand first, then his mother's.

"Will I see you back at school?" he asked quietly. Digger looked again at Reba, who stared blankly at her son. He slowly shook his head again. AC paused for a moment, then spoke. "If it matters, I want you to know how much I regret all of this happening."

"This is not your fault," she offered. "Trust me, we've battled this a whole lotta times, and it always ends the same. They win, and we lose."

"But don't you see, it is. I am responsible. Remember, I referred Digger for the assessment, and then suggested Denise help out."

"You were the best thing that happened to Digger this year. And I mean that," Reba sighed in appreciation.

There was an uncomfortable silence before AC opened the door to let himself out, looking back at Digger.

"If it's easier for you, I'll clean out your locker." Digger and Reba nodded in unison, and like the rare man who influenced the Adlers in a positive way, he exited their life and went on with his.

That Friday marked the beginning of years of moving, switching schools and jobs, and dependency on family handouts to fill in the gaps between social assistance. Yet through their many ups and downs, mother and son worked hard to keep each other's spirits buoyant with encouragement and goodwill.

A Nova Scotia friend of a friend told Reba about the 'balmy' weather in southern Ontario. Lured with the promise of employment, the Adlers moved to Niagara

Falls, the heart of the tourist industry, complete with fabricated adventures and international visitors. It wasn't long before they both grew tired of the flashing neon signs and seasonal hoopla.

Ziggy Winerowski, Reba's Niagara Falls employer and pizza franchise owner, also owned a little eatery, unofficially dubbed the Winer Diner by the regulars, in New Abino. It had a weathered outdoor patio overlooking Lake Erie. The diner reminded Reba of the calmer pace they left behind in Nova Scotia. Ziggy's brother Joe ran 'New Abino Groceries & More' just down the road, with Ziggy being his biggest customer. Ziggy relocated Reba, a good employee, to the diner and told Joe about her peculiar but hard-working son. The brothers negotiated an arrangement: Digger would work the same hours stocking shelves at the grocery store as Reba did, serving at the diner. Another win-win situation. Reba would text Digger when she left work, and on cue, he'd be leaning against the newspaper stand at the grocer's front door, black apron in hand, when Reba retrieved him.

Life got even better when Reba met Cousin Al at the diner. Always kind and never inappropriate, she stopped charging him for coffee after he told her about the Polly's Lane cabin for rent. That was two years ago; the lake still resembled the Nova Scotia coastline and stacks of chopped logs for the fireplace kept being replenished on their deck, courtesy of Cousin Al.

All was routine and almost perfect until Reba messed up a few customer orders. Rather than disciplining her or docking her pay, Ziggy told her to see his doctor. When she went, the semi-retired practitioner challenged her alcohol intake, especially because he knew from experience that it flowed freely at the diner. He suggested she stop drinking and wrote her a note for a month off for stress leave, which she ignored and returned to work the following morning.

NOVEMBER 7TH

Gracie Sheehan
(At a Niagara Falls library branch)
9:00 AM

Gracie used her key to enter the back door of the library, ready for today's staff meeting. At fifty-four, she was one of the oldest employees, and since starting there two years ago, she had no bad days, earned a decent wage and blended in nicely with her colleagues. She peeked through a window near the main door, where members, visitors and the unhoused gathered on benches, with or without belongings. Neil Gaiman's famous quote was posted within view: *"Google can bring you back 100,000 answers. A librarian can bring you back the right one."* It made Gracie smile every time she passed it. The library offered a peaceful space for readers and a reprieve from the troubles people faced outside. Regulars bonded with the like-minded; the homeless often sheltered there during the day from scorching heat or winter storms.

She scanned the weekly agenda as the meeting started: recruitment of volunteers, planning a community garden, and the repeat item of overdue returns. Suggestions were brought to the table, some good and some not, but after the pandemic, everyone agreed that they wanted the library to be as it was.

Gracie took a long sip of her tea. While others debated workshop dates, her thoughts wandered back to the chronology of events that brought her to this place in time. She commuted by foot from her Park Street condo, the same historic building where Winnie Firestone, a feisty octogenarian, lived. Through Winnie, she met Mason, the son of Winnie's dear, deceased friends.

Gracie's first husband died four years ago of lung cancer, leaving her to support their daughter Tess through university and help her gain her independence in Toronto. To complicate matters, Gracie lost her job when her employer relocated, all of which happened within a span of eight weeks. While she worked tirelessly to start life on her own again, she accidentally fell in love with a man named Fred, leaving all things familiar in Toronto to live with him in the country. Fred was who he was, and she soon discovered that she could never 'fix' him or his life. After many sleepless nights and heart-wrenching discussions, they parted ways with wounded hearts. That was two years ago. Wilson, a golden retriever Gracie inherited, remained with Fred when she moved to Niagara Falls. And once again, she re-learned the importance of caring for herself before others. Gracie spun the heirloom eternity band that Fred gave her, now on her right ring finger; it was a constant reminder to never compromise her values, integrity and goals.

Still oblivious to the meeting happening around her, she thought about Mason. Like Fred, he entered her world at a vulnerable time and when she was not looking to share it. As Winnie's lawyer and guardian, Mason first spotted Gracie, an attractive woman with auburn hair and brown eyes, when she was standing, pensive and poised, in Winnie and Gracie's condo building foyer. *What a nice man,* Gracie thought at the time. *What a beautiful woman,* Mason thought at the same time.

Mason was not sophisticated at the dating game after his wife passed away, but after helping Gracie with a landlord issue and billing her the cost of a lunch, they both felt something. They shared the opinion that everlasting happiness was an elusive goal. They had accumulated enough life experiences to be realistic, tread carefully, and trust their judgement. Mason also appreciated that Gracie was not chasing rainbows and bank accounts to cushion her sunset years.

Mason's childless marriage was solid, and he was devastated when his wife passed away. Gracie's marital history was messier, and she appreciated his experience in litigating divorces involving infidelity, addiction and violence. Those, he explained, were choices people made; the consequences Gracie suffered from her deceased husband's indiscretions were not her fault.

Combining their wisdom and accumulated experiences, Mason and Gracie grew into each other like old souls. Quiet evenings apart became quiet evenings together, peeling away the layers of discomfort that came with acclimatizing to someone new, yet his home gave Gracie the distinct impression that there was still another occupant. There were countless photographs of Mason and his wife. In his study, two well-worn leather recliners still had her knitting basket nestled between them. Mason readily admitted his difficulty in letting things go. There was no one to inherit his wife's treasures, and Gracie respected that. So, their relationship inched forward cautiously, sanctioned by their biggest critic, who was Winnie.

"Gracie ...?"
"Earth to Grace Sheehan ... are you with us?"
Gracie returned to the present when a co-worker tapped her shoulder. The meeting had evaporated into silence, and until then, Gracie was unaware that all eyes were on her.
"Welcome back. You left us a while ago." Gracie flushed, apologizing. "We're on your item. Number six, the outreach program proposal."
It was indeed Gracie's agenda item.
During the pandemic, she willingly agreed to deliver books to people with no means or ability to get them. Her efforts gained momentum even though it had never been discussed with the library's board. Mason suggested Gracie raise it at today's meeting because of its liabilities, including library staff driving in bad weather. After some positive discussion, it was added to the next board meeting's agenda for the same reasons as Mason offered and hopefully secure some funding. Gracie was thrilled and shared this with Mason, who anticipated his concerns would be addressed quickly.

Sonnet O'Brien
(Lot 1, closest to the main road)
9:00 AM

It was morning again, and just like the days before, Sonnet had nothing to look forward to. She left her bunkie once last week to run errands, and that was also the last day she showered. She shifted between her bed and the sofa, occasionally looking through her bedroom window towards the lake to see how high the waves were near the shoreline. She thought, rarely of nothing, sometimes about a memorable patient, but mostly she sank into the crevices of her unforgettable past.

The hospital's human resources department left her numerous messages, as did her manager, requesting that Sonnet consent to switching her no-show shifts to vacation time. These preceded urgent texts from her union president, pleading with her to submit a sick note to justify her absence. A few kind co-workers also called to voice their worries about her. She ignored them all.

Sonnet heard the bang of a vehicle's undercarriage hitting a big rut in the road, and then the engine revving to force its way out. She knew it wasn't the familiar sound of Reba's Toyota, and it was too early for Fletcher's predictable meal delivery. As the white SUV slowed down, she recognized the modern logo of a bird or an airplane wing that identified it as the mail vehicle. Its yellow roof light flashed as it backed into Sonnet's driveway, half in it, half still in the lane. Marty, the only mailman she was aware of since moving to Lot 1, knew enough to leave her mail in between her doors if it was important, even though door-to-door delivery didn't exist there. He also knew that the three neglected mailboxes on their mismatched posts were rarely opened, often overstuffed with junk mail, and served more as a marker to the Polly's Lane entrance than their intended purpose.

Sonnet put on her slightly more presentable housecoat, covering the threadbare nightgown she'd been living in. She watched Marty exit the passenger door, which in rural settings was, in fact, the postal worker's driver's door. He left it open with the vehicle running while singer Ed Sheeran cooed his *Perfect* song on the car's radio. Sonnet smiled, even though there was nothing perfect about today—or this week. Standing out of sight of the front door, she heard the wooden deck boards groan under his footsteps. One, two, three steps, then a purposeful knock. Sonnet wrapped her housecoat tighter and answered Marty's third knock. Her parked car in the driveway made him wonder if she was sleeping off a night shift. He opened the screen door just as Sonnet opened the wooden one, and for a few minutes neither knew what to say. Marty smelled garbage, and the malodorous woman facing him. Sonnet inhaled the crispness of the morning air that blended with Marty's scent.

"Morning, Sonnet," he chirped in his best Marty-the-mailman voice. She first saw the white envelope, plastered with multi-layered labels, then looked into his faded blue eyes for the reason why he delivered it. With no response from Sonnet, Marty held up his offering.

"I've got some registered mail for you." Sonnet's eyebrows arched in response. Marty slowly turned the envelope to face her; she scanned the hospital's address in the sender's lines.

"Hmmm …" was all she could muster. She attempted to clear her throat to say something, but because she hadn't spoken for days, nothing resembling words came out. Marty pulled a pen out from his breast pocket and handed it to her with the envelope, pointing to the spot for her signature to confirm proof of delivery. She fumbled with which way to click the pen point open. Marty gently took it from her, twisted it open and handed it back. She signed her name against the stiff, sealed envelope while Marty evaluated the crown of her unkempt hair. He'd only met her a few times at her door, but knew of Sonnet from when he visited his mother on the same hospital chronic care floor where she worked. Her unusual name and Irish lilt were unforgettable. Out of her scrubs and smelling older than the people she cared for, this was not the prim and proper Sonnet he knew.

"Is everything alright?" he asked softly as she returned his pen. He hesitated for a moment to give her time, carefully separating her copy of the slip from its serrated edge. Ed Sheeran's sultry voice on the radio and Marty's concern made Sonnet a little emotional. Letter carriers weren't supposed to inquire about the resident's mail, but Marty suspected it wasn't good news.

Sonnet cleared her throat again, her voice barely above a whisper as she pulled the strip to open the envelope.

"Hmmm… I suspect it's not." She slid her finger under the sealed flap and removed the white envelope. Marty waited, then took one step back. The wooden deck board squeaked as he shifted his weight on it.

"I..." he paused. "It's none of my business."

"It doesn't really matter." She removed the letter from its envelope and unfolded the crisp stationery. "They're probably telling me that I'm fired ..." She swallowed, but nothing in her throat moved up or down. Marty took another step back, zipping up a jacket branded with the same logo as his vehicle.

"Jeez, not at a time like this, and especially with all the shortages," he scoffed. Again, he had no right to ask if something went wrong, but he witnessed her work ethic and the pace she kept up, running between patient rooms. To Marty, Sonnet O'Brien was not only a good nurse but a saintly one. He stood still, his portly stature patiently shielding the wind from whipping against her thin frame while she read the letter to herself. She folded it, returned it to its envelope and slid it back into the cardboard courier mailer. She took a few deep breaths before looking up at him. He searched her moist grey eyes to interpret what they might share, which was nothing. He held her attention longer than was comfortable for either of them. She wavered between thinking if he was nosy or genuinely concerned. She decided on the latter because he looked more worried than nosy.

"It says that if I'm not back to work in two days, I'm considered AWOL."

"Like absent without a good excuse?"

"Just like that."

"Hmmm... just like that," he repeated. He hoped for more but wasn't getting it. He held up the receipt she signed. "You know, I can hold on to this for a bit. It might give you a few extra days if you need it." Sonnet feigned a smile that showed her unbrushed teeth.

"Then two of us will get fired. So, best to be on your way, but thank you for offering."

After another uncomfortable pause, Marty returned to his vehicle, closed the door and zig-zagged across the narrow road, then sped away.

Still holding her mail, Sonnet put a windbreaker on over her ankle-length housecoat and nightgown. She slipped her socked feet into the muddied rubber clogs that lay askew outside her door. She fastened her jacket buttons, unaligned with their respective holes, and walked slowly between the Reese's and Hope's tired manors. The wind had rearranged some of the discarded construction material, sweeping some across the leaf-covered steps and verandas. She treaded carefully to avoid slipping on mossy patches creeping over the flagstone path that led to the lake. She held her coat tighter as the wind lifted her hair, greying since Sonnet turned thirty. She had only dyed it once after Stan, her ex, insisted she needed to look younger. That was another time and another failure.

The lake was alive with choppy waves, and seagulls swooped in search of a meal. Sonnet hoped the view would soothe her, as it often did. She stood on a disintegrating wooden dock, the end of which the lake had absorbed over time. She tested half of her weight on the first board and then each consecutive board until she stood over the water. She looked left along the shore. Most docks had been removed for the winter. On her right, far down the horizon, was the historic Point Abino lighthouse, shuttered from the tourists for the season. A few faded remnants of a Canadian flag flew on the Polly's flag pole at the end of the lane. Far beyond that, on a separate private property, a huge new American one flew high in the air.

A strong gust of lake wind, laden with spray from the waves that came from her left, yanked her housecoat wide open under her windbreaker, then ripped the cardboard envelope from her hand. Sonnet cried out as it flew high in the air, then skipped over and over across the water, landing flat like a missed Frisbee on the rolling waves. It would be fatal to tackle the frigid waves and try to retrieve it. A quick end to her life without being discovered, until perhaps her decomposed corpse surfaced in the spring on some American shore. She shivered and dismissed the thought, watching the envelope dance in the water. She waited, hoping it might work its way back to shore, but instead, it disappeared.

Limbs numb, she hurried back to the bunkie as quickly as her exhausted body would move, wet feet sloshing in loose clogs. She kicked them off on her deck, opened the doors and stood shaking, not knowing what to do next. Fumbling to open her windbreaker, her fingers were too frozen to pass the buttons through their holes. She finally yanked her soaked jacket up over her head, her housecoat coming with it. Sonnet let them fall to the floor instead of separating them and hanging them over her kitchen chairs to dry. Her wet wool socks came off, then her nightgown. She walked naked and shivering to her bedroom to get a clean nightgown and her favourite thick grey wool socks. Rather than dressing, she ran a hot bath, soaking her painful body until she felt warm and slightly calmer. She shampooed and conditioned her hair in anticipation of

Marty returning with another registered letter in the days ahead—to confirm what she already knew would happen.

Drying herself, her normally hollow abdomen felt full and tender, more so on the right and, although she'd always been deathly pale, her skin had taken on a hint of yellow. Sonnet O'Brien inspected herself in the mirror and acknowledged how very ill she was.

Fletcher Hope
(Lot 2: middle bunkie)
Noon

Fletcher rolled around in his bed a few times before deciding to leave it. His sheets told him he'd had a rough night, but he wasn't sure why. He popped a dark roast puck into his upscale coffee barista and filled his thermal travel mug. He slid coordinated wind pants and a waterproof coat over his cozy sweats, wedged his feet into unlaced boots and went outside. Coffee, lidded and in hand, he followed the narrow flagstone path past the main house down to the raised sections of the aluminum dock, lying on the ground and not far from the lake. He skipped back to the wide wooden steps of the manor's veranda; his father wanted the outside porch screens boarded up before winter. Fletcher passively considered working on it that day, if he wasn't distracted by something more interesting.

Fletcher turned the lights off inside the manor, closed the door, then took two blankets from a storage box, tucked them into a red, folding Adirondack chair and went to the section of the dock that sat closest to the lake.

He cocooned himself in one blanket and sat down in the chair, tucking the other blanket snugly around him. His first steaming sip of coffee was delicious. He watched the waves splash against the shore, then recede. Back and forth they went. The sun beamed straight over him from a cloudless sky; the wind had calmed completely since the morning. It was almost pleasant outside, considering winter was coming soon. He watched the last of the tree leaves swirling down in gentle circles and land on the water.

Fletcher found his phone between the blankets and got lost in his social media apps. An old classmate posted another climb up the corporate ladder, and an old high school flame gave birth, while others hopped in and out of relationships. Some days, Fletcher longed to be them, but usually, after an hour near the lake on a day like today, there was nowhere else he'd rather be. He missed his family and the girl who dumped him after his arrest, but not his father's demeaning comments or the marriage prospects his mother scouted out for him. His father sent him job postings where he could work remotely from the bunkie; he also overheard his father, Frederick, tell his mother, when she forgot to end the call, that he did not want Fletcher to be employed at any of Frederick's companies to further humiliate him.

Fletcher passed his days watching the sun set and rise, that is, if he got up in time. The reliable stream of Hope cash kept his bank account mostly in the black, and he occasionally siphoned extra money from his mother. Because his father's creative accountants wrote Fletcher off as a business expense, he felt no guilt and was as content to bask on the shores of New Abino as his family was to keep him there.

Even though Fletcher lived in an adult body, his level of maturity was not fully developed. Morally bankrupt, he had recovered from his addictions but not quite his behaviours. Prison had a big impact on him, but not in the way others in jail were affected. He was not abused, thanks to his father funding monthly pizza nights for the whole cell block, and nobody wanted that compromised. His father wrote the cheque; the warden ordered the pizzas, and everyone ate, albeit in the pecking order. Another one of those win-win-win arrangements.

He left prison with a permanent aversion to hamburger helper, canned vegetables and his worst, prison toilet paper. The one-ply kind that fell apart and offered no resistance to a man's "code-brown" jobs, as they were known among the inmates. He vowed he would never buy another square of cheap toilet paper again. He'd also taken to grooming himself after some bad haircuts and thought he looked quite sharp once he figured out how to crop his own locks.

Fletcher let the waves ease his worries, meditating a little before approaching the shore. He spotted what he initially thought was driftwood bobbing up against a partially submerged tree, but it was too flat, and the sun reflected off it. He walked around the aluminum dock sections and over the slippery rocks, relocated there to slow the shore erosion. It was not driftwood he scooped up, but rather a cardboard mailer, folded like a waterlogged rag and held together mostly by shipping labels.

He waited until he was on safe ground before examining his find. He read yesterday's date, the hospital's return address and his neighbour as the receiver. This O'Brien woman seemed nice enough, but he sensed she didn't feel the same way about him. He squeezed the package between his hands to drain the water, placed it on the dock under multiple layers of his blankets, and then sat down on it while he tapped her name into his phone's search engine. He found nothing on social media, but she was recently recognized by the local hospital for twenty years of exemplary nursing service. Fletcher scrolled down and found a dated media release where police listed her as an assault victim. Her husband, Stanley, who owned a different surname, was arrested for bodily harm, a charge she later dropped. Digging for more dirt, he read that Stan was also charged with bank fraud.

Fletcher stood up and debated whether to deliver the package back to her or eat. He opted for breakfast, giving him time to decide if he should have a little peek in the package before returning it. He headed back to his bunkie, the aroma of coffee still lingering while he made French toast, drizzling it with cinnamon and locally sourced organic maple syrup. While he ate, he examined the envelope and tried carefully to unseal the top and bottom, but wide bands of tape kept it intact.

This left him options: he could open it and then throw it back in the water because Sonnet didn't know he had it; he could open and reseal it as best as he could, and then return it to her; or he could still open it and deliver only the contents, telling her that whatever was inside came away from its package. His last option was to return it just as he found it.

Maple syrup dribbled off his fork, landing on the package. He considered his choices as he watched the viscous liquid blend into the soggy surface. Somehow, the stickiness made the package less desirable to handle. He took the package, rinsed it under the sink and set it to dry on the heat register, feeling quite righteous about his decision not to open it.

Digger and Reba Adler
4:00 PM

Reba and Digger were both in their final hour of today's shift. Digger's day was going well; he loved his shelf-stocking job. The Adlers took AC's advice when they moved to New Abino and told the people who frequently interacted with Digger that he had some special abilities. Instead of being chastised like they were back home, the opposite happened. Joe and his co-workers welcomed Digger with curiosity and, more importantly, respect. At a staff meeting, he anxiously explained why and how he did things the way he did, matching labels on the shelves and methodically rotating new stock. His co-workers eagerly accommodated him, and Joe added new responsibilities in manageable increments. When Digger was happy, Reba was happy, and when they both were happy, the world was theirs for the taking. It was like magic.

As well as Digger's shift went, Reba didn't know that hers wouldn't end the same way as her son's. When Cousin

Al came in for breakfast that morning, she remembered to ask about borrowing his chainsaw to trim back the choking overgrowth narrowing the lane, but forgot to return his change. His breakfast was always $8.50, with unlimited coffee. Al usually gave her a ten-dollar bill, and she always produced the exact change from her secret pocket, which she never kept until he told her to. Today, he only had a twenty-dollar bill. Reba got busy with other customers, and when she didn't return his change, he sat at the diner counter wondering how to handle this sensitive issue without bruising either of their egos. He loved Reba as much as any of the regulars did, and it was she, not Ziggy, that kept them coming back. He knew her, Digger, their bunkie and the history that brought them to New Abino. This distressed him even more than it did about his change dilemma, or lack thereof.

While Al sat staring at the pies in the display case facing him, Ziggy appeared from the kitchen, clean apron strings secured above his wide middle. He sat on the round, red vinyl-covered stool beside Al. Once they got past the weather, Al asked if things were going well, and Ziggy said, "Fine." But there was a long pause, and as Ziggy ran his tongue over his top teeth, sucking in his breakfast residue, he thought that all was not fine. Neither one to sugar-coat words, they both dove straight into the issue at hand.

Ziggy solved half of the problem by giving Al his change from the cash register, which made Al feel even worse. In a hushed voice, Ziggy divulged to Al that Reba had messed up some other orders, so Al's situation didn't surprise him. The two men sat for a while, like the wise old sages that they thought they were, and eventually came up with a plan. Reba had already asked Al to borrow his chainsaw, which both men agreed would never touch Reba or Digger's hands. Al would bring the chainsaw over on Reba's next day off and do some 'investigating'. Ziggy supported the plan, and both agreed not to mention the money misunderstanding, because that's what they both agreed that it was.

Reba finished her shift, emptied the tips from her apron into her little change purse and gathered her belongings, which included meatloaf and mashed again, plus five little ketchup packets for Digger. She texted Digger that she was on her way and, as usual, he was ready when she arrived. A forlorn-looking dog was sitting on the Adlers' porch when they came home, thumping his tail against the wooden deck, almost as if he were expecting they would bring his supper home.

"There's that damn dog again," Reba snarled.

"You've seen him before?"

"Yup. Don't touch him. I'm sure he's full of fleas."

"But he looks friendly." Digger wanted to pet the dog, who was more interested in their meal than either of them.

"Get away, you useless animal," Reba warned, hoisting the food well beyond the dog's reach. He stood up, tail and hips wagging with even greater momentum.

"Mom, we should call him Useless."

"Well, that's what he is to me," Reba grumbled.

"Can't we give him some food?"

"Nope. If we feed him, he'll keep hanging around. He needs to go back to wherever he came from. They'll feed him over there."

"But what if he doesn't have a home?" Reba hadn't thought of that, but wanted no part of this discussion now. She was exhausted, hungry and sore. "He's no mangy dog, so he must have a home, and there's no way he's setting foot through this door."

Dinner was consumed as usual in front of the TV, and after the dishes and *Wheel of Fortune* were done, she brought out her little change purse and spilled its contents onto the kitchen table. She put five dollars into the emergency fund in the peanut butter jar over the sink and counted out the rest. She couldn't recall where the twenty dollars came from. In her memory, she sorted through her customers, who ordered what, unable to source out who gave her the biggest bill. It bothered her even more than Digger and the dog staring at each other through the front window with the same sad eyes.

Before her shower, Reba scrutinized herself in the mirror. Rather than looking to discover what had changed, she hoped to find what hadn't. With her baby fingernail, she scraped a speck of dried food from her forehead, then followed the deeper lines crossing it. She dressed for bed and went to sleep, still thinking about the twenty-dollar bill.

NOVEMBER 13TH

Gracie Sheehan
(at the library)
Noon

Gracie read the email carefully, then leaned back in her chair at the library's front counter, beaming that the library's outreach program was approved by the board. Minutes later, her supervisor waved her over to the quiet space behind the counter and offered her the program, with an official start date of December 1st. Despite her excitement to accept it immediately, Gracie wanted to include Mason because it was his suggestion and he was now such an important part of her life.

Gracie learned in her early library days not to judge who came through its doors. Her philosophy was that every story, published or not, had a life, and every life had a story. Often, people's shoes or what they carried past her at the front desk told their story. Today, a tired mother rushed in with her gaggle of offspring, apologizing for misplaced books that were now overdue. Her children hovered behind her in order of height, outfitted in new shoes while hers were old and outdated. The next family, in contrast, included a well-dressed father; following him were three girls, weighted with overstuffed knapsacks of returned books, due on time. With wild hair and untied sneakers, they swarmed Gracie, armed with library cards and an inventory of new book requests.

Working behind the front desk gave her a vantage point. The regulars were predictable, devouring new releases by best-selling authors and offering their own reviews. She also found receipts in returned books that served as bookmarks or mysterious notes with edits and mistakes that authors made.

She walked around to stretch her legs and absorb her surroundings. Lonely or bored souls, sometimes a combination of both, wandered in and found a strategic chair within earshot of the children's story hour. Others chose a study kiosk, hoping to overhear snippets of normal communication. Refugees met each other, sharing words of hope in their native tongue. One middle-aged man parked himself at a reading table, opened a magazine and sat without turning a page, lost among his private thoughts in a very public place.

Octogenarians, like Winnie from Gracie's building, usually arrived midmorning. Walking or assisted by wheeled devices, their physical abilities dictated what they could transport home. Stretchy outfits matched, fully accessorized. They were not worth worrying about unless they forgot where they were, where they were going, or their clothing did not match the weather. The library and the bank next door had reciprocal agreements to keep these visitors occupied, sometimes at the bank with a library book, until someone could pick them up or deliver them safely home.

Then there were those who sheltered from the weather, or whatever and whoever preyed on them. For reasons she had yet to understand, they made the greatest impact on her. They came once, or often. Their eyes matched their clothes and shoes, worn down and worn out. Sometimes Gracie discreetly rationed out leftovers in the staff kitchen from meetings, wrapping a croissant or cookie in a serviette and sliding it across the desk with their library card. They understood her gentle shoulder shrug or frown if the kitchen was bare. There was no need for either to speak - the language of need was universal.

Sonnet O'Brien
1:00 PM

Sonnet had two visitors in the last week—one expected, the other not expected or welcomed. Marty delivered a second registered letter from the hospital four days after the first one, which reiterated the same ultimatum. Sonnet must return to work, be approved for sick leave, or be terminated. She also read a text message from Candace, her union rep, the day before, insisting she take sick leave. This contradicted what Sonnet repeatedly told her—that she wasn't coming back.

Today, Candace arrived unannounced at Sonnet's bunkie with a heavy cardboard box, banging against the screen door frame with her foot until Sonnet opened the door. She set the box on Sonnet's tiny, cluttered kitchen table. There was no exchange of pleasantries as the two women looked at everything in the room except each other. Candace finally spoke.

"As you can see, you're missed at work. Now, open it." Sonnet hesitated for what seemed too long for Candace, then peeled away the hospital tape and lifted the flaps of the box. It was packed to the top. Both women were surprised by the carefully arranged books and get-well treats from co-workers. "No wonder it was so heavy. This shows you that they want you back."

"Wow," Sonnet whispered in awe.

"Look, I'm sorry for blowing up at you after that meeting. Seriously, I mean it."

"I forgive you."

"I'm off today, so let's go out for a bit. I'm sure you need stuff."

"I'm good."

"No, you're not. You need to get out," Candace said, and eventually persuaded her to get some groceries.

Glad she had recently bathed, Sonnet changed from her sleepwear into presentable clothing, combed her hair and slid into a warm coat for the blustery weather.

Sonnet initially felt claustrophobic after fastening her seatbelt in Candace's car, but settled after making a shopping list while Candace drove. Sonnet bought what she needed and then, instead of Candace heading in the direction of Polly's Lane, Candace pulled into the parking lot of a medical building and confessed her underlying motive for getting Sonnet out of the house. Candace insisted that Sonnet see her family doctor, Dr. Torres, to complete some sick benefit forms; Candace also produced a duplicate of the same form that Marty delivered a few days earlier.

Candace coerced a livid Sonnet into the second-floor clinic, pointed her towards a vacant waiting room chair, then antagonized Dr. Torres's receptionist to "squeeze" Sonnet in without an appointment. The receptionist glared at an equally infuriated Sonnet for being "squeezed in". Candace sat down heavily beside Sonnet, ready to wrestle her down if she bolted.

The pair waited a tense and silent hour until Sonnet was ushered alone into a spacious exam room that doubled as the doctor's own office. Form in hand, she stood at the window, wanting nothing more than to escape through the window and across the gold leaves carpeting the woods. Another half-hour passed before her well-respected physician walked in. Dr. Torres disarmed her with his familiar, crooked smile. She watched him wash and dry his hands, fill his mug with tap water and gulp it down. He perched his fit frame on the corner of his desk to face her at eye level.

"So, let's see if my receptionist got this right. You've been dragged in here because you're a no-show at work, and your bulldog union rep thinks you're deeply depressed." By then, he'd already noted the dark circles around her eyes, loose skin below her chin and could only guess how emaciated she looked under her baggy sweater and denim leggings. She raised one eyebrow and smiled feebly before looking back out the window.

"Your receptionist is very perceptive."

"You and I know each other well from the hospital. We both pride ourselves on our work ethic, don't we?"

"We do."

"And, we're both strong people."

"We are."

"That is, until we aren't anymore." She glanced at him, then blankly at his credentials on the wall behind him. "Agreed?"

"Agreed," she whispered as he sat down at his desk.

"I'm wondering if there's some merit to what your rep said." He rolled his chair closer to his desk, then clicked at his keyboard with two fingers while scanning his desktop screen. "You know, the last time I physically saw you in this office as a patient was eight years ago."

"What can I say?" Her gaze shifted passively between the autumn view and him, folding her lips into a thin line. She desperately wanted to leave, but respected him too much to do so.

"Can I ask you a few questions?"

"You may."

"Have you lost interest in being the good nurse I know you are... maybe finding it harder and harder to come to work?" He hoped, with his inquisitive facial expression, that she would answer. Sonnet raised her glassy eyes to the ceiling, unable to speak. He responded for her. "I'll assume that is a yes... and this graph on my screen says you weigh 144 pounds." He walked slowly over to the chipped, white antique scale, then waited patiently until Sonnet stepped on it. "So, if I knocked off five pounds for your clothes, my math tells me you're down forty pounds."

"I didn't realize I'd lost that much."

"And I'm assuming this wasn't planned."

Sonnet stared numbly at the numbers between her feet. When Dr. Torres asked about her thoughts of dying, or if life would be easier if she just didn't wake up in the morning, both caught the moment when her tears splashed off the scale's magnified weight display. He gently touched her shoulder, then extended his hand to exchange her disability form for a box of tissues. He sat down again and completed the form while Sonnet wept softly at the window. His fingers tapped quickly on his keyboard, followed by a hum from his printer, spitting paper out. His empathetic eyes followed her.

"You know, I still vividly remember our conversations about your past. You carried such a heavy history even before becoming a nurse, and to be frank, I'm not only impressed, but intrigued that you survived this second calling for as long as you have. Those Sister Mary Agnes years were not all good ones, and your years with Stan were worse. I still admire you for finding your way out and moving on. But it'll take you longer, and with help this time around, before you start feeling better." He passed Sonnet the prescription from the printer, which she recognized was for an antidepressant. "It's your choice to take it or not, but my advice is that you do. I've also signed you off for a month," he said, rechecking his notes on her disability form and then signing it. "I'd never force anyone to act against their will, but I'd be lying if I said I wasn't worried about you." Sonnet watched the tiny scar below his mouth as the words flowed out. "Can I ask you to do something?" Sonnet's eyes met his, not answering. "Will you eat at least twice a day?"

"I'll try."

"We should do some bloodwork, too. Your colour's a bit off."

"Not today."

"Okay, but maybe one more 'ask'." She held his eyes, trying to stifle more tears. "Will you come back and see me in three weeks? It will give the meds time to start working." His mouth slowly formed into that uneven smile. "I wish we had a hundred of you, Sonnet, but we don't. And when I see you again, if you are sure that you can't, or choose not to go back to work, I'll support your choice."

He patiently granted Sonnet the time she needed to compose herself despite knowing how late his day would end. She smiled wearily and thanked him for seeing her. He followed her, still holding her form. He grinned sheepishly, reminded her that she was delinquent by three pap tests and four years of mammograms, and asked her to schedule one of each. She nodded, wiped her face dry, then waited while he made a copy of the sick form behind the receptionist's desk. As he gave Sonnet the original, a lab and a mammogram requisition, he said quietly to her, "Your rep did the right thing dragging you in here. Maybe not the bullying part, but I'm glad I was able to see you."

Sonnet thanked him again and folded her papers before entering the overstuffed waiting room.

Sonnet passed all of her papers into Candace's extended hand, who, without reviewing them, tucked them into a file folder labelled 'O'Brien' below the union's logo. The mood during their thirty-minute drive back to Sonnet's bunkie was a tense extension of the waiting room. Regardless of which way they faced, the car's ventilation failed to filter out Sonnet's neglected dental care or the stale air from her driver's cigarettes. Sonnet asked Candace to drop her off where the main road met

Polly's Lane, mostly to shorten their mutual anguish, and she did. Sonnet heaved her grocery bags out of the car and, more from manners than appreciation, thanked her before heading home.

Five steps in, Sonnet knew it was impossible to carry everything in one trip to her bunkie. She set one bag on a dry patch of tall grass just off the lane. She hoisted the heaviest bag up by the handles using both hands and swung it around with enough momentum to land against her upper back. Minutes later and, alarmed at how winded she became from managing this task, she slid the bag off her back and onto her kitchen floor. She put the kettle on and leaned against the counter until she caught her breath. Retracing her steps, she spotted a dog, a yellow lab mix, for the second time in a week. This time, his head was buried in her grocery bag. She yelled as she hurried to salvage her provisions, the inside of the bag flapping as vigorously as his tail. He poked his head out, a bagel evenly framing the outline of his mouth. *Better that than the stewing beef,* she thought, unsuccessful at shooing him away. She picked the remaining bag up again by its handles and settled it against her back. The dog happily trailed her home, his meal consumed in a few hearty chews.

"That was tomorrow's breakfast," she scolded him as she closed both the screen door and wooden doors between them. He groaned loudly, sank down onto her deck and waited patiently, optimistic for anything more.

Sonnet re-boiled the kettle and sat for a few moments to recover. She put her groceries away, then opened a tin of assorted shortbreads to have with her tea. She moved a kitchen chair to the window for a strategic view of the dog, who reminded her of a friend's pet. *He must live nearby and eat better than me,* she thought, tapping on her living room window. He responded by initially turning his head towards her, then rose with an exaggerated effort, lumbering over to face her. She set her hot mug of tea on the window ledge, and both watched the steam form a silhouette of a teardrop on the glass. The dog attempted to lick it. Curious about each other, both returned to the kitchen door; she watched him favour his left front leg, which had a bare patch of skin on the elbow. His hopeful brown eyes pleaded, tail wagging slowly in anticipation of something. Anything. She opened the door just enough to put her hand on his head, and he leaned heavily into her palm. She felt around his neck. It was a while, if ever, that he'd worn a collar.

"Where's your home?" Her voice was compassionate. His tail wagged to signal he was quite comfortable at hers. "Okay, then, what's your name?"

His tail thumped hard against the door, and he whimpered loudly when she closed it. Sonnet pulled her least favourite shape of shortbread from the tin, returned to the door and offered it to him. The dog swallowed it without chewing, appreciating the treat with a slobbery woof.

"That's it, no more."

He allowed her to gently examine his hairless joint in return for a second cookie. There was no obvious sign of injury, but the area was warm to her touch. "I'm no doctor," she offered softly as his dark eyes bore into hers, "but in my humble opinion, you've got arthritis." She scratched him behind both ears. "Best be on your way home, young lad, before someone realizes that you're gone."

The dog returned to the steamy film on the window and lay down again. Just as she was closing the door, she saw a crumpled cardboard package jammed in the space where her deck ended and her door was framed. She recognized the package from the hospital that had blown into the lake. The outer address seals had sloughed off, and the documents inside had stuck to the cardboard envelope. She tossed it onto the kitchen counter with a pile of unopened mail. She also hadn't thought again about the papers she left with Candace, including the mammogram and lab she had no desire to complete or the prescription she couldn't be bothered filling.

Sonnet finished her tea at the front window where the dog had repositioned himself to a sunny patch and was deep into a nap. She tapped lightly on the glass and saw his jowls waffling with each snore. "You look like a Rufus," she said, watching his blond fur shine in the sun as it slid over his ribs with each breath. Like Rufus, Sonnet went for a nap, hoping her pain and bloating would allow her to sleep.

When she woke, Rufus was gone. She opened the door to look for him, noticing a small white plastic bag hanging from her doorknob. Inside it was her prescription, which had been filled and delivered. She hadn't heard a vehicle, which would normally have woken her. She took the receipt from the bag and flipped it over to read a handwritten note on the blank side.

Sonnet:

*You'll feel better taking this, which also increases your
chances of your sick claim being accepted.
Remember, we've got your back.
Candace*

Sonnet rubbed her forehead, then scratched her scalp in frustration. She didn't know whether to call and challenge the pharmacy for having someone else fill her prescription or appreciate Candace's investment in her. She argued with herself about acknowledging her doctor's insight – that her low mood was affecting her ability to make rational decisions, namely, accepting help.

Sonnet stood in socked feet on the sunny deck, inhaling the crispness of late fall. She looked casually up and down the lane, wondering if Rufus might reappear. She returned inside, slid her feet into worn slippers, and wrapped herself in a blanket. She put the kettle on again, then sat down in the other chair at her kitchen table. She pulled the box Candace had delivered closer and emptied its contents into piles: a stack of books, a jar with a hand-written label identifying the contents as *Bernie's Black Raspberry Jam,* cards and cellophane-wrapped packages of indulgences, all with her name written on them. For her. For Sonnet.

Her attention shifted to the books. Good books by good authors, including two in a red bag with a note addressed to her from her favourite ward clerk, the same one who told her about the bunkie rental. Her note told Sonnet that the books in the bag were on loan from the library, and new books would be delivered to her if she wasn't well enough to go out. The clerk encouraged Sonnet to read the books that she chose before December 1st, when two new books would be exchanged for the ones in her hand. Sonnet read the familiar titles; they shared similar reading interests, and although Sonnet doubted that she could concentrate long enough to read, she was touched by the gesture. She read the note again, and her name on the envelope. Fourteen people took the time to write her name, if she included the note from Candace on her medication receipt. She couldn't remember an event, not even a Valentine's Day in elementary school when she'd seen her name written so many times. Fourteen times—one more than a baker's dozen.

December 1st

Early Storm Warning
(Current temperature: slightly above the freezing mark)
7:45 AM

Sonnet's night flashed into day when she drew the living room curtains open, just as the Adlers drove by. Based on her microwave clock, they were heading to work. She had a to-do list today, which included buying food and replacing her worn tires.

In the middle bunkie, Fletcher remained glued to his screen all night, polishing off a tub of gourmet ice cream while watching whatever the influencers were influencing him about and ignoring the local newsfeeds. While most people in his time zone were starting their day, his was ending. Without leaving his warm bed, he ordered dinner online, which was to be delivered at 6:00 pm, and anticipating the Korean delivery girl was his dessert.

The Adlers didn't invest a lot of time exploring what existed beyond their world. They gleaned what was important to them in their own unique ways; Digger's mind filtered information on his terms, while Reba siphoned through the barrage of diner gossip, then interpreted what she thought was fact versus fiction.

She savoured a rare, five-minute pause, skimming through the first section of someone's breakfast-stained newspaper while a local farmer worried aloud about a storm brewing on the New York side of Lake Erie. The lake usually carried whatever happened in the Buffalo area to Point Abino but left a milder imprint. Because it was early December, and based on the scuttlebutt, more people were interested in embellishing past generational blizzards than preparing for this one. A police officer polished off a syrup-soaked heap of pancakes and Ziggy's homemade sausage links, mentioning that the municipal snowplows were ready to roll. As he tipped Reba, he also said that there were no emergency plans.

Noon
(Temperature dips below the freezing mark)

Sonnet debated whether she should buy groceries first, but decided to have her tires replaced. Donning an extra sweater, her jacket and worn sneakers, she drove into town. Inexperienced in the knowledge of car maintenance, she didn't think to pre-book an appointment during the busiest tire-switching week. She pulled into the shop's congested parking lot and then approached the chubby middle-aged man behind the service desk. The badge on his navy golf shirt identified him as Cliff, the shop manager.

"I'm here to buy some snow tires," she said carefully. His harried look told her that he'd already done a good day's work. She followed his eyes across the overcrowded waiting room.

"No appointment?" He squinted at his screen, already knowing her answer.

"I've never done this before. My husband…" She didn't finish.

"I'm sorry for your loss," he misinterpreted, and she didn't correct him as he extended his hand for her keys. Glancing at the Ford logo on her key, he scanned the jammed parking lot. "The red or the white SUV?"

"The white one."

"We can't do it today, but I'll check your tires against our stock before we book you."

"Thank you," she said and hurried outside with him. Squatting down, he ran his fingers over her front tire. He leaned against the hood for support to stand his unfit frame up to his full height.

"I said we can't do this today," he repeated, shaking his head and wanting to scold her for driving on bald tires.

"I know," she said helplessly, "but I'm not sure when I can come back."

He circled her vehicle; the first tire he checked was the best of the four. He popped off his baseball cap, scratched his forehead and replaced it while arguing with his conscience. He would never forgive himself if Sonnet left and something bad happened.

"You'll have to wait. All those people inside booked their appointments long ago."

"How long would—?" She stopped herself mid-sentence.

"Could be hours."

"I see."

"Look, if you were my wife, I wouldn't have let you leave the driveway," he said with concern rather than criticism. He persuaded her to stay and corralled her cautiously to the waiting room, glaring long and hard at a muscle-bound man until he surrendered his seat. Clearly the outlier and only female, she stared into her purse for a few minutes until her breathing calmed. Soiled automotive flyers and abandoned cups littered the dusty coffee table, such a contrast to the sanitized hospital environment she left a month ago. She zoned out the loud, low voices boasting of their foresight to schedule their tire switch, especially with today's weather forecast.

1:00 PM

Back at the diner, some weather addicts escalated the storm to a blizzard, heightening the lunch crowd chatter. Reba heard the wind picking up through gaps in the window seals but had to look hard to find a snowflake.

At New Abino Groceries & More, Digger was busy at the end of the cereal aisle. He lined up a new breakfast cereal display at eye level, marketed there to sell best, instead of the bottom shelf where he thought they should go. Challenged by this, he ignored his environment, inside and outside.

2:00 PM

Because of the weather reports, the library suspended the day's programs, including the outreach book deliveries, and closed its doors at noon. Gracie portioned out leftover treats from the lunch room onto serviettes and passed them to the unhoused visitors as she escorted them out. She reminded them where the nearest shelter was and encouraged them to go early because beds would be scarce that night.

Although she had dressed warmly for her fifteen-minute walk to work, she was relieved when Mason drove her home to her Park Street condo. He then left for the stately house he'd shared with his wife until she passed away. Both thought it best to maintain separate residences despite frequent sleepovers. Neither was preoccupied with marrying again or their financial status, that being Mason's wealth or Gracie's lack of it. Gracie kept Mason out of her daughter Tess's life, and Mason kept Gracie out of his public life, except for the rare crossover of a few cherished friends.

At his bunkie, Fletcher napped as soundly as a newborn with a dry diaper and a full belly.

5:30 PM
(Freezing rain, and the sun has set)

Sonnet alternated between crying and praying, sometimes simultaneously, through her ninety-minute drive back to Polly's Lane, a commute that normally spanned a third of that. The darkness, her blurred vision and the sleet on her windshield were a treacherous combination. She prayed because of her devout Catholicism, certain that only a miracle kept her vehicle on the road. But mostly, she prayed to give thanks to Cliff at the tire store for insisting she wait to have her tires replaced. If not for him, she'd be stranded at the garage, spending the night smelling old, worn-out tires and sleeping between even older, worn-out men.

Almost at the entrance to Polly's Lane, she spotted two of the three mailboxes, knocked over and scattered across the main road. Every slap of wind and rain threatened to topple the third box off its rickety post, hanging on by nothing more than a bent nail and a promise. Slamming on the brakes to avoid hitting the debris, her SUV slid across a solid layer of ice before it stopped, wedging a mailbox, minus its post, between her right front tire and the car's undercarriage.

She geared into Park, opened her door and shifted her left foot from her car onto the road. Before she could stand fully upright, she slipped on the ice and fell hard onto her left side, one leg buckling against her front tire while the other remained in her car. She lay contorted on the ice-covered pavement, gasping for breath from the blow. Stunned, she remained still, overcome first with pain and then with terror.

After taking inventory of what vulnerable organs occupied her points of impact, she brought her knees together and then raised them to her hips, grateful they still functioned. Using the car tire as an anchor and fueled with adrenaline, she kicked hard to propel herself out from under her vehicle. She succeeded, but the force also dislodged the mailbox from her vehicle's undercarriage. She screamed as her car slowly turned sideways and away from her, off the main road, then down the gradual slope of Polly's Lane. She heard the threatening sound of her vehicle gaining momentum, then horrendous cracking noises when it landed against something too dark and far away to see. Her shrill cries pierced the wind, ending with exhausted sighs.

Meanwhile, in his bunkie, Fletcher heard the loud crunch next door. Assuming an old tree snapped off its trunk, he readjusted his earbuds and continued tapping his hands against his thighs to the beat of the song *I Like Me Better*. He decided he'd investigate when his motivation and daylight converged.

Sonnet rolled gingerly onto her soaked knees and freezing hands. Sleet was pelting bullets of ice against her back. She crawled to where the rougher gravel met overgrown roadside weeds, then became fixated on her last name lettered across her dented mailbox. The red flag, indicating she had mail, was frozen in place, as was the partially open box. Sonnet rarely received genuine mail, so despite the crisis brewing around and within her, she slid her frigid, stiff hand inside the box. She pulled out two white envelopes tucked into grocery flyers. Folding the envelopes into the waistband of her jeans, she gasped from the cold paper, then jammed the junk mail back into the mailbox.

In slow motion, and again with great care, she stood up. She inched along the road's edge, taking baby steps sideways down the gradual decline. This took forever, but moving slower was wiser than falling twice. She spotted her vehicle's headlights two hundred feet away, the engine still running and the car upright; even the turn signal light was still flashing. The SUV sat wedged between trees, roughly twenty feet from the ice-covered grass surrounding her deck. Pacing herself and her breathing, she approached the driver's door. Access to the front passenger door was obstructed by thick evergreen branches. She could open the driver's door but not reach far enough to turn the vehicle off. Fingers numb, with no remote key fob for her dated model, she fiddled with the inside door buttons until she activated the one to open her driver's window. Still, she could not reach in far enough to turn the car off. Making the sign of the cross, as if it would help, she dragged her soaked, freezing body through the window, rolled her window back up and shut the car off.

She breathed deeply for the first time since her vehicle escaped her—until the pain in her side caught her. Remaining inside to absorb what warmth the car still offered, she planned her next task. She popped open the trunk and exited the car, cautiously stepping around the layers of ice covering the holes in her driveway.

Choosing a bag of potatoes first, she inched ahead to the deck, by now looking like thick glass. She gingerly climbed the two rickety wooden steps to the deck and paused. A wave of panic rolled through her. Petrified of falling again, she knelt and slid each grocery bag across the deck until it landed near the bunkie door. She shuffled along the wooden planks to the screen door. It was frozen shut. She reached into her grocery bag, retrieved a can of stewed tomatoes and whacked it repeatedly along the door frame until the ice broke away.

After unlocking her main door, she moved each of the wet bags onto the kitchen counter. Shaking from her inner core to her extremities, she pulled her stiff, wet coat off over her head and hung it on the doorknob. Her shoes came off next, followed by every piece of clothing that was plastered to her bony frame. She forgot about the envelopes, now drenched, until they separated from her skin and fell to the floor. She plugged the kettle in and wrestled her aching body into a thick flannel nightgown, over which she put on a second one. Socked and slippered, she retrieved an oversized grey wool cardigan from the closet by the kitchen door. Owned by a previous tenant, it was the only thing nearby that would warm her stiffening muscles up quickly.

She groaned as she wiped wet spots from the floor and picked up both envelopes. The first one was a glorified ad discounting a rural internet provider. The other was addressed directly to her; she shook her head in disbelief after she tore the envelope open and read the letter slowly and aloud to herself, then silently again. Her sick time insurance claim was approved, excluding the five-day waiting period, provided that she adhered to her doctor's treatment plan. By the time she set the letter down, the kettle had boiled. While her tea steeped, she inspected the carton of eggs she purchased, marvelling how each one had remained intact in its little cardboard nest. She poured milk into her tea, then placed the container and eggs away, closing the fridge door just minutes before the power went out.

At the Diner
6:00 PM
(Freezing rain, whipping wind)

Reba sensed by now that she wasn't going anywhere, and neither were the worried diners. Most of them were eating the spaghetti special, while the outside sign advertising it rattled in the wind. Loosely measured servings of house wine and coffee were still flowing. She snuck into the kitchen while Ziggy was cruising through the patrons in the dining room, looking for weather updates. Reba called her agitated son, by now marooned at the grocery store.

"Hi. You okay?"

"No. Joe closed the store because of the storm."

"Ziggy's deciding whether to do the same here."

"When are you coming?"

"Whenever I can leave here safely. The roads are getting bad."

"But we still need to get home."

"I know. But not 'til it's safe. Who's left at the store?"

"Six of us, and some customers."

"I'll get there as soon as I can. Got your spinner?"

"It's in my pocket."

"Good idea to use it when we hang up."

"Mom!"

"What?!"

"The power just went out!"

"Damn it! Ours too! Our generator just kicked in. Did yours?"

"What's a generator?"

"It's the box that keeps the emergency lights on."

"Mom! The super bright lights over the exit signs just came on!"

"Great! That's the generator. Use your spinner, honey. And your alphabet of calming words."

"I will, but I'm still upset."

"Me too, honey."

"Mom? It's still kinda dark here. Are we safe?"

"Of course we are. And aren't we super lucky to have lots of food both at my diner and your store?"

"Yup."

"Okay, let's start with your happy alphabet."

"A is for awesome."

"B is for belly breathing."

"C is for calm, D is for, for, for …

"You're doing great, and I want you to keep going until you feel better. I gotta go. Love you!"

"Mom?"

"Yes?" Reba impatiently picked a piece of something sticky off her uniform.

"I want to go home. And I'm worried about Useless."

"I'm sure he's fine."

"Mom?"

"Yup?"

"Love you too."

Reba ended the call and heaved a big sigh. She used her phone flashlight to find candles to augment the emergency lighting - it made the diner cozy and hid its sins. Besides Ziggy and Kat, the pretty, young server, she counted a dozen mostly fed customers gravitating towards the window to watch a vehicle creep along the main road.

One young man paid with what cash he had because the machines were down. Determined to leave, he started his black, dual-wheeled truck remotely, then ventured outside with his girlfriend, arms locked together. With less ice coating the passenger door, they climbed in and closed it. Minutes passed, but the truck remained. The girlfriend returned to the diner, with all eyes on her.

"Hey, we're heading to Fort Erie and there's room for four more if anybody's interested." A set of tired parents consoling two cranky toddlers instantly raised their hands. The girlfriend waited while her boyfriend scraped the ice-laden windshield and the young family bundled up. Reba slid their burgers from the grill into buns and packed them into bags with water for the grateful family.

Of the six patrons remaining, three were unknown men of assorted ages, wearing green work shirts with identical logos. They mopped up the sauce on their plates with garlic bread and then approached the window. An older couple joined them, leaving an even older mother seated and oblivious to what was troubling the others. The pickup truck backed up carefully, and then made its way onto the main road. Engine roaring, the truck fishtailed, straightened out and crawled into the night.

"Well, folks, we've got exactly three pieces of cherry pie and three pieces of apple. And, it's on the house," Reba announced proudly, deciding to make the best of a bad situation.

"Cherry for me," said the youngest of the three workmen.

"Me too," piped in the tall worker beside him, likely the oldest of the three.

A pudgy man, whom Reba recognized from previous visits, approached her at the counter as she plated the desserts. Eyebrows raised high, he shouted across the room to his wife that today he wasn't a diabetic, then asked for apple pie a la mode. A nervous laugh broke out.

"Today's your lucky day," Reba grinned and handed him the biggest serving. She slid more pie and ice cream onto plates and brought them to his table. His wife took one and passed the other to her mother.

"Momma isn't fussy, as long as it's sweet."

With a round of thanks, they dug in. Reba brought the remaining dessert to the last workman, whose lean, rugged appearance gave her the impression that he didn't eat what wasn't good for him. Sure enough, he declined but accepted coffee.

"Good thing, 'cause it's still hot." She emptied the remains into his cup; he reciprocated with a warm smile. "I don't recall seeing you guys in here before."

"We're working on the new house over near the lighthouse. About twenty minutes from here." The lettering on his shirt identified an electrical contracting company.

"I've seen it. That's one big mansion that somebody's building. Another celebrity moving in?" she asked as the three men exchanged glances.

"She's a famous author. Don't think she's local. She's looking for a quiet retreat to write."

"Well, she picked the right spot. Are you gonna be there long?"

The oldest of the workers, whom Reba estimated to be on the short side of sixty, answered.

"Probably a month this time around, providing the hydro comes back on soon. Once the wiring is finished, we're done until the walls are up and painted, then two of us will come back to install the light fixtures and tie the wires in the panel." Reba scratched her head, having no idea what he meant, and switched the subject.

"Well, Thursday's special is always spaghetti, and Ziggy's homemade soups are long gone before supper."

"Then, I'm sure you'll see us back."

She cleared their plates and made an effort to remember that the most handsome of the three, at least in her eyes, drank his coffee black. She gathered the remaining dishes and cutlery from the tables and loaded them into a grey plastic tub. She set it on the stainless-steel counter in the kitchen while Ziggy and Kat, a well-endowed student whom he hired for just that, used soup spoons to devour the rest of the ice cream.

Without power, water was in short supply. Without water, there was no dishwashing and limited bathroom flushes. The diner employees knew this, as did the electricians, but the party of three seniors hadn't figured this out until Ziggy suggested the males go outside and the women avoid flushing unless they absolutely had to.

Fletcher was parked in his armchair, watching the waves crash against the shore, wondering where his dinner was. The dog he named Tucker, but Digger named Useless, and Sonnet named Rufus, was curled up between him and the back door mat, thinking the same.

At the grocery store, things were a little less lively. All the customers left when the power went out, some with a handwritten bill to square up when the cashier could process a payment. The store's young staff, who couldn't leave, plugged themselves into their devices and found a corner to brood in. Joe, the store owner, lived minutes away but wouldn't leave because of the others. He sat down in his office with the meat manager, each worrying about their families at home. Digger, being Digger, kept on stacking shelves in perfect order, worrying slightly more about Useless than his mother.

8:00 PM
(Freezing rain, changing to snow, and all roads are closed)

Fletcher started following the newsfeeds more closely, despite his sketchy reception. He received a text that his Korean dinner was freezing up in a snow bank along with the lovely driver, whom he had hoped would sweeten his night. She was all prettied-up, but unprepared for the blast of winter and therefore unable to get herself and their dinner to Fletcher.

A burly tow-truck driver rescued her and, in lieu of payment, consumed Fletcher's meal after driving her home and before his next stop. Only a few drivers who ventured out after sunset arrived at their destination, despite repeated posts warning the public that first responders were no longer responding. Police advised the public to stop driving and take shelter wherever they were, noting that even some officers got stuck and had to abandon their vehicles. Snow-plow drivers returned to their municipal yards, unable to see beyond the blade on their trucks.

New Abino and the surrounding region had effectively shut down.

8:30 PM

At the grocery store, Digger washed down a bag of potato chips with a carton of milk. He also designated the sundry aisle as his bedroom. On the floor, he lined up the length of his height with supersized packages of toilet paper. He exchanged texts with Reba, who added another layer of reassurance that everyone, including Useless, was fine. He carefully straddled the bundled toilet paper and lay down, impressed by his ability to make such a fine bed. He fretted for a few minutes because his phone battery life was lower than his comfort zone of fifty percent. Mittens on, eyes darkened under his hat, he covered what he could with his coat and recited calming phrases to lull himself to sleep. Among other thoughts was the realization that at thirty-five, it was the first night he would spend without his mother or Nana Becca under the same roof.

The diner received word that the pickup truck occupants arrived home safely in Fort Erie. The trio of seniors had already settled down to sleep, sprawled across the floor in one corner, using coats and other items pilfered from the lost and found bin. Kat, the young server, made her bed from chairs in another corner and zoned in on her phone, uninterested in the amorous glances of the young electrical apprentice. The men took turns stepping out the back and onto the patio to relieve themselves in the snow.

Ziggy barricaded himself in the kitchen, which left Reba and the workmen to sort themselves out. She found a deck of cards and took the liberty of assuming they would appreciate a round of draft beer. Each paid their share and tipped her generously. One moved a table under the emergency light. Introductions followed – they knew she was Reba by the dozen times they'd heard it. The only card games they all recognized were Fish and Euchre, and no one was playing Fish. Young Tom, the electrical apprentice, sat strategically to Reba's right and within Kat's sightline, still feeling hopeful. Big Tom, appropriately labelled for his height, took the chair on Reba's left, leaving the electrician with the nice teeth and closely cropped, greying hair as her partner.

"These jokers call me Montana," he grinned, shuffling the worn deck.

"There must be a reason."

"Yes, ma'am, there is," he answered, keeping her wondering.

9:00 PM

Sonnet saw nothing but her reflection when she held a candle at her window – everything outside was blackened by night and layered with ice. She read the local news reminders on her phone to stay put, emphasizing that tow trucks would only respond when it was safe and calls would be prioritized in order of urgency. She heard ferocious waves crashing over crumbling break walls, the most threatening storm since she moved there.

She was reminded of her early years in Ireland, when she summered at her grandparents' thatch-roofed cottage on the ocean, more so after her mother died. The weather was often as cruel as it was today, and it was not unusual for the drafty fireplace to be extinguished by wind and rain. Sonnet loved those days, feeling safe in the arms of her granny when her grandad's tales of shipwrecks and sunken treasures lulled Sonnet and her brothers to sleep.

Raised in a conservative Catholic rural home near Dublin, Sonnet's mother, whom she called 'mam', looked after the beef and barley farm, the house and three children, birthed in three consecutive years. Her father, known as her 'Da', needed the car for work, leaving her mam on the farm. Mam ran errands on Saturday, and Sunday was a day of rest. She passed away when Sonnet, the youngest, was eleven. Sonnet reflected on how her own mood mirrored her mam's, and how both caregivers gave and gave until there was nothing left to give. Sonnet eventually learned the devastating truth from the village gossip—that her mam died by suicide rather than the boating accident she was told about as a child.

Her Da, a good father, relied on Sonnet to parent her brothers and do the cooking and cleaning while he worked. Her auntie educated her on the facts of life, namely that periods were a blessing and a curse, without explaining either. In Ireland at that time, it was considered as prestigious to have a daughter in the family enter the convent than it was for sons to become priests. With her father's gentle urging and a paltry dowry, she was accepted at a convent, not only to escape from mothering her brothers but the hardship of remaining on the farm. Her oldest brother had already run amok, so Da, with the help of the local authorities, "persuaded" him to join the priesthood. The other brother followed suit, which left no one at home. In her father's mind, he scored the trifecta and then sold the farm.

At fifteen, Sonnet became a novice in a religious order - she took vows of chastity, poverty, modesty and obedience to God. She progressed at the convent to become Sister Mary Agnes, including the name Mary, because spiritually, she was the mother of Jesus. Agnes was associated with the Latin word 'agnus', meaning lamb, which accurately described her personality. Saint Agnes was also a miracle worker, and as much as Sonnet wanted to aspire to that, she knew in real life that miracles were unlikely to happen. She wore a dark, full habit and white headdress, the symbol of purity.

The convent, although far from extravagant, felt palatial compared to her rustic family home. Most nuns there lived in harmony and gentle comfort. Sonnet enjoyed nutritious meals and a warm bed in a small room and felt loved by all. Her chores, helping at the church and adjacent rectory, were shared with her mentor, an elderly nun, until she fell ill and left Sonnet to carry on alone.

A young and darkly handsome Father Francis, ten years Sonnet's senior, recently transferred to the parish. He was instantly admired by his congregation and the nuns. Mass attendance tripled, as did the offerings in the collection plate. His humility, slight stature and kindness were so opposite to Sonnet's overbearing and intimidating brothers.

Father Francis and Sonnet made a concerted effort to maintain a physical distance, with the exception of afternoon tea at the small kitchen table. They alternated stories of their families with Bible discussions. On quiet Tuesdays, Sonnet lingered, and Father Francis found stories to keep her there. It started with the innocent touch of a hand, then a brush against shoulders, and after months of tense praying to preserve their vow of celibacy, they failed. It happened ironically, Sonnet thought now, during a winter storm. Neither quite knew what they were doing, but every time skin touched skin, both felt helpless in their need. Sonnet and Francis's prior knowledge of love came from family and faith, but now, this was a very different love. And intense. They longed for each other when apart, and their days apart were long. Their sexual encounters spanned two years until Sonnet, by then eighteen, became pregnant. It wasn't until she was certain that she confessed to an equally distraught Francis. Abortion was a sin, marriage wasn't an option, and the church's donations kept increasing. The outcome was obvious and predictable. Their secret was locked by her fate. The adulated Father Francis stayed put, and Sonnet, camouflaged with a newly assigned identity, was banished to one of Ireland's Catholic-run homes for unmarried teens.

When Sonnet's pregnancy reached term, the onset of labour was immediate, with strong, regular contractions – different from what little she knew or expected about birthing. Without a doctor or anesthesia available, after hours of intense pain, one tiny foot presented itself. A hushed flurry of comments about the foot ensued, followed by a frantic chorus of prayer. An hour later, or at least what Sonnet estimated was, an elderly man dressed in a crumpled tweed suit, tie askew and adorned with a stethoscope arrived. He briefly assessed the state of terror in the room, pulled out his rosary, and concentrated more on the hard black beads in his hand than on his patient. A nun draped a sheet to shield Sonnet's face from the rest of her body. Sonnet tried to pray, the speed of her silent words fluctuating with her contractions.

A second man arrived shortly after, conversed in hushed, hurried tones with the doctor. A dark rubber mask appeared from nowhere and was applied firmly to Sonnet's face. Following a scuffle of resistance, mostly fuelled by fear, everything went black.

When Sonnet regained consciousness in the same cramped and humid room, she felt the hollowness within her body first, then the desperation of loss. Persisting, she was told that she delivered a girl who needed resuscitation. She wasn't allowed to look or touch her infant, but overheard a nun christen her as Mary, like all the other babies born that week and the weeks before and after hers. When the baby was swaddled and before being whisked away, Sonnet caught a glimpse of her hair – it was as black and curly as Francis's.

Sonnet hemorrhaged after the delivery and was transported in the local dairy's delivery truck to a hospital, where the first doctor, an oversized white apron protecting his suit, "fixed her up good" so that she'd never conceive again. She interpreted that his "fixing" comment was primarily intended to make her pay for what he implied was her mistake. Unworthy and unwelcome anywhere else, she was kept there for a few days to recuperate while the nuns at her convent packed up her possessions. She was transferred from the hospital to a different, run-down convent north of Dublin, a stark contrast to the old historic structure that Sonnet left.

As with some other hand-picked, beautiful babies born out of wedlock, Sonnet learned from a sympathetic maid that her tiny Mary was hidden in a special nursery for disabled babies and those of mixed race, who were eventually sold to wealthy, desperate couples, often American. This was arranged by an illegal adoption agency that fabricated birth certificates listing the mothers as deceased from childbirth and the fathers as unknown, effectively eradicating any historical connection to a priest or a nun.

Sonnet's crumbling convent was attached to an equally decrepit orphanage by a walkway, covered by a leaky thatched roof which offered users minimal protection from the elements. The buildings were isolated away from a village; no one except its inhabitants could distinguish between the wind blowing and the administering of human suffering.

Sonnet toiled her days away in the scullery. Other than being excused for Mass, meals and vespers, her greatest luxury was to mind the library where, in a rare moment, she felt content tucking a little one into a corner and reading to them. It also allowed her to cherish a sliver of her own childhood, remembering when her mam did the same.

At nineteen, after grieving the memory of her baby's birth and the passing of her father, Sonnet made a plan. She no longer felt obligated to him, nor could she tolerate what she witnessed at the orphanage. She transferred the simple gold band from her right hand to her left hand to ward off any questions and to give her a false sense of protection. She moved to Dublin, where she hid and worked for a year, long enough to save for a flight to Canada. During that time, only once did she read about Father Francis in a bulletin that announced his transfer to a church in County Cork. But with so many other priests who took the name Francis and no photo validation, she couldn't confirm that he was alive, nor the one she still loved.

Arriving in Canada in her twenty-first year, a Catholic hospital in Ontario welcomed her as a health care aide. The culture she was accustomed to as a nun, then shifting to her work in health care, allowed for a smooth transition. Assigned to the nursery on the night shift, she bathed newborns and relieved exhausted mothers by rocking the colicky ones to sleep with Irish lullabies. More than once, she turned her head to find a tired soul, head propped against the door, listening to her songs. After a year, she earned enough income to fund another dream. While still working weekends, she began her nursing education and a new role in life.

A loud crack of a falling branch outside brought Sonnet back to the present. She checked her phone and realized she had spent an hour absorbed by her past. After nibbling on a lemon scone and a pear, her right side and gut reacted with pain again. With nowhere to go and nothing to do, it wasn't until after her pain and the wind settled that she could fall into a deep sleep.

At the Diner
10:00 PM
(Wind settling, heavy snowfall continues)

The last round of euchre ended as quietly as it began, with the two Toms splitting the twenty-dollar pot. All was silent in the diner around the foursome, who scrutinized the remaining floor space between the tables to find enough room to spend the night. The three men took their final trip outside to drain their bladders of beer. The Toms claimed two rows of floor space between tables seating eight, also closest to the front door. This left Montana and Reba with the last corner, which measured slightly more than the length and width of a double-sized mattress.

Reba grabbed her jacket, purse and a half-dozen clean tea towels from under the diner counter. She offered three of them to Montana to use as a pillow. He pushed their euchre table against an adjacent table. Reba remained standing as he sat on the floor, stretched out his lean denim-covered legs, and propped his back up against the wall. He scraped the melting snow off his boots and used it to wash his hands. Reconsidering his location, he stood back up.

"You should stay here," he whispered, drying his hands and then some small puddles with a towel before pointing to the same spot.

"Then where will you sleep?"

He scanned the parameters of the diner again, glancing reluctantly in the direction of the bathroom.

"Don't worry about me."

"It still leaves you with nowhere to sleep."

"No, ma'am. I insist." Awkwardly, Reba kneeled, then sat with her back against the wall, pulling her navy and white checkered uniform down over her knees.

"Okay, now what?" she said quietly through a grin, looking up at Montana. He stifled a quiet laugh and took another look around – there was no other option. She took charge and slapped the floor beside her. "Now, sit."

With greater effort this time, he sat as far apart as he could from her. She heard his knees crack, followed by a low groan when he straightened his long legs again. They sat in silence, neither moving. All of the candles had melted, leaving only the emergency lighting and the lingering scent of the spaghetti special to remind them of where they were. The oldest woman of those present snored intermittently, and somewhere, someone released a tirade of gas. Montana and Reba chuckled, then sat stiffly for another few minutes before Montana whispered in her direction.

"So, how ya doin' over there?"

"Just chipper."

"Me too."

"How's your back?"

"It's killing me."

"Mine too. And are your feet hurtin' too?"

"As much as my back."

"Mine too, especially in these boots." He positioned the heel of one wet boot, toe facing up, on top of the steel cap of the other, as if he were walking a line. "And they stink."

"Is that a bonus?"

They grinned, peeking quickly at each other, then straight ahead. Another few minutes passed.

"This might be a long night," he suggested.

Reba reacted with a barely audible grunt and zipped her jacket right up to her neck.

"I'm sorry, I didn't mean anything by that."

"I know you didn't. It's okay."

"No, ma'am, it's not okay," he insisted, which frustrated Reba. The top of her head was parallel to his shoulders, which left him looking down towards her.

"Really, it's fine," she said.

The gap between his next comment lasted another few minutes.

"I just want to be clear. You're safe."

She took a deep breath, turned her head away from him and rolled her eyes. "With six other people in this room, I feel safe, too. Now, let's just try to get some sleep."

"Great idea."

Montana slid down on his back to a lying position and doubled the dry tea towel folds under his head. Reba rolled over on her right side, facing away from him. It was her bad side to sleep on, even in a comfortable bed, but she was too stubborn to ask him to switch. She waited for what seemed like thirty minutes until she heard him shuffle his position. A soft snore told her he had fallen asleep. As quietly as she could, she rolled over onto her left side, only to find him facing her. His eyes were closed.

At last, she thought, readjusting her coat to cover her shoulders. She rubbed her mascara-coated eyelashes, expecting her makeup to be smeared everywhere but where it should be by the morning. Her phone, still in her hand but on silent mode, lit up. It was Digger, unable to sleep. She tapped a quick message to remind him not to worry, that she was sleepy and would text him in the morning. She tucked her phone between the tea towels and the wall, then looked at Montana. His eyes were wide open.

"I'm so sorry."

"Don't be," he answered as she rubbed her eyes again. Another brief pause. "Everything okay?"

"Yup."

"You sure?"

"It's my son. He works at the grocery store up the road, and he's stranded there, too."

"And he looks just like you."

"You've seen him?"

"Yes, ma'am. He's tall."

"Sure is."

"I thought he was your brother."

"That's because I was twelve when I had him," she smiled, not far from confessing the truth to this stranger.

"Okay, then. Good night, Reba."

"Good night." She closed her eyes and tried to force herself to sleep. It didn't work. She opened one eye to see Montana still watching her. He smiled, and she reciprocated. He didn't look away, and neither did she.

"Reba?"

"This better be a good question."

"It's not a question."

"Then what is it?"

"You have garlic breath."

She rolled her eyes again, stifling a hearty laugh with her cupped hands. Montana lifted his left index finger and drew an imaginary line on the floor, starting with the wall above their heads and ending near his knees. He pointed to the side of the imaginary line that was closest to her.

"What are you doing?"

"Showing you where your side of the bed is."

"Oh. I see."

"So, now I'm going to roll over and try to sleep. You can sleep any way you want, but I'm apologizing ahead of time if any part of me lands across that line when I'm sleeping."

"Apology accepted ahead of time."

"Good night, Reba."

"Good night, Montana, or whatever your real name is."

As before, Montana kept her wondering. She was acutely aware of the presence of this man lying so close to her, a man whom she knew nothing about. She peeked at him periodically, each time finding him wearing a mischievous smile. Sleep didn't come to the pair until well into the night, and by the time morning illuminated the icy windows, both backs were leaning heavily against each other.

December 2nd

6:00 AM
(Roads remain closed, still no power in New Abino)

Digger opened his eyes and saw the shelving units above him, reminding him of where he was. He jumped up and rearranged the bulky packages of toilet paper in a neat row, hoping they would fluff back up before he replaced them on the shelf. He texted his mother for the third time since waking up, tucked his phone in his pocket and started his workday routine.

Things were also coming back to life at the diner. The trio of seniors was up first, toileted and ready for breakfast. Ziggy was grumpy and, to everyone's benefit, remained secluded behind the kitchen door, preoccupied with the dwindling water supply and the limited things he could prepare with the emergency generator. Kat had no intention of getting up until she had to, shifting her view so she could watch young Tom sleep. Big Tom was sitting up, rationing his phone life to quick texts.

Reba woke up but kept her eyes closed, not uncomfortable with Montana's back leaning against hers. He'd been awake for a while, unintentionally encroaching on Reba's side of the floor. She felt a little push of his hips against her bottom, wondering if it was innocent or intended. He solved her dilemma by gently edging away, his body creaking and cracking until he sat upright. She grasped her uniform hem, pulling it down as best as she could without lifting her hips. She leaned up on one elbow, then sat up and yanked again at her hemline, cursing Ziggy in her mind for forcing her to show her knees. Without exposing more than she already had, she shimmied up to a sitting position. Everything hurt from sleeping on the cold, hard floor.

"Mornin', Reba."

"Morning." She rummaged through her purse, not for her brush, not for her cheaters, but until she found her small compact mirror. She opened it and used the magnifying side to evaluate what the night had done to her, and it wasn't pretty. She chose the cleanest of the three tissues in her apron pocket and wiped off what makeup didn't belong. The brush came out next; Montana felt a small tingle watching her work through her thick copper hair, pile it high on top of her head and work a twisted scrunchie into it. Considering the circumstances, she was as groomed as she was going to get.

She peeked at Montana's chin stubble, following his fit form from there down past his thick work socks - his safety boots stood neatly paired about three feet from him and even farther from Reba. Her eyes moved back up the frayed hem of his jeans, past the unbuttoned shirt under his open coat and to his face. Appearing unchanged from last night, he watched her watching him, his mouth forming the hint of a smile as he spoke.

"I'll bet you the price of a cuppa coffee that the kitchen door will open in under a minute."

"Why would you say that?"

"Because he's already opened it twice."

And that Ziggy did, ignoring Kat and summoning Reba to the kitchen. Reassembling herself, she kneeled for a few seconds, then planted one hand on her bent knee, feeling every aching body part. Montana kneeled, then stood upright first, extending his powerful right hand to help her up. It was easier to accept it than not. She noticed that his index finger was permanently flexed.

"Thank you." She straightened her uniform and gave those already awake her best "I'm not a morning person" frown, and that she wasn't answering questions yet. She knocked on the swinging kitchen door and then pushed it open. Ziggy was barking orders even before it shut, questioning why the coffee wasn't on.

"I'm not overloading the generator, so everyone's getting juice, cereal, toast and fruit. No eggs. No fried stuff. And no substitutes!" He handed her bread and bagels along with dessert cups for fruit cocktail, which ultimately shifted the division of labour away from him and onto her and Kat.

"Okay to make coffee, and boil water?"

"Should be enough for that. One cup each."

Reba ignored his ration order, left the kitchen and announced the menu. No one objected. She put the coffee and kettle on and brought the cutlery over to Kat, who grudgingly sat up, yawning, stretched, and patted her tousled hair. Montana put his boots on, then adjusted the louvred blinds to let the daylight in. His co-workers followed him out the side door to relieve themselves. Once back inside, they made good use of the hand sanitizer before straddling the red stools at the counter.

"Oh, Reba... I've got two free hands... and nothing in them," Montana sang in a country drawl. Wondering if he was flirting, she turned to see him wink as he pointed towards the coffee maker. "I can handle the hot stuff."

Reba shot him a look he couldn't interpret, then slid mugs and a box of tea his way. He sashayed around her in the cramped space, pouring boiled water into stainless-steel teapots for the old folks and coffee for the Toms, mocking a curtsey as he served them. He returned to Reba, hesitated with his hands on his hips, then returned to her side of the counter.

"And where's the juice?"

Reba pointed to the fridge and the tray of glasses beside it. By the time he'd served everyone their choice of beverage, Reba had toasted the bagels and breads and plated them. Montana rifled through the drawers, finding peanut butter and jam packets as Reba ladled fruit cocktail from a big can into small bowls and passed them to Montana, who centred them on plates, added the condiments and served them. Whistling between grins, Montana poured Reba's first coffee, then served himself.

"Much obliged for your help," Reba said as she took a sip, leaning against the back counter. He gently brushed past her and circled back to the customer side of the counter.

"No complaints yet, but no tips either," he grinned, empty palms open, before joining his colleagues by the window seats to eat everything on their plates. Kat came to life only after young Tom brought her coffee and lingered.

Reba texted Digger, who had already polished off a box of breakfast bars between tasks at the grocery store. Everyone was anxious to go home, which was pretty much the same as it was at the diner.

Outside, the small world of New Abino remained frozen. The storm had knocked out its power, but not its spirit. Snowplows from nearby Fort Erie started rumbling out to clear access for emergency vehicles. The local hospital's afternoon shift staff had forged on through the night shift, and, although physically and emotionally exhausted, relied on their reserves to carry them through the day shift or until relief arrived.

7:05 AM
(The power is on in Niagara Falls)

Gracie's phone alarm woke her at the same time as it did every day. She lay in her big bed at her Park Street condo and procrastinated another five minutes before sitting up and swinging her legs over and onto the carpet runner. Running her hand through her matted, shoulder-length mop of auburn hair, she curled up her toes, and then extended them, back and forth through the soft rug fibres, wondering what the day looked like behind her draped window. Her phone pinged; a text from the library confirmed it would remain closed. She flopped back on her bed, welcoming the thought of having no other plans for the day. She messaged Mason.

"The library's closed."

"Lucky you."

"My bed's still warm … and there's lots of room."

"Have you looked outside?"

"Not yet."

"Have a look - you'll see why I'm not joining you."

"Too bad."

"Same here."

"Maybe dinner?"

"I'm assuming you mean tomorrow after you look outside."

"I think I'd better. Lots to work on today?"

"Two divorce mediations, a custody case and court to prepare for."

"Then I'll leave you alone."

"Miss you."

"Miss you too."

They exchanged heart emojis before Gracie put her phone down. Instead of dressing, she wrapped herself in the thick, white bathrobe she'd gifted Mason for sleepovers. Opening the drapes, she marvelled at how the force of nature sculpted the snow on her street into large, frozen waves. None of the streets were plowed, and not one foot, paw or claw had disturbed them. Mason was right – she was staying home. She imagined the thundering Niagara River, just minutes from Park Street, responding to the storm. The wind whipped thin layers of snow up high into the air, sparkling in the sun like a shaken snow globe. She knotted Mason's bathrobe belt and paused at each huge, arched window while her coffee brewed, mesmerized by the frigid outside, such a contrast to the dry warmth of her historic condo setting.

Her phone pinged again.

> "Good morning. Can I call you?"

The number was blocked.

> "Who is this?"
> "Sorry. It's Fred. Had to change my # again."
> "Sure."

Gracie sat down with her coffee, answering the third ring. The deep male voice matched that of the teacher she accidentally fell in love with after her husband, Blair, died. Gracie and Fred parted ways two years ago. Wilson, the golden retriever Gracie inherited after his owner passed away, remained with Fred.

"Good morning. Lots of snow in Niagara Falls?"

"Probably as much as in New Pelham. You have a new number."

"I do. A mischievous student hacked into my phone again. It's easier to block my data and get a new number. Are you alright?"

"I am." For the cordial relationship that she and Fred maintained after she moved out, Gracie felt unsettled by his question. They rarely communicated now, the last time being six months ago. She stood up and returned to the window. "Is something wrong?" There was a pause, then she immediately knew. "Is it Wilson?"

"It is."

"Oh no."

"I'm sorry, but I thought you'd appreciate this call."

"What happened?"

"A week or so ago, I touched his ear to scratch behind it. He whipped his head around and barked. I thought he was going to bite me."

"Wilson did that? That's not like him."

"That's exactly what I thought. I let him settle down, felt the same spot a bit later, and he did the same thing. Then two days ago, he had some wobbly steps, and then the sound of his paws when he followed me around started changing, so I knew something was wrong. I took him to the vet, who sedated him enough to do a thorough exam. That's when he found the tumours."

"Tumours? Oh, Fred," she sighed, tears forming. As much as Gracie loved Wilson, they agreed he was happiest remaining at Fred's rural home instead of moving to Gracie's condo.

"I'm sorry to have to tell you. He's such a great dog, and I know you love him."

"Where is he now?" She could barely speak.

"At the veterinary clinic. He spent the night there because he was so off balance that he couldn't walk. The vet offered to put him to sleep last night, but I thought you'd appreciate knowing. It won't change the outcome, but he's still legally your dog."

"Poor Wilson."

"The vet said he could run some tests, but I didn't think it was fair to Wilson. He said we could hold off and keep him alive until he passes on his own - he called it watchful waiting, but thought what was best for Wilson was to put him to sleep today." Gracie paced between windows as Fred continued. "So, that's where I need your help. If you'd prefer to see him one last time, I'll wait for you. The vet's office is closed, but a vet technician is stranded there and caring for him until we decide." Gracie stared blankly at the cold, still life outside, the unplowed streets, and knew it was cruel to prolong Wilson's suffering. Fred's voice quivered, with long pauses between words.

"He wasn't himself ... and Grace, he just kept looking straight at me. I can't read a dog's mind, but I think he was trying to tell me he'd had enough and just wanted to die." His words cracked, and then she heard muffled sobs. "I've cried a lot in my life, but he's the first animal that's brought me to tears. You both did something for me that no one else was able to."

"What was that?"

"You... and Wilson, you kept me grounded."

Fred and Gracie were in different places, living different lives, yet, on this winter morning, they inhaled and exhaled slowly, together, grieving a beautiful golden retriever that was partially responsible for bringing their lives together.

"I can't make him wait for me to see him. It's not fair," she whispered.

"I thought that's what you would say... and I truly understand."

"Fred?"

"Yes?"

"Thank you for calling me."

"It was important for me to let you know. I'm sorry things didn't work out for us, but I would never knowingly hurt you or him."

"I know Fred … I know." There was a long moment of composing silence.

"I'm assuming the library's closed today?"

"It is. And the school?"

"Thank goodness, yes. The kids won't see my red eyes."

"You're a kind soul, Fred."

"Thank you. Some days I don't feel that way. Are you going to be alright?"

"I will, after today, and maybe tomorrow … and I appreciate everything you've done, not only for me but for Wilson."

"I still care about you."

"Me too. Fred?"

"Yes?"

"Is it true all good dogs go to heaven?"

"Absolutely."

There was a quiet pause after they exchanged goodbyes before their call ended. Gracie brought her knees up to her chest, buried her head in Mason's soft robe and sobbed for her losses. For Wilson, and also for the separate paths that she and Fred continued on. She shared Fred's sentiment; had their circumstances been different, they may have remained together. Mason was as devoted to her now as Fred was in her past. Yet, even though Gracie was moving forward, both Mason and Fred's marriages kept them looking back.

8:10 AM

Fletcher woke up with something warm against his calf. It wasn't his pillow or his Korean delivery friend. He looked down at his feet to see the dog curled up at the damp bottom of his bed, one eye open to meet Fletcher's gaze. He couldn't recall what time he let the snow-crusted dog inside. He sat up, as did the dog; Fletcher yawned, and the dog followed suit. As soon as Fletcher stood up, the dog jumped off the bed, sauntered to the door and whimpered.

"Me too, Tucker." He approached the wooden door and opened it. The screen door was frozen in place. "Shit."

The dog whimpered to indicate his urgency. Fletcher pushed against the screen, accomplishing little. With the combined barriers of snow and ice, it would take longer to get them out than their bladders would hold. He walked to the living room window, unlocked one of the side windows and, with a few good tugs, it rattled open. The screen was coated with ice and frozen in its frame. Fletcher banged at it until the ice fell off, then kept whacking at the frame with the handle of a heavy meat cleaver until the screen came loose in one piece. Fletcher used the cleaver to slice away at the snow and eventually created a U-shaped opening. Tucker's tail wagged against Fletcher as he propped a kitchen chair up against the window. With a little help, Tucker disappeared to do his business.

Fletcher brought a Colombian dark-roast coffee pod to the coffee machine, then called himself an idiot. He texted his mother about the power outage, as if she could help; she encouraged him to be patient. She texted his father, who called Fletcher back and told him to check if the snowblower was still at the very back of the toolshed. Frederick, his father, had outlined very specific instructions on mixing the correct amount of gasoline and two-cycle engine oil to make it run safely. Frederick silently wondered if it would even start, but felt no need to extinguish what ambition his son might have and said that machines performed best with a "real good work-out". He added a few college football quotes of encouragement and asked Fletcher to text him back when he was finished. Fletcher and his father's definitions of "finished" were very different, but that didn't matter. Frederick had already checked the New Abino weather and felt vindicated, knowing his son could only rely on himself to clear the snow. Frederick returned to more pressing matters, like the mega-million-dollar proposals on his desk needing signatures.

Fletcher would rather have enjoyed a coffee latte, but since that wasn't possible, he fueled himself with some organic guava juice and two protein bars. He suited up in his favourite winter gear, branded with a dinosaur skeleton. He found his new rubber-soled boots, yanked the tags off and laced them up. Mittens and gloves on, he exited by the same side window Tucker did. By this time, the sun was out and the view was magical. Icicles hung from everything, and all of the bunkies looked like gingerbread houses. The snow came up to Fletcher's waist, and he felt energized while forging a hundred-foot path with his legs from the bunkie to the tool shed. It was locked, so he hacked at the padlock with the meat cleaver until one of the clasps anchoring the lock broke off.

The door opened inward, making access easier. He switched his phone flashlight on. A wave of nostalgia swept over him when he saw his old bicycle, fishing gear, and pool toys before spotting the cherry-red snowblower deep in the corner. Casting ladders, a boat engine, and lawn chairs aside, he manoeuvred the snowblower out to the sunlight.

A red plastic, five-litre jerry can of gasoline and a six-pack of little oil bottles were on the shelf, exactly where his father said they would be. Fletcher followed Frederick's instructions, also embossed on the snow blower's fuel cap. He added one bottle of oil to the five litres of gas for the recommended fifty-to-one ratio mix, spilling only a bit of fuel. He was pleased not only because he followed the instructions, but he also managed to combine the correct amounts without using his phone's calculator to translate the Canadian metric system to gallons and ounces. He waited a few minutes for the spilled fuel to evaporate, giving him time to post a proud selfie beside the snow blower on his social media sites and wait for compliments.

He opened the snowblower's choke, set the throttle, and pushed the primer bulb twice, his father's instructions ringing in his ears. The snow blower did nothing on the first, second and third time he yanked on the cord to start it. On the fourth pull, it responded with such a loud backfire that Fletcher and Tucker took cover in the snow. He waited, researching his phone long enough to rule out a gas explosion, and on the fifth pull of the cord, the snow blower roared to life. Its blades started to whirl, blowing the dirt underneath it into the air. Coughing to clear his throat, Fletcher navigated the machine out of the shed and into the snow, where it promptly ground to a halt. Heeding his father's repeated warning to blow away only a bit of snow at a time, the blower came to life again on the next try, and Fletcher embarked on his arduous task.

10:35 AM

Sonnet had been up for an hour, still wearing both layers of yesterday's nightgowns. Everything ached. With no power or heat, she remained buried under her bed covers until the sound of an engine lured her to look outside, pleased by the sparkling icicles that the sun was persuading to melt.

Her phone rang four times before she answered. Dr. Torres's office wanted her in for a follow-up appointment. Reluctant to go, she explained that her car had collided with a tree. The same receptionist who Candace insisted squeeze Sonnet in last time suggested that her friend should bring her back again. After a blunt reminder of the fine for missed appointments and her doctor's insistence that she attend, they settled on an appointment for December 15th.

Sonnet opened her wooden front door, mostly from curiosity, and faced the same dilemma that Fletcher had faced. A wall of ice on the screen had formed a third door. She banged at the screen - the ice shattered like glass onto the deck. She heard engine sounds coming from Fletcher's way. She cranked her neck left and spotted the plume of snow flying across the lane, moving very slowly in her direction. She guessed it was Fletcher, crusted in snow, followed by the very tip of a wagging tail; Sonnet watched the activity until the cold forced her back inside.

Noon

At the diner, the generator was working hard to provide minimal surges of power. The senior trio was negotiating lunch with Kat, who'd rather be anywhere else than there. She'd already accepted a ride home from the persistent young Tom once the roads opened. Ziggy, calculating his lost revenues, offered only tuna sandwiches on white or whole wheat, whether the diners liked it or not. Everyone except the electricians was restless. They had already shovelled a path to their white work truck and took turns widening it.

Montana rubbed his throbbing knees, then arched his aching back. Hands on his forehead to shield the bright daylight, he hoped the sun would melt the ice-covered power lines before they collapsed. He scanned the vehicles in the parking lot; a blue handicapped sticker was affixed to the back window of an older van, matching the physical limitations of the senior trio. A beat-up pickup truck sported the same hockey logo on the rear window as Ziggy's baseball cap. This left the owner of the dated blue Toyota, front facing the diner, to be Reba. He relieved young Tom, who had cleared an impressive amount of snow, and sent him inside. Montana and Big Tom continued shovelling until they had cleared around all the vehicles.

"Back tire's real low on this side," Big Tom said, brushing more snow away from Reba's Toyota.

"Not in the best shape," Montana contributed, kicking the other three.

"Hope she's got a donut for a spare." Big Tom rapped the tire case attached to her rear door, then shook his head. "Might be hollow in there."

Montana squatted down to inspect the tire and spotted an embedded piece of metal reflecting in the sun.

"If I yank this out, it'll flatten like a pancake."

The quicker the ice on the windows melted, the broader Reba's view became. Between tidying up and listening to the news, Reba caught the two men huddling around her vehicle. Seconds later, she heard young Tom's phone ping. He left Kat and asked for Reba's keys, and considering that she owned the least desirable vehicle there, theft was off her radar. She dropped them into his open palm, and he rejoined his workmates. She watched the electricians gather for a short conversation before Big Tom manually opened her tailgate. The men stood abreast, broad shoulders obstructing her view until Big Tom came inside.

"Should I be worried?" she asked.

"Worried?" he laughed. "Not yet, that is, but what does a guy have to do to get a cup of coffee around here?"

Reba brewed a fresh pot while she worried, anticipating the others would come in soon, and they did, dripping from melting snow and sweat. Their backs filled the spaces between the red stools they occupied. No one complained about the tuna sandwiches, which disappeared as quickly as she served them. Montana wiped the crumbs off his face with a serviette and, with a nod, motioned her over.

"I have something in my right pocket and something in my left pocket. Pick a pocket." Reba rolled her eyes and tilted her head.

"Left." Montana dug deep, opened a closed fist and produced her ring of keys. "Well, if that's the prize, I can hardly wait to see what's in the other hand."

From his right pocket, he produced another closed fist.

"What do you think it is?"

Reba put her hands on her hips, more impatient than inquisitive.

"I give up." He arched his eyebrows, slowly opening his hand. She picked up and examined a zig-zagged piece of metal. "That's easy. It's half of a cotter pin." She recognized it from the show-and-tell games she played with her father and brothers; she'd also seen some clipped to baseball caps.

"I'm impressed. Did you also know it wrecked your tire?" he asked, watching her pride wilt when he pointed to the broken pin.

"No. Which one?" she groaned, as if it mattered, because replacing any tire was expensive. She never checked her tires.

"Back left."

Her shoulders sagged.

"Can I drive it?"

"You can't drive with a flat, but we replaced it with your donut."

"My donut?"

"Yup - it's your little emergency tire. You can drive it only as far as you need to go to fix the flat, and ASAP."

"That might take a day or two. How much would that cost?"

She calculated her next paycheck date. There wasn't enough money in her account, even with the mystery twenty dollars she'd brought home and stashed in the peanut butter jar at home. She rubbed her bottom lip with her index finger as her eyes flitted across the room. Ziggy rarely gave paycheck advances unless it was for a reason he approved of. Reba rationalized that this was a very good reason, but would mull it over. Montana glanced from Reba's worried eyes to his empty cup. Age, hard work, and fatigue created two vertical creases between his eyebrows. A solid number eleven was how young Tom described them - Reba noticed them as he spoke.

"I heard the snowplows will clear the highways today, but unlikely they'll get to these secondary roads until tomorrow. Not great news, but it'll buy you an extra day on that spare."

Reba cringed at the idea of spending the rest of the day and another night at the diner with eight others, all desperately needing a good shower.

"I sure hope the plows get out here today."

"Don't count on it."

Montana and his peers suited back up for the next round of shovelling, not expecting help from the others inside. Reba felt out of sorts, massaged her throbbing temples, and popped another headache pill.

Meanwhile, at the grocery store, Digger's manager Joe drafted a schedule of thirty-minute, snow-clearing rotations. Like the diner, they had more brooms than shovels. Determined to set a good example, Joe and the produce manager led the pack. Both unfit and fifty, they accomplished very little. After a twinge in one's heart and the other one's back, they came in and sent the next pair out, one of whom was Digger. In half the time, he cleared twice the area of his counterpart. He tackled the next patch, and the next patch and the next patch after that, more than everyone combined. Winning praise from the others, mostly because it meant less work for them, Joe insisted that he come in and eat as much of whatever he wanted. Beaming, Digger picked his favourite raspberry ripple ice cream and didn't stop spooning it into his frozen mouth until the tub was empty.

3:00 PM

Excluding snack breaks, Fletcher remained engrossed in his snow-blowing adventure. He cleared a path from his bunkie to the lane, then to Sonnet's, including the extra twenty feet to her vehicle. The dog she called Rufus dutifully trailed him.

Sonnet watched Fletcher work, then take selfies with Rufus and her wedged vehicle as his backdrop. As much as she detested him, she appreciated his effort. She rubbed her painful bruises and watched Fletcher until he spotted her through the window. He gave her a wave; she joined her palms to create a thank you symbol. He nodded and kept going, Rufus trailing him to catch the blowing snow in his mouth.

Back in the kitchen, Sonnet reread the letter from the insurance company, which stressed the importance of adhering to her doctor's treatment plan. The antidepressants Candace brought sat untouched on the counter. She picked the bottle up and checked the label for accuracy, something she'd done repeatedly before administering the same dose to her patients. If she took just one, she could feign compliance, which was better than lying to a doctor she respected. She opened the bottle and looked at its contents. She poured them all into her left hand and counted them out. Thirty tablets matched the quantity printed on the label, another task she'd repeated countless times while doing medication inventory at work.

Her thoughts darkened. If she swallowed all the pills, she might conceivably end her problems and her life. She wasn't absolutely certain that thirty tablets would have a guaranteed outcome; checking online may prompt a suicide helpline. She stared blankly at her palm, then at Fletcher playing with Rufus, both full of energy, gently stirring the pills around with her right index finger. She returned all but one to the bottle and then swallowed the little outlier with yesterday's abandoned cup of frigid tea.

6:00 PM

At the diner, the local radio station marked twenty-four hours without power by playing Bruce Springsteen's *Darkness on the Edge of Town* while New Abino relied on generators and patience. The night was black, and none of the roads, or at least those important to the locals, had been cleared. Electrical crews worked overtime to restore power, albeit more slowly than everyone predicted.

Joe corralled everyone into the grocery store lunchroom to acknowledge the hardship of being away from all things important. He thanked everyone, especially an exhausted Digger, also agitated from being squeezed into a cramped room. When he tried to leave, Joe insisted that he stay. Although it was only December 2, Joe awarded Digger *Employee of the Month* for his snow-clearing efforts. Digger's anxiety escalated, knees knocking as fast as his hands tapped against them.

Joe understood Digger's abilities from both the Adlers and the internet, but most of his co-workers didn't, misinterpreting his avoidance behaviours as ignoring them. Joe took this as a learning opportunity and kindly suggested Digger tell his co-workers more about himself. Digger froze, his knees bouncing faster. In the past, he repeatedly faced failure and frustration in explaining himself. When Joe offered, Digger reluctantly permitted him to start the conversation.

"The best way I know to tell you about Digger is that he is different." The room became very still as Joe paused, cautiously praising his best employee without discrediting the others. "Digger is super smart. He has many abilities, not disabilities, that make people see him differently." The slower Joe spoke to emphasize his point, the less Digger's knees bounced. "Situations, especially like this, make lots of people uncomfortable. If Digger's frustrated, he might seem angry. Am I right?" he said as he turned to Digger, who nodded repeatedly.

One single mother asked Digger how he managed at school.

"Not too good." His head hung down as his shoulders rolled inward.

"And did they bully you too?" she asked, thinking of her own young son.

"Yup." Those who were texting discreetly stopped, and the faces of those who were listening sagged.

"And were some teachers mean to you?" Digger's chin dropped lower.

"Yup, times two."

"Just like my little guy," the young mother answered softly, a tear following the crease near her eye. A teenaged female clerk looked up from her phone.

"Have you ever had a girlfriend?" Digger sucked loudly on his bottom lip until Joe intercepted.

"I don't think that's an appropriate question."

He ended the meeting with appreciation for everyone and promised a bonus on their paychecks. He reassigned restless staff to keep them more distracted than productive. Digger chose his regular job without being told. He whirled his spinner and exchanged a few texts with Reba, reassured by her that things would be better tomorrow.

He headed back out the door, in the dark, to recover from the meeting by shovelling snow.

Joe lingered, alone in the lunchroom, hoping he had made some progress in unifying his team. He checked in with his wife at home, worrying less about her than how his staff would survive another long night.

7:00 PM

Sonnet rose from the sofa with the worn quilt she'd slept under and wrapped it around her shoulders. She put her slippers on and shuffled into the kitchen, fumbling around in her junk drawer until she found what she was looking for—a bag of small candles. Feeling nauseated and peculiar from the antidepressant, she arranged six candles in a circle on a sturdy aluminum pie plate, lit them and warmed a small pot of bottled water over the flames, flavouring it with a tea bag. She watched the water change to a brandy colour, filled her mug with it and added a few drops of milk. She took a sip and closed her eyes. Three small pleasures soothed her: her hands securing the warm cup, its steam bathing her face, and the taste of good tea on her tongue. Still wearing two nightgowns, she brought her tea and the half-eaten tin of shortbreads back to the sofa. The moon illuminated her cabin, she pulled the quilt tighter and sat down to think about nothing and then everything, all mixed up together.

Fletcher was more pleased with himself than he'd been in a long time. He was cold, wet, and hungry from clearing snow around the three bunkies and then a path wide enough for a vehicle to access the lane. He left the snowblower outside, intending to return it to the tool shed.

He weighed out the complexities of two ideas he had to heat his home. He found a small gas-fueled generator in the tool shed and carried it indoors, thinking he could run both a space heater and his cappuccino maker from it. Another option was to move his propane barbeque inside, light it, and leave the lid open to provide heat while he boiled water for coffee and packages of ramen soup. He decided to do both.

He brought the generator inside first, then the barbecue, leaving a trail of snow tracks across the old Persian rug left behind from his grandmother's estate. Rufus added to the snow on the carpet by giving himself a few good shakes. He then lay down by the window and worked at removing the clumps of crusty snow embedded between his paws.

Fletcher had no idea how much fuel was in the barbeque tank. He opened the tank's valve, and with three quick lighter clicks, he whistled aloud when the flames swept across the food residue coating the steel grilling surface.

Snowplows slowly expanded their territories to begin clearing the secondary roads. Media alerts still threatened that police would issue stiff fines for anyone venturing out, and there was no guarantee that emergency vehicles would respond to calls.

9:00 PM

As the hours of confinement increased at the diner, so did its malodorous and miserable occupants. Dinner was a hodgepodge of perishables, at least in Ziggy's mind, which activated a hushed debate about why tuna sandwiches were served at lunch.

The oldest woman from the senior trio of seniors grew more confused and irritable; her daughter rationed out two happy pills from her depleting stash. They worked quickly, settling her into a noisy slumber.

There was a rerun of yesterday's euchre game, its participants, and winners. No one was interested in expanding the conversation beyond who was dealing and the score. Young Tom made headway with Kat, using his phone's dwindling life by sending playful texts, in the hopes of warming up next to her that night. When the card game ended, Big Tom admitted he was missing his wife's nattering, but more than her, he was missing his bed. Sleep-deprived, he pilfered a few headache tablets from the diabetic man's wife, adjusted and readjusted his position on the floor, selfishly hoping for more space if young Tom cozied up with Kat.

Reba's only bedtime option was returning to her little corner beside Montana. Shortly after dinner was cleared away, she found a small treasure in the back of the supply closet — a pair of faded red and white checked window curtains, removed long before her debut at the diner. She laid one curtain on the floor to use as a bed sheet for both of them. She created a floor-length skirt with the second one, intending to cover most of her legs, but definitely her bottom while she slept. Montana stood about six feet away, humoured by watching Reba awkwardly lowering herself to the floor. He followed suit, his exhausted and stiffening muscles unsuccessful in keeping the curtain in place on the floor.

"I've messed it up," he apologized, pointing to the curtain.

"I don't care."

"I also stink."

"I already knew that."

They lay quietly for a few minutes, both on their backs, staring at the ceiling. Montana turned on his side, facing away from her, and after a few minutes, rolled over towards her.

"I can't do this."

"Do what?"

"Sleep on that side."

"Then don't."

"You don't mind?"

"Do I have a choice?"

"I'm sorry."

"Why are you apologizing?"

"Because I have bar-rag breath, and I'm afraid to take my boots off because the stench will clear out the room."

"And I'm as fresh as a daisy? Get over it."

"Okay. So, can I take off my boots?"

"Go for it."

"Thank you."

"Stop thanking me."

Reba followed the same repositioning sequence as Montana did. She first rolled away from him, then back to face him. He watched her watch him in the dim light.

"Say something, or go to sleep," she muttered.

"You're stuck here with all of us. And when this blows over, you'll have to keep coming back here and be reminded of this."

"What's wrong with that?"

"Nothing, I suppose."

"Okay, then."

"Do you like working here?"

"It pays the bills, or at least most of them."

There was another long pause, and instead of looking at Montana's face, she was drawn to his hands. She noticed that the skin from his knuckles to his fingertips was blanched, and his nails were clubbed. Montana rolled up his fingers so that only his fists were visible, except for the mangled right index finger she'd noticed before. She made a sour face.

"Why did you do that?"

"Do what?"

"Hide your hands."

"Because they're ugly."

"I wouldn't call them ugly. They're more like ... like interesting. What happened to this one?" She touched the crooked one gently.

"It was in the wrong place at the wrong time."

"That doesn't explain much. What did you do?"

"Got it caught."

"In what?"

"Machinery ... a hydraulic post digger." She cringed, clamping her teeth shut.

"Whatever that hydraulic post thing is, it sounds bad. Can I see it?"

Grudgingly, he unfolded his right hand onto hers; she examined the sheath of scars covering his fingers.

"Must've been messy when it happened."

"These broke," he said quietly, pointing to all but his baby finger.

"All of them?" He nodded as she skimmed her fingers over his nails. "Can I see your left hand?"

He hesitated, then complied. She held both his large hands, marred from decades of electrical burns, an adverse effect of his trade. The warmth of her soft skin soothed him.

"Why are your nails curled like that?"

"From long hours working to restore power in ice storms. Like I said, they're ugly."

"Well, they're not pretty, but they tell a story."

"And what story is that?"

"That you're a hard worker. You should be proud of that." Reba nodded at his hands, held them a little longer, then slid them out of hers. Montana smiled.

"That felt nice."

"What did?"

"You touching my hands."

"Huh."

"I have a suggestion."

"I can hardly wait," she said.

"Maybe if we switch sides again, we both might sleep a little better tonight."

"Why?"

"Because my ex-wife slept on this side, and I've always slept on your side."

"Huh."

"Huh, what?"

"Nothing."

"So, is that a 'yes'?"

"I guess it is."

With great effort to keep a respectful distance and not entangle their body parts, Reba sat up, drew her knees up to her chest and leaned her back straight against the wall. He saw her stiffen, then stare ahead.

"What's wrong?" he whispered, with no response. Her eyes fluttered repeatedly, but she remained still. He sat up and watched until she relaxed. By that time, a few minutes had passed. "Are you alright?" he repeated, gently touching her shoulder. Again, she didn't respond. Concerned, he held her rigid hand in his until it became limp.

"Hey, Reba, are you okay?" He turned to face her directly. As with her hand, her facial lines softened. She stared directly at him. He did the same until she rewarded him with a weary smile.

"Hi," he said quietly.

"Hi," she mouthed back.

"You scared me. I thought you were on another planet."

"I think I fell asleep."

"I sure hope that's what it was."

She looked confused, frowned at him, then yawned softly.

"I'm so tired," she said. "I just want to go to sleep." Montana began to crawl around her to move to her other side. "What are you doing?" She eyed him, then the curtain fabric on the floor as if she'd not seen it before.

"Switching sides."

"What for?" she asked, oblivious to their previous conversation.

"So that we'll both sleep a little better tonight?"

"Oh. Okay."

He carefully avoided touching her as he repositioned himself on the floor.

"Reba?" Montana whispered.

"What now?"

"It's okay if you lean your back against mine."

There was a long pause before she answered.

"If it happens, it happens."

Montana wasn't sure what Reba meant by that, but by the time sleep came to the pair, their backs were leaning heavily against each other.

Their movements caught Big Tom's attention across the room, who was the last awake person in the diner. He hoped Montana would garner a sliver of comfort from Reba, if even just a pleasant thought, which he knew not only his friend, but his co-worker hadn't felt in a long, long time.

9:30 PM

Fletcher savoured his cappuccino while four sirloin beef burgers sizzled on the barbeque in the middle of his living room. Gourmet Thai noodles swelled in the cast iron pot of boiling water beside the meat. He cranked up the volume on his smart speakers and was dancing when an excruciating sound exploded from somewhere in the bunkie. Rufus bolted for the door, barking frantically to escape the wailing.

Fletcher looked at the ceiling's smoke detector, instantly reminded that he had removed its expiring battery instead of changing it. He dashed between rooms, hands cupping his ears until he isolated the noise to a carbon monoxide monitor behind his sofa. He yanked it out of the socket, infuriated when the piercing noise continued. He threw it across the room; the alarm continued. He retrieved it from where it landed behind a heavy recliner and fumbled with it until he ejected the batteries. Finally, the room became silent; the residual effect ringing in both his and the dog's ears. Rufus howled while Fletcher suddenly thought that both of them were being poisoned.

He quickly closed the propane tank seal under the barbeque, then unplugged the devices he had attached to the generator, which he also shut off. He opened the front door wide; Rufus ran fifty feet away from the bunkie, paused and then kept running. Fletcher inhaled deep, exaggerated breaths while he keyed 'carbon monoxide poisoning' into his phone, then shoved the barbecue onto the deck.

He evaluated his dinner. Some water spilled out from the noodle pot, hissing steam evaporating off the grill. Using tea towels, he transferred the pot to the stove, then flipped the burgers onto a plate and came inside. He took a knife and, using his phone flashlight, inspected the inside of the burgers. He decided they were cooked and edible. Instead of eating two and saving two, he became a good Samaritan—with an agenda.

He packaged two burgers in foil and scooped some of the Thai noodles into a take-out container, then retraced the moonlit path he cleared to Sonnet's bunkie, which was dark, except for a circle of candles he saw through her window. He knocked softly on the door with Rufus in tow, who hoped the burgers were his.

Sonnet heard the knocks, fearfully edging along an inside wall. She waited, mistaking the sound for Rufus's tail whacking against it, then saw him pacing back and forth in front of her window. With no need to make herself presentable for a dog, she tightened the quilt around her and listened by the door. In the dark of night, there were no shadows on the other side. She opened the door, immediately startled by Fletcher's bulky, down-filled coat, magnifying his size. He stood inches apart from her, separated only by a frost-covered screen. She hesitated, watching him impatiently shift his weight from foot to foot. After his display of a few hopeful grins, she opened the door a crack. Rufus nosed through the door opening and sprinted inside. The scent of food redirected her focus from Rufus to Fletcher's face, and then his hands.

"Thought you'd like something hot to eat." He raised his offering to her eye level.

"You frightened me! Is … is … is your power on? How in Heaven's name did you make this?"

"Nope, no power yet. I cooked it on the barbeque."

Sonnet's gut groaned loudly when she inhaled. Even though he'd lived beside her for a year or more, their communication was rare. She attempted to process his intentions, tightening her quilt around her night clothes.

"You should eat this while it's hot," he said, arms still extended.

"I'm, I'm … I'm not sure what to say. Thank you," she finally mumbled.

"You know, I made a stupid mistake. I brought the barbeque inside, and while I was cooking, the carbon monoxide alarm went off."

"I thought I heard something."

"It's all my fault. Ah …" he said, just as a snow-crusted Rufus vigorously shook himself, spraying water and bits of ice across the room, then made himself comfortable on her sagging sofa. Sonnet shook her head, then turned back to Fletcher, who was scanning the contents of her home.

"Yes? Is there something you want?"

"You're a nurse, right?"

"Why do you ask?"

"Well, because I'm wondering if, like, you don't think I could have poisoned myself with carbon monoxide?"

"I don't think so, but you're best to call the poison control centre."

"I know that, but just looking at me, do you think I'm, like, okay?" Sonnet couldn't help but sigh. She gave him a reassuring once-over, like a mother before sending her eight-year-old off to school.

"If you were able to cook this good food, dress yourself and be kind enough to bring it over here, I would think you're just fine," she said, instead of suggesting he call the poison control centre again.

"Whew. That's really good. I needed to hear that." A mild gust of wind swept some snow up against the door behind Fletcher, hitting it like coarse salt.

"Thank you for the food and for clearing my driveway. Do I owe you anything?"

"Oh, no. Nice place you've got here."

"Well, again, I thank you." She moved slightly closer to him, hoping he would take her gesture as a sign to leave.

"And you got the envelope I found washed up on the beach."

"Ah, so it was you who left it by the door."

"I figured it was important, and I didn't want to open it," he lied.

"It was important. Thank you again for everything, and now I need to rest," she said impatiently.

"Well, don't forget to eat. You need some meat on your bones, as my mother would say," he chuckled, and opened the door. Rufus stayed put, warm and cozy on Sonnet's wet sofa.

Food in hand, Sonnet nodded once more in appreciation and closed and locked the door. She turned around to see Rufus slide off the couch and swagger towards her. He stood beside her, then leaned against her thigh before looking up. Her tired, grey eyes stared into his big, black pupils. His tail twitched, then wagged slightly from side to side, followed by a soft whine. Another knock distracted them both – it was Fletcher returning.

"Tucker, come on, boy," he beckoned. The dog leaned against Sonnet again, not moving.

"Tucker? Is that his name?"

"I don't know, but he comes when I call him Tucker."

"He also does when I call him Rufus. He's not yours?"

"No. I thought he might be yours."

She shook her head and looked at the dog's pleading eyes.

"Well, Rufus, make up your mind. Are you staying or going?" The dog lay down and placed his head on the floor between his paws, in no hurry to return to where the alarm startled him.

"I guess he's staying," she said, edging the door closed.

Fletcher, clearly disappointed, left. Seconds after Sonnet closed the door, Rufus resumed his anticipatory stance, confident that not only could he win Sonnet over, but half of her dinner as well. She placed Fletcher's offerings on the counter and opened the foil-covered burgers and broth-infused noodles. She scooped half of the noodles into an old stainless-steel pot, added one burger and cut everything into smaller pieces for him.

"Now, eat slowly, young man. Not good for the digestion," she scolded him quietly. She transferred the second burger into the take-out container of noodles and cut her serving into the same size as Rufus's while she lectured her guest.

"In this house, regardless of who you are, we pray before we eat." And so, she prayed as he waited, then put his pot on the floor beside her seat at the table. "Bonne Appétit."

He gobbled up his meal and had the pot licked clean by the time she had swallowed her third mouthful.

"That's it. No more," she scolded him, then changed her mind and scraped the rest of her dinner into his pot.

DECEMBER 3ᴿᴰ

6:00 AM
(Sunny, but cold)

Montana and Reba woke up at about the same time, facing each other. Montana's right hand lay extended over his bent knees; it was the first thing Reba saw when she opened her eyes. She observed it again, wondering how he managed not to get that bent index finger caught in the everyday things he did.

"Morning, Reba."

"Morning." She slid her hand out from cradling her head, reached over and covered his finger as if to shield it.

"Does it hurt?"

"Only when I whack it with a hammer," he grinned softly. She curled her hand into the palm of his; he wrapped it entirely with his. "Do you remember what happened last night?"

Her eyes opened wide. She poked her head up and scanned her environment, then looked under the curtain that was barely covering her. "Why? What happened?"

"You had a little spell. Like you were in a trance."

"A trance? I don't remember that."

"I didn't think you would."

"Hmmm, that's never happened before."

"Maybe nobody's been close enough to you to notice."

"Huh?" She didn't know whether to be insulted, frightened or reassured to learn this. Before she gave it more thought, Montana pointed to the kitchen door. She saw Ziggy's head poking out, motioning for her to hurry up and put the coffee on.

"I think I hear a snow plow!" yelled Kat, jumping up and peering out the window. Behind her popped up young Tom, followed by the others in order of how quickly they could rise to their feet. Reba came over, more intent on luring Kat to help her than seeing the day begin. Reba's phone rang in her pocket. Predictably, it was Digger.

"Mom, our hydro is back on!"

"The grocery store has power!" Reba yelled loudly to anyone who would listen. "That's great news, honey, so ours should come back on any minute. When that happens, I'll let you know. Are you okay?"

"Yup. You okay too, Mom?"

"I'm just fine."

Within minutes, power was restored to the diner, accompanied by the cheers of its occupants. Just as the noise settled, all eyes focused out the window towards the approaching sound of a big engine. More cheering erupted, then loud groans as the snow spiralled high off the plow's curved blade like a white tidal wave and dumped it right back on the diner's driveway.

Reba jump-started the three electricians with the first round of coffee, which they gulped down while zipping up their outdoor gear, still soaked from yesterday's labours. They were as motivated to clear the barrier as everyone was to watch them.

The diner's ambience was that of eager anticipation. Reba hummed, thinking that the quicker the stinky people left, the better. She packed up three servings of toast, peanut butter and jam for the seniors as young Tom warmed up their van. The seniors gushed over Reba's care package and left for home.

Ziggy used a thick, black marker to scrawl a message on the grease-stained flap he tore off a cardboard box of frozen bacon:

Closed.
Open tomorrow for breakfast.

He taped it to the glass front door. Never short of loud opinions, he told Reba to lock up and left in his pickup truck. She removed and read his sign, dated it and reattached it with more tape as the exhausted shovelers stamped the snow off their boots and came in.

Backpack straddling her shoulders, Kat was dressed and impatient for young Tom to drive her home. Montana rested his scarred hands on his lean hips.

"So, how are we doing this? Our crew cab can hold four people, including toolboxes."

"I gotta get home first. I've got an English exam tomorrow, and I haven't started studying," Kat whined.

"Any other emergencies?" Big Tom quipped with a hint of sarcasm, thinking about Reba but looking at Montana. "Reba, your car's got that small donut tire. Montana, should she even be driving on these roads?"

"But I need my car. My son's been stuck at the grocery store as long as I've been here, and he doesn't drive."

Montana heard her desperation. There was a silent gap while he and Big Tom exchanged pensive stares.

"Here's my suggestion," he said, turning to Big Tom. "Drop Kat home first, then take young Tom to our trailer to clear out a parking spot, then come back and get us."

"Where's your trailer?" Reba asked.

"At our job site. About twenty minutes from here."

"But I've gotta be back here in the morning," she persisted. Montana checked Ziggy's sign on the front door.

"It doesn't say what time it opens, so if we pick you both up and get Digger to work, maybe you'll make us breakfast?" Reba's eyes grew wide.

"You'd do that for us?"

"It might cost Ziggy an extra pound of bacon."

"It'll cost him whatever you want. On the house," she said.

Kat and the two Toms left within minutes, just as Digger let Reba know that Joe was driving him home. Reba reminded her son to thank him from both of them. She locked the front door and dimmed the lights. She made fresh coffee, then faced Montana. Recurrent layers of sweat stained his shirt. He undid the top two buttons and lowered his aching body onto the stool across her.

"So, here we are, just the two of us," he said, looking around. "Stinky and cranky, and sleep-deprived. Not so romantic."

She put her palms to her eyes and rubbed them, then took in his appearance, feeling mildly odd about being alone with him.

"Well, I've never slept with a guy whose real name I didn't know," she cackled, instantly regretting her words.

"Now that's helpful to know."

"Sorry, that was a stupid thing to say." She backed up a few steps.

"You're not afraid of me, are you?"

"Not quite, but maybe a little nervous."

"Why? Because we're alone? I told you that you're safe with me." She relaxed slightly.

"What I meant was, should I know if there is another name that people, like maybe your kids, call you?"

"My kids call me Dad." He grinned, and she rolled her eyes.

"Then what does, or what did your mother call you?"

"Thayer."

"Thayer? Is that your real name?" She repeated it slowly.

"Yes, ma'am, that's what she called me, especially when she was mad. It was her interpretation of an old name meaning a brave, strong hunter."

"Huh. And what did she call you when she wasn't mad?"

"Her little ray of sunshine."

Reba giggled loudly, and despite their fatigue, Montana was taken by Reba's eyes, sparkling like iridescent green marbles.

"Okay then, Sunshine. How about some of that bacon that Ziggy won't realize he's missing?"

"Only if I can help."

"You can help by staying put, where you won't distract me," Reba chirped, knowing in fact that she was more than a little distracted by him.

With a new surge of energy, she disappeared into the kitchen. Montana heaved himself up, spread his soaked coat across a heat register to dry and stood at the window, hands on his hips, where the icicles were dripping in the rising sun. Exhausted yet restless, he found a broom in the closet and put it to use. Reba opened the kitchen door to ask which way he wanted his eggs cooked. Silenced by his unprompted initiative, she became mesmerized by the impressive back muscles under his damp shirt swaying in unison with the broom's rhythmic swish, swish, swish across the floor. She closed the door quietly, cracked three eggs on the grill and toasted some rye bread; the freshest and biggest up-charge on the menu.

6:45 AM

Delivered by Joe to the top of Polly's Lane, Digger was relieved to know Reba's Toyota could make it down to their bunkie. He assumed Cousin Al cleared the path until he saw the snow blower in Fletcher's driveway. Digger thought Fletcher was weird; Fletcher thought Digger was peculiar, each so different from the other.

Digger stared in wonder when he saw Sonnet's car, lodged between the trees, then whispered Yay to only himself when he spotted the illuminated light above her door.

From her front window, Sonnet saw him walk by, then stop and stare at her car. She'd only seen him without Reba at the grocery store and felt troubled that he was walking home alone at this early hour. Unconcerned about her bedraggled appearance, and Digger looking no better, she startled him when she opened her door.

"Good morning," she said, her voice hoarse. "Are you alright?" He stared blankly at her, initially saying nothing, then spewed out his last two days in one long, rambling sentence.

"Our power is back on. Would you like to have some coffee?" She surprised even herself with the offer.

"I know." He pointed to her light. "And I don't drink coffee."

Relieved, she let it rest.

"You're not driving home with your mom?" She pointed her chin in the direction of her car, one slippered foot on the deck to hold the door ajar.

"She'll be here soon," he said defensively and continued heading home.

Just as Sonnet was closing the door, Rufus ran outside towards Digger, hooking his front paw on Sonnet's torn housecoat hem.

"Oh!" she yelled as the dog yelped loudly - both lost their balance, tumbling onto the wet deck. "Oww!!" she screamed, landing on the same bruised side that she fell on two days ago. While she moaned in pain, Rufus rolled over in slow motion, then jumped up and ran towards Digger. Sonnet extended her right hand to push herself into a sitting position; a jolt of pain shocked her.

"Oww!!"

Digger turned, hearing the commotion.

"Useless!" He stooped to hug the dog.

"Useless?" Sonnet cried, insulted by his comment.

Digger cocked his head to one side.

"That's what my mom says."

Sonnet sat up, overwhelmed with pain and confusion. Both Digger and the dog returned.

"My mother named the dog Useless," he explained, his hand resting on the dog's head. Both watched Sonnet attempt to get up. Using her left arm, she grasped the door handle, pulled herself up onto her knees, and then onto her feet. She held her right arm against her body and opened the door. Digger shrugged his shoulders and turned towards home. Rufus eyed Sonnet directly, locked into her teary stare as if debating his loyalty, then opted to follow Digger.

7:01 AM

Gracie and Mason's phones played different tunes to wake them. Silencing their alarms, each turned over and folded their arms and legs together. Their skin, softened with age, easily moulded into each other's curves. Mason's first kiss landed on Gracie's forehead. Her eyes remained closed as she moaned softly. He kissed her eyelids, then her nose, cheek, and chin. He followed the outline of her neck, kissed her collarbones, and then gently tugged at the sheets to uncover her breasts. He kissed each nipple slowly, savouring the taste in his mouth. His phone pinged. He hesitated, distracted by the interruption for a split second, then continued to savour her body. He rested his hand across the soft mound between her legs. His phone pinged again.

"I hate this thing," he groaned, lying on his back and stretching as far as he could to reach his device. He squinted, but couldn't see the message on his screen without sitting up to find his glasses. Instead, he passed it to Gracie, who read it to him.

"It says your phone bill is due," she giggled and handed his phone back. He silenced it, dropped it onto the sheets and snuggled back into Gracie's arms.

"Now, where were we?"

"Almost at third base," she whispered, nuzzling into his neck and moving one hand slowly down his torso.

"Hmmm ... you might not find what you're hoping for ... because I've kind of lost my momentum."

"But I haven't," she giggled again and gently searched, then took his wilting member in her hand. Some days, Mason struggled with intimacy, not from lack of desire, but from the cumulative effect of his stressful legal career, heredity, and blood pressure woes. Medication sometimes dampened his performance, and in his opinion, ruined their first cruise. Gracie disagreed, having never been overseas. She cherished Mason, constantly reassuring him that all forms of intimacy, regardless of how and where the opportunity arose, were important.

Gracie calmed Mason, kissed and fondled him until his body responded.

Success, she thought, proud of her skill in pleasuring him.

Success, he thought, relieved, as he entered her.

Success, they both thought, after a satisfactory romp in Gracie's big bed, cuddling a little longer before showering together to make up the time they lost before facing their day.

7:45 AM

By the time Big Tom returned to the diner, Reba and Montana had shared enough history and breakfast to forget their fatigue. Reba's story totalled fifteen minutes; her questions to Montana filled in his gaps. He was divorced and adored his children. His employer constructed luxury homes, including the author's primary residence in Montana, which brought him to Canada to build her retreat. He was a humble man, respected by others in the industry for his pride and perfectionism, and was in high demand.

Montana unlocked the diner door to let Big Tom in, and Reba had packaged up enough breakfast for both Toms. She was as grateful for the ride home as they were for her and Ziggy's unknowing hospitality.

As happy as she was to leave, Reba regretted that their quiet morning had ended. They'd exchanged phone numbers, but at this point, nothing more, and nothing less, was expected.

Big Tom drove, with Reba nestled between the men. In awe of the huge, ice-clad snow drifts, she was relieved not to have driven.

"Did you manage to get Kat and young Tom home?" she asked.

"You bet, but they sure were cranky being separated," he answered, looking above Reba's head, winking at Montana. "Hopefully young Tom worked off his frustration shovelling snow."

As the truck passed the grocery store, two compact cars resembling snow-covered igloos remained in the driveway. The red glow of the CLOSED sign shone brightly above the entrance doors. Ten minutes later, the truck arrived at the top of Polly's Lane. Reba insisted that Tom not drive down the lane to avoid getting stuck and complicating things. Even with no boots, hat or gloves, she insisted on walking home.

"It'll do me good," she lied as Montana got out. His hand clasped her upper arm to support her as she first stepped onto the running board of the truck's high carriage, then, in front of his boot, planted there to prevent her from slipping. She thanked Tom, then rewarded Montana with the best smile she could muster. They set a pick-up time the following morning for the men to deliver both Adlers to work. She watched the truck drive away and then made her way home, but what she didn't see was that her flat tire lay in the back of their truck.

Reba assessed the damage from the storm as she walked. Lots of fallen branches pierced the snow drifts. A stray roof shingle and other unknown debris lay in places they didn't belong.

Digger was sound asleep in his bed when she peeked in on him. She didn't see the dog, lying hidden between his bed and the wall. Reba stripped her soiled clothes off, relished a hot shower and headed to bed, for once without setting an alarm.

Young Tom had shovelled as much as his energy reserves could muster, and just enough room to park the truck. In single file, the men followed the narrow path from the truck to the heated trailer. Montana lingered outside to absorb the expansive view of Lake Erie. He imagined the author taking a break and stretching her limbs on the massive balcony of the A-frame home. This pristine sight, with no distraction beyond nature itself, was indeed a writer's paradise.

When he entered the trailer, the rancid smell told him neither of the Toms had showered, and both were already in their berths at the back of the trailer. Montana understood why when he turned the taps on – the water was only tepid, but still felt luxurious. His thoughts shifted to Reba's emerald eyes, her maritime demeanour and her hesitancy when she was near him. Their intimate moments were summed up by a few prolonged looks, some hand-holding primarily focused on curiosity, and the warmth of her back sleeping against his.

He thought about her spell and her lack of awareness about it, or at least, what she admitted. *She's a protective mother bear of Digger,* he thought, drying himself off. He compared her son to his children; his work took him miles away from them, and by virtue of his long absences, they'd learned early to fend for themselves. He had his own little quirks, just as Reba labelled Digger's. And, just like Digger's orange spinner, the little cross Montana carried in his pocket always made him feel better.

Montana climbed up to his elevated bed at the front of the trailer. He layered himself with all the blankets he had and fell asleep, thinking that if he'd been home more, maybe his own relationships would be as solid as Reba and her son.

10:00 AM

Shocks vibrated down Sonnet's right arm, and by now, the swelling obliterated any definition in her wrist. She was too cold to ice her injuries. She couldn't remember when she last bathed or showered, and it wasn't going to happen today. As a consolation measure, she carefully removed both soiled nightgowns and replaced them with clean, baggy flannel pyjamas and the same pilled, bulky sweater. She put the kettle on, splinted her right hand between the buttons of her pyjama top, then picked the strands of her hair and Rufus's fur off of her sweater while she waited.

She eased herself into a kitchen chair and stared at the box of things that Candace brought. She couldn't move the heavy box with one hand. Groaning and in pain everywhere, she rose and pulled the box closer.

On top was a bag stamped with the library's logo, and in it were books. She removed a folded slip of printed paper from the bag's clear outer sleeve, stating the books were due back on December 1st. This shifted Sonnet into a worry mode.

Sipping tea, she stared at the phone number on the library slip. She got up again, found her phone on the sofa arm and checked her battery life: twenty percent. She set it on speaker mode and leaned it against her mug, then pecked out the number with a shaky finger. The call was answered quickly by a woman at the library who identified herself as Gracie. Sonnet explained her dilemma and was reassured that there was no penalty for her books because of the storm. Those books would be exchanged for six new ones, which, weather permitting, Gracie would deliver on December 7th. She apologized for not having called Sonnet yet to introduce herself; Gracie gave her a brief orientation to the library's outreach program and told Sonnet she could choose her own books from the online inventory if she preferred.

Sonnet thanked her and hung up, pleased that she'd accomplished something. She carried her tea to her front window, hoping to see Rufus loitering near her door and spoke to no one but herself.

Rufus, whom the Adlers call Useless, and then there is Tucker, what Fletcher calls him. Good Lord, the dog has three different names, and he responds to them all…

2:00 PM

Reba woke up, reassured that she was in her own bed. The faint aroma of something good wafted out of the kitchen. Bundled up in her fluffy housecoat, tied tightly over her flimsy nightgown, she tucked her feet into sloppy, fur-lined slippers and shuffled to find Digger toasting frozen waffles.

"Boy, those have never smelled so good." She leaned against the counter and looked into the empty box. Only two of the dozen waffles were left in their plastic wrapper. "Is that your tenth waffle?"

"I'm hungry."

"I bet you are."

"Coffee's ready to go, Mom." He'd already set her favourite mug out.

Reba ran a few soft scratches across Digger's upper back as she passed him to turn the old coffee maker on. The mixed aromas of caffeine and toasting waffles cued her hunger. She filled her large, chipped mug with coffee, toasted the two remaining waffles and sat down facing Digger.

"I'm proud of you. Our last two days weren't easy."

"I shovelled almost the whole parking lot at work."

"You did that?"

"Yup."

"Wow. No wonder you ate ten waffles."

"I found Useless, too."

"You did? Where?"

"At Mrs. O'Brien's house. He was in such a hurry to see me that he knocked her over."

"That's not good. Is she okay?"

"She fell, and then she yelled at me."

"At you? Why?"

"She asked where you were, and then she asked me if I wanted a cup of coffee. When Useless heard me and ran out, they both fell. And, and, and then she called me useless. So, I just went home."

"I'm sure she didn't mean it."

"She screamed pretty loudly."

"And you didn't let the dog in here, did you?" Guilt covered Digger's face.

"He was hungry."

"What did you give him?"

"Cereal. But after he ate, and we had a little sleep, I let him out."

Reba spotted the empty cereal box beside the garbage can. It was hard to be angry with him after two hellish days, probably worse for him.

"I hope Sonnet's okay. I saw her car - looks like it was purposely driven between those fir trees," she said.

"I think it slid into the trees," he answered, drenching the rest of his waffle with maple-flavoured syrup. "Where's our car?"

"Still at the diner. It's gotta flat tire, so some nice guys told me not to drive it. They drove me home and will take us to work tomorrow. We'll get it fixed after that, so no need to worry about it now."

But she did worry as she plucked her waffles out of the toaster and tossed them onto Digger's empty plate, which she scraped across the table until it was in front of her, and then sat down. Enough syrup was left to coat both sides of her waffles. When she went to stand up to get a fork, Digger passed her his.

December 4th

3:00 AM

Sonnet prided herself on having a high tolerance for both physical and psychological pain. Until now. The discomfort and swelling in her right lower arm made it impossible for her to sleep. She paced the moonlit floors of her small surroundings. She prayed. She turned the bathroom light on and saw her desperate self in the mirror-clad cabinet above the sink – grey skin and a grey, knotted mess of hair surrounding gaunt, grey eyes. She opened the cabinet; behind a crumpled toothpaste tube, she found anti-inflammatory pills, prescribed eight years ago for a shoulder injury she sustained while moving an obese patient. She remembered the incident because there were so few overweight cancer patients, unlike the patients in the chronic care unit.

The bottle's warning label threatened death by hemorrhage unless she swallowed each expired dose with copious amounts of food and stayed mobile for longer than she knew she could. She tucked the bottle in her pocket and shuffled to the kitchen. She opened an upper cupboard near her sink where the bottle of antidepressants sat on the bottom shelf between multivitamins and tea-stained china cups. On a higher shelf was a brown bottle of Irish whiskey from a staff gathering she attended years ago, recalling the others sharing copious amounts of liquor and hospital gossip.

She raised her left arm, halting mid-reach when pain pierced her right side. She breathed out slowly until it eased, then used a footstool to retrieve the grimy bottle. The cap, sealed with age and dried whiskey, wouldn't budge. She sat down, and despite anchoring the bottle using her hands and knees, couldn't loosen the top. She retrieved a chopping knife from the kitchen drawer and stood the glass bottle upright on the chair's seat. Blunt side down, she whacked the plastic cap. It shattered into small pieces, miraculously leaving the bottle upright and intact. A loud sigh passed through her pursed lips. She emptied her tea dregs down the sink, then, with a trembling hand, filled her entire cup with the golden liquid. When she set the bottle down in the sink, it tipped over, spilling most of its contents into the drain.

On either side of the cup of whiskey, Sonnet set the two yellow pill bottles down and stared at her poisons. Their child-proof caps were almost impossible to open with her left hand. She grasped one bottle, depressed the safety tab with her left thumb, secured the cap between her teeth and rotated it until it came loose. Repeating the process with the second bottle was easier. She took a few shallow breaths and reflected on her plan. *Do I want to die, or just ease my pain? If my pain settles, I might not want to die, but with this wrist and all my other symptoms, I know I'm seriously ill and probably dying anyway. I know I need an X-ray... but I'm certainly not calling Dr. Torres in the middle of the night, nor 911 ... and I don't have a car to drive myself to the overcrowded ER and have them scrutinize me before they order it, especially at the hospital I worked at...*

Sonnet was so very, very tired. She tipped one pill bottle sideways and coaxed three tablets into her palm. For good measure, she tapped three more out, then took six more pills out of the other bottle. Staring at the twelve tablets in her hand, the nurse part of her brain rationalized that if she lived, she'd develop a stomach bleed from the anti-inflammatories, but wasn't sure what six antidepressants would do and, like before, had no intention of researching it online. She settled on three of each, popped them in her mouth and swallowed the whiskey, not stopping until the cup was empty. She smacked her lips, her face souring from the liquor's aftertaste.

She walked to the living room and opened her front window curtains to see the star-lit night, mildly disappointed that Rufus was not nearby. She wanted his warmth against her. She scanned the cloudless sky, free of winter interference. Such a beautiful sight, a wide halo circling the moon. When her cocktail began to take hold, she found some soft classical music on the radio. She gingerly laid her wounded body on her sofa, placed a lumpy pillow over her belly and rested her injured arm over it, covering herself up with her tattered quilt. Ten minutes in, she felt only peace, obliterating any thought of what the outcome of her night would bring.

7:30 AM

Three rested, clean and very hungry tradesmen drove down Polly's Lane to pick up the Adlers. Big Tom, behind the wheel, passed Sonnet's bunkie on the left, noticing her wedged car. "Looks like someone got stuck there."

"Or slid there during the storm," Montana mused as he looked up quickly from reading Reba's text - the Adlers were waiting as Big Tom circled the dead end.

Approaching the truck, Digger towered over Reba's average size, but by their wavy copper hair and green eyes, anyone would know that the Adlers were related.

"Morning, folks. This is Digger," Reba said. Minus toolboxes, the back offered ample seating for them. Montana held the door open, and Digger slid in behind Big Tom.

"I don't need help," Reba said, tugging at her uniform. "I hate this get-up. No one else wears a dress to work, except for maybe the Pope."

Montana raised one eyebrow as she turned her back to him, determined to climb up unassisted.

"Okay, ma'am, then you're on your own." He watched her bottom twist back and forth with a rush of pleasure as the Toms in front watched; then Digger offered his hand, and she grasped it without objection. Montana resumed his spot in front, and as the truck bounced over the ruts, they all looked at the spectacular sunrise reflecting across the calm, unfrozen lake.

"It's beautiful here," Big Tom lamented. "You'd never know we had such a terrible storm just days ago. So, what's with the white car in your neighbour's yard? Kind of a tight parking spot between those fir trees." He slowed down to take another look.

"Not sure. Digger? You said Sonnet fell."

"Yes, Mom," Digger muttered, unsettled in the back seat of an unfamiliar truck, behind unfamiliar men. The orange fidget spinner whirled furiously between his thumb and index finger.

"Is she okay?" Montana asked, and Reba answered.

"I hope so. Keeps to herself, so we barely know her. Huh, that's odd."

"What's odd?"

"Her outside light is on. And she never leaves her curtains open, especially at night."

"Should we stop?"

"No, that's okay." But as soon as the words left her, guilt took over. She poked her head forward to check the truck's dashboard clock. "I'm sure she's fine, but maybe I could just run over and have a quick peek in her window." Digger stared at Reba as Tom shifted the truck into park.

"But Mom, Joe doesn't like us being late for work."

"Honey, we're never late for work," she said soothingly, then opened the door. Montana jumped out and, without asking, grabbed her arm for support. Waiting by the truck, he watched her quick, cautious prance down Sonnet's short driveway; only a few small snow drifts had formed since Fletcher cleared it. Her deck was mostly bare. Reba stepped around the patches of ice, then knocked on her door. No answer. She waited, then moved to Sonnet's window, blocking the sun's glare with her hand. She saw Sonnet sprawled across the sofa, right arm precariously extended, while the back of her hand lay on the floor.

Reba knocked on the window. No response. She knocked harder, and harder again, watching for movement. There was none. Hands on her hips, Reba turned towards the truck, raised both arms up high and shook her head.

Assuming she needed another opinion, Montana responded, leaving his door open, and crossed the deck to stand beside Reba. Shoulders touching, both peered inside.

"She looks pretty grey."

"She always looks grey."

"Either she's a really sound sleeper or …" Montana banged his flat hand against the window. No part of Sonnet budged. He moved to the screen door and whacked his fist against the frame. "Gee, not even a twitch."

He opened the screen door, but the wooden one was locked. He returned to the picture window. Fingering the smaller, adjacent window, he removed one screen and then tried the window. It was rickety and loose. He hooked his fingers through the four small round holes at the bottom of the frame and tugged. Nothing. He flicked open his pocket knife blade and ran it along the perimeter of the window, which had been painted shut a few layers ago; this time it opened.

"I'm a little nervous," Reba said.

"Me too. Let's hope she's just passed out."

The Toms left the truck open and approached; Digger double-checked that the truck gear was in park, closed the doors and concentrated on calming himself.

"She looks dead," young Tom said, upsetting Reba.

"Reba, I'll boost you through the window to check that she's … okay," suggested Montana. She cocked her head, pointed to her uniform hem, already above her knees.

"Nope. Someone else can do it." The Toms were eliminated because of their size, so Montana manipulated his lanky frame through the tight opening, then poked his head out.

"What's her name again?"

"Sonnet. Sonnet O'Brien."

They watched Montana walk slowly, calling Sonnet. No response. He reached down and lifted her cool right hand from the floor. Her lips parted slightly. He gently placed his hand across her forehead, then patted her cheek. He felt her right wrist for a pulse, laid it gently across her abdomen and then came to the window.

"I think there's a pulse, but I'm no nurse," he reported to his onlookers.

"But she's a nurse," Reba blurted out, realizing her statement had no benefit.

"We should either call 911 or take her to the hospital."

"Let's just drive her there. By the time help comes here, she might be … in worse shape," Big Tom said.

Young Tom replaced the bunkie window and screen as Montana unlocked her door and looked at Reba.

"What about ID? They'll ask for that," Reba offered as she entered the sparse kitchen, a contrast to her homey clutter, but laid out the same as hers. She picked up the open pill bottles, her eyes widening as she saw the broad chopping knife on the counter, inspecting its blade.

"Whew. No blood," she whispered.

She resealed the bottles, relieved they still contained pills. She stepped on a hard piece of shattered whiskey cap chips on the floor, then spotted the mostly empty bottle in the sink, whistling softly and shaking her head.

Based on where Reba stored her own purse at home, she opened Sonnet's kitchen closet and found a small purse in the same spot. Clipped to Sonnet's purse strap was a hospital-labelled lanyard and badge, and a set of keys, one of which looked like Reba's own door key. She grabbed it all, and Sonnet's coat.

Montana gently picked Sonnet up, dressed in worn flannel pyjamas and an oversized grey sweater, and slowly carried her out to the truck. Reba closed Sonnet's door and shadowed him, hearing quiet moans while he lifted her up and onto the back seat. He propped her up like a rag doll until Reba squeezed up from behind him and sat beside Sonnet, anchoring herself snugly against her barefoot passenger.

"I've got her now," Reba said.

"She weighs next to nothing," he said, shutting her door and hopping into the front seat. Young Tom programmed the hospital's address from his phone into the truck's navigation system.

Reba felt Sonnet's cold skin against hers, even through her night clothes and sweater. Sonnet's jaw sagged, exhaling shallow breaths of stale alcohol; her head swaying as the truck swerved to avoid potholes.

Digger stared at Sonnet's thick, coated tongue. Unbrushed residue caked her teeth, and Reba mouthed a warning for him to keep his opinions to himself in case she could hear.

"Hold her for a second," Reba whispered, shifting Sonnet's weight against him so she could remove her winter coat to cover Sonnet's lower legs.

"Oh! My dear God!" she gasped. Sonnet's night clothes had slid up her back, exposing deep purple, bruised skin. Digger held her while Reba pulled her sweater down. "Something terrible happened to her."

"What?" young Tom asked, cranking his neck around.

"Digger, when did you see her fall?" Reba asked.

"Yesterday."

"These can't be from yesterday. What in the world happened to her? Maybe we should've called 911." Sonnet winced when Reba moved her right arm, noticing it was twice the size of her thin left wrist. "I think she's got a broken arm, and Good Lord, maybe someone beat her up with that meat cleaver in her kitchen.'

"We're eighteen minutes away," young Tom reported, activating the orange warning lights on the truck's roof, thinking that if nothing else, it made him feel more useful. He urged Big Tom to pick up the speed as Reba swaddled Sonnet's cyanotic feet.

Reba texted Ziggy while she told Digger to let Joe know that he'd be late. Seconds later, Ziggy and Joe texted each other, reassuring the other brother about their best employees' identical excuse about running late and hoping to report for work by 9:00 AM.

8:30 AM

Eighteen minutes seemed like double that, even as the truck sped to the hospital. Arriving, Tom pulled into the emergency entrance and Montana rushed through its sliding glass doors, plastered with posters about infection control and respect for staff. After a long delay, he and a young, uniformed man hurried over with a wheeled stretcher. Digger got out so that Montana could transfer Sonnet onto the stretcher; Reba followed, gasping again when she saw Sonnet's deeply bruised shin.

"What happened?" the uniformed man asked the group as he and Montana wheeled Sonnet through sliding doors. The Adlers trailed behind them, Digger following his mother.

Reba pointed to Montana, but spoke first.

"He knows nothing, and I don't know much more than her name. She's a neighbour. My son here says she fell yesterday, or the day before. We found her about a half hour ago, passed out, just like this." She pointed to Sonnet. "And, and she's all black and blue, and, look here, she might even have a broken arm."

Reba became tearful, not from Sonnet's unresponsiveness, but because they lived so close as strangers. She wondered how Sonnet's injuries happened.

"Wait!" Reba cried out, then ran back to the truck with Digger, left him there and returned with Sonnet's purse. She handed her hospital ID badge to the young man named Xavier, according to his badge.

He compared Sonnet's photo to her ashen appearance.

"She works here? Wow, she sure looks different."

With a pen and diner order pad she plucked from her apron pocket, Reba scrawled out her own name and phone number, ripped off the slip and thrust it at Xavier as he raised the stretcher railings and rattled them until they locked in place.

"What we know about her is everything you now know. I don't think she has any family," Reba said, sensing a fuzziness in her head.

"Thank you. Anything helps," Xavier replied as he turned, wheeling Sonnet through automatic doors marked 'NO UNAUTHORIZED ENTRY'.

Montana shrugged his shoulders, gently touching Reba's back, suggesting they return to the truck. Reba didn't move. He looked directly at her, seeing the same blank stare she had at the diner during the blackout. Her eyelids fluttered slightly.

"Hey you," he said softly, squeezing her upper arm, with no response. He felt her bicep muscle wilt. Concerned she may fall, his arm circled her waist, and sat her down in a waiting room chair. "Reba?"

"Is she okay?" asked a chubby young mother with a bundled baby, sitting across from them. He didn't answer.

Reba's eyes flitted under her lids. He held her securely, feeling her stiffen and then relax. She remained still, then opened her eyes. She scanned her unfamiliar surroundings, then Montana, and then the half-dozen people in the waiting room, including the young mother, baby on her hip, heading to the patient registration desk.

Other than slow nods, Montana watched her recover from whatever was happening. A petite woman in crisp, sky-blue scrubs and a stethoscope around her neck approached, wheeling a chair. Reba looked blankly at the chair, then at the woman and finally at Montana, who squatted down beside her.

"What's this? Where am I?" Reba said, rubbing her forehead and looking around.

"You're in the ER, and I'm a nurse," she replied, then looked to Montana.

"She had a spell. It's the second time I've seen it happen."

"Like a seizure?" asked Erica, RN, according to the embroidery on her scrubs. Reba frowned.

"I don't know what a seizure looks like, but it just happened, over there." Montana pointed toward the glass doors.

"Well, let's get her seen while she's still recovering from it. And she's registered already?"

"No. We just brought her neighbour in, and then this happened." Reba became more agitated with the awareness of her environment.

"Okay, then please register at the desk, and ..."

"No disrespect, but how did you find out she was ..." he started, then noticed the young mother observing them, just as Reba yanked Montana's sleeve.

"What's going on here?" Reba asked, eyelids half-shut. Erica checked her watch.

"Your companion is worried about you, and rightfully so. Once you register, we can all figure out what happened."

Reba's head rolled back; both Erica and Montana leaned in, hovering protectively over her. She then leaned forward and they retracted back. Montana leaned on his achy knees and then stood up cautiously.

"There's nothing wrong with me. I'm overworked, underpaid, and just survived three pretty shitty days," Reba blurted out. Montana's hands rested on his hips.

Erica spoke kindly, but firmly.

"I spent that whole storm here because my co-workers couldn't make it in. I'm not complaining, but I am explaining that everyone suffered some hardship. Now, would you like to register so you can be seen?"

"No!"

Both Montana and Erica took two steps back.

"Reba," Montana tried to reason with her; she shot up an open palm and glared at him.

"Don't you Reba me!"

Erica pointed to a screen displaying a rotating series of messages above the registration window, unnoticed by Reba or Montana until then.

"Look, the current ER wait time is six hours. I'm offering you urgent care. Right now. So, I can either bring you in immediately, based on your symptoms and providing you register, or you can wait in line behind everyone else. What would you prefer?"

Reba pulled her phone out of her pocket, blinked her eyes a few times, then focused on the lock screen; it was 8:56 am. She circled the edge of her phone with her index finger, then pivoted the time display screen to Montana's face.

"I'm late for work."

"You can't be serious," he said.

Erica's eyes opened wide as she spoke. "So, what I understand you're telling me is that you are declining care."

"Yes."

Montana shook his head in frustration.

"Well, in that case, I'm going on to call the next patient. For the record, Reba, can you please tell me your full name and date of birth?"

"No."

Erica looked to Montana for an answer, hoping at minimum that she could chart Reba's refusal of care. He shrugged his shoulders, then quietly said that her son was outside.

"Stop talking about me," Reba growled.

Erica glanced down at her, then to Montana, blinking her eyes a few times. Reba pressed her palms over her eyes and rubbed them.

"Good luck to the both of you," Erica said in a professional tone, spun around and expertly wheeled the chair back through the same door she came from.

Montana looked down at Reba, moved both hands to his thighs, and took the chair beside her. "You know, I don't know if I should be quiet, or argue with you, or just walk away."

Reba hung her head low, twisting the fraying lace strands hanging from her apron.

"Why don't you want the doctor to check you out?" he asked softly. There was a very long pause, and both leaned back in their vinyl seats. Montana raised his hand to place on her shoulder, changed his mind and set it back on his thigh. "I can understand if you lived where I do and have to pay for all this, but you're right here," he said, extending his open hand around the waiting room.

"It's available, and you don't have to pull out your wallet. I just don't get it."

Reba turned her head away from him, fingering the outline of an apron stain.

"No, you don't get it. At all," she squeaked.

"Then help me understand. What is it?"

"It, as you just called it, would mess up my life even more than it already is."

"Okay, now I'm totally confused. Who and what would mess up your life?"

"Montana, why did you drive both of us to work today?"

"Because you had a flat tire, and it wasn't safe to drive in the storm."

"And, tell me another reason."

"I don't know, and I give up."

"Because between Digger and me, I'm the only one that drives."

"So, what's that got to do with any of this?" Exasperated, he threw his arms up, just as Big Tom and Digger walked inside. Reba stood up and walked cautiously towards them.

"Forget it. Just forget that any of this happened," she said, turning back to Montana, who was following her. "Just take me, ah, me and Digger to work," she said to Tom, then softened her tone. "Please."

Digger read her anguish; something was not right. Again. Tom and Montana turned away from them to converse, allowing the Adlers a moment alone.

"Mom, what's wrong?"

"Nothing. I just have a headache," she answered softly, then turned back to the men and raised her voice. "Now let's giddee-up, guys, 'cause we're already late for work." She caught Montana's glare before they headed for the exit doors, all four silently fighting their own battles.

"Reba? Reba Adler? Is there a Reba Adler here?" Xavier, the ER attendant, called out as loudly as he could without sounding offensive. He stood, digital tablet in hand, at the open 'NO UNAUTHORIZED ENTRY' doorway, his voice carrying Reba's name across the entire waiting room. He scanned the occupants within his sightlines and saw Reba stop abruptly before the glass doors, just as Tom and Montana were passing through them. They all turned around to see who was calling her name.

"Shit, shit, shit," Reba muttered under her breath. Xavier's eyes locked into Reba's; he motioned with his free hand for her to approach him. She hesitated long enough for Xavier to repeat his gesture, emphasizing that he needed her. Instead, she grabbed Digger's arm, hurried around Tom and Montana and out the glass doors. Montana shrugged his shoulders and raised his hands yet again, indicating to Xavier that he couldn't help.

The young mother, holding her sleeping baby, watched curiously as Xavier scratched his head and tried to figure out what had just happened.

9:15 AM

The sterile triage cubicle of the emergency department where Sonnet lay was devoid of anything resembling comfort. She felt a small pillow under her head that smelled and felt different than her lumpy one at home. Her eyes squinted open, then quickly shut to block the blinding ceiling lights. Arousing slowly and still very groggy, she touched the cold steel railings confining her, then scanned the tiny, curtained space. She became aware of the IV line taped to the back of her left hand, a frigid solution coursing into the insertion site and up her arm. White paper tape pulled her skin tight, securing the needle in place.

She attempted to lift her right arm across the blanket, vaguely remembering that she should feel pain. Instead, it was weighted and immobilized in bright purple. She attempted to decipher the words on a fluorescent label taped to her IV bag. *There must be meds dripping into this solution. My head is pounding ... good Lord, I'm not only drugged, but hung over.* She inhaled the faint but familiar cleaning smells of her work environment, closed her eyes and drifted off into oblivion again.

9:45 AM

When Sonnet stirred again, she sensed she was not alone. Soft rustling on both sides of her stretcher was followed by heavenly layers of blankets warming her from neck to toe. A quiet noise hummed in the background between intermittent pings, reminding her she was not home, but safe.

"Hey there," said a soft female voice. Sonnet opened her eyes just enough to watch her caregiver press a button to silence the monitor, overhead lights preventing her from seeing more. The woman, as if on cue, pulled a cord to turn on the dim light behind Sonnet's stretcher, then shut the ceiling light off.

"Urine colour is still pretty dark …" said another low, male voice. After a pause, "and none of her lab values are settling, but …" Sonnet turned her head towards the male voice. "Ah, Ms. O'Brien, can you hear me?" She nodded. He identified himself as a doctor she didn't know. "Do you know why you're here?"

Sonnet attempted to turn her head up to look his way, then lifted her immobilized arm.

"That's part of it," he said calmly, and tapped his pen against her cast. She looked at the tall, brown-skinned doctor, his torso buried in oversized green scrubs. He swiftly picked up his buzzing phone, texted something into it with the speed and manual agility of one hand. "Do you remember what happened to you?"

"I'm not well." It was all she could process to say.

"And you're covered in bruises."

"I know."

"How did those happen?"

"I fell."

"Where did you fall?" he asked, mild impatience registering on his face.

"On the road."

"When was that?"

Sonnet tried to lift her right hand to her face, abandoned that idea, tried with the other hand, then gave up.

"What day is it?" she asked.

"That was actually my next question to you. Can you tell me?"

This time, she tried harder to bring her splinted hand to her forehead, accidentally hitting her eyebrow, and harder than expected. She winced. The female offered her a sip of cold water through a straw from a lidded plastic cup. She sputtered a little, swallowed it, then answered the question.

"December 4th, or maybe the fifth?"

"Good enough. It's actually the fourth. And I'm assuming you know where you are," the doctor asked.

"I do." Sonnet looked at the IV line, then stared straight ahead.

"Knock, knock."

His soft, familiar voice came from the other side of the billowing privacy curtain. Dr. Torres parted the striped panels and slipped through the opening and tugged at the curtain until it closed completely.

"Good morning," he said, facing Sonnet directly.

"Sonnet, you obviously know this man," the young ER doctor said.

"Hello there," Dr. Torres said quietly, dressed in wrinkled, green scrubs that matched his colleague. Sonnet's mouth managed a slight upturn. He placed his hand on Sonnet's blanket-covered ankle. "Ooh, still warm. First-class."

"I hope you don't mind my asking Dr. Torres to sit in on this conversation," the ER doctor said. "He's more familiar with you than I am, and we've often consulted together."

"And, full disclosure, our kids play hockey on the same team," Dr. Torres piped in, delaying the inevitable conversation.

"I'll leave you for a few minutes," the female said, looping the call bell cord around the top rail of Sonnet's stretcher and within easy reach. "I'm sure you know how this works. I'll come back in a little while."

Dr. Torres assumed the vacant side of Sonnet's stretcher, enabling both physicians to look directly at her and over her at each other. The ER doctor spoke first.

"I couldn't find any labs in the system, other than what we did today." Sonnet was unaware that her blood was drawn until she noticed the cotton ball taped in the crook of her elbow. "You were unresponsive when your neighbours brought you in."

She furrowed her eyebrows in confusion.

"My neighbours?"

"Do you know how you got here?" The physicians eyed each other.

She shook her head. The ER doctor plucked Reba's diner slip from the clipboard holding her paper chart. "Reba Adler? Do you know her?"

"No, other than her living near me," Sonnet replied, wondering how her neighbour became involved.

"Okay, so at least you know who she is." He quickly checked a message on his phone, pocketed it, and resumed his assessment. "According to the admission notes, she was one of the people who brought you in." He skimmed through the pages on his clipboard.

"People? I don't recall any of that," Sonnet said blankly, watching the doctor scribble furiously.

"Noted, but let's leave that for another time. It seems like you've got a lot going on here," he said, looking quickly at Dr. Torres, then back at Sonnet. "You said you fell on the road, and by the progression of your bruises, I'm guessing that happened two or three days ago. Would that be about right, if today is the fourth?"

"I, I ... think so. It was when the storm had just started. I was driving home ... and the roads were sheer ice. My car slid off the road, but first, I fell on my side. No, no. No, that doesn't make sense." She rubbed her forehead. "I was trying to get out of my car, and fell on the ice. Yes, that's what happened." She pointed to the same hip where her oldest bruises were.

"And your broken wrist?"

"So, it is broken ... I thought it was."

"When did that happen?" She paused, assembling her timelines.

"One ... or maybe it was two days ago ... I think."

"And how did that happen?" he asked.

Her brain worked to piece the details together.

"I fell. Yes, I fell on my deck. On the ice."

"Okay. Anything else?" He stopped writing and made a point, looking directly at her.

"No."

He looked across the stretcher to Dr. Torres, who gently took over with the next batch of questions.

"Sonnet, the reason we're worried about you is that so much of your body is covered in bruises and soft tissue injuries, as well as this," he said, pointing to her cast. "Other than this x-ray, we haven't ordered any more diagnostics, but we have to ask you. Did someone hurt you?" Sonnet looked up at him, eyes wide with alarm. "I'm sorry, but I have to ask. We talked before about Stan …" He let the words sink in as both physicians watched her carefully. "You told me in my office that the police were involved before, but you refused, I mean, declined to press charges."

"I haven't seen Stan for years." She shook her pounding head.

"So, he's not stalking you, badgering you for money, harassing you?" Dr. Torres asked quietly.

"No. I told him that I haven't got any money left to give him," she said, turning her head away from him in shame.

"I know it's painful to talk about it, but your answers are so, so reassuring, and important to hear," he said, resting his hand on her shoulder.

Her blankets were cooling, as was the tension in the room, until the ER physician took over.

"Okay, so now that assault is off our radar, we need to talk about this bloodwork …"

Sonnet interrupted him.

"I don't need, or want to hear it. I know it," she whispered.

"Know what?" Both doctors asked her the same question.

"That my labs are out of whack. My CBC, ALT, and AST serum levels are up, and my …"

"Now, just hang on a second. What are you trying to tell us? There's no record in the system that you've seen someone, or had these done," the ER doctor said, growing impatient and very aware that Sonnet was overstepping her boundary as a nurse. She took a painfully deep breath, supporting her right side with her left arm.

"After all my years of working in oncology, I've come to know the signs."

"The signs of what, Sonnet?" Dr. Torres asked quietly. That morning, he had checked her electronic medical records in his office; there were no bloodwork results, and specifically what he'd previously requested that she complete.

"Cancer. Pancreatic cancer. Look at me, and you've seen my labs," she said despondently, as both physicians leaned in.

"Sonnet, that's …" Dr. Torres stopped, his hand still on her shoulder.

She looked at the ceiling, then followed the steel rod the privacy curtain was looped through, back and forth and then around him, but not meeting his eyes. "I've got all the markers. You weighed me. Forty pounds fell off of me, my belly distends and aches, I'm nauseated, my poop is pale and unpredictable … and I can't get off the couch. What more proof do you need?"

Dr. Torres' face sagged; every symptom she named mirrored his concern on the day her union rep brought her to his office, and was also the reason he wanted her to come back for a follow-up appointment. The ER doctor interrupted.

"It's still not a good idea to jump to conclusions. Let's order some more tests before we confirm anything, and we'll keep you on the admissions roster ASAP, rather than as an outpatient."

"What does it matter? I don't need to have these done to know I'm dying."

"I wouldn't make that assumption yet," he responded assertively. "We'll let the test results guide us to some answers first."

"No. I'm declining them."

"Pardon?"

"I'm sorry. I'm not consenting to having them."

"Well, then, let's get on to our next concern. Your blood alcohol level was elevated when you came in, and your neighbour gave us two medication bottles, including some antidepressants Dr. Torres prescribed. Do you remember how much you drank?" he asked bluntly. Feeling equally as uncomfortable as Dr. Torres was standing silently beside her, she didn't answer. The ER doctor persisted.

"Then what about the meds? Based on the preliminary labs I ordered, and your unresponsiveness when they brought you in, am I guessing correctly that you, being a nurse, took way more than your prescribed dose?" The ER doctor pressed on. "Let's get right to the point. Were you trying to end your life?"

Sonnet's face turned to stone. She shook her head slightly, hoping to give them the answer they needed, so that they would leave her alone. The only noise resonating in the room, otherwise suffocatingly silent, came from the monitors.

Dr. Torres took over the conversation, wondering in his own mind if she was being truthful, yet not wanting to offend her.

"I get it, Sonnet. I understand. We all have coping mechanisms, and we've all made mistakes. It's not our role to judge you, but rather to help you." Both doctors waited patiently, allowing her a few extra minutes to digest the gravity of their conversation. "I have great respect for you, and I know you know that," Dr. Torres continued softly. "Let's just take this one step at a time." There was yet another long lapse.

"So, no psych referral?" the ER doctor asked Dr. Torres across Sonnet's bed; she and Dr. Torres both shook their heads. "Okay, then," he said, and without any acknowledgment, slipped through the curtains and left his patient alone with her own doctor.

"Please let me help you," he said quietly again. "I'll do anything I can in my power to help you." He took her cold hand, then warmed it with both of his. Neither pulled away; he felt her squeeze his fingers and hold them for support.

"I know," she mouthed meekly. "I know."

The thick air in her tiny cubicle began to cool and recirculate after both doctors left. Sonnet, mentally exhausted, medicated and still slightly impaired in her judgement, dozed off again while the porter arrived to roll her stretcher away for tests. He checked her chart, and after reading that she had declined consent for any testing, he pushed her stretcher back to where it had been. He left, just as the predictable noises of the overstuffed emergency department ramped up to full volume.

10:00 AM

Neither the Adlers nor the electricians spoke during the drive from the hospital to New Abino. Outside, the roads were blanketed with fog and inside, the truck cabin was rife with tension. Reba was delivered to the diner first, the cab's stress level easing significantly as she exited the truck, then even more so when the men declined her bland offer of breakfast.

Digger's agitation also settled once he was dropped off at the grocery store, but not before Montana followed Digger out of the truck and spoke to him alone. Facing the grocery store parking lot and a few feet from the truck, Montana and Digger exchanged phone numbers while Montana explained calmly what he had witnessed in the ER. Nodding his head, Digger agreed to watch his mother and call Montana if he needed help. What he meant by the offer of help was unclear, but uncomplicated; if Digger noticed anything different about Reba, or was afraid, he could call Montana. Anytime, day or night. Montana put his hand firmly on Digger's shoulder just before he turned towards the grocery store's front door.

"I've got your back, son," Montana said quietly.

Digger looked at Montana, confused.

"I am my father's son," he replied, literally interpreting Montana's statement.

"Right. What I meant was a figure of speech ... like an expression."

Digger didn't respond, but took one step back. He watched Montana reach deep into the front pocket of his jeans, pulling out a closed fist. Digger leaned in as

Montana opened the palm of his hand to display a small, asymmetrical wooden cross with round carved corners and a bottom post only slightly longer than its crosspiece. The worn varnish exposed smooth, dark-grained wood. Digger concentrated on Montana's face, waiting for an explanation. Montana pointed to the pocket of Digger's uniform pants, confusing him even more.

"You know that orange thing you just shoved in your pocket?"

"You can't have it," Digger snapped, clamping his hand over his pocket. His gaze followed Montana's hand as he lifted the worn cross piece to eye level.

"I don't want it. I only wanted to show you mine. It looks different, but instead of spinning yours like you do, I turn mine slowly over and over." Digger's lips parted as Montana demonstrated by flipping the cross slowly and methodically over and over in one hand. "See, they accomplish the same. It's my worry monk. Somebody gave it to me a long time ago, and turning it round and round helped me when I was going through a tough time."

Montana repeated the rotation, slowly at first, then quicker. Mouth ajar, Digger watched, then pulled his spinner out.

"AC, my best coach gave me this," he said. Digger's memory of AC was quickly overshadowed by the groping incident with Denise at his old high school, which ultimately prompted the Adlers to leave Nova Scotia.

"Lucky you had AC," Montana said, forming a reassuring smile. "I used to need this a lot, but now I just keep it in my pocket to remind myself. And it's got some good words engraved into it that I still read now and then."

"Oh."

"Would you like to have this? I have another one."

"Do I have to give you mine?"

"Oh, no. You keep yours." Montana watched the concern on Digger's face fade away.

Digger eyed the cross with a mild interest. Slightly less than three inches long, he knew it would fit easily in his pocket, a backup to the security of his own spinner. He would hide it in his room at home until he felt safe showing his mother. Montana held the cross out for Digger to take.

"The words are worn, but I hope you can still read them. I have them memorized." Digger squinted, but followed Montana's lead as he closed his eyes and recited them, while Digger read the words on the little cross with him. By the end of the script, their voices blended together.

> May God grant you always a sunbeam to warm you, a moonbeam to charm you, a sheltering angel so nothing can harm you. Laughter to cheer you, faithful friends near you, and wherever you pray, heaven to hear you.

"Are you sure I can have this?" Digger asked.

"I wouldn't have offered it if I weren't sure."

"Thank you, Mr. Montana."

"It's just Montana."

"Okay, Montana."

Digger smiled for the first time that day, a smile that Montana saw was just like his mother's. Montana extended his hand to Digger, who shook it, then hustled through the grocery store's front door, popping his head back out to offer a hasty 'thank you for the ride' to all three electricians. Montana hoped it would be a better day for everyone.

When Digger entered the storage room to load his cart of products to stock shelves, he took the gift out to examine it more carefully. Alone and undisturbed, he whispered the inscribed words as best as he could read them. Everything made sense to him except the line about faithful friends, because he had none, but when he looked closer at the cross, he spotted the most worn areas of the wood; a tiny pair of four-leaf clovers were etched into the grain. One to give him good luck, and the second for his mother. He hid the worry monk back in the front pocket of his pants, patting it down for security.

Famished, the electricians knew that the Winer Diner was the sole eatery within miles, so instead, young Tom was sent back to the grocery store to buy breakfast. He returned with the only combination of hot deli options available that early: Asian stir-fry, cabbage rolls and spicy Jamaican meat patties. The trio tackled their meal in the truck using plastic utensils, supplemented with orange juice and chewable heartburn tablets.

10:45 AM

Approaching their job site driveway, a twenty-minute drive from the diner, the electricians noticed a red pickup with the municipal building inspector's sign on the side door, idling near their trailer. Unanimously, they voted to keep driving and leave the inspector to inspect whatever it was that he could. Relieved to pass unnoticed, two-thirds of them also voted to volunteer their time helping the residents of Polly's Lane.

Their first stop was Sonnet's driveway. Working cautiously, they hooked a heavy chain between her vehicle's undercarriage and their truck, easily freeing her car. Other than scraped doors and hardened spots of leaked sap from broken branches, Sonnet's vehicle sustained minimal damage. Her car sat at a precarious angle in her driveway, however, after the three men voted with confidence that any woman, regardless of skill set, could navigate it out without further damage, they unhooked the chains, dumped them into the truck's bed beside Reba's flat tire and drove to the tire shop.

It took twenty dollars, and a leftover Jamaican meat patty for Montana to bribe the front desk staff to push the work order to the front of the line. Bellies battling indigestion, they paced impatiently and were back at the diner within the hour. Blocking the parking lot view with their truck, no one noticed them replacing her tire. They returned the spare to the unlocked tire case on her rear door, and Reba's car was ready for the road in nineteen minutes.

Finally, back at the author's house with the day half over and no violations posted by the building inspector, the men were quite content to carry on with their day.

DECEMBER 5TH

10:00 AM

Gracie checked the time on the library's clock, then hurried to the front doors and unlocked them. Only a handful of people were waiting for the library to open, and she recognized all of them. A few came to read and stay warm there after the shelters closed to replenish supplies and prepare for the night ahead.

Gracie was startled to see eighty-year-old Winnie from their condo building compete with the others to enter first. Before Gracie could question her motive for leaving home on such a wintery day, she slipped past Gracie and headed for the Fiction section. About to close the door, she spotted Mason, bundled up and leaning against his dated black Cadillac.

"Are you driving our Miss Daisy around this morning?" she asked, tightening her sweater around her.

"We both know that what Miss Daisy wants, Miss Daisy gets," he quipped as he walked the fifteen feet towards her. "Winnie called me after I dropped you off at the library, during the five minutes it took me to drive to my office. She said you were responsible for this."

"Me? How?"

"You keep reminding her that reading is good for her brain. She summoned me back to Park Street to pick her up because she had nothing good left to read, and here we are."

"Well, at least come inside and stay warm until she picks out what she wants to read."

"I've got a meeting in twenty-two minutes," he said, brushing his lips against her cheek. Both of them looked around, hoping no one noticed.

"Kissing is strictly prohibited in the library," she warned, responding with a swift kiss against his cheek. "That should carry you through the day. I'll help Winnie out and hurry her back to you." Gracie rushed inside to track Winnie down while Mason returned to guard his post as her impatient chauffeur.

Sonnet's Bunkie
1:00 PM

Fletcher thought that Sonnet might need a little cheering up after he saw her looking so forlorn a few days ago. They would never be friends, but perhaps his Good Samaritan status for bringing her burgers would keep him in good standing. He decided to pop over to check on her. He was halfway out the door when he remembered that his mother never paid a visit empty-handed. He opened his kitchen cupboards, briefly considered his new travel mug, then changed his mind. Fortune cookies filled a bowl on the counter, courtesy of the Korean delivery girl. He chose a handful of unbroken ones with crisp wrappers, tossed them into a clear plastic bag, and headed to Sonnet's house. He hadn't reached the lane before Rufus, alias

Tucker, came running from the Adlers' deck. Content with a few good scratches behind his ears, Tucker sniffed everything, leaving slobber on the cookie bag and Fletcher.

When they arrived at Sonnet's door, no one answered Fletcher's knocks. Tucker circled her vehicle, marking each tire while Fletcher wondered who moved it. He inspected her front door and knocked again. He jiggled her doorknob; it was loose and unlocked. He opened it halfway, then knocked again. Silence. He called Sonnet's name - no response, then sent Tucker in first, expecting her to scream and shoo him back outside. Nothing happened.

After Tucker's uneventful snoop, Fletcher took his turn. The little house smelled like his grandparents; old people camouflaged with lavender. His own bunkie's outdated, upscale furnishings contrasted sharply with what resembled rejects discarded from a yard sale. He set the bag of cookies on a small water-stained table and wandered through each room with Tucker at his heels.

Sonnet's bedroom dressers were loaded with lumpy piles of clothes, some folded. Another messy heap was crowned with a discarded bra, still fastened at the back. He picked it up, examining its sweat-stained, misshapen fabric. It had outlived its purpose long ago - so different from the Korean delivery girl's hot pink, lace-lined, underwired cups. He opened a bedside table to find the usual: a box of tissues, a partially completed crossword puzzle bookmarked with a pencil, a novel and a very worn Bible. Raised without any religious affiliation, he was curious about the Bible, and if it had any monetary value. He opened the navy leather cover, its cracked spine separating from what it protected and gilded pages worn from use. He was puzzled why Sonnet owned a Bible gifted to a 'Sister Mary Agnes' from a guy named Father Francis.

Fletcher wandered into the bathroom; she kept it as clean and neat as his. And as he did with everyone's bathroom, he peeked inside her drawers and medicine cabinet. He recognized the name on an old prescription bottle of antibiotics—nothing that would give him a buzz in his old days of drug abuse.

The second bedroom was lined with heavy, taped boxes labelled Sewing Room, China Cabinet, Appliances, Basement - unappealing to him. He pulled the faded curtains open, likely hung when the bunkie was built, and took in the lake - a better view than from his place.

Ooooh, he cooed to himself as he returned to the kitchen, spotting the sharp edges of the cracked whiskey bottle cap that he hadn't noticed before on the floor. Glad he kept his boots on, he set a chair on its side in the doorway separating the kitchen and living room to prevent Tucker from puncturing his paws.

In the sink, he found the empty whiskey bottle.

"Oh Tucker, she's been on a bender," he reported softly, ignoring the sounds coming from the living room.

Fletcher picked up a few broken pieces, dumping them in a ramen noodle container, dropped into the garbage under the sink, the same one that he brought her food in a few days ago.

He opened and closed Sonnet's barren fridge, moving on to the box of books and treats on her kitchen table. He finished off the peanut brittle gifted by someone named Andrea, leaving the empty package in the box. He read a few get-well cards littering the table, which confirmed that Sonnet was sick and, as Fletcher thought, not recovering anytime soon.

Reading the cards turned his intrusion into remorse. He replaced Sonnet's chair under her table and called Tucker, who by then had consumed her fortune cookies, most still sealed in their wrappers. Both sporting guilt-laden faces, they slithered out the door. Assuming there was nothing of hers worth stealing, he considered leaving it unlocked, then rationalized that someone else might think otherwise. He turned the inside knob and shut the door, then checked that it locked behind him. A spark of curiosity motivated him to reach into his coat pocket, retrieve his house key and insert it into Sonnet's worn keyhole. It unlocked effortlessly, without even a jiggle. A sudden rush of pleasure coursed through him, replaced again with regret.

He quickly locked it and walked to his home, hesitated, then casually walked to the Adlers to check if their car was in the driveway. It wasn't. He walked over and stepped onto their deck, peeking through their window, his key still in hand. A rustling sound, then an odd noise near the house, unnerved him. He walked swiftly to the lane and in the direction of home, Rufus catching up after literally losing his cookies, wrappers still around them, all over the Adlers' yard. It was enough excitement for both of them in one day.

December 7th

10:00 AM

On her drive to the library, Gracie topped up her gas tank, then loaded her dated white Volvo with six bundles of well-read books, tucked into flashy new bags with clear sleeves, funded by a library grant. She slid two crisp slips of paper into each sleeve, one of which named book titles of the presumably read and due back, and the other printout providing a record of the next exchange date for the soon-to-be-enjoyed. Five of the six neighbourhoods on her route were familiar; she scheduled the remote, rural address on Polly's Lane as her last destination before returning to the library. A flutter of excitement filled her, confident that her day would be a good one.

11:30 AM

At the hospital's emergency department, Sonnet received a thread of good news. Despite protests from Dr. Torres and the revolving ER team of providers, she was being discharged, even though some bloodwork results were still pending. Discharged, as opposed to signing herself out without medical clearance, like she was planning. She couldn't remember a time when she wanted so desperately to go home.

The only inpatient hospital beds available during her stay were on the cancer floor where she previously worked, and with the good fortune of Dr. Torres advocating for her, she remained in the ER holding area instead of being admitted. Being a patient on her own unit, with her medical records exposed to coworkers assigned to her care, would only compound her burden.

Rehydrated, fed and showered, Sonnet regained two pounds and some colour in her cheeks, which her caregivers didn't realize was slightly more yellow than pink. The ER staff made a concerted effort to protect Sonnet's privacy, a difficult task to do, until Roberta, her nurse manager and Candace, her union rep, paid a visit together. Oddly, today they were both kind and genuinely concerned, such a stark contrast to their last meeting in Roberta's tiny office.

When Sonnet told them she was being released, Candace insisted on driving her home. She reluctantly accepted because it was the most expedient way to leave. Within the hour, Candace returned, armed with hospital-issued scrubs, bright red, non-skid patient-issued socks and a pair of her own duty shoes, too big for Sonnet, but still an appreciated gesture. Candace left the cramped cubicle to allow Sonnet privacy to dress. Not expecting clean underwear, Sonnet left her soiled ones off. She secured the pair of scrub bottoms tightly around her waist, double-knotting the drawstring and rolling up the pant legs to avoid tripping over them. Standing up, she clung to the stretcher railing until her head stopped spinning, then finished dressing. Three days in the ER felt like ten, she mused, pulling back the curtain. Candace's nails clicked against her phone as Sonnet gathered her meagre possessions into a white plastic bag. About to cover her shoulders with the same baggy, old sweater she wore when she was admitted, Candace gently intervened.

"Oh, no. You won't need that - my car's toasty warm and in the first pick-up spot."

"Thank you, and I really mean it."

"I know. Now hand me your bag and let's get the hell out of here."

Candace stuffed the ragged sweater into the plastic bag, identical to the bags Sonnet helped fill when sending patients home. She also laid them on stretchers to accompany the deceased to the morgue, to be handed over to mourning families, or destroyed when there was no one to collect them.

Noon

The New Abino regulars began trickling back into the Winer Diner after the storm. They returned to their favourite table and re-ordered their favourite 'soup of the day' from Reba, their very favourite server. They also gossiped, in hushed whispers, that Reba was not her chipper self. They blamed her demeanour on stories from the storm seeping in, some stirring in their own creative versions. The prime chatter revolved around her spending two busy nights sleeping with three men from out of town, who wore her out. All that activity culminated in a visit to the hospital, where she was driven by, of all people, the three culprits.

Reba was unaware of the hushed chatter and peculiar looks; she floated between tables, refilling beverages. Distracted, she indeed was not herself and was feeling vulnerable, something she had not experienced for a while. She was always the strong leader and protector of Digger, but instead, in the last few days, they switched roles. Only the Adlers and Montana knew what happened at the hospital; to the two Toms, Reba was delayed in the ER because of Sonnet.

Reba had a vague recollection of what Montana described as a "spell", but since refusing to be seen, she was more aware that these were not isolated incidents. She didn't mind the spells, or whatever they were, but what petrified her was if something was really wrong. Wrong meant taking unaffordable time off work. Wrong meant medical investigations, which she and Digger feared equally. Wrong meant, like Digger after his seizure at age thirteen, that her ability to drive might be suspended indefinitely. Digger never pursued getting his driver's license because he hadn't needed one, and never admitted he wanted it. Too many things were going wrong and messing up their sheltered world.

Reba continued rushing from table to table, ensuring everyone got what they ordered, delivered with an artificial smile and more caffeine. Only when each table was served, and she had the chance to observe the patrons from her perch between the pie display and the beverage counter, did she permit a single tear to escape.

The only person to catch Reba brushing the wetness from her cheek was Montana when he and the two Toms arrived. They chose a table farthest away from the counter and spoke in low tones. They attracted suspicious glances and busy nattering from the regulars, who wondered if they were indeed the thugs who took advantage of their Reba during the storm. Montana noticed her stiff walk and stoic stance when she took their orders.

"What's the special, Reba?" Big Tom asked.

"Fish and chips," she replied curtly, her back rigid.

"Then it's fish and chips for me."

"And me too," added young Tom.

"I'll have the same," Montana said quietly.

"Coffee for everyone?" Reba said, shoving their plastic menus under her arm. They all nodded, ignored by their server, who was already heading back to forward Ziggy their orders.

By the time the electricians finished eating, most of the lunch bunch had dissipated. Reba hovered behind the counter, avoiding Montana's efforts at eye contact. When she brought the coffee pot with their tabs, the Toms declined refills, thanked her politely and laid cash on the table without checking the bill. As if on cue, they left Montana sitting alone. He fished out more than enough and passed it to her. As she was picking up the Toms' cash from the table, he placed his hand over hers. She slid it away, wiping the back of it on her apron.

"Reba."

"What?'

"Please sit down."

"Can't you see I'm busy?"

"Almost everybody's gone."

"Which means there's lots of cleaning up."

"It can wait. Look at me." She glanced at him, then just as quickly, away. "Please, just sit for one minute." She conceded, taking the chair farthest from him. Posture rigid, she folded her arms tightly across her chest and waited.

"Hurry up. What do you want?"

"I want nothing. Well, maybe I just want to know that you and Digger are doing okay."

"We're fine."

"That's good. That's very good," he said quietly. "That's all I wanted to hear."

"Can I go now?" she asked. He sat quietly, not responding. Slowly, she rose from her chair, and he did the same. She lowered her head; he placed two fingers gently under her chin, lifting it to face him. Her eyes pooled, about to spill.

"Why are you so sad?"

Tears rolled down her cheeks. She yanked a wad of serviettes from the dispenser and pushed her hand into her face.

"Because I'm afraid," she squeaked, then hurried off before he found the right words to console her.

Ziggy caught the interaction, forming mixed opinions about the man who shovelled out his driveway twice, but also spent two nights on the floor with his best employee. As Montana slid into his coat, they exchanged awkward glances. Ziggy waved Reba into the kitchen, then nodded to Montana, who was unsure if the message he was sending meant "Goodbye" or "Get lost".

12:30 PM

Candace drove down the slope of Polly's Lane and pulled her car in behind Sonnet's precariously positioned vehicle, exactly as the electricians had left it.

"That's an odd angle," Candace quipped, then saw Sonnet's hands grasp her face. "What's wrong?"

"My car slid down from the main road during the storm and landed in those trees ... and while I was ... gone, somebody pulled it out," she said, pointing to the tire tracks and shaking her head in disbelief.

"Who pulled it out?"

"I don't know. Somebody did. Maybe my next-door neighbour ... but he doesn't have a car ... and Reba, she lives farther down, but it couldn't be Reba ..."

"Maybe they called someone, but regardless, they're good neighbours to have." Candace shut her car off, popped her trunk open and grabbed Sonnet's white plastic bag. "Go, unlock your door, and I'll bring your stuff inside," she said.

Sonnet found her keys, still clipped into the loop in her purse. She placed both feet on the ground, waddling towards her bunkie in Candace's oversized shoes. She suddenly remembered the toppled whiskey bottle in her sink, something she didn't want Candace to see. She unlocked her door with one hand and tried to block Candace from coming inside. Candace ignored her, following closely behind while swinging the bag of soiled clothes in one hand, discharge papers and a new bottle of antidepressant medications they'd picked up at the pharmacy in the other.

Sonnet stepped inside onto the small, worn mat. She froze when she saw a tuft of blond fur on the black edge of the mat. She was sure it wasn't there before.

"Can you move forward a little? I don't want to drop your stuff," Candace said, slightly irritated. Ready to gently nudge her forward, she noticed Sonnet's gaping mouth. "If you're going to faint, sit down on that chair."

"Someone's been in my house."

"Of course, they were. Remember, they rescued you, and maybe even saved your life."

"Yes, but…" Puzzled how Candace knew those details, she scanned the floor, spotting only one bottle cap chip under a kitchen baseboard. She peeked into the sink; the empty bottle was still there. Candace, purposely peeking over Sonnet's shoulder to see what she was hiding, also saw it.

"Yikes. Did you drink all that by yourself?"

Sonnet ignored her, alarmed again when she spotted a few clear crumpled wrappers scattered across the floor. She kicked off Candace's shoes and shuffled towards the mess, holding on to the door frame to pick up a wrapper.

"What is it? What are those?" Candace asked, setting Sonnet's things on her kitchen table and watching Sonnet examine her find. Candace also picked a wrapper up, tearing a torn slip of words away from a dried wad of congealed dough. "You like fortune cookies?"

"They aren't mine. Someone's been in my house," Sonnet whimpered repeatedly. Candace saw Sonnet's colour turn paler than it already was when she stood in her spare bedroom doorway, pointing to the open curtains.

"I never, ever open these because they're so sun-damaged that they crumble in my hand."

"Well, then check your valuables, like maybe your jewelry?" Sonnet shuddered from the reference to her past. After years of possessing nothing at the convent, then Stan hawking her few, ancestral treasures to fuel his addictions, she owned nothing of value to check for.

"What about your bedroom? You don't have a gold rosary or a big cross, or something like that?"

Sonnet was unsure whether her agnostic union rep was mocking her or offering a suggestion. It didn't matter. Candace gave her space while she padded across the braided rug towards her bed. More dog fur and cellophane wrappings littered the rug. *Rufus. How, or who would have let him in?*

She opened the bedside table's top drawer, where she arranged her Bible, front always facing up towards Heaven, spine and top edge tucked tightly into the front corner of the drawer. It had been moved. Her lower jaw slackened again as she picked it up – the bookmark had also been moved from the last paragraph she read to the front, where Francis's inscription was. She sat on the bed, fear and despair swirling in her head.

"Everything's still where it should be in there?" Candace asked softly.

"No. It's not."

"That's not good. So, what was taken?" Sonnet looked up briefly but directly at her, then stared at her most cherished possession.

"You'd like to know what was taken? My privacy, my dignity ... and my safety. That's what was taken. No, it was not taken. It was stolen."

Her shoulders sagged forward into her sunken chest. Supporting the worn Bible between her casted and good arm, Sonnet mouthed the inscription quietly to herself, fingers gently following Francis's signature. She stopped at the faded 'i' in his name. Instead of dotting that letter, he'd drawn a minuscule heart with a fine-tipped pen, so tiny that it was only when Sonnet began wearing reading glasses that she'd noticed it - and the slightly different hue of black ink. It was the only present she'd received on her eighteenth birthday, as precious as the love she was gifted with it. She looked up at Candace, who thought it best not to interfere with her thoughts.

It was another minute before she had the strength to rise from the bed. Candace followed her silently around the rest of the house, Sonnet still clutching the Bible.

"I can stay with you if that will make you feel any better."

"No, it won't."

"Do you need some groceries? Some milk?"

"I'll be fine. There's food in the freezer." Candace walked towards the fridge. "Stop. I said I'll be fine."

"Okay, then," she said sheepishly and backed up towards the door.

"Thank you for bringing me home."

"I'm sorry about whoever rifled through your stuff. I hope you figure out who it was."

"I hope so, too."

"And don't forget to call the police." Sonnet stared at her awkwardly.

"What for? So, yet another stranger can, as you said, rifle through my stuff?"

"No. So they can file a report. Maybe you're not the only victim."

Sonnet brushed her hand in the air to dismiss Candace's suggestion. Out of words, Candace left, shutting the door tightly behind her. Sonnet watched through her front window as Candace drove away, neither woman bothering to wave.

Sonnet moved cautiously around her house again, taking inventory and wondering who would invade her privacy, but not take anything. She checked the door and lock – there were no new marks or signs of forced entry. *Did Cousin Al have a key? But he never overstepped his boundaries. Was it Rufus's real owner, who rented this place before me and didn't return the key? Or was it Fletcher? Rufus would surely follow him inside.*

She wrapped herself in the oversized sweater she retrieved from the plastic hospital bag and settled into her worn-out sofa. As she stared out the window, she was stunned by how, in these last few weeks, her life had turned upside down and was very unlikely to right itself again.

2:00 PM

Gracie enjoyed driving the scenic route along the river from Niagara Falls to Polly's Lane. She had completed the first five deliveries, as content to see the shut-ins as they were to welcome her. She drove along, catching glimpses of lingering sailboats, less loved by their owners than in years gone by, masts waltzing with the wind in the marina slips. She loved her job as much as hiking along this river with Mason. And, after two failed relationships, she appreciated the love he gave her.

Approaching the weathered road sign pointing towards Polly's Lane, she signalled her turn, even though no one was around to notice. She kept her foot on the brake, easing her car cautiously down the slope, more slowly after hitting the first big rut in the road. When the lane ended after only three driveways, she circled around, wondering which little bunkie belonged to Sonnet O'Brien.

There were no numbers marking the second and third bunkie; however, a reflective green marker, labelled 'Lot 1', stuck out of an overgrown bush in front of the first house. She pulled over, thinking that if she pulled into the driveway behind the angle-parked vehicle, her car would obstruct the lane, which she reasoned was no different than leaving her car where it was. She turned it off, hooked the last bag of books over her shoulder, and locked her car.

She stood facing the bunkie, hoping that Sonnet lived there. Only animal footprints led to the big lake house behind it. Edging her way carefully around the dirty car, she crossed the deck and knocked softly on the door. No one answered. She waited patiently; sometimes shut-ins were slowed by mobility challenges. She knocked again and again waited calmly, encouraged when she saw a figure in the window focus on her car, which had a magnetic sign linking her to the library service. She waited longer, heard the door lock click, then open. Her best customer service smile faded when she saw the unravelled woman on the other side. Her hair was as dishevelled as the wrinkled green hospital scrubs and hair-covered sweater hanging off her skeletal frame.

"I am so, so sorry to bother you."

Sonnet blinked with droopy eyes as Gracie lifted her bag of books to defend her presence, then pointed to her car.

"I'm Gracie from the library, delivering your books." Sonnet used her pale, thin fingers to smooth out her grey hair. Gracie discreetly noticed the bruises and tape marks on her hand, then the purple cast on her other arm.

"I won't keep you long. I chose some books that you may like to read, and I understand by this list," she said, pulling it out, "that you have some that are due back." She held her foot under the door frame to keep it propped open.

"Oh, yes," Sonnet responded, her throat thick from sleep. "I remember." Gracie's eyes met hers, with the same sorrow that Gracie saw in her husband, Blair, before he passed away. But she also saw something in Sonnet that reminded her of her friend Livy, who died suddenly the same year that Blair did.

"There are just six books due back. I don't want to keep you, but if you have them handy, I'd be happy to return them today."

"Of course. Come in." Gracie stepped onto the mat in the kitchen, holding the book bag in one hand and the list in the other. Their eyes met again. Sonnet appreciated Gracie's smile – genuine, with nothing hiding behind it.

"What a beautiful drive from the Falls to come here. I made this my last stop in case I got lost, and so I wouldn't have to hurry back. I never knew this little road existed."

"It's pretty in every season, although winter makes the lane more treacherous than it already is." Sonnet moved to the old box on her kitchen table. She took three library-coded books from the top and stacked them on the table. She rummaged through unlabeled books, creating a separate pile. Gracie, lover of all things written, recognized most of the titles – many were bestsellers.

"Wow. You've got a lot of good books here."

"My co-workers filled this box – it'll just take a minute to give you back the other three."

"I noticed your uniform. Just coming home?"

"Oh. Sort of."

"From the hospital?"

"Yes, well, it's not … not quite what it looks like." Sonnet saw Gracie's understanding brown eyes. "I was a patient there for a bit," she said, pointing to the plastic bag. "Came in wearing pyjamas, and was discharged just a few hours ago wearing these."

"Oh, no. I'm so, so sorry to bother you. I'm glad you were able to come home, maybe not fashionably, but at least wearing clothes."

Gracie smiled empathically, knowing it was unethical and against the rules to ask personal questions. Sonnet returned the smile and then found the three remaining books. Gracie traded the new bag for those due back, aware of Sonnet's cold hands against her own.

"There's a new date on this slip, if you're okay with it."

"I'm sure it's fine."

"My note says someone else registered you for this program and picked out your books, so I chose similar ones. I hope you'll like them."

"I'm sure they'll be fine."

"And, if you'd like something different, you can reserve it online or just leave me a message, and I'll try to get it for you."

There was a long pause; Sonnet poked her head into the new bag of books.

"Do I give you this bag back now?"

"No. Not until I exchange it for a new bag of books in a month."

Sonnet nodded her head, and again she paused.

"You said you could bring me specific books?"

"Yes, as long as we have it, or can get it from our neighbouring libraries. Did you have one in mind?" Again, a long minute of silence lapsed, which Gracie interpreted as Sonnet trying to remember a book or author.

"Do you, I mean the library, keep a permanent record of my books?" Gracie looked puzzled.

"I'm not sure what you mean. Like the items you borrow?"

"Yes. If I borrow and return the book, does the library keep a record of it?"

"Only if you keep an online record of your borrowing history. We don't normally retain what is borrowed and returned. Hmmm, I've never been asked that before."

"There's always a first time."

"I'm sensing you have something in mind, but are hesitant to ask me. Lots of people ask for steamy novels or books on controversial subjects. Our library has a whole roster of topics."

"It's called MAiD."

"Do you mean *Maid* or *The Maid*? They're both great novels and currently in our inventory."

"Neither. I mean books about MAiD: medical assistance in dying."

"Oh, now I understand." Gracie swallowed and tried to maintain a neutral expression. "I'll have to check to see what we have. Is there a specific one that you found in our system, or online?"

"With all due respect, I don't care to look online. I don't have a tablet, and I'm leery of my phone tracking what I search for." Gracie wondered what difference that would make, but said nothing.

"Of course. I will find some. Non-fiction, I presume?"

"Yes."

"And hard copies, rather than digital?"

"Yes. Please."

"I can do that." Gracie hesitated for a few moments, wording her next question with caution. "Hmmm ... I'm scheduled to come back here in a month. Can this wait until then, or rather, I mean, would you like me to bring these sooner than the next delivery date?" Sonnet heard the concern in Gracie's voice.

"Please, don't worry about me."

Gracie's expression remained unchanged. Sonnet ran her tongue between her teeth and her lips, then pointed to her scrubs. "I've been an oncology nurse for years, and wanted to do more research on it." Her intention to settle Gracie's mind worked; her face and shoulders relaxed.

"I'm sorry. It's just that you caught me off guard."

"It wasn't my intention."

"I know. I mean, I understand."

"It's alright."

"So, to clarify, if I'm heading out this way sooner than a month from now, would you like me to deliver these to you?"

"That would be very kind of you."

"Okay. Should I see what we have, and email you first?" Gracie asked, instantly regretting what she had just said.

"No need. I'd prefer it if you just called me with the new date you were coming. I really don't want anything recorded."

"Of course."

"It's Grace, right?"

"Yes, but most people call me Gracie."

"If you don't mind, I'd like to call you Grace. It's a beautiful name, and it was also my mother's."

Gracie smiled. "Yes, of course, Grace is fine."

"Thank you, Grace. When I saw your car, I didn't want to answer the door, but I'm so glad that I did. You're very kind, and I appreciate that it was you who came by today."

As Gracie opened the door a crack, she saw Rufus waiting on the other side, wagging his tail.

"Oh! You have a dog," Gracie exclaimed as Rufus did his best to squeeze his snout through the door's small gap.

"Rufus! Now behave," Sonnet said in a matronly voice. "He likes to steal food."

"I used to have one like that."

"You like dogs too?"

"I love them – even the ugly ones."

"Well, this young man loves everybody. You can let him in." Before Gracie opened the door to accommodate Rufus's girth, he slid between them and sat down closely beside Sonnet.

"Thank you, again, Grace," she said, resting a fragile hand on the dog's head. He pressed his body against her.

"You are most welcome, and it was a pleasure to meet you."

Gracie walked across the deck, noticing the small mound of vomit deposited on the top step that wasn't there when she came. Fearful Sonnet may slip in it, she called Sonnet, just as she was closing the door. Sonnet, still wearing the red non-skid hospital socks, approached the pile with Gracie. They bent over, heads close together, to dissect it, identifying not only undigested food but bits of cookie wrappings and torn fortunes. From inside, Rufus barked and watched the women turn to him, wagging his tail because he felt better after vomiting.

Gracie shooed Sonnet inside, who returned with a pot of warm water. Gracie pushed the mess off the deck with Sonnet's shovel, then washed the residual bits off the deck and stairs. Sonnet thanked her several times and waved as Gracie drove away. Closing her door, Sonnet picked up the tuft of dog hair she saw earlier on the doormat just as Rufus groaned and lowered himself onto it. It matched

Rufus's colour and texture exactly, but how it got there still unnerved her.

Gracie reflected on Polly's Lane while returning to the library; Sonnet unsettled and intrigued her in equal measures. She unloaded the bags of returned books onto the restocking cart at the back door and then checked in with her co-workers.

"How did your first official outreach day go?" one of her colleagues asked.

"Actually, good," Gracie said, not willing to share more.

"Before you head home," she said, handing her a square box, big enough to hold four beverage coasters. It was wrapped in plain, brown paper. "This was mailed to you."

"Hmmm ... that's not a familiar return address."

"And it's too small to be a bomb," she joked, then apologized immediately because a recent rash of bomb threats had cycled through some public buildings.

"Then maybe I should open it here."

"We agree, and we've taken bets on what we think it is."

"What do you think it is?"

"We won't tell you, but if you open it now, we'll tell you what we thought."

Gracie took the hint. She stood on the customer side of the checkout counter and unwrapped the package as her co-workers leaned in. Inside was a small white box with a tiny paw print on it.

"I was right," one co-worker said.

"You haven't even seen what's inside," Gracie answered. She opened the box, immediately connecting the clay mould to Wilson's paw. "Oh my, what a sweet thing to do." She became emotional, humbled by Fred's kind gesture.

"Yup, I was right. And that must have been one big dog."

Gracie had many fond memories of Wilson, whom she inherited from her close friend Livy, before she died suddenly. It was the second time in one day that Gracie was reminded of her. So odd, she thought as she gathered her things and headed home for the night.

5:15 PM

By the time Reba left the diner, texted Digger and picked him up at the grocery store, she figured she had shed enough tears to fill a coffee cup. She avoided Ziggy's raised eyebrows and wouldn't talk to him after Montana left, even after he yanked her by the elbow into the kitchen and interrogated her about "those electrician guys in the white truck", assuming by the gossip that they had hurt her. She cried harder, shaking her head, which confused him even more. She retaliated by hiding in the kitchen until near closing, leaving an agitated Ziggy to clean up after the late lunchers.

Reba couldn't wrap her thoughts around why she was so upset. She repeatedly felt the weight of Montana's hand cupping hers, then pulling hers out from under his. His hold wasn't forceful, like Ziggy's on her elbow. He hadn't hurt her, physically or emotionally, but somehow her mind was flooded with bad memories of other men. She half-ran to her car, as if to escape the negativity of her day.

Digger climbed into Reba's car, instantly aware of her fragile demeanour. There was no food scent until he put his deli leftovers on the back seat, and their predictable twenty-minute chat on the drive home was saturated with a series of uncomfortable silences. He worked his fidget spinner in one front pant pocket and rotated the worry monk in the other. At one point, Reba stared at his lap, covered by his winter jacket, for reassurance that he wasn't fondling himself. When Digger clued in, the ride felt even longer.

When they turned onto Polly's Lane, Reba noticed Sonnet standing in her window. They traded waves.

"Sonnet's home. That's good news." Reba parked in her driveway, then heaved her exhausted self out of the car. Digger followed her inside with dinner, feeling like he either owed her an apology or an explanation.

"Mom, I want to show you something."

"Oh no. What is it?"

"Nothing bad. Just this." He pulled the worry monk from his pocket and set it on the table. Reba eyed it suspiciously, then picked it up, still warm from Digger's hand.

"Looks like a cross to me." She thought the best place for it was in the junk drawer with the three other crosses she was given when she left Nova Scotia.

"It's a worry monk."

"A what?"

"A worry monk. Watch how I can turn it over and over in my hand." She passed it back to him to demonstrate.

"Huh. I bet someone lost it while praying that they had enough money to pay for their groceries."

"Nope."

"So, where'd you find it? It's so worn."

Digger hesitated before telling her more, hoping Reba would approve of what he said.

"Montana gave it to me. It used to be his. And look, Mom. See these four-leafed clovers? This one's for good luck for you, and the other one's for me." He pointed to the engravings. "Would you like me to read it to you?" Even though literacy was still a challenge, he hoped that reading the inscription would make his mother happier.

"Sure," she said, tears escaping the reserves she thought had run dry.

He slowly and carefully pronounced each word.

"May God grant you always a sun... sunbeam to warm you, a moonbeam to charm you, a shel... tering angel so nothing can harm you. Laughter to cheer you, faith ...ful friends near you, and wherever you pray, heaven to hear you."

By the time Digger finished, Reba's apron was over her face, muffling her sobs. Digger moved closer, pointing to the words he'd successfully read. She hugged him harder and longer than she had done for a long, long time.

"Pretty good, eh, Mom?"

"It's better than good. It's perfect."

Pleased with himself and her affection, mother and son felt strength in their special bond. Digger took a chipped,

Niagara Falls souvenir shot glass from the kitchen and set the worry monk in it, then placed it on his bedroom dresser with the cross's top leaning against the mirror. Still in the kitchen, Reba filled his plate with all of the food he brought home, including five little packets of ketchup. While her bagel toasted, Digger turned the TV on. They ate in silence, watching the news and *Wheel of Fortune.* In those ninety minutes, while Digger watched the wheel spin on TV as fast as his own gadget, his mother was preoccupied with only one thought: that Montana genuinely cared not only for and about her, but also about her son. And that also hadn't happened in a long, long time.

6:30 PM

After work, Gracie laid the dishes and cutlery on two place mats at Mason's kitchen island while he made a salad. They had already finished a bottle of Merlot while chatting about work. Wine during weekdays, whether at Mason's home or Gracie's condo, was usually rationed to one bottle between them. On weekends, their rules were made to be broken.

During their first year of dating, dinner at Mason's was prepared by his housekeeper and served in the dining room, situated just down the hall from his inviting bedroom—and easily visible from Gracie's seat. His housekeeper eventually weaned herself from the pair after she spent enough time eavesdropping to approve of Gracie and her culinary skills. And after devoting three decades to Mason and his now-deceased wife, she deserved to rest.

When the housekeeper retired from dinner duty, it also decreased the number of times they used the dining room. Because the kitchen provided no view of the bedroom, the frequency and duration of trips there fluctuated, like their wine consumption. Lower quality and quantity during the week were traded for higher quality, but fewer occasions in the bedroom on their days off. Regardless, like in many relationships, they adjusted.

Gracie filled their plates with poached salmon and rice while Mason scooped an arugula and pear salad into bowls. They moved clumsily around each other; Mason in the kitchen was so opposite to his impeccable dining room etiquette. Mason in the kitchen was just Mason, but Mason in the dining room behaved as if he were in public. Charismatic, polite, and usually better-dressed.

Today, he vented at length about his day in court, negotiating a tumultuous divorce involving two blended families, complicated by an unplanned set of twins. After days like this, he spoke until he ran out of words, or he was silent. Gracie worried about those silent days; broken marriages and their drama depleted him. She was a patient listener, and he was a better one after he shared his day. Today was a day when he needed a lot of patience, and he apologized for rambling.

"How was your first official book run?" he asked, finally appreciating his meal.

"Very interesting."

"I'm relieved the board upped your mileage and insurance coverage."

"Especially on a day like today. My car hit a pothole on a bumpy little laneway I'd never heard of. It was my last stop, and at such a beautiful, but neglected little hideaway."

"The car's okay?"

"Seems to be."

"And the customer? A little old man who wanted company for tea?"

"Just the opposite. A woman, actually a nurse, who looked so undone. She had just come back from the hospital, and I felt terrible because I woke her up."

"Why was she in the hospital?"

"I don't know, and didn't feel I should ask. Maybe she'll tell me the next time I see her."

"These are monthly visits, right?"

"They're supposed to be, but she asked me for specific books, and if we have them, I offered to bring them sooner."

"About what?" Gracie looked at Mason, wondering if she should share Sonnet's request.

"Medical assistance in dying."

Mason's fork, laden with a chunk of salmon, stopped halfway between his plate and his mouth. She immediately regretted telling him.

"You mean medically assisted suicide."

"I don't like that expression. The acronym is M.A.I.D – and with a small 'i'."

"I know what it is. It's a legal approval to kill another human being."

Gracie shook her head but remained quiet as Mason finished his dinner. After she collected their plates, rinsed and put them in the dishwasher, she took the little box of Wilson's paw print out of her purse and gently placed it in front of Mason. He opened the box and fingered the clay imprint.

"That's nice. Were you expecting this?"

"Not at all. Fred had it delivered to the library."

"Nice of him. You loved that dog."

"I did, but he was much happier there than in a condo with me."

"He died of old age?"

"No. He had cancer."

"And Fred had him put down."

"Yes," she said, feeling the wine. "Fred asked my permission first, then allowed the vet to assist with his death." Mason kept his eyes on his plate as Gracie continued. "You know, when people know their pets are suffering, no one questions how the vets help them die. They hold them in their arms so they know they are loved. So, how is that different with people?"

Mason, spent from his day arguing in court, was in no mood to initiate another battle. He picked up the cutlery, tossed them in the dishwasher, and then splayed both palms on the granite island across from Gracie.

"One way or another, Grace, with people, it's still suicide. Whether they end their lives alone or with help, suicide is suicide," he said, leaving what little remained in his wine glass and heading to his bedroom to change.

Gracie removed the cutlery, rinsed them and spaced them out in the dishwasher. She cleared the island and refrigerated the leftovers, and by the time she had wiped the counters clean, Mason returned, wearing jogging pants and a matching hoodie.

"I'm overdue for a long, brisk walk. Care to join me?"

"I've got the wrong shoes, so I'll pass."

Mason laced up his winter walking shoes and slid into a bright orange ski jacket. He smoothed down the reflective strips on his coat sleeves as Gracie grabbed her purse. Mason took her parka off a laundry room door hook and helped her into it. Despite the good-sized area they stood in, it felt as congested as the last few minutes of their conversation. Mason kissed her lightly on the cheek, more for politeness than passion, and they left the house together, neither saying another word.

9:30 PM

Reba was fast asleep by 9:00 pm, an early night for her. Digger played video games while lying on his bed, occasionally glancing over at the worry monk. He loved how smooth the wood felt in his hand. Unsure if he thanked Montana, he scrolled through his paltry contact list and texted him.

> "This is Digger. Thank u for the wury munk u gave me."
> "No prob. Did u get to use it?"
> "Yup. Works good."
> "How's your mom?"
> "OK. She went to bed early."
> "Musta been tired."
> "And quiet."

"Everything okay?"
"She cried a lot."
"Sorry to hear that. Why?"
"Don't know."
"Hope she feels better soon. Good night."
"Me too. Good night."

Digger felt better and played video games until he fell asleep. Montana felt worse.

DECEMBER 15TH

8:50 AM

Sonnet stopped her dented car in the middle lane of Dr. Torres's clinic parking lot, arguing with herself until the logical side of her brain won. Because she'd already paid five dollars to park, she kept her promise and her appointment to see him. He was her advocate, and she needed him now more than ever.

As usual, his waiting room was full. She stepped around a young mother and her toddler, perched on low stools and sliding beads across an abacus. The receptionist swiped Sonnet's plastic health card through the scanner, but instead of scowling, asked how she was feeling. Sonnet sensed that not only did the receptionist know her lab work was in her medical record, but she'd also read it and formed her own opinion.

"I'm here," was all Sonnet offered, then leaned against a wall to wait.

She was eventually ushered into the same spacious exam room and office as she had during her last visit. Sonnet walked to the corner window, its high ledge allowing both privacy and the diversion of a picturesque ravine view. Sonnet leaned her elbows on the ledge and took in the deep snow covering the fluttering leaves she recalled from her last visit. Broken branches from old trees stuck out from the snow.

After an endless wait, Dr. Torres rushed in with enough momentum that his long white lab coat floated in the air. He repeated the same rituals as before: he filled his mug with tap water, gulped it down, then apologized for keeping her waiting. He sat at his desk, tapped four keys on his keyboard, then abruptly stopped. He walked over and stood to her right at the window. Taller than Sonnet by a good six inches, he crossed his arms and, like her, rested his elbows on the window ledge. A potted plant, with a 'thank-you' note poking into the soil, separated the doctor from his patient.

"You know, it's so pretty out there," he sighed and leaned closer to the glass, taking in the landscape. Sonnet inhaled the scent of his breath bouncing off the window, a mix of mint and coffee.

"I doubt you get to stand here often."

"You're right. Neither of us is good at stopping long enough to watch the sunset, or smell those proverbial roses." Sonnet nodded, forcing a smile. The pair stood beside each other, as they had done many times at a dying patient's bedside. Their poignant moment was interrupted by his receptionist's knock and immediate entrance. They remained where they stood, just their heads turning towards her.

"Oh, sorry, but the call you're waiting for is holding on line one."

"I'll call him back."

"Okay, but ..."

"But we'll need a few quiet minutes here first." Dr. Torres turned back to face the window. Sonnet caught the frustrated woman shaking her head before closing the door. "Lots of drama, but she's good at what she does. Now, where were we?"

"Talking about all the sunsets we missed."

"That's right."

"And how many sunsets I have left."

"Not all of your tests are in."

"Remember, I didn't agree to have anything done besides bloodwork, and my arm was casted as soon as I came in."

"That's right, and explains why I'm not finding any tests. I'd like to order them now, if you're okay with that." Sonnet shook her head.

"Why bother? This conversation, be it now or two weeks from now, will inevitably lead to the same outcome, which is dying."

Dr. Torres took a deep breath and rubbed his furrowed forehead. A lone deer sauntered into and out of their view of the ravine.

"But that might not be true. You've convinced yourself that you're terminally ill."

"Because I am."

"But there's no definitive or final diagnosis. And nothing to confirm it."

"I have every symptom. I know I am dying."

"Sonnet, please tell me how I can help you," he said softly, his right arm still leaning on the ledge while his left hand found his lab coat pocket.

"I'd like you to refer me to the medically-assisted death program."

"Whoa. I didn't expect you to ask me that." He swallowed, then faced her directly.

"I'm sorry," she said quietly, her hollow eyes expressing what she couldn't say.

"Don't be."

"Please consider this as my formal, voluntary request."

"But there's only bloodwork and no tests."

"What difference will it make?"

"Because we'll know what's going on – and there are treatment options."

"With all due respect, the medical system will do what the medical system does. We've both witnessed those interventions, and let's be honest, even if they extend my life, which I don't want, none of them are pleasant."

"I appreciate that, Sonnet."

"As I said, I do not want to prolong my life. It's not about quantity, but my quality of life, which is none."

"You've obviously been thinking about this."

"And I've made up my mind." There was a very long pause, during which both turned back to stare out the window.

"Sonnet, you're Catholic, and you know I'm a Catholic, too. Maybe not quite the church-going kind, but I still believe in our faith."

"What's that got to do with this?"

"The church's position on it."

Sonnet hoisted her purse strap over her shoulder – she saw his instant regret about raising the issue.

"But we're not in church. We're here, in your office, and you are my doctor. There's no room for religion in this medical discussion. This is between you, as my physician, and me, your patient. And as for faith, hope, and we might as well throw in charity, I have none of those left."

"I'm sorry that I offended you."

His head and shoulders drooped. Sonnet looked deeply into his eyes, as weary as hers, then walked towards the door.

"Wait," he whispered. "Please wait." She turned partially around, hand on the doorknob, avoiding eye contact.

"I don't want to wait," she whispered back.

She left before he could review her chart, or at the very least, her casted right wrist. He sat down and leaned back in his office chair, raising his hands and clasping them together behind his head. He looked up, fixated on an old, water-stained ceiling tile. He wondered how medicine had progressed, or perhaps regressed, since his graduation, where he had recited the Hippocratic Oath to do no harm. It was only when his receptionist interrupted his thoughts with a perfunctory knock that he stood up, feeling like he did after finishing a gruelling double shift. He took a deep breath, guzzled his tap water down and faced the rest of his day.

Sonnet descended the stairs to the clinic's main floor and was at the exit door when her phone rang. Hoping to ignore it, she changed her mind when her phone display identified the caller as the library

"Sonnet O'Brien speaking."

"Hi. It's Gracie, I mean Grace, from the library. I have the books you requested."

Sonnet scrutinized the people moving nearby, too preoccupied to listen to her.

"Thank you."

"I won't be able to drop them off today, but maybe soon?"

"I'm actually in town for a medical appointment."

"Oh. I hope everything's okay." Gracie also hoped Sonnet might elaborate, but she didn't.

"I can pick the books up in a bit."

"That's great, and you don't even have to leave your car. The library's not open yet, so just call when you arrive and I'll pop out." Gracie confirmed the library location and entrance to use.

"I don't have any books with me to return."

"No need to worry about that."

"Ah, can I ask you one more thing?"

"Of course."

"I don't have a printer at home. There are some sample forms I would appreciate regarding medically assisted death." Sonnet relayed the website she memorized and told Gracie exactly where in the menu the application referral forms were listed.

"Just to be clear, am I understanding that you're asking me to print these forms for you?'

"Yes. And if it's not too much to ask, may I ask you for two copies?"

Gracie breathed deeply but silently before she answered. "Of course. I'll try to have them ready for you when you come."

"I know we don't know each other, but may I ask for your discretion in not sharing this request with anyone?"

"Yes, of course, I understand." They both heard someone laughing loudly in the background at the library.

"Thank you kindly. I'll be there shortly."

Ten minutes later, Sonnet parked in the library pick-up zone and dialed the number Gracie gave her. Gracie hurried out, not wearing a coat, and approached Sonnet's car with a new red library bag. She passed Sonnet two slips of paper after she rolled down her window.

"Nice to see you. I hope you're feeling okay today," she offered, for lack of anything better to say.

"Thank you."

"One book receipt has a revised due date for the books you have at home, and this one is for today's books, as you requested. Now they're all due on the same day."

"So, one is for last week's books, and this one is for today."

"Yes." Gracie paused for a moment, then leaned closer to Sonnet. "And today's books are reserved under my own name to avoid having any connection to you. Not exactly library protocol, but either way, I'll share the responsibility for getting them back."

"That's very considerate of you."

"And, the two copies of the forms you requested are tucked into your books." She handed the bag to Sonnet.

"Thank you."

"And, lastly, I have a little something for you." Gracie presented her with a plastic library card, decorated with a miniature green bow. Sonnet appreciated the gesture.

"Thank you, yet again." Sonnet fingered the curves of the bow. "Until now, today was not pleasant."

"Well, I hope your day gets better, and I'll see you after Christmas, on …" Sonnet checked the top book slip date before answering, revealing her purple cast.

"January 4th."

"Hope the cast comes off soon."

"Me too," said Sonnet, not offering Gracie anything more.

After exchanging Christmas pleasantries, Gracie hurried indoors, shivering without her coat. She passed the checkout desk on her way to unlock the main entrance door, where the sun warmed those waiting for the library to open. She recognized most visitors, especially those seeking comfort and, unlike Sonnet, a brief reprieve from their worries.

10:05 AM

Yesterday, Kat and Reba hung tired Christmas ornaments during an unusually quiet lull at the diner. In contrast, this morning, every table was occupied. Reba's feet ached, and her mind hurt from the regulars complaining about their "table" being taken by strangers. She noticed a new red poinsettia plant that Kat or Ziggy had squeezed into a tight space between a wall and the coffee machine. She wiped the counters down, then moved the plant closer to the front entrance, but noticed that some of the foliage was sagging from the coffee maker's heat. She rotated it so incoming guests saw only the good side, and it was only then that she saw a crumpled red envelope shoved in between the blooms. REBA was printed on it. She tucked it into her apron pocket, then fussed over her plant to make it appear healthier. She poked a finger into the dry soil and emptied a full glass of water someone left on the counter, which pooled in the green foil covering the pot.

Reba scraped food off plates, dumping dirty dishes into her grey rubber bin. She pointed to the plant when she and Kat were both near the old cash register.

"Who left this?" she asked.

"I dunno."

Determined, Reba walked into the kitchen and asked Ziggy.

"That greenhouse guy," he answered, flipping hash browns.

"What greenhouse guy?"

"Comes after delivering to the grocery store. Sits by the window."

"That really tall guy?"

"Yup. Sweet potato fries, and no mayo on his BLT."

"Ah, right. When?"

Reba instantly made the connection – Finn was Dutch and married, with a half-dozen children. She frowned reluctantly and left, ignoring Ziggy, unsure if he answered her last question. She studied her name on the card and flipped it over to read the stamped greenhouse name, which also matched Finn's sweatshirts. Putting her damp rag down, she opened the envelope seal with a steak knife. Inside was a recipe for fried oatmeal, hand-printed on a lined page, torn out of an outdated journal. She turned it over.

> *"Any chance we can have this for breakfast tomorrow?"*

Reba sighed. She didn't know what it was, because nobody asked for fried oatmeal. She looked back at the gifted plant and tried to think of who left it. She tucked the recipe in her pocket, then looked up to see two customers waving her over, impatient for service.

When the new diners were accommodated, Reba popped back into the kitchen and poked her nose into the half-full pot of oatmeal on the stove's warming element. She checked the recipe ingredients in her pocket – there was lots of leftover oatmeal, and everything else on the list was already in Ziggy's kitchen. She approached him, holding the recipe facing his eye level, while he slapped frozen burger patties on a cooking surface.

"Think you can make this with what's left in that pot? Looks pretty easy." Ziggy scowled, concentrating on his task.

"Then what are my pigs going to eat?"

Reba leaned past the corner of the cooking surface and lifted a white bucket of scraps, which Ziggy filled daily for his farm animals.

"Look - there's already a Christmas feast in there for them." Ziggy's face didn't change.

"They need oatmeal for digestion."

"So, does that mean no?"

"Why do you want me to make that? Nobody will eat that."

"Well, look at this. Somebody will." She flipped the recipe over to show him the message. "Can we try it just once, tomorrow? If people like it, we can make it a Sunday morning special. And if they don't like it, I won't bring it up again."

Ziggy grumbled under his breath, wiped the sweat off his brow, and looked at her over the top of his grease-spattered glasses.

"I'll tell you what. You come in half an hour early, on your own time, get everything ready, make the recipe, and I'll fry them up. But if there's so much as one pancake left, no more fried oatmeal. You hear me?'

"Loud and clear," she chirped, rushing out of the kitchen before he could change his mind.

10:30 AM

Fletcher rolled over in bed to see the Korean delivery girl gazing at him. He yawned loudly and pulled her porcelain body up against his, her features arousing him all over again.

"How long have you been up?" he asked, nuzzling his face into her hair. She smelled like his soap and shampoo because she arrived late last night, saturated with ginger soy sauce from a leaky container. A perfect misfortune for sharing a sensuous bath and the pleasures that followed, well into the wee hours of the night.

Fletcher's phone lay under his pillow, and when the ring tone identified his mother, he groaned. By four rings, he had gulped some fizzy water, cleared his throat and had the phone on speaker mode. He propped himself up on one elbow, centred the phone between his bedmate's breasts and began to massage them.

"Oh, Fletcher darling, were you still sleeping?"

"Morning, Mom. Nope, was just in the middle of brushing my teeth," he lied.

"I'm glad, because we spent a lot of money fixing them."

"I miss you. How are you and Dad? And how's my sister?"

"All good. Faith just finished her PhD dissertation - we're so excited for her! And ... you won't be missing us for long, because we're flying to Niagara Falls for Christmas!" she squealed. Fletcher laid his head back on the pillow and put his palm to his forehead while the Korean delivery girl covered her mouth to stifle her laugh.

"That's great news. I'm so excited," he lied again. He picked up his phone and turned off the speaker for fear his mother would hear him react as the girl beside him slid her hand slowly down his body until she found what she was looking for.

"Yes. You remember George, our pilot? Well, he's flying us into Buffalo and we'll rent a car to cross the border."

"Now I'm really excited," he giggled as his lover planted kisses down his body until her lips replaced her hand. "And when are you coming?" he asked. His lover poked her head up from his erection and silently mimicked his mother's question before resuming her task.

"I knew you'd be excited. We'll fly up early on the 24th. I'll text you when we clear through Customs. Is Polly's Lane still so bumpy?" On cue, Fletcher's lover mounted him and mouthed 'bump, bump, bump' in sync with her moves, hands and ponytail swaying in the air.

"Yes, there are lots and lots of bumps." Fletcher's hips moved with hers.

"Then maybe we should just book a hotel?"

"Good idea, Mom, and you don't want to wreck the rental car. I can meet you at the main road and stay at the hotel so we can all be together as one happy family, if that's not an inconvenience."

"Wonderful idea, honey. And, Faith is bringing her new friend Jessica."

"Mom, my neighbour's just walking up the driveway. She's been sick, so I need to check that she's okay. Can I call you back?" Fletcher's third lie slid past his mother as smoothly as the previous two.

"That's sweet of you, honey, but don't keep me waiting."

"I shouldn't be too long. Bye."

Fletcher double-checked that his phone was indeed off before losing it between the sheets. He anchored his hands to his lover's breasts and completed the euphoric ride, vaguely distracted about whether Jessica was his sister's new partner or intended for him.

He also conveniently forgot to call his mother back.

11:00 AM

Sonnet left the library and drove a few short blocks to the bank to deposit her first disability cheque. She manoeuvred her car between the narrow spaces, for once unconcerned about it being hit or keyed. She came out ten minutes later to see the back of a male figure assessing her car.

She waited long enough to recognize Stan, whom she had separated from five years ago. The seams of their marriage became irreparable after small cracks expanded to craters, then erupted like volcanoes. She fled, not only for her safety but her sanity, and paid the price by inheriting his bankrupted debt.

He turned completely around to see her; she had feared him for so many years that she recognized that look, even before he inhaled to spew what she predicted would be insults about her driving. But instead, he exhaled loudly when he did a once-over of her emaciated frame.

They faced each other, ten steps between them. He looked at her, just like he did back when she thought he cared enough about her to let her know if he was running late. That was until she overheard him brag to his drinking buddies about his "nurse with a purse wife" before hanging up.

Stan was a torturer, and Sonnet was his victim. The insults from his mouth were as significant as the blows from his feet. He knew only some of her past, at a time when she felt she could confide in him, but nothing about Father Francis or the child their love conceived.

Rather than divorcing him and, by default, the Catholic church, she stayed and sought solace in her work, while Stan found it in the bottle. When she finally said she was leaving, he responded with laughter and words laced with poison. She remembered those words, as clearly as if he said them now: "If you leave me, you'll end up with nothing but that shit-covered uniform on your back."

That was the same night Stan stopped coming home, after beating and raping her as a parting gift. She couldn't work because of her wounds, but needed a doctor's note to be allowed to recover at home. This brought her to her first humiliating encounter with Dr. Torres, who called the police. She refused to have him charged; she was certain it would only make matters worse for her.

Dr. Torres's unwavering support earned her trust in him, sometimes as subtle as a quiet nod across a hospital bed, or a kind word when he passed her in the hall. They appreciated and respected each other's clinical skills. Their patient-physician relationship, Sonnet as his patient, and he as her doctor, also strengthened on the days in his office when he had more time to give her, and she had more to say. He understood her Catholicism, failures and rejections resulting in her low self-worth. Trash was what Stan called her; unworthy of developing another relationship, or even a closer kinship with her work family.

And even after her appointment this morning and their conversation, she knew Dr. Torres would never, ever judge her.

Stan's mouth opened to show the progressing decay of his nicotine-stained teeth, and when his eyes narrowed and his lips thinned, her legs and hands began to shake.

"Lost some weight." Stan's voice pierced the air between them, like many times before.

"That's what happens when you're dying," she whispered, surprised at how easily those words slipped out.

"Jesus Christ, Sonnet. I didn't need to hear that."

"I don't need to hear you speak the Lord's name in vain."

"Oh, get off your holy ..." he paused, unnerved by the purple cast on her hand, "I meant ... I mean ..." He didn't finish his sentence.

"Excuse me, I need to get to my car."

"Who'd you hit? Or, ah, what happened?" She had no energy to provide details.

"The car slid off the road and got wedged in some trees during the storm."

"Where did that happen?"

When Sonnet moved to Polly's Lane, she never disclosed her new address, unless it was mandatory, and still sensed he had no idea where she lived.

"On a side street," was all she offered.

"You shouldn't have been driving then." Sonnet rarely swore, and if there was a moment she'd like to, it was now. Instead, she pursed her lips, exhaled slowly and walked cautiously towards her car. He stood firm, blocking her path.

"Excuse me," she said meekly, stepping sideways to go around him. She was repulsed by the old booze and rotting teeth on his breath; that familiar glare of retaliation covered his face, re-traumatizing her. He lifted his hand. She flinched.

"Jesus, you didn't think I was gonna hit ya'?" His hand touched her hair, brushing it off her forehead as she stood frozen, praying for an approaching person or vehicle to distract him.

"Please let me through. I feel faint. I just got out of the hospital."

"Then I'll help you." He pinned her against her car, expecting more of her size than he remembered. "There, now you won't fall." The hard pressure of his legs and protruding belly against her hollow abdomen drained what little energy she had to push him away. He yanked at her purse handles, still hooked through her elbow. He rummaged through her bag, producing her wallet. "I was lookin' for your keys, but I'm sure you can help me out with a little cash until my check comes in." Numbed by another flashback, she watched helplessly as he removed the five twenty-dollar bills she had just withdrawn. He separated four of the crisp bills with a filthy thumb, stuffed them in his pocket, and returned the last one to her wallet. Her fear intensified, similar to those years he came home late and wanting, whether he was capable or not. Like today, succumbing was less painful than fighting him off.

He found her car keys in her coat pocket and unlocked her door, still anchoring her with his leg between hers. He then released her, but only after groping at her chest with his hands.

"Geez, there's nothing left of your tits," he scoffed as he pried open her dented door and shoved her in. Feet still on the asphalt, Sonnet fell sideways into the front seat, her ribs striking the console. Muffling a painful scream with her fist, she held her breath, stiff as a mannequin, until she heard Stan's footsteps stop at his vehicle, his door open and slam shut, and his untuned engine sputter to life. She exhaled only after the last rumble of his rusty truck faded away.

She rearranged herself and untangled her casted right arm from her purse. Feet back in the car and doors locked, she waited and waited until she gathered enough energy and courage to leave the parking lot.

Sonnet drove home, blanched hands locked around the steering wheel. Sloping down Polly's Lane, she pulled into her driveway, having no recall of how she got there. Rufus, roused from his nap on her sunny deck, lumbered over to her, his rear end waddling from side to side. Sonnet put her grocery bag down to pet him, needing to touch something living, warm, and harmless. He leaned heavily against her, sniffing the parts of her coat that Stan had pawed. Rufus lifted his head, looking directly at her as if he knew of her ordeal.

"You have no idea how much I hoped you'd be here. Were you waiting for me?" He lost interest in her when he heard her voice, turning his attention to her purchases. "Ah, now you smell what I brought you."

She formed a withered smile as he ran to her open trunk, propping his front paws up on her bumper. His head and tail bobbed when he caught the scent from the bag of dog food. She struggled not to drop it, a casted hand and a good arm carrying it. She tested her bunkie's door, relieved it was locked. Groceries inside and kettle on, she scooped a generous helping of kibble into one metal mixing bowl, water in the other. Rufus finished both before the kettle boiled.

"That's it, no more," she chirped. His pleading eyes won her over, and another half-cup landed in his dish. "This time, I mean it, young man. No more."

He finished it in a minute, then stood politely by the door. She let him out, where he vanished across the lane to do his business, then returned. She bent over so their noses were inches apart. He offered her a paw, first the one where his swollen elbow had since settled, then replaced it with the other one.

"You're quite the gentleman, aren't you?" His jowls spread wide across his teeth, wrinkling his nose.

"Are you smiling at me?" He held his expression. "Oh, my goodness, you are smiling." And the dog's floppy grin, she mused, gave her just a wee reprieve from her sadness.

Rufus followed her to the bedroom, yawning loudly as Sonnet sat on the bed and pulled her Bible out. She slid her hand between the pages until the weight of not only God's but Father Francis's words warmed her fingers; she closed her eyes and imagined the heaviness of his hand over hers. She tucked her feet under the unmade covers. Rufus nudged her thigh, then lay his head there, her free hand gently stroking his fur until he curled up on the braided rug. She watched the rhythm of his breathing, feeling protected. They fell asleep without sensing they were tired, even though it was still just the morning.

Noon

Fletcher stood on the deck in his Australian sheepskin slippers and waved goodbye to the Korean delivery girl. As usual, he had no agenda, and his entertainment just left, so when a delivery truck stopped at Sonnet's address, he gave it his full attention.

The middle-aged, pot-bellied driver climbed out, unbothered about obstructing the lane. He carefully manoeuvred a large square box onto a dolly and down a retractable ramp, then up the two wooden steps to Sonnet's deck. He knocked repeatedly on the door until it opened. Rufus slid out first, sniffed the box and positioned his hind leg against it just before the driver chased him away. He barked back a few times, then sauntered over towards Fletcher's bunkie, marking each tree along the way.

Fletcher couldn't hear the driver or Sonnet, but saw her repeatedly point his way. The driver pushed his heavy load back onto the dolly, but unable to move it up the ramp, wheeled it down the bumpy lane and over to Fletcher's house. Since he wasn't expecting anything, Fletcher watched excitedly, rather than help the driver wheel the box up two steps and across his deck. Depositing the box, the driver extended a small tablet for Fletcher to sign. The driver checked the tablet and disappeared, leaving Fletcher to transfer the box inside on his own.

Once indoors, he unpacked a solar-powered generator. His father's blunt message, noted on the packing slip, said: 'Merry Christmas. This stays on Polly's Lane.' It made sense after Fletcher recalled telling his mother about the blackout, except the part about almost burning the bunkie down. Fletcher scratched his head, wondering if his mother had called to be thanked for the delivery he hadn't received yet. He also wondered whether he should appreciate the delivery or deepen his parental resentment. He compared it against the year when he received an ugly Christmas sweater his mother bought just before he was deported, then was forced to wear it for the family portrait while his sister wore cashmere.

Fletcher put his shoes on and went outside. He called Rufus, and when the dog didn't respond, he circled his property and then Sonnet's, partially because he hoped the dog would appear, and partially because he was frustrated. He saw her in the light of the kitchen window, drying her eyes with a tea towel. Thinking there may be another opportunity for him to be helpful, he walked onto her deck and waited, hoping she'd come to the door without him having to knock. And when he didn't leave, she opened the door just a foot's width.

"Just checking in. Everything alright?" He saw fresh sleep lines across her hollow cheek, but no sign of the dog. Sonnet's flat affect shifted to revenge when she noticed his tattoo, a hideous spiderweb on his neck. She also wondered what motivated him to come. She looked down at his feet; he followed her gaze, eyes eventually meeting.

"Is something wrong?" he asked.

"Well, I was just wondering if those were the boots that muddied my house."

By his stunned expression, no answer was needed. She stunned him even more by opening the door wide and beckoning him in. A minute ago, he wouldn't have hesitated, but now regretted his stupidity.

"I'm just looking for the dog," he half-lied, hoping to redirect her train of thought.

"Tucker, as you call him?"

"Yah, I mean, yes."

"Well, then you better come in." For the first time in forever, other than during sex and when the bunkie's carbon monoxide alarm went off, his heart pounded wildly. Sonnet saw his fear and loved the feeling of power over him. "What do you think I'm going to do to you, shoot you?" She raised her casted arm, instinctively, and he recoiled.

"No, but …"

"Then come inside, because I'm cold." He immediately obeyed. "Now, Mr. Hope, what in God's good name made you break in here?" she grilled him, topping up the kettle. There was no way he would confess that his key also fit her door.

"I, I don't know. I was just looking for the dog, and when you didn't answer the door, I began to worry if you were okay. And besides that, your door was unlocked, so it's not like I forced myself in." Sonnet felt a sudden urge to whack him in the head with her kettle, then remembered she'd once been on the receiving end of it from Stan.

"And why didn't you think I was okay?"

"Well, because you looked really sick, and no disrespect, but you also looked terrible the last time I saw you. And the dog might have been stuck inside."

Her grey eyes bored into his, making him want to run. She read his fear, put her hand on the doorknob, blocking his exit. Fletcher's heart, circulating blood through a body at least double Sonnet's weight, pounded harder.

"I really should leave. I didn't mean to interfere."

"No need to, because you've already interfered. Would you like a cup of tea? You look like a frightened dog."

Sonnet moved the library bag that Gracie brought from the kitchen table to the floor, pointing to the chair she wanted him to sit in. He chose her usual chair instead – it was closest to the door, and offered him an unobstructed view of her, thinking that if he watched her brew the tea, maybe she wouldn't poison him. He debated telling her that he'd preferred coffee latte, but she'd already rinsed the teapot with hot water, made tea and set it on the table.

"I like it steeped for five minutes, so we've got lots of time to talk," she said, repositioning the other chair to face him directly.

Five minutes of agony and then five minutes to drink the tea, he thought, *and then I'm gone. Ten minutes of misery,* she thought, should give him enough time to show some remorse.

"You violated my privacy."

"I'm sorry."

"You also moved my things."

"I'm sorry about that, too."

"There were fortune cookie wrappers all over the floor."

"Well, they were actually for you, but the dog ate them first."

She stifled a smile, but wondered again about his motive. It didn't matter, she thought, while she set some mismatched china on the table. "What made you look in my bedside drawer?" It gave her satisfaction to watch him squirm. "Be honest with me, now."

"Well, that's usually where people hide interesting things."

"And what did you expect to find in there?" She opened a red plaid tin of shortbreads, arranging an assortment on a plate.

"I don't know."

"I see. And why did you touch my Bible?"

"I don't have an answer for that. It was just there. The last time I saw one of those was in a hotel room I stayed in when I played football. I didn't think people actually read them," he said, choosing a layered cookie with a dab of red jelly in the middle. Assuming it was stale, he took a tiny bite. It was crisp and fresh. "There's always a Do Not Remove stamp in the front of the Bible, so I checked to see if it came from a hotel." She covered her lips with her good hand to hide her amusement.

"Rest assured. I didn't steal it."

"I figured that out when there was no stamp. But who's Sister Mary Agnes?" Hearing the name unsettled her.

"Me."

"You? You're a nun?"

"I was."

"Holy shit. I mean, sorry …"

"Holy shit describes it accurately." Shared smiles lightened their tension.

"When was that?"

"Long ago, in another life and another country."

"So that explains the accent. I'm guessing English?" He chose another cookie, this one coated with chocolate, watching Sonnet cautiously while she reached into the library bag.

"Close. I'm Irish, but the shortbreads are Scottish."

"How many years were you in the, um, nunnery?" Again, she grinned.

"Twenty."

"So, like, for twenty years, you prayed and had no, ah, I mean," he stuttered.

"Are you asking me if I was celibate?" She watched him flush.

"Bad question. You don't have to answer that."

"And I won't." As he chose a third cookie, he hoped she would.

She rummaged through the library bag again, then carefully pulled the forms out that Gracie had printed for her. She turned to the pages that needed signatures, covering the page headings so that only what she wanted him to see was visible. She tried one of the two pens lying on the table, but the ink was dry when she scribbled on the back of a card. The second pen worked.

"Now, young man, do you promise never to set foot in my house uninvited?" He sat up straight.

"I promise. Really, I do."

"And are you truly sorry for invading my privacy?"

"I am. I'm truly sorry," he lied.

"So, if you're apology is sincere, I will forgive you, if you kindly witness my signature on this form?"

"Sure. What kind of form is it?"

"Insurance. A guaranteed life to death insurance."

"Oh. Is that a new kind?"

"It is. It became law in 2016."

"Wow. You've done your homework. It must be good insurance."

"I have, and it's guaranteed."

"Guaranteed, that's great. So where do I sign?" Reading nothing but the lines she pointed to, Fletcher notarized and dated Sonnet's application for medical assistance in dying.

Rufus waited patiently by the outside door until Sonnet let Fletcher out, satiated with cookies and confidence that he was in good standing again with his neighbour. It was the scent of his crumbs that helped Rufus decide who to follow.

DECEMBER 16ᵀᴴ

6:50 AM

Digger couldn't understand why his mother got up so early and hurried them both out the door. Never the first one at the grocery store, Reba waited impatiently with him until Joe arrived, hugged him prematurely, and sped off.

She unlocked the diner's side door and hustled into Ziggy's kitchen to prep the fried oatmeal ingredients. She pulled the handwritten recipe card from her apron pocket and double-checked the ingredients, expecting Ziggy to barge in shortly and take over. She washed her hands, then sank one deep into the porridge pot she'd removed from the fridge. She held the cold pot with one arm as she tried to loosen the gluey mixture with the other. She felt a little funny, ignoring it until a rainbow of electric stars formed across her line of vision. Sensing another spell, she squatted down on the clay floor tiles, just seconds before her world went black.

7:20 AM

Ziggy was in a foul state of mind when he pulled into the diner's parking lot because the night before, his son had borrowed his pickup truck to get into what Ziggy knew was trouble, then returned late with an empty gas gauge. He also swore loudly when he saw Reba's "shit-box" parked where he usually did, layering on the bitterness. He slammed his truck shut, opened the kitchen's exit door, ready to strip a lecture off his tongue, but forgot everything when he found Reba sprawled on her back across the floor. Legs askew, like her mouth, she lay with her head angled against her shoulder.

"Reba!" He also felt lightheaded, kneeling down, not only to tend to her, but to prevent himself from falling over her. "Reba!"

Reba moaned, stirring slowly, then worked her eyes open as if she was ungluing them. She rubbed them, trying to identify the sweaty jowls hovering over her. She lifted her head up, recognizing him, then shoved a weak arm against him, forcing him to move out of her path quicker than he was prepared to do.

"What, what's going on?" she mumbled, squinting at him and then at her low-lying environment.

A knock on the kitchen door distracted them, and Montana was even more surprised when he swung it open, just a few feet from where Reba was trying to prop herself up on her elbows. She clamped her exposed legs together, her checkered uniform hem hiked up near her hips. Ziggy was still positioned on his hands and knees at her side, one shoulder leaning over hers.

"Gee, this isn't quite what I expected," Montana said, instead of what he wanted to say and knew he would later regret.

"Why am I on the floor?" Reba said groggily.

"Because I found you here! Right here! Look!" Ziggy boasted in defence, pointing to a toppled step stool and various dollops of spilled oatmeal. He turned to Montana. "And you, get the hell out of my kitchen!"

Montana ignored him, feeling certain that if Reba had suffered another spell, Ziggy was unaware, or worse, ignoring them at the expense of her health and safety.

Reba, more alert and aware by now, felt her uniform. Realizing what it did and didn't cover, she sat up and yanked it down as the two men watched. As the last buttonhole tore in the process, Reba retaliated at Ziggy.

"I am never wearing this stupid uniform again. You hear me? Never!" She hooked her finger into the buttonhole and tore it further to ensure it was unrepairable. She then turned to Montana. "What are you doing here?! And, what the hell are you looking at?!"

Montana moved his hands to his hips. He looked at the pair on the floor, splattered oatmeal around them, and covered his mouth to conceal an unexpected grin.

"Are you laughing at me?!" she yelled.

"No, ma'am," he mumbled behind his hand, keeping it there until he could manage a concerned look. "But I'll pass on the fried oatmeal."

Reba became even more unravelled for two reasons: it wasn't obvious until Montana's comment that she linked the recipe to him, and she was on the floor because of another spell. She drew her caked hand towards her face, stopping before touching it. Nearest to a sink, Montana moistened some paper towels and passed them to Reba while Ziggy grunted, grabbed the steel counter for support and, with great effort, heaved his flaccid body up to a standing position. He puffed his barrelled chest out and faced Montana.

"You're not welcome here."

"In your kitchen?" He leaned against the counter in a casual stance, hands pocketed.

"In my whole diner."

"Why?" Montana extended a hand to assist Reba off the floor – she pretended to ignore him and the conflict brewing between the men.

"For taking advantage of my waitress." This ignited Reba's fire.

"I'm not your waitress. First of all, we're called servers these days … and second, how did he take advantage of me?" she shouted, by then on her knees, this time accepting Montana's help. Ziggy ignored her, leering at Montana, which made her even angrier.

"You know why." His words concerned both Montana and Reba.

"No, sir, I don't," Montana said, then Reba piped in.

"And I'd like to know why, too." She looked back and forth between the men, thoroughly confused. Ziggy pointed an accusatory index finger at his opponent.

"You slept with her. You went first, and then you let your friends take a turn."

"You're an idiot! In case you hadn't noticed, because you hogged the kitchen all to yourself, we all slept together in that room during that wretched storm," Reba snarled, trying to clean her slimy hands with the wet paper towel.

"So, it's true!" Ziggy reeled his head back, looking at the pair with seething resentment. Reba's jaw dropped. She looked to Montana, who lifted his baseball cap calmly, scratching his forehead with the same hand. He took one step back from Ziggy just as Reba took one step closer, her head held high. She poked Ziggy in the chest as she spoke.

"What's true?"

"I just told you."

Montana interjected.

"Are you insinuating that we had sex?"

Ziggy cocked his head to one side and stared accusingly at him. Reba smacked her forehead with the palm of her hand at the same time Montana raised his hands in the air.

"Now just a minute here. Let's get this straight. It's none of your damn business what your employees do outside of here, and for the record, I didn't sleep with her out there," he said, pointing to the dining room, "or for that matter, anywhere else. But since we're on that subject, I'm dying to know who, or what, gave you that impression." Ziggy cowered back; Montana didn't let up. "You brought this up, so you better speak now. I, no, we both need to hear exactly what you have to say." Reba felt bold and poked Ziggy twice this time to emphasize she was siding with Montana.

"Yah, Ziggy, you better spit it out."

Her boss leaned a hand on the steel counter for support, picked a few chunks of oatmeal off the floor, and then eyed his employee.

"You're not going to want to hear this, Reba."

"Oh yes, I do. Now, let's have it," she egged him on. Ziggy looked at Reba, but pointed his thumb in Montana's direction.

"The regulars are telling me that these electrical guys had their way with you so rough that you ended up at the hospital. And, they felt so bad about what they had done to you that they even brought you there to get fixed up."

Reba and Montana's mouths opened simultaneously.

"And you believed those lies?" Reba blurted, face flushed with anger and resentment. Montana shook his head slowly, more concerned for Reba than himself, then spoke up in defense of everyone involved.

"So, Ziggy, it's your job as the leader here to fix this mess and set the record straight. You not only have to investigate, but also correct what the regulars say about your staff, as well as out-of-town customers like us." Ziggy looked sheepishly at the floor and scooped up another chunk of oatmeal. "Look at Reba, not the floor, Ziggy. I've heard more than once that she's your best server, and that everybody loves her." He then turned to face Reba. "Have I ever done anything inappropriate?"

"Never!" Reba stood as tall as she could.

"And have the two Toms ever been anything other than respectable towards you and Kat?"

"Never!" she shouted, coincidentally, just as Kat swung the kitchen door open and hesitated.

"Coffee's ready, and did I just hear my name? Am I in trouble?" Kat asked, but no one answered. "Oh-oh, is everything okay in here?"

A red-faced Ziggy pointed sharply to the door, and Kat vanished back into the dining area, leaving only the aroma of fresh coffee behind.

Montana took control. He pointed to Reba, still livid from anger and betrayal.

"You've got one fine server here, Ziggy, and if you don't make amends to her for not only killing those rumours, but worse, letting them fester, I promise you that I'll start enough rumours around here to kill your business." Ziggy's eyes grew wide with hatred, and Reba moved closer to Montana as he continued. "So, have you figured out how you're going to fix this mess, Ziggy?"

"Well, not yet."

"Well, I have. First, you're going to give Reba the rest of today off, with full pay for her troubles. Then, Ziggy, you're going to post a sign that's going to stay on the door until the New Year to tell your customers that your servers have been slandered by false rumours and that anyone who disrespects your establishment and its staff will not be welcomed back."

"You can't make me do that!" Ziggy blurted out, to which Montana instantly fired back.

"You don't think so? Just give me a month, and you won't have to worry about a Valentine's Day menu, because I'll make sure there'll be no one coming here to eat it."

Reba eyed both men, back and forth, thinking she should leave the kitchen before things got physical. She lowered her head and exited quietly, favouring a sore hip. Kat stood still behind the front counter, distracting two seated regular patrons who wanted the early bird breakfast.

"Are you okay?" Kat asked, looking concerned as Reba felt a bump above her ear.

"I think so," she said, rubbing it.

Both women heard muffled shouting from the kitchen, but not loud enough for anyone to interpret their dialogue. Montana came out shortly, asked Kat for three take-out coffees, and then motioned for Reba to approach him.

"You're coming with me."

"I can't. I have to work."

"Not today. He gave you the day off. With pay."

"You're joking."

"No ma'am. I'm dead serious. Now get your coat on."

"Wow. I guess he means business," she said to Kat, who was less than enthusiastic about Reba leaving. She took her coat and purse out of the storage closet, returned to Kat, and pointed in the direction of the kitchen. "Good luck with him. See you tomorrow."

Kat nodded, transferring a full take-out tray of coffee and a bag of muffins to Montana. He headed for the door with Reba, passing two farmers perched on their favourite stools, fixated on their coffee cups. She wondered if they knew about the rumours, or worse, were contributors. She dismissed the thought, having heard enough to unnerve her. Montana held the diner door open for her.

"Thanks for bailing me out. I'll see you, whenever," she said, zipping her jacket up and heading towards her car.

"Oh no, you don't."

She threw an odd look his way.

"You said he gave me the day off."

"He did."

"Then I'm going home."

"No, you're not." She shot him a confused look. "You're coming with me." She raised her eyebrows. He approached her slowly, gently put his hand on her back and guided her towards his truck.

"And where might that be?"

"You'll see when we get there."

"Should I be worried?"

"Did I not just stick my neck and my reputation out for you? And did you not also agree with me, with Ziggy as our witness, that I never did anything inappropriate?" She lowered her shoulders and looked up at him, feeling only slightly less rattled. "Okay, now in return, I'd appreciate a few hours of your time. Agreed?"

"Huh. Agreed."

As Kat and the farmers stole glances outside, and Ziggy from the kitchen's back door, Montana opened the door for his passenger. Wanting to leave her to her own stubbornness to climb up into the truck, he waited until she asked for his help. After she buckled her seatbelt, he passed her the full tray of coffees Kat poured, then shut her door. She read the cup lids as he circled the truck and hopped into the driver's seat. One lid was marked only with a heart, the second said "BT", the third with a single "M", and "Reba" was lettered on the fourth lid. The truck engine roared to life, idling while Montana adjusted the heater settings, then turned onto the main road.

"I guess 'M' would be you," she said, checking that the lid was secure before handing it to him.

"Thank you," he said. She took a sip of hers.

"And by the heart on this lid, I'm guessing Kat hooked up with Tom."

"And good for them," he chirped, eating the top of a raisin bran muffin in three bites. She took the bottom from him, peeled the ribbed paper off and passed it back.

They rode in silence for about ten minutes, sipping their coffee. Reba felt fatigued after her disastrous morning, while Montana thought of their last tense ride. He pulled into the driveway of his job site, delivered the coffee and breakfast to the two Toms, and they were back on the road within minutes.

"Thank you," she said softly.

"For what?"

"Oh, for everything."

"Everything? Such as?" he asked, thinking more about the verbal war about to erupt.

"Such as sticking up for me."

"That I did. And?"

"Letting me touch your hands during the storm." He grinned, wondering what prompted her to bring that up. He examined his scarred fingers, balancing the steering wheel.

"And what else?"

"Not coming on to me." Surprised again, he looked at her, letting their thoughts rest for a moment.

"And?"

"Oh, let's see, how about for worrying about me?" He looked at the odometer and calculated the eight-minute distance from their destination.

"And why do you think I worry about you?"

"Because ... I don't know why, because ... I give up."

"So, should I answer my own question?" Seven minutes away. She paused for another half a minute before answering him.

"Sure."

"I worry about you ... because you're a good person and a good mother, and you've got a good kid for a son. I worry about your health, and I know Digger does too."

"Huh."

"What I'm saying is that we both worry about you, sometimes at the same time."

"Is that why you gave him that little wooden cross?"

"The worry monk? Partially. It still works for me," he said, pulling another small replica from his right pocket and holding it up. "I carved this one last night." He hid it seconds later. "It's my safety net."

"You, needing a safety net? Huh."

"For many years, but less so, now. And I never forget where I came from."

"Digger likes it, too."

"Did he tell you that he wanted to learn to drive?" A wide-eyed Reba turned to Montana.

"No, he did not. He never, ever said that to me."

"Have you ever asked him?" They were two minutes away.

"No, because he never brought it up. What else did he tell you?"

"That he appreciates everything you do for him and, and that you're the most important person in the world to him." Reba looked down, copper hair obstructing his view of her face. "And did he also tell you that he's petrified of losing you?" He saw the tear land on the lid of her cup. "And you know what else?" he asked, his destination just down the street.

"What?" she whispered.

"I'm also afraid for both of you, especially if one of you were to lose the other."

She looked up and saw the sign for the hospital, their destination not registering with her until she heard the clicking of the turn signal.

"Oh no," she moaned. He pulled in the lot and parked the truck. "No, no, please don't make me do this again."

"You fell this morning, by yourself, on that hard floor, and not a soul around you. Ziggy told me."

"That's not fair."

"Life's not fair, Reba, but here we are. You might not remember, but the last time it happened, the nurse suggested you come right in after you had a spell so they could figure out what was going on."

"Please, I know what they'll do!" Her uncontrolled sobs made him emotional.

"They probably will, but I'm no doctor, Reba. What's worse, losing your license or losing your life, or even worse than that, what if both you and Digger were together in the car and you hit a tree?"

"But, but... I just can't do this. I'll probably lose my job."

"Not if I can help it. I just stuck my neck out for you, not even an hour ago. I barely know you, but there's something about you, Reba, that makes me want to fight for you."

"I'm not worth it."

"How can you say that? Is that what you would tell your son, who loves you very much?" She cried harder, her hands covering her face. Montana gave her a few quiet minutes while he used one finger to tap on his phone. "What time does Digger finish work?"

"Five."

"Good. That means we've got eight hours before we have to pick him up."

"I don't want to go."

"Then you won't get paid for today, because that's how I persuaded Ziggy to give you the rest of the day off." She shook her head.

"That's blackmail."

"Actually, it's a combination of coercion and blackmail, but that's between us." Montana came around and opened Reba's door for her. She didn't budge, and neither did he.

"I'm afraid."

"So am I, but that's why we're here together."

Reluctantly, she came out. He followed her, hand against her back, through the same Emergency Department sliding doors as before. He stood beside her as she registered, listening to her accurately describe why she needed care. She mentioned feeling faint, this time from fear; while Montana quickly located a wheelchair, she was bumped up on the triage urgency rating scale. They were escorted into a cubicle, her caregivers assuming he was part of her process. A nurse patted the stretcher for her to climb up on, then took her history. Montana listened, raising his eyebrows when he calculated Reba was fourteen when Digger was conceived, then continued nodding to corroborate her description of the spells.

An hour later, a petite female doctor in black scrubs appeared, dark hair tucked into a black surgical cap decorated with pink flamingos. She spent a few inquisitive minutes expanding on Reba's history. She ordered tests and, in a kind voice, explained that she'd like to review them before offering a diagnosis. Reba, wiping her tear-stained face with the back of her hand, nodded silently.

"I know you're scared, but I'm really glad you came. Sometimes not knowing is worse than knowing," the doctor said, reassuringly. "I'll come back and see you with some answers. Is there anything you need?" Reba said no, and Montana thanked her before she slipped away as quietly as she came, pulling the curtains shut to give them privacy in a very un-private place. Montana leaned his shoulder against the wall facing Reba, the intimidating medical equipment behind her. They stayed silent for a few minutes until the lab technician came in. Reba's shoulders lifted, and she tucked her hands under her seat.

"I hate needles, I really do," she said to the compassionate stranger. Her blue face mask was the same colour as her eyes.

"You're not alone. Most people do exactly what you did when they see me, but I'm very good at this, so if you allow me just ten seconds, I should be done. Would that be okay with you?"

Montana offered his hand to Reba. She hesitated, then took it and closed her eyes, squeezing it tightly while the technician drew multiple vials of blood.

"Did you count?" she asked Reba.

"No."

"Whew, because that took eleven seconds instead of ten."

"Wow. That wasn't so bad."

"I told you I was good at this, and you've got this handsome guy to look at. Quite the distraction," she winked at Reba, then smiled appreciatively at Montana. She stuck labels onto vials, threw her used supplies into a sharps container, and disappeared without a sound.

Reba's hand remained tucked into Montana's; he leaned closer and offered her his other hand. He warmed her cold fingers, then moved his palms gradually up her forearms. Their eyes met, his expression soothing her.

"I'd like to kiss your forehead," he said.

"Why?"

"To see if it's as cold as your arms."

"Go for it." And he did, gently planting three soft kisses across her forehead. Her hair smelled clean. He reached forward and gingerly pulled a small beige lump out of her hair.

"I think this was supposed to be my oatmeal pancake."

She smiled shyly. His face was inches from hers, and despite all of the beeping monitors and chaos around them, she felt a tingle from his touch. She slowly closed her eyes, hoping and waiting, until she felt his lips gently brush against her cheek. Sighing, she moved her mouth to meet his. He reciprocated, allowing a soft moan to tell her he appreciated it. He placed his hand on her shoulder and kissed her again, softly moving his crooked fingers across her lips. He blinked a few times, then smiled, placing his finger across her lips to hush her from saying anything to break that peaceful moment. He closed her bright green eyes with his fingers and watched the features of her face soften.

Neither of them noticed the man's feet waiting on the other side of the curtain until he cleared his throat.

"Knock, knock," a well-built black man said, separating the curtain slowly and then evaluating Reba's torn uniform. He left, returning within seconds with a folded patient gown. "Reba Adler?" he asked, checking her wristband against his requisition forms. She confirmed her identity and date of birth. "I'm here to take you for some tests, but you need to change into this, which is probably more comfortable and in better shape than what you're wearing. Everything off but your underwear, opening at the back, and we'll be gone at least an hour," he said, his voice directed to Montana while checking two forms on his clipboard. "I'll be back in one minute to get you," he said to Reba.

There was an awkward moment of silence as Reba held up the oversized gown.

"It'll be lovely," Montana said, "especially with you in it."

"Matches my eyes," she said.

"Now, I'm going to find some breakfast, and I'll be back." He saw her fear return. "Do you have your phone?" She rummaged through her purse.

"Yes." She looked at the lock screen. "Fully charged."

"Good. I promise you I'll come back."

"I know."

The feet belonging to the porter were hovering behind the curtain, waiting patiently.

11:15 AM

Fletcher did a walkabout on his property, then went down to watch the stillness of the lake. His gaze followed the shoreline to the century-old lighthouse where he used to hide out with his seasonal friends. He walked back, whistling loudly as he circled his family's summer home, hoping Tucker would respond. Muddy paw prints were visible across the wide veranda steps, and he felt confident his canine friend was nearby. Fletcher followed the paw prints through clusters of trees and boundaries, down by the lake, then crossed back and forth between the three large manors and their bunkies, unfazed that he, Fletcher, was trespassing again.

Rufus poked his snout through the curtains in Sonnet's bedroom, tail drooping and body still as he watched Fletcher walk back and forth, then out of sight. He sauntered back to Sonnet's bed, nudging her awake with his cold, wet nose. She rose slowly, then shuffled to her kitchen with him at her heels until he got to her door.

"Again? You're worse than me," she said aloud, letting him out. Instead of his usual scamper into the woods, she watched him circle around the residences through her windows. She was distracted by a call, displaying Dr. Torres's office number. Instead of the receptionist, it was his voice she heard.

"I was hoping you'd pick up. Are you home?"

"Yes."

"And did you get some groceries?"

"I did. You're worrying about me again."

"I never stopped." There was an awkward stillness before he continued. "I'm feeling terrible."

"You? Why?"

"I've short-changed you."

"Why?"

"I should have followed you out my door and persuaded you to have some tests."

"I'm sure they'd be abnormal."

"Can I at least refer you to a specialist?" He knew an internist would be suggesting the same, but at least he'd feel like he'd offered her another opinion.

"No, thank you. I'm sure I have cancer. Of my pancreas."

"And may I ask how you came to that conclusion?" He did not want to judge her or suggest she was diagnosing herself. And there was nothing tangible in her medical file, besides abnormal bloodwork, to confirm or deny it.

"Does it matter?" She didn't lie, but also didn't say that she also knew anything beyond what he had last told her. She sat down, right elbow leaning on her thigh and casted hand supporting her heavy head. She felt guilty and disrespectful towards of him, scratching her forehead until it hurt. She asked him the question most relevant to her. Again.

"I've completed my application and signed my consent form for a medically assisted death. It's been witnessed. I know this is difficult for you, but I'm asking you again to complete the medical portion of my application." There was such a prolonged silence that Sonnet checked her phone screen to see that the call duration was progressing.

"Sonnet, because I have so little information, there will be blank lines and gaps between what answers I have to write on it. You still have time to investigate this, and there are options. I think I explained that I'm not the…"

"The one to complete the forms? But you're the doctor who knows me best."

"I know, but it goes against my personal, ethical and professional values. Remember the 'do no harm' oaths we both took? It counters that, just like it would counter our faith in God…"

"Please, let's leave God out of this."

"I'm sorry, and I feel terrible about causing you more distress than you deserve."

"It is what it is."

"Can I make a few calls and refer you to someone else for the assessment?"

"I have the medically assisted death contact information."

"Sonnet, I'm sorry. And, I will understand if you decide you want another family doctor." She stared at the seconds accumulating on her phone display screen, even more upset by his suggestion. "I don't know what else to do for you. Again, I'm so sorry." Her hands trembled, either from physical hunger or from the frank confession of someone she respected far longer than herself.

"So am I."

"I don't want to lose you, but I don't know how to help you."

"You can't. I know it's your job to inspire hope, regardless of the diagnosis."

"The medication I prescribed for your mood…"

"Is not helping." She didn't mention that she hadn't opened the new bottle she picked up from the pharmacy on her way home from the hospital.

"Is there anything that gives you just a little bit of, maybe of joy?" It was not a question she anticipated.

"No. Nothing." She thought passively of Rufus but didn't mention him. Another long pause offered both doctor and patient time to evaluate the impact of their words.

"Would you consider some palliative therapy?"

"Not at this point, thank you. I need to process this conversation first." Another long gap of silence. Rufus came to her side, laying his head in her lap. She ran her fingers gently over his soft ears.

"I understand. Sonnet?"

"Yes?"

"Are you thinking of taking your own life?" His question hit her like a rock.

"I can't answer that right now."

"Please don't."

"Not your worry, Dr. Torres. And I have the phone number to call."

The final gap in their conversation was at least a minute long, followed by an exchange of professional pleasantries, just as if they were still at the hospital and things between them were normal. He ended the call first. Rufus stared intently at her with a ruffled brow, as if he knew how she felt. He put a warm paw on her knee, and she covered it with her hand, drawing on his support as if he were human, that is, until he meandered over to the cupboard where the dog food was.

4:00 PM

Montana didn't waste time after he left Reba at the hospital and rejoined her. By then, she was dressed in a hospital gown, restless, and playing games on her phone.

"Well? Are you behaving?" he asked.

"Yes, I am."

"That's good, because no one likes a mean-spirited woman."

"You were gone a long time."

"Well, ma'am, I spoke with your kid, worked, showered, and here I am."

"He told me you stopped by."

"Nice outfit."

Defensively, she pulled the covers over her chest.

"It's better than that useless excuse of a uniform I came in wearing. It's going in the trash as soon as I get home."

"I believe you. Any news?"

"Still waiting for the doctor to tell me nothing's wrong and I can go home."

"Okay if I stay?"

"Yes, I want you to stay."

He pulled the chair next to her and sat down, hands still in his jacket pockets. "You know, we've all had rigours to make us who we are."

"What are rigours?"

"Hardships."

The curtain parted, and the young doctor with the flamingo surgical cap returned. Both she and Montana saw Reba's fear return; Reba grasped the hand Montana offered.

"How are you feeling, Reba?"

"Well, I'm told we all have rigours and hardships."

"We do, and thanks for being so patient. You've been here all day."

"Yes, siree."

"So, you've had an MRI and an EEG, which measures brain activity, because you came in after having a spell or what I think was a seizure this morning, and possibly a few times before today?"

Reba didn't answer, but Montana nodded, hesitant to add that he'd witnessed three of them. "The two tests you just had can show a seizure if you experience one during the tests, but that didn't happen during either of them, and we can't find any structural cause to indicate …" Reba took her hand from Montana and held it up.

"Wait. Can you talk in plain English? I don't understand those medical words."

"My apologies. Overall, it's good news. All your tests are normal, and don't show anything, like a tumour, a brain leak, or a blockage to explain your seizures."

"Okay, that's great, and all I needed to hear," she said, looking at Montana and swinging her bare legs over the side of the stretcher. "So, we can go now?"

"In just a minute."

"Now what?"

"Do you drive?"

Reba's eyes grew wide, glaring at Montana not to interfere, as the doctor watched their interaction.

"A little bit. Just far enough to get me and my son to work and home again."

"But you are driving?"

"Like I said, just to work and back. You have to understand that my son doesn't drive."

"I do, but here lies the problem. If you were to have a seizure while driving, there is a very strong possibility that you would hurt not only yourself, but also others, like your son, or worse yet, cause the loss of a life. That's called manslaughter." Reba cringed at her words, dropping her head back into the pillow. "So, let's focus on the good news, and my recommendations, some of which I suspect you might already know."

"So, let's get on with it," she said impatiently, her knees bobbing up and down like Digger's when he was anxious.

"The first good news, which I mentioned already, is that all your tests are normal."

"Yes, I know that."

"The second good news is that I can prescribe medication to hopefully stop the seizures."

"Is there a third good news?"

"There is. If the medication indeed stops your seizures, you'll be able to drive again."

"Perfect. Then give me the pills and I promise I'll start taking them. Today."

Montana asked the next question, feeling certain that Reba wouldn't. "Once Reba starts the medication, when can she drive again?"

"In six months, providing she remains seizure-free." Reba fired caustic glares at both of them.

"Six months! I can't do that."

"I'm sorry to tell you that you really have no choice. Six months of taking your medication without missing it, and having no seizures, will get you back in the driver's seat in no time."

"How about two months?"

"Mrs. Adler, the six-month duration is medically and, I will add, legally non-negotiable. And to be perfectly clear, it means no driving, none at all, not even just a little bit. I have no choice but to notify the Ministry of Transportation today, so if you're caught driving, you'll pay a hefty fine, have your license suspension extended, or worse, go to jail."

Reba put her head in her hands and sobbed. Montana watched the doctor write a prescription and pass it to Reba. After some more words of encouragement and stressing to both that they did the right thing by coming to the hospital, Reba was cleared to leave.

Montana stepped out, allowing Reba privacy to change. She emerged, red-eyed, in her torn uniform, backside soiled from her fall earlier that morning. She threw her apron in the garbage can at the hospital entrance and didn't resist when Montana's arm found its way around her shoulders. He guided her to the truck, opened her door and helped her in. When a second button popped off her uniform, he went to search for it.

"Don't bother."

He obeyed, shut her door, and climbed into his side. He started the truck and let it idle in the parking lot. "Want to talk about it?"

"About what, those rigours and hardships I've been dealt?"

"How about something easier, like what you're wearing to work tomorrow?"

"Pants. Pants tomorrow, pants the next day, and forever after that. Baggy black pants."

"Good. Now, can I ask you something?"

"Depends."

"When did these spells really start?"

She looked left at his hands, looped into the base of the steering wheel, then to his serious eyes and the lips that had kissed her so tenderly. There was no value in lying.

"Shortly before we moved to the lane."

"When was that?"

"Oh, about two years ago." She watched him consider her answer, then offered her excuse. "Lots of stress. Couldn't sleep. Worrying about money, stuff and Digger."

"But why did …"

"Why did I ignore them?" He nodded slowly. "Because. As long as nobody knew they were happening, there was no reason to tell anyone."

"Wow. So, nobody, even Digger, figured something was wrong?"

"Digger wouldn't notice things like that. And nobody else cared."

"What about Ziggy?"

Reba shook her head vigorously, then shifted her position to face him. "Do you know what he cared about, why he hired me?"

"Because you're good at what you do?" She startled him by slapping her open palms against her breasts.

"Wrong. These are why Ziggy first hired me at his pizza place in Niagara Falls. He didn't know I was a damn good server until after the people at the diner told him. Why do you think he made me wear this stupid outfit?"

"What are you telling me?"

"I'm telling you that he'd be a much happier man if his hands were on these and other places, too."

Montana looked to her, waiting for her to answer what he was wondering before he had to ask. "And?"

"He didn't force himself on me, but he groped me when he could get away with it at the pizza place. Remember, we had just moved from Nova Scotia, and I needed to put food on the table. He finally stopped when the kids working there called him out for making dirty suggestions. They all threatened to quit and tell their parents. And then report him."

"And what did you do?"

"Nothing. Better him harassing me than them."

"Why would you say that? Because you're not as important as they are?"

"They were just young kids. They had their whole life ahead of them. I was already used up and knocked up by the time I was their age." She hung her head and folded her hands together.

"Reba, why do you think that way?"

"Well, it's true, isn't it?"

"I disagree. Look, I was not the chosen one in my family. In fact, I was at the bottom of the rung."

"Are we still talking about rigours and hardships?" she asked. He couldn't help but laugh.

"In a sense, but some of those hardships, plus a decade or two of living, made me realize that it wasn't all my fault. I'm no saint, but when someone else kept knocking me off the ladder, I eventually learned to stay away from it. Now, I look after myself first."

"What are you saying?"

"That nobody has the right to step all over you." She didn't respond, and he felt that he'd lectured her enough.

He paused, then spoke again. "Thank you for trusting me … and staying at the hospital … and even though the next six months will be tough, everything is going to be alright."

"Huh."

"Now, shall we get these pills first, or go pick up Digger?"

December 17th

7:40 AM

Montana woke the two Toms early, their reward being breakfast at the diner as opposed to protein bars. Big Tom turned onto Polly's Lane to find the Adlers walking past Fletcher's bunkie to meet them. He turned around in Sonnet's driveway, noticing her car parked straight. The truck's loud engine woke her; she peeked between her living room curtains to see her neighbours climb into the truck.

Digger saw the top and bottom of Sonnet's curtain move, certain that he saw a dog's head poke through as the truck drove them away.

Digger arrived in time for his 8:00 am shift. Montana took his place in the back seat behind Big Tom, keeping a respectable distance from Reba.

"No necking back there," Big Tom chirped from the front.

"The last time that happened … never mind," Montana said, lightening the atmosphere in the cab, which was more pleasant than their last ride all together. Reba vividly recalled her last sexual encounter in a back seat, completed during a fifteen-minute work break, and before either was missed.

Reba left the truck first, rushing in through the diner's back door before Ziggy noticed how she got to work. He gave her a once-over, frowning when she took one of his clean white aprons and covered her black jeans and black T-shirt.

"Feeling better?"

"Yup, and nothing that a few pills won't fix."

"Good."

She came into the dining area, just as Kat was looking for the pen she had misplaced.

"Hey, am I ever happy to see you again. Nice uniform. Can I wear those too?"

"I would, 'cause you'll never see me in that again," Reba said, pointing to Kat's checkered uniform.

"Everything okay now?"

"It will be. How was yesterday?"

"Pure chaos. Ziggy had to cook and help bring the orders out, and he sure was mad."

"Perfect," Reba said, just as the three men came through the front entrance. Ziggy hadn't posted the notice Montana insisted that he tape to the door. The men walked over to their favourite table, and Reba followed with mugs and coffee. They declined menus, knowing they all wanted the 'Happy Waitress Breakfast', which included three eggs, toast, sausages and bacon. Montana asked Reba for a blank order slip, and while they were waiting for their meals, he wrote on the back of the slip.

"Does Kat have access to a printer?" he asked young Tom, who immediately texted her.

"Yup."

"Can you ask her to type up a bold sign with these words and give it back to you?"

"Sure." He texted Kat a picture of the slip when she returned to the counter. After reading the words, she smiled, nodding her head at the men and raising two thumbs in agreement.

"She can fancy up the words, as long as the message is clear." Young Tom checked his phone again.

"She says, consider it done."

Reba delivered the men's breakfast and then the checks. Montana lingered after the two Toms headed out, and Reba returned to collect the tips.

"Are you gonna be okay?"

"I'll be fine."

"And Ziggy?"

"Hasn't said a word."

"Text me when you're almost finished, and I'll pick you and Digger up."

"That'll be much appreciated, and I mean it."

"But I also want you to think about getting someone else to help with driving." She nodded, looking at him to say more. He opened the calendar on his phone. "Our job will wrap up before the week is done, and the three of us will head home to other jobs for about a month. Then, when the other contractors are finished in the author's place, we'll come back to finish the last phase of the job here." He checked his calendar again. "Today's the 17th, and my guess is that we'll leave here at the earliest, the day after tomorrow. He scrolled down the calendar. "Then I'm hoping we'll be back here around the same time in January."

"I'll have to work on the rides. The diner shuts down between Christmas and New Year's because Ziggy's family visits from out of town," she said, with sadness in her eyes.

"That'll help. And Digger?"

"The store only closes on the actual holidays."

"Maybe Joe can help out with Digger."

"Yup."

She looked at the other customers waiting for her. She also caught Ziggy spying on them from a crack in the kitchen door, and he immediately slipped back into the kitchen.

"We'll talk more tonight. See you then," he said, placing his hand over hers and squeezing it. Unlike the last time, she didn't pull away.

Earlier that morning, Sonnet was momentarily distracted from her thoughts when she saw the Adlers drive away in a strange truck, then returned to consider her demise. Yesterday, Dr. Torres was persistent, but didn't deny what she was certain of. Cancer, she always predicted, would end her life. She felt terrible because Dr. Torres's call didn't end well, and now she'd made two people, including herself, feel miserable. She questioned her own judgment because she had no confirmation of what she was convinced would kill her. Of course, any wise sage involved in her care should question her—and her reasoning. After all, medicine was based on objective data, not the subjective thoughts of a nurse. Yet, Sonnet had made up her mind soon after starting on the cancer unit that she was not interested in extending her life with chemotherapy or palliative surgery. After her accumulated traumas in life, she did not want or need more. She thought of Dr. Torres again. He apologized to her; this man whom she respected for his intelligence, professionalism, and dignity. It should have been her apologizing to him.

She got up, fed her overnight guest and let him out to explore the neighbourhood. She freshened his water bowl, then washed his breakfast dish, thinking about her own. She picked up the pill bottle that Candace had purposely left on Sonnet's counter when she delivered her home. It was the same antidepressant she'd been prescribed. She swallowed one pill with water, only to tell Dr. Torres if he called that she had started them. She opened her refrigerator, thinking boiled potatoes and eggs were staples in her childhood. She peeled and chopped up a potato, boiling it in a small pot with an egg, while she tried to decide what to do with a life she no longer wanted, nor expected to continue.

Noon

Gracie stood at the library doors, waiting for Mason to pick her up for a lunch date. Just as his car pulled up, she recognized a young woman who took refuge there from whatever she felt her dangers were.

"You're always welcome, and it's not busy today." Gracie chose her words in a way to let the woman know the on-site counsellor was available. The woman turned away, burying herself deep into the coat folds of a much older man.

"Her pimp?" Mason asked as Gracie slid into the front seat, waiting until he drove away before kissing him on the cheek.

"I don't know. She's a smart kid, but easily misled."

"How do you know her?"

"She's volunteering at the library for her probation."

"Isn't she the one responsible for your property manager landing up in jail? The girl the police found in his basement office?"

"Yes. She's come a long way, but occasionally slips into a relapse."

Mason parked at a local eatery and escorted Gracie to a quiet booth. A sign saying 'Remember Who & Where You Are' was posted at the entrance, underlining the owner's philosophy for staff and patrons to mind their own business and avoid the drama of others. For that reason, his business profited from the clandestine meetings of lovers, unsavoury clients and people from all sides of the law.

"Good day, so far?" Gracie asked as they examined the menu. It was a safe conversation starter, as their last few were strained. They both enjoyed healthy debates, but their opinions about assisted death were weighted on opposite ends of the spectrum, with Mason still adamantly opposing it.

"It is. How's Winnie doing?"

"Very good. She's convinced her silver-haired friends that coming to the library is as important as going to church."

"That's my Winnie."

"She told me that because they've all got one foot through Heaven's gate, their brains have to stay sharp so they'll remember where the other foot should go."

Mason glanced up from the menu, dismissing the thought that she'd purposely mentioned death as a lead-in to a related debate. Gracie caught his glance, then decided it wasn't worth ruining lunch.

6:00 PM

Montana dropped his co-workers off at home, then hurried to pick up the Adlers from work, apologizing for being late. As promised, Kat had printed, laminated and taped the sign about rumours and respect to the front door after Ziggy left. Reba's much less appealing black work outfit also sent a different message to the male diners than Ziggy's choice of uniform, but not to Montana. He was attracted to her, regardless of what she wore.

Montana drove the Adlers home, with Reba in the front seat between him and Digger. She placed her palm on the seat beside Montana's thigh; a thrill shot through her when his warm, calloused hand discreetly enveloped hers.

Leftovers, anchored in containers between Digger's feet, came courtesy of both the diner and the grocery deli. The truck interior was filled with a mixed scent of fried potatoes, fabric-softened clothes, and male sweat. Easing down the lane, Montana expertly avoided every pothole, pulling into the last driveway.

"Digger, bring the food in, and I'll be there in just a minute." He looked at his mother, questioning her reasoning, because they always walked in the bunkie together.

"But supper will get cold."

"I'll be only a minute. I just need to speak to Montana."

"But…"

Montana spoke up. "It's okay, Digger. I just want to check that your mom remembers what the doctor told her to do." His reassuring voice worked, and Digger obediently headed for the bunkie.

"What's this?" Montana circled a red patch on the base of her thumb.

"Coffee slurping on me. I put an ice pack on it. Twice."

"Good. And what's this?" His thumb followed the fabric piping around her top's neckline, then gently fingered her collarbone.

"This," she said, pointing to her neck, "is about six inches away from where your mouth should be." She reached over and held his face in her hands. "I have as much ketchup on my clothes as you have dirt on your face."

"I showered this morning."

"That was a long time ago."

"And that was just before I brushed my teeth."

"That means we both stink."

"It does."

"Should I invite you in for leftovers? You smelled what's already on the table."

"And deprive that kid of yours? No, ma'am, I don't think so." Montana reached over and put his hand on her cheek. It was smooth and soft against his rough skin. She leaned in and kissed him first, and he responded, moving closer to her. His hands enveloped her head, his lips kissed her eyes, nose, and lingered on her lips. Condensation from the heat and their bodies steaming up the cab offered a small measure of privacy. "Do you think Digger's watching us?"

"Probably not. He's got his routines, but I doubt he'd object unless he overheard you hurting me."

"I sense that's happened before." She counted the number of times on his fingers, stopping at seven. "I would never, ever hurt you." She turned towards him, allowing their kisses to deepen. Her hand reached around his neck, pressing her body against his.

"I know that already. You make me feel good, and I haven't felt good in a long time." He kissed her again.

"I'd like to make you feel even better," he suggested, her eyes sparkling in anticipation.

"Well, we'll have to figure out when and where that might happen, 'cause it sure won't be here."

"And not only would we have company if we went to the trailer, but it's also about seven stars below a five-star hotel."

She laughed. "Want to feel like a teenager again?"

"Sure do," he grinned, arching his brows.

"Then pick me up at seven-thirty."

Reba and Montana returned to their respective homes. Reba had dinner with Digger, then begged off their regular evening routine, using the excuse that Montana needed help with an errand. He wasn't pleased until she suggested he pretend it was the weekend and follow that routine.

She showered and put her best bra on, even though the matching underwear had long been discarded. A dark green sweater, buttons fastened right to the top, and her good jeans completed her ensemble. She skipped applying cologne or her 'Hot Night' lipstick until Digger was settled in his chair with the remote, and she was at the kitchen door. She waited impatiently there, not opening her top four sweater buttons until she heard the familiar engine sound rolling down the lane.

7:25 PM

Reba hopped into Montana's front seat like she was sixteen again, the food and hard work smells replaced by Montana's clean body and clothes. The distance between them seemed so far, and by the time he turned onto the main road, she had shimmied over next to him. Lady Gaga and Bradley Cooper sang *Shallow* on the radio, and when Reba and Montana's voices blended in, Reba felt shivers until the last piano note faded away. She also wanted to cry instead of letting her hands wander to Montana. His amorous intentions were also interrupted, paralleling hers with a different sense of longing.

"Don't you think that song just described a little bit of you and me?" he asked, the dashboard reflection illuminating their faces.

"Like how?" she asked, not wanting to believe that he felt the same.

"Like, maybe hoping to dive a little deeper than just a one-night, or even a three-night stand?"

Reba looked ahead, blinking away the moisture in her eyes. "That's a loaded question. I was just kinda hoping that we could…"

He kept driving, gently resting a hand on her knee. "That we could relieve, ah, some sexual tension?"

She laughed nervously. "Well, in Canada, we don't say it straight up like that, but I'm sure the message is the same."

"Hmmm… I'll be very honest with you and tell you that even though I'm ready and willing, I was afraid to make that assumption and book a hotel."

"There are none around here, anyway, unless we drive into Niagara Falls", she said, feeling slightly disappointed.

"It's such a calm night. Clear skies and warmer than I expected, considering the wild storm we had last week," he said, pointing to the outdoor temperature displayed on the screen in front of them. "Let's just drive a bit."

"Then turn here," she said quickly, and he did.

"Where are we going?"

"You'll see," she said, but it was too dark for him to notice her mischievous smile.

He drove onto a newly paved road heading towards the lake. Most of the snow had melted or been cleared away. The road curved to the right, separating the lake on the left side from the well-kept summer homes, abandoned until spring beckoned their owners back. The iridescent moon awarded the pair with a magical reflection against the still lake.

"It's dark and mysterious," he said, then immediately stopped; a metal barricade blocked his ability to drive further along the lake.

"That road's closed, but look on the left - there's a small parking area. Ignore the private parking signs - nobody's here anyway."

And she was right. Maintenance crews had cleared a path into the lot, mostly to dump snow from the storm. The piles, mixed with dirty sand, obstructed the marina, but not the lake. He pulled into the lot and parked near the water's edge. She got out, and he cautiously followed suit, both walking close enough to the water to see up and down the shoreline.

"There's the lighthouse. We've got a nice view of it at the construction site," he said.

"It's also my favourite place to come alone."

"Why?"

"Because it reminds me of home. We've got lots of lighthouses in Nova Scotia, but none quite as pretty as this one."

"So, home's pretty far from here."

"A short flight, or a very long drive," she said.

He pointed to the metal road barrier. "Do those gates ever open?"

"During the warm weather. But, when it gets cold, everybody goes back to their big city life, and it's just us regulars left here."

"How lucky you are."

"Except when the power goes out," she lamented.

"Well, I'd like to think the power failure brought us a little luck, curled up for two nights on that diner floor."

"You call that luck?"

"Sure do." From somewhere, he produced two cans of local craft beer and popped them open. "Did you know I wanted to kiss you in that first hour we were on the floor?"

"Nope," she said, and took a sip, smiling like a satisfied cat.

"But then I thought, if that didn't go over well, there was no place to run."

Reba took a swig, raised her eyebrows, and looked directly at him. "Huh. But it was okay to kiss me at the hospital? I couldn't run away from you when I was there either."

"That was different. I wanted you to know that I cared about you."

"Huh."

"I like you because you make the best of things. You've got a great kid, a little quirky as you call him, but I wouldn't want to mess with him or his momma."

Reba had never heard that before. "You can bet your motorcycle, your horses, and whatever else you guys ride on down home, that nobody messes with us. I defend him, and he protects me." Reba tightened her coat and lifted her collar to cover her ears.

"And that's exactly why you make me want to…" He stepped close enough to see the want in her eyes. He kissed her, and she responded. He kissed her again, reviving the urgency of their needs. He covered her shoulders with his arm and led her back to the warmth of the truck, where he embraced her with desire.

"So, okay if we find a hotel?" he asked.

"No."

"Oh. Okay, then. Did I just do something wrong?"

"Nope. You did everything right," she said as she reached under his coat and around his waist to warm her hands.

He unzipped his jacket, as she undid hers, pressing her body into his. "Am I still thinking what I think you're thinking?"

"Yup."

"Like, here in this pickup truck?"

"Yup."

"Really? But it's not like my nice, clean truck at home."

"I want to stay right here with you, where no one can see us, talk to us, or talk about us."

She felt his body responding to her, moving his hands around her neck. When he waited for permission to progress to her breasts, she helped him along. Awkwardly, and in the cramped cab, they fumbled to undo whatever parts of their clothes they could to satisfy their urgent and suppressed needs. They made love to a Canadian crooner romancing them over the airwaves, the moonlit night above them, and the solace of no one invading their privacy.

8:35 PM

It was just five minutes after the time Reba promised Digger when she would be home that Montana delivered her there. Clothes reassembled, she asked him to thank his friends for fixing her tire and returning her car, now realizing why he was late picking her up. They parted with a long embrace and hope for more days like this.

Reba kept her coat on as she walked between Digger and the TV to her bedroom, aware that her sweater was on backwards. She changed into her flannel nightgown and housecoat, as she always did around this time of night.

"Did you get your errand done, Mom?"

"Yup, it took a little longer, but we accomplished everything we needed to."

"That's good. Montana texted me that you were coming home soon." Her eyes widened.

"He did?" She thought he was texting Big Tom about work.

"He's nice, and he doesn't make me worry." She stooped over and planted a kiss on her son's forehead before getting cozy in her chair. "You smell like perfume."

"It was on my sweater from the last time I wore it."

"And you smell like beer. And… Montana."

"I do? I'm not sure why," she answered, leaving both Adlers thinking about Montana.

DECEMBER 18TH

8:00 AM

Reba and Montana were equally happy to see each other when all three workmen picked the Adlers up in the morning. First, they dropped Digger off at work, then Reba at the diner and followed her in for breakfast. Reba ignored any reference to the night before, but by the looks on the two Toms' faces, she had a pretty good idea they knew that something had changed.

The diner regulars were in a jovial holiday mood, and not one customer mentioned the sign on the diner's front door. Kat and Reba didn't want to explain it, and Ziggy holed up in the kitchen to avoid supporting or disputing it.

Just as the workmen were paying for their meal, Reba heard young Tom telling Kat about the crew leaving soon for Christmas break. Montana watched Reba watch the pair, and when their own eyes met, she spoke.

"Soon you'll be heading home, too," she said, noisily tossing dishes into her grey bin.

"And like I said, we're coming back. When we pick you up after work today, I'll be able to tell you more."

After the men left and throughout the day, Reba continued to feel Montana's presence surrounding her.

10:00 AM

Sonnet sat at the kitchen table with her tea, flipping mindlessly through cards from her colleagues. The staff Christmas party had come and gone, as had other festive invites. She'd also ignored the hospital's calls. Her brothers and childhood friend, still in her homeland, rarely communicated. Why would she add to their burden until they called her?

Passing the living room, she opened her curtains to see Rufus sleeping on the deck, his ribs no longer visible, thanks to the lane's dining opportunities. In Sonnet's spare bedroom, labelled boxes of possessions stood exactly where they did when she'd moved in, storing nothing that she needed, or wanted. The wind was picking up, whistling through the weathered window caulking, especially where Montana had opened the window to rescue her. She peeked between the disintegrating fabric towards the lake, where angry waves splashed against the shoreline. Her gut ached with nausea. Christmas was a week away, and would be no different than today.

Dr. Torres's call did not change her mood – it only reinforced how much she did not want to wake up each morning. She thought of those dark days after birthing her daughter, whom she never saw or knew. Back in the kitchen, she picked up the bottle of antidepressants, unknown at both the convent and home for mothers – prayer was the only prescription to remedy sorrow. She returned to watch Rufus, undisturbed by the wind's rhythm ruffling his fur. She tapped lightly on the glass, and he responded, first with a yawn, then hoisting himself up and heading to her door. She let him in and as predicted, he headed straight to his food cupboard.

"Such bad manners you have. Not even a hello." He gave her a forlorn look, sat down and waited. She rested against the counter near him and crossed her arms. He moved closer, leaning into her. "Now, that's showing a little more courtesy." She opened the cupboard and scooped out the amount of kibble recommended on the dog food label. "That's it, no more", she repeated as she always did, and as always, gave in when he begged for more.

12:15 PM

Overhead, the weather became threatening again. Dark clouds swirled at an alarming pace, and the wind tossed stray construction debris around like confetti at the author's retreat. Montana and the Toms quickly packed up their tools and possessions, vacating the trailer for other trades to occupy for the next building phase. Home was a three-day drive or a four-hour flight; their contractor opted to fly them and their overweight baggage home instead of funding their wages and accommodation if they drove. Montana texted Reba at work.

> "Hey there. Warnings of another bad storm."
> "Regulars saying strong winds."
> "What's Ziggy saying?"
> "Nothing. Crabby as usual."

"Short notice - boss is flying us home. Not driving."

"When?"

"Not sure. Maybe even tonight? I think we're on standby."

"☹️"

"Ask Ziggy if you can leave. Digger too, so I can get u home ASAP."

"He'll squawk."

"He won't want a repeat of last time."

"Gimme a minute."

It was two minutes before Reba responded.

"He's letting me go. No pay after I leave."

"Great."

Dig's OK to go too. Kat's driving me to his store."

"K. See you in less than an hour."

Reba shuddered at the thought of being stranded at the diner again, this time without medication. But to Ziggy, the local farmers' predictions and gossip took precedence over any weather app. Finally, after consulting with those present, he banged on an empty table in the middle of the diner, soiled white apron covering his girth, and announced that the diner was closing in five minutes. It took Reba and Kat ten minutes to pack up unserved orders and leftovers, then tidy up.

As each set of customers left, their dread increased under the indigo sky - neither wanted to be stuck with Ziggy or hear him grumble about losing money again.

Kat ignored her mother's "no passengers in my car" rule and, before Ziggy changed his mind, shuttled Reba away to the grocery store.

1:05 PM

By the time the truck pulled up at the grocery store, the parking lot was almost empty, and the CLOSED sign was lit up again. Digger loaded an overstuffed box of partially prepared deli food between tool boxes in the truck bed, then sat beside Reba in the back, where they listened to the men chatter about getting to the airport on time. Montana and Reba exchanged glances in the rear-view mirror, neither able to interpret the other's thoughts. Montana dropped the Toms off first, then sped to Polly's Lane. Digger lingered in the truck until Reba shooed him and their food into the house, then hopped into the front seat with Montana.

"I feel bad that we need to leave so quickly," he started.

"Me too."

"I'm not sure when, but we're coming back for sure to finish the electrical work."

"In a month?"

"I hope so. Depends on how fast the other trades finish. If I'm not working crazy hours on another site, maybe we could meet up for a weekend?"

Her head drooped, copper hair shielding her face from him.

"Where would we meet? And who's going to get me there?"

"Reba, Reba, Reba … you're overthinking this."

"No, I'm not. I've played this game a few times."

"Hey, I didn't predict this storm, and I am coming back."

"Yeah, right. And then what?"

"Reba, let's not do this. Look at me." She did, with glassy eyes. "I'm not that kind of guy, and you're not a hustlin' woman. You have to trust me, and not look at me the wrong way."

"It's just that …" she said, just as he checked the dashboard clock, which upset her even more. "Go. You've got a plane to catch." He lifted his hands off the steering wheel in frustration.

"In less than two hours, I have to leave you, get my act together and catch a plane. The guys will hate me if we miss that flight, so what do you need me to say that will make you feel better?" She looked up at him, tears rolling down her cheeks. He melted when women cried.

"Nothing. If I knew you were leaving today, I wouldn't have done it with you last night."

"I think we both got what we needed – and wanted last night." He pulled her towards him, wiping her face with the hood of his sweatshirt. "Now, instead of tears, let's look forward to the next time we can get together." He lifted her chin with his fingers. "Can the guy next door, or that nurse we rescued, help you out until we come back? Better yet, maybe Digger can start some driving lessons? I'll gladly take him out when I come back."

"Maybe."

Montana regretted leaving her bitter, but had nothing else to offer. He took her face in his hands and kissed her forehead, then her nose and her mouth.

"I'll text you when we're at the airport. Look at me." And she did.

"What?"

"Remember, I care about you. I'll tell Digger it's his responsibility to help you, too. Anything else?"

"Yes."

"What is it?"

"Why did you text him last night before you drove me home?"

"Two reasons. First, so he wouldn't worry, and second, so he'd let the dog out before you came home."

"What a little shit."

"Who? The dog, Digger or me?" He grinned widely after planting a final kiss on her cheek. "I knew it. It's me."

Reba left the truck and waved to Montana when he drove away, as did Digger from the doorway. She walked inside, from the arms of a man so different than those of her past, into the embrace of a son she loved and so desperately needed. She went to the bathroom and buried her tears in a towel, her emotions spinning, just like anything untethered outside.

3:00 PM

There was no precipitation this time around; however, horrendous gusts of wind made it possible only to hear and see what it was destroying. It gained enough momentum to rob the New Abino hamlet of power again. Never in the history of those folks still possessing a memory had a power outage happened twice in two weeks. Game shows and soap operas vanished from TV screens again, just as social media exploded with predictions, long before the hydro company posted the exact cause.

Digger had already methodically unpacked the deli food, and Reba managed to prepare it all before the power failed. They ate a late lunch by candlelight, consoling themselves with generous servings. Reba began packing leftover portions into freezer bags while Digger went onto the deck. He leaned against the bunkie wall as he evaluated his surroundings, hoping Useless was nearby and seeking shelter. He spotted Fletcher standing on his deck, doing the same. After neighbourly nods, Digger came inside and reported to Reba that the outage wasn't theirs alone.

Rufus and Sonnet paced restlessly, trailing each other between windows, watching until the inevitable confirmation; the blue microwave clock display disappeared and the kettle's heating element grew silent. Rufus looked directly at her, as if he knew these were unwanted signs. She placed her hands against the kettle, as tepid as her tea would be if she made some, then warmed her cool face with her open palms.

Fletcher inhaled the Adlers' culinary aromas sweeping past him in the wind, wondering what was on their menu. He was famished and hoped his manners might weasel a meal out of them. They were beneath his self-imposed intellectual and socioeconomic status, even though they were employed and he was not. They rarely spoke beyond quick exchanges about nothing important; however, his growling stomach motivated him to head next door.

Digger half-expected it would be Fletcher when he knocked. Reba, licking a spatula clean after emptying a pot of saucy meatballs, hoped Montana missed his flight. Bad news for him, good news for her.

"Hi, there. No power over here either?" Fletcher inquired politely.

"Lost it ten minutes ago," Reba said, as Digger felt Fletcher provoking his anxiety. Like his mother, he would have preferred to see Montana instead.

"Something smells amazing. Italian, I presume?" As he kicked off his boots, Reba compared his charm to somewhere between Eddie Haskell on an old TV show and a telemarketer.

"Just filling the freezer with leftovers," she said, moving his boots with her foot so she could close the door behind him.

Fletcher didn't hesitate to sit down at the table – he found the room cluttered, but warm and inviting. Digger didn't like Fletcher because he took his seat at the table. He stood in the living room doorway, his hand slowly rotating the worry monk in his pocket.

As if planned, Fletcher's belly rumbled loud enough for all to hear.

"Excuse me, I didn't have breakfast yet."

"It's already past lunchtime," Digger implied.

"I only woke up an hour ago."

Digger, who thrived on rigid routines, liked him even less. Reba emptied meatballs from a still-warm freezer bag into a soup bowl with two pieces of garlic bread she hadn't frozen yet, and set it before Fletcher.

"Sorry, there's no pasta."

"Oh, that's quite alright, but is there any parm?"

Reba opened the fridge and handed him a plastic jar of commercially grated Parmesan cheese. Fletcher examined the jar, then thought it would be bad manners to run home and get his own imported chunk. The Adlers watched Fletcher eat, then mop up the sauce with his bread.

"That was delicious, Mrs. Adler. You're an excellent chef." She debated whether he should call her Reba, but since no one called her Mrs. Adler, she said nothing about that, nor the food she didn't make.

"Thank you." Reba winked at Digger. "Have you seen your other neighbour?"

"Sonnet? I mean, Miss O'Brien?" He looked around, hoping dessert would appear from somewhere.

"Yes. How's she doing?" Reba wondered first about her health, then about Montana's suggestion to ask her for help with driving while he was away.

"I saw her a few days ago. She looked pretty sick. Very grey."

"She is, and I see that her car rarely leaves the driveway. I wonder if she's still working."

"She's a nurse, you know," he said.

"I do."

"She asked me to sign some life insurance forms."

"Well, that's none of our business, is it?" Reba cautioned, relying on her Nana Becca's rules about nosiness. She avoided mentioning Sonnet's hospital trip.

Digger frowned, but for other reasons.

"Mom, if there's no power here, there's probably no power at her house, either."

"Why don't you run over and see?" Reba instantly saw Digger's reluctance. "Oh! I forgot I wanted you to do something else for me. Fletcher, would you run over there and check on her? If she's hungry, tell her there's still warm food here."

Fletcher looked at Digger, wondering what the "something else" could be during a power failure, then back at Reba, whose face told him nothing.

"Sure, Mrs. Adler." She decided she liked how Fletcher addressed her as she handed him his boots.

Fletcher zipped up his jacket and hurried to Sonnet's bunkie. The wind was merciless, catching anything movable and hurling it high above him. It took a few loud knocks before two faces peeked out of the living room window. While Sonnet would have preferred to ignore Fletcher, Rufus barked until she opened the door, pyjamas and housecoat hiding skin and bones.

"Hi, Miss O'Brien. Your power's out too?" Rufus's tail wagged furiously at the potential.

"It is."

"So's mine, and the Adlers'."

"I assumed that much."

"It's pretty cold already in here."

"It is. Is there something you want?" She felt no need to be cordial, after all, it was he who invaded her privacy. She watched him scan her bunkie, stopping at the open pill bottles on her kitchen counter. She felt very vulnerable in her own cool, unlit room, hoping he wouldn't pick up on it.

"No. I'm okay. And you?"

"Considering we have no power, I'm coping. Why are you here?"

"Oh, yes. Mrs. Adler was doing a lot of cooking just before the power went out. She's got some food that's still warm and wants you to come over and eat something."

"Oh, I don't think so." Fletcher looked at Sonnet more carefully than he had before. She did look unwell, and based on the forms she asked him to sign, he started to think that she was dying. And soon. He glanced back at the pill bottles.

"You don't leave your place much."

"I have nowhere to go. Now, if that's everything…"

"I really think you and Tuck, I mean Rufus, should come over to the Adlers."

"But I don't want to."

"Look, it's none of my business, but I think you could use a little food. Your kitchen looks like you also don't cook much." She was growing not only more uncomfortable but irritated with him, and Rufus scratching his paw against the door only heightened the feeling.

"And you don't either."

"No, I like Korean. Mrs. Adler's a great cook, so if I were you, I'd take her offer. And, I wouldn't even bother to get changed. You're a nice lady. Maybe we can have a little neighbourhood get-together until the power comes back on." He spoke on behalf of the Adlers, assuming they felt the same way. "I'll walk you over there, you can eat something, and if you don't want to stay, I'd be happy to walk you back home."

"I really don't …"

"I insist. I might not be your favourite person right now, but if it makes any difference, even I'd feel better if you eat something."

Sonnet caught a faint whiff of food on his clothes. She looked up at him, then down at Rufus, seeing the same anticipation in both males.

"I can't believe you want me to leave the house like this, and in this weather."

"I'll take that as a yes." Fletcher flashed her a broad enough smile to display most of his perfectly aligned, whitened and fluoride-coated teeth. He opened the closet door and pulled out her heavy winter coat and scarf.

"But I have to get dressed."

"No, you don't, and Mrs. Adler isn't dressed much better. It's just us," he bargained as he held her coat open.

She looked at him, lips pursed; he reminded her briefly of a salesman who manipulated extra time from her when she had none, nor patience. She shook her head, thinking the sooner she went, and maybe even ate a little, the quicker she'd return and be left alone.

In one sweep, Fletcher helped Sonnet into her coat and plucked a pair of slip-on shoes from the closet. Instead of passing them to her, he squatted down to help her into them.

"Please get up. I can manage myself, thank you." She leaned against the wall, shuffled them around until they were facing the right way and put them on.

"There you go, you're ready for a night on the town."

"It's not night. It's only …" She protested, but couldn't tell him the time because the microwave and stove clocks were out.

"Three-thirty, but it still looks like night."

He opened the door, and Rufus ran out first into the wind, then returned and positioned himself between the pair, content to be protected rather than the protector.

The wind was frigid against them as they walked to the Adlers. Rufus's tail stayed low and between his legs. Fletcher held Sonnet's arm as if she were his granny, while Sonnet wondered if he had one. She held her scarf across her face with her casted arm, which to Fletcher made her look even more fragile. Fletcher spoke, but she couldn't hear him. She glanced over at the black lake between the bunkies. Waves crashed high and angrily against the shoreline. She desperately wanted to turn around, questioning how in heaven's name Fletcher coerced her into walking over to someone's house that she barely knew, in her pyjamas and even worse, during a power failure.

When they arrived, Fletcher opened the door without knocking and ushered Sonnet in. Rufus slithered around them and headed to Digger and the bag of dog treats he kept stashed in the side pocket of his recliner.

Reba estimated by the length of time Fletcher was gone that Sonnet either needed persuading to come, time to dress or, as before, to be roused. Whichever the outcome, it gave Reba time to change from work clothes into clean layers of sweaters and jeans and run a comb through her hair, predicting Sonnet would do the same.

That was not the case, both women realized. Sonnet shot Fletcher a hopeless look that he ignored. Reba quickly slid a chair over to her newest guest. Sonnet stepped away from Fletcher when he tried to remove her shoes.

"Please keep them on," Reba said, and Sonnet did. "I'm glad you came. I'm sorry I can't make you some hot coffee." Sonnet waved her hand, still embarrassed by her pyjamas hidden under her coat.

"I appreciate the thought, thank you."

"We don't have a generator, but with another power failure, maybe we should consider buying a used one," Reba mused.

"Wait! My parents just had one delivered. They're coming here for Christmas." Fletcher said loudly. All eyes turned to him. "I'll run home and check if it works. Then you can come over and we'll all warm up." He ran out the door, the dog preferring to stay with Digger, following him to the living room while the women remained in the kitchen.

"How're you feeling? You were sick," Reba said kindly.

"I've had better days, and this blackout doesn't help."

"I cooked up some food just before the power went out, and some of it is still warm. Chicken fried rice, meatballs, potato wedges, and samosas. Oh, and there's a bit of garlic bread left. What can I get you?"

"Lots of choices, but I'm..."

"Maybe just the fried rice? Easy to digest, if you can't eat a lot." Before Sonnet could consider her options, Reba spooned the rice into a cereal bowl. "Warm is better than cold." Sonnet looked at the medley of vegetables, chicken and rice. She picked up her fork and tasted it, not only warm but full of flavour and comfort.

"Thank you."

"Water or pop? That's about all we have. Oh, there's also beer."

"A bit of water, thank you." Reba filled two glasses and returned to the table. She glanced discreetly at Sonnet, warning herself not to ask what she wasn't entitled to, regardless of her curiosity.

"I hope it's only a few hours without power. Last time was awful. Digger was stuck at the grocery store for two nights, and I spent the night at the diner with a bunch of strangers."

"That must've been very uncomfortable." Sonnet took a third forkful of food; Reba happily watched her eat.

"I'll tell you, it was no picnic, and then I got a flat tire. Some nice guys drove us home, and even fixed my tire."

"What good souls. Did they drive a white pickup truck?" Reba instantly thought of how much she already missed Montana.

"They sure did. And we saw your car. Did it slide into the trees?" Sonnet perked up.

"It did. Miraculously, the branches saved it from hitting more trees."

"But we couldn't figure out how you got out."

"I didn't." Sonnet sighed heavily, shaking her head. "I drove home on those icy roads. Ironic that your tire was flat, because I had new tires installed that same day. The store manager insisted I stay until he replaced my worn ones, and I'm so grateful."

"They noticed you had new tires."

"They?"

"The guys in the white truck. They pulled you out." Sonnet put her fork down and stared at Reba.

"They did? Oh, my. You must thank them. I should pay them."

"No need. Trust me, I already did." Reba thought of her last night with Montana.

"Thank you. It was not a good day for anyone."

"So, if you didn't drive your car down the slope, who did?"

"No one. When I slowed down to turn off the main road, my car slid into the mailboxes—the storm had toppled them over. But when I left my car to move them, I fell under it. I pushed my feet as hard as I could against the tire to get out from under it, and unbelievably, I moved not only the mailboxes but the car—enough to move it down the slope. It was sheer ice."

"So that explains the bruises ... and the broken arm." Their eyes locked, Reba's from concern, and Sonnet's from alarm as well as suspicion. She buried herself deeper into her coat and grew still.

"How did you know that?"

"Who do you think brought you to the hospital? The guys in the white truck did. They were bringing us to work, but when we saw your car, and Digger saw you fall on the deck, we got worried. I also left my name there if you needed a ride." Sonnet rubbed her forehead, trying to patch bits of memories together.

"That explains why the doctor mentioned it. Thank you. Now, I remember falling." She pointed to Rufus. "I tripped over him."

"That must've hurt."

"It was terrible." She looked carefully at Reba, considering how to frame her next question. "So did you come into my house?" She nodded.

"Yup. Montana and I came together. He's one of three guys in the truck. He rescued you—plucked you right up like a wounded sparrow and carried you to the truck. I brought your purse, which you keep right here," she said, opening her closet door and pointing to her own purse. I shut the door and off we went."

Sonnet tried hard to assemble the chronology of what Reba may or may not have seen. She had a flashback of Fletcher rummaging through her house, but felt very doubtful that Reba would do the same, especially after divulging where she kept her own purse. There was no reason not to trust her.

"Thank you again," Sonnet said, even though she didn't want to be rescued that day. "And, please thank the man who helped." Reba nodded.

"I will, if I see him again. Yeah, you were pretty much out of it." Her voice softened while Sonnet stared at her feet.

"I was in a lot of pain." Her throat ached; she'd spoken more today than in days.

"I believe you. Look, why don't you finish your rice before it's ice cold?"

Sonnet smiled meekly, placed her fork in her bowl and pushed it away. Reba leaned in, parking her elbows on the table. Sonnet pulled at the exposed, fraying tip of her cast. Reba slowly extended her hand and placed it on the same arm. Sonnet, usually the one to console a grieving patient's mood, kept her eyes downcast.

"I know it's none of my business, so I won't ask, but I hope you're okay."

"Thank you for the rice." She stood up and zipped her coat up higher.

"I'm sorry for asking, but you don't have to leave. It's just as cold here as your place, but at least you're around people here."

"You've been very kind, but I need to go home." Reba looked over at Digger, debating whether she should ask him to walk Sonnet home. He and the dog were snuggled up beside each other, not a moment she wanted to interrupt.

"Looks like what's his name next door isn't coming back anytime soon."

"Thank you again." Sonnet leaned against the table. It was an effort to get up, and Reba saw how frail she was.

"Are you sure you don't want to stay?"

"No. I must be on my way." Reba stood up and opened the closet door to get her coat. "Please, you don't have to walk me home."

"Oh yes, I do. If the wind blows you away, I'll never forgive myself." She passed Sonnet a pair of oversized mittens and was rewarded with a weak smile.

Reba opened the door to a gust of wind that hit them both with such force that both knew it was wiser to stay where they were. Yet, Sonnet grasped the railing and crossed the deck; Reba had no intention of letting her go alone. They descended the steps. Without much thought, Reba looped her arm through Sonnet's unbroken one. Preferring to have pushed it away, Sonnet knew Reba was right; the strength of the wind would topple her over. The two women inched forward, heads bent, arm in arm and shoulder to shoulder, until they arrived at Sonnet's deck.

"I'm fine from here!" she yelled to Reba, who either didn't hear or didn't listen to her; she held the screen door as Sonnet opened the wooden one. Reba looked beyond Sonnet into the kitchen, straining in the darkening room to see the open bottle of pills beside it on the counter. Sonnet turned her head to meet Reba's gaze, easing herself from her tight grasp. Instead of leaving, Reba closed the door and stood in the kitchen, which felt much colder now compared to that of her own.

"I'll be fine now," Sonnet said firmly, not convincing Reba that she would be.

"I hope so." Sonnet wanted her to leave, but she didn't. "You know, I've been there, too."

"Where?"

"In that terrible state."

"What state?" Sonnet sensed that she knew where Reba was heading.

"That state of not wanting to be here." Sonnet wanted to push her out the door, but instead, Reba leaned against it. "You see, I once had this tiny baby boy that I, nor anyone in my family wanted around. Truth be told, they didn't even want me around anymore." Sonnet couldn't think of how to respond kindly, and she wasn't in a frame of mind to be a good listener. "I got sent to my grandmother's house because there wasn't any room for another child in my own house, even though I was just a child myself."

That triggered the terrible, stabbing memory in Sonnet's heart. No one, not a soul, knew about her own tiny baby; not Stan after her twenty years with him and not even Dr. Torres. They never asked, and she never confessed. Sonnet raised her head, each searching deep for a connection in the other's eyes. They recognized the same pain.

"How old were you, Reba?"

"Fourteen."

"God help you."

"Well, he certainly didn't, but he sent a nurse. And when that nurse told me Digger wasn't normal, I just stopped caring." Sonnet side-stepped the emotional turmoil churning inside her.

"A nurse told you that?"

"She did. And when that happened, my immature, horny body went wild. There would have been six more Diggers if not for her. She was the one who helped me understand that I needed to be a mother first, even though I wasn't ready or wanted to be one. But in her magical way, she taught me how to love that kid. She also told me that my body was mine alone and not fresh meat to be taken at will by others. She got me out of messes, over and over and over again. Penny was her name, and to this day, every time I feel down in the dumps, I think of her." Sonnet absorbed everything she said.

"God bless her."

"And now here you are, another nurse close by." Sonnet didn't understand the relevance—it was coincidental to her, but significant to Reba.

"Yes. So close."

"Kids?" Reba asked.

"I beg your pardon?"

"Kids. Have you got any kids?" Sonnet froze, staring at the floor. It was a sin to lie, yet she'd repeatedly lied for forty years. Reba read the answer on her troubled face and continued. "Where are they?" *What did it matter now,* Sonnet thought.

"One. There was only one," she divulged, then immediately felt like she'd been punched in the chest. She'd confessed her secret to practically a stranger.

"Also a boy?" Overwhelmed, Sonnet sat down. Feeling faint, she bowed her head into her hands, wanting so badly to retract her words. Reba's empathic, emerald eyes understood her grief.

"A girl." Reba sat down beside her, placing her hand on Sonnet's shoulder.

"You knew, Sonnet. At least you knew." Reba took her freezing hands. "It's okay, really it is." Sonnet removed her hands. They were trembling.

"No. No, it wasn't okay."

Reba knew she'd already asked too many questions and broken her family's 'mind your own business' rules. Still, she didn't feel safe leaving her.

"I'm sorry."

"Me, too."

"For what it's worth, I love my son and always will more than anyone else, even with all his issues." Sonnet's face showed only sadness. "And, for all the bad things that happened to me and him, dragging our baggage around from place to place, I've learned something every time. But most of all, I know now that he's the best thing that ever happened to me."

"You're very fortunate."

"I am, but it also took me years to figure out that the answer to life is about continuing to live until you die."

They both grasped that fragile bond, just a thin layer of glue that connected their souls. That bit of glue to keep Sonnet together, and allow Reba to leave. She stood up before she spoke again.

"I know I've asked you way too many questions, and I also sense that you didn't want to answer any of them, but I'm glad you did." Sonnet placed the palm of her good hand against her face. "You don't have to say anything else, but I'm also glad you came over, pyjamas and all."

They exchanged quiet nods and gentle smiles. Reba walked two steps over to the counter and picked up the pill bottle. She furrowed her brow as she tried to pronounce the five-syllabled generic name for the antidepressant, then read the warnings boldly printed on the label.

"Are these supposed to be good for you?"

"It depends. They could be."

"Like if you take them when you're supposed to?"

"Correct."

"As opposed to taking them all at once?" Sonnet didn't answer. "If I left them here, would you take them like you're supposed to?" Sonnet considered whether to answer her.

"I hope so."

"I hope so is the answer I needed to hear."

Reba bundled herself up and looked out her back door window. Unsure if she was imagining it, she thought the wind gusts were not as strong, making her walk home easier. Just before she opened the door, she looked at Sonnet.

"Whatever happened to your little girl, and even if you weren't able to give her a name, I'm sorry."

Sonnet didn't answer, and without another word, Reba left, securing the door tightly in its frame.

"Mary. They named her Mary," Sonnet said to no one but the wind.

6:00 PM

It took some time for Fletcher to realize that the solar-powered generator did not include a battery pack, and without light to charge the solar panels, he was out of luck for being a hero. He did some research online, then got caught up in trolling useless posts on social media when the power outage ended. There was no point returning to the Adlers, so he tried to order food. His favourite eateries were closed, including the one employing the Korean delivery girl. He texted her directly, even more disappointed when she didn't respond. He waited another hour, then rummaged through his cupboards until he found some artisan crackers to put imported Camembert cheese and fig jam on. Something, anything to replace the taste of processed meatballs and garlic bread.

Reba returned home to find Useless and Digger asleep on the couch, arms and legs intertwined; not one appendage twitched. She opened the cupboard under the sink to rearrange some flattened boxes lying against the garbage can so she could close the door. She pulled the can out; an open bag of dog food was hidden behind it. No sense scolding Digger; if Useless made his day a happier one, then he wasn't so useless after all.

After a few delays caused by high winds, a plane carrying the three men took flight from Buffalo. Montana was crammed into a middle-row seat between two portly strangers, quite certain that the two Toms were in the same predicament. The aircraft rocked precariously as it climbed through high winds into the black sky, its engines roaring to achieve a safe and calmer altitude.

Montana sedated his anxious thoughts by creating a mental list of the things he could see: the chubby toddler's fingers fussing in his mother's arms in the seat ahead, a fallen piece of chocolate melting on the white fleece covering the pendulous breasts of the woman on his right, the wringing hands of the man praying on his left as he held a religious medallion.

The visual distractions worked until they didn't, prompting him to touch three things. He fingered his coat zipper first, up and down, then the varied, embroidered textures of his jacket's logo before reaching into his pocket for the worry monk. As always, it worked best, but not long enough; the plane continued to climb, and the turbulence persisted.

Smell, he needed two things to smell. He pulled his flannel collar up to his nostrils, the same shirt he wore when he and Reba made love by the lake. He inhaled his own cleanliness first, and then hers. Her faint cologne stirred him, and he breathed it in, slowly and deeply. Clean skin and fulfillment of needs and wants. No remorse, and no regrets. She was a woman he would not normally have pursued, but someone he was already missing.

He combined those feelings with something he could taste. He closed his eyes and moistened his lips, imagining them on hers, then the rest of every part he explored. He savoured her taste and her scent until the aircraft was flying high, horizontal and calm enough to put him to sleep.

6:30 PM

The power brought life back to Polly's Lane.

Sonnet gradually warmed her socked feet over the heat register, waiting for the kettle to boil. Hot tea in hand, she buried herself under blankets on the sofa, unable to erase the last hour with Reba. She compared their histories. Both birthed children, with starkly different outcomes. Sonnet rarely allowed herself thoughts about Mary, yet now she couldn't suppress them.

Digger mirrored Reba's features, but who did my Mary resemble, and if, at forty, Mary was still her name? Is she alive, in Ireland, or living the dream somewhere closer? But why wouldn't she be alive—or well? Did she have her own family to love, and was she loved? Had she struggled with unforeseen obstacles, like me? She has no idea who Francis or I are or if we are dead or alive. And she will never know. No, I can't think any more about Mary ... nor can I think whether Francis is dead or alive.

Sonnet breathed deeply, then yawned aloud. She had witnessed and suffered so many losses. What was left for her to gain or lose? She only knew that she longed for relief from her pain, and today underscored again what she never had; the love and support of a family.

She got up and walked to the kitchen counter where the pills were. When she made tea, she hadn't noticed the folded piece of paper under the bottle. She opened it to see a diner order slip with a scratched-out grocery list on the lined side and a pencilled note on the back:

> *"1 pill each day.*
> *Will check in tomorrow.*
> *R."*

Her phone number was scrawled in the bottom corner - another tiny bit of glue connecting them. She knew Reba meant no harm.

Sonnet entered the number in her phone, then swallowed one antidepressant with her tea, replaced the cap, and set the bottle back on top of the slip of paper. She leaned against the counter and texted Reba.

> "My power is back on." Reba texted her back immediately.
> "Ours too."
> Thank you for the nourishment and for escorting me home."
> "NP. Go to your door now and wait for a bit. 5 min max."

Sonnet scratched her head—she didn't want Reba to return, and Reba was already checking in with her tomorrow. Sonnet wanted to be alone, desperate for isolation, not human contact. She went to the door and waited, thinking how she would say, as kindly as possible, that she was not the type to engage in frequent chit-chats. Five minutes passed, and no knock on the door – this further irritated Sonnet. The wind had settled even more, making it easier to hear noise.

She opened the light above her door. In the dark, her eyes adjusted to see Digger standing in her driveway with Rufus at his side. Digger cautiously crossed Sonnet's deck.

"My mom said you needed him with you tonight. He ate and just pooped," Digger reported, as Rufus slid around Sonnet and into her kitchen. Digger ran home without hearing Sonnet's thank you.

Rufus tilted his head to one side and eyed Sonnet, just as she eyed him. She folded her hands across her chest.

"And I suppose you think that you're spending the night?" Lowering his head and batting his brown eyes as if he was granted forgiveness over permission, Rufus sauntered to her bedroom, turned around in the doorway, sat and waited for her to follow. She set the half-read book about dying that Gracie had provided her back on the table. She then checked that her doors were locked, filled a hot water bottle to keep her feet warm and padded off to join Rufus.

8:00 PM

Digger messaged his store manager, who agreed to drive the Adlers to and from work for the next two days but encouraged them to make alternate plans after that. Pleased not to worry for two days, Reba readied herself for bed. She took her antiseizure medication, which she'd done diligently for two days; even though she didn't always know when her spells, as Montana called them, happened, she felt confident that the medication was working. She considered texting Sonnet again, but changed her mind. She insisted that Digger bringing the dog over to her bunkie would motivate Sonnet to be responsible for him as well as distract her from thoughts of self-harm.

Tucked under the covers much earlier than normal, she thought of Montana, who was probably home, preoccupied with his big family somewhere in that big state with unpredictable cellular service. She questioned if that was an excuse to avoid communicating with her. Christmas was a week away, and would likely be spent the same way as it was since they moved to the Niagara region, just mother and son holding each other up until the season was over.

December 21st

7:30 AM

A small war erupted between the Adlers from the time they woke up, got dressed for work and piled into Reba's car—with her in the driver's seat. The battle continued until Reba dropped Digger off at the grocery store, leaving only herself to argue with. She had no intention of relying on the charity of others, as they had for the last five days, nor was she going to pay for something she felt perfectly competent to do herself. Besides the doctor and Montana, no one but the Adlers knew of the real reason she'd stopped driving. Ziggy didn't know, and there was no need to heighten the conflicts mounting between them.

Not once had Digger raised the issue of driving lessons since he spoke with Montana, and she wasn't about to either. She had enough to worry about—and pay for. She turned into the diner's lot, parked beside Ziggy's truck so that her car was not visible from the road, and casually walked into work. Nothing lost, nothing gained, and in her mind, nothing had changed.

10:00 AM

Sonnet dressed warmly, packed up all the library books, including those about dying, into her car. She overfed Rufus and sent him on his way, then drove into town, her first stop being the library. The front doors opened at 10:00 am, and Sonnet waited until everyone else paraded inside. Red book bags weighed her down, and her purse strap slid off her shoulder and dragged beside her as she ambled over to the counter, labelled 'Returns.' She rested one bag on the floor, hoisting the other onto the counter. The young man behind the desk scanned the first pile of books back into circulation before she passed him the bag hiding the books about death. He alternated scanning and glancing at Sonnet until she gratefully saw Gracie approaching them.

"Good morning," Gracie said, as the young man pointed to the books about death. "Yes, I checked those out under my name," she murmured, then left him to lead Sonnet into the common area.

"Thank you," Sonnet said.

"If those weren't helpful, there's a new book I set aside."

"That won't be necessary." Sonnet wanted to run, or rather, just politely step around Gracie, and then run.

"So that must mean good news. And, hopefully, your illness will be easier to manage."

"Yes." It was all Sonnet was willing to offer.

"It's not my business to ask, but I hope you're okay."

She didn't answer, but by Sonnet's hollow eyes, Gracie sensed there was something more burdening Sonnet. She placed a hand on Sonnet's shoulder, herself feeling tearful for reasons unknown. "No one goes through life unscathed," she said softly, unsure if it was meant for herself or Sonnet; she stepped aside and let Sonnet go without waiting for an answer. Sonnet left quickly, with no books, no red library bag, and no courage to tell this woman that most days, including today, she had lost her desire to live.

Gracie picked up the books Sonnet returned, and as she carried them to the restocking cart, she noticed some paper sticking out of the pages. Expecting a bookmark, she opened the page, partially to remove it, but more to see what Sonnet had marked. A faint vertical pencil line ran down a third of the page. A hand-written list, transcribed from a template in the book, was personalized and itemized.

My Last Wishes

- *<u>No</u> funeral, but please request a Mass be said in my memory at the Cathedral*
- *Please donate the Bible lying on or beside me to Trinity College Library in Dublin, Ireland (to be dispersed as the library sees fit)*
- *Contact the Reese family, who owns the place I rent, to claim what furnishings belong to them*
- *Please donate all my clothes and other possessions, already labelled and packed in boxes in the adjacent room to the women's shelter*

When Gracie read a small yellow sticker attached to the bottom of the notarized and dated page, she felt faint. It read: *'Ask Grace Sheehan to forward this to the parish secretary at the Cathedral'*. She returned the piece of paper to its original spot in the book, signed the book out again under her name, printed the return date slip, and tucked it into her book bag. She then keyed in the return date of January 11 in her calendar – she needed to speak with Sonnet before the date the book was due back.

6:00 PM

The tension in Reba's car was as thick when she picked Digger up from work as it was when she had dropped him off that morning. Ziggy stayed clear of her, just like he did from his wife on days like this; why further aggravate an already aggravated woman?

There was none of the usual discussion on the way home; nothing about the grocery flyer specials, how their workday went, or what leftovers the containers sitting on his knees held. Reba stayed within the speed limit during their commute and flicked the turn signal on when she left the main road for Polly's Lane, anomalies from her normal behaviours. She drove slowly past Sonnet's dark, snow-dusted house and car, assuming she'd been home all day.

Reba parked her car and looked in the trunk for no reason other than to distance herself from Digger. He unpacked dinner while she changed from her standard black clothes into flannel pajamas, topped with a sweatshirt to camouflage her untethered breasts. She busied herself until Digger plated his food, then Reba emptied what little remained into one of the takeout containers and sat down in her living room chair. The news on TV was always depressing; although she hated political wars and had enough in her own world, it was Digger who fired the first missile.

"Joe said you shouldn't be driving."

Reba threw her fork into her stir-fried meal. "How does Joe know anything about my driving?!"

"Remember, he drove us to work? I asked him for another ride."

"Why?"

"Because Montana also told me you shouldn't be driving."

"Montana? When did Montana tell you that?"

"When I texted him."

She stood up and took herself and her meal to the kitchen, finishing it at the sink while she debated who she wanted to punch more—Digger for texting Montana, or Montana for mentioning to Reba before he left that because his cell phone service at his rural home was unreliable, their contact would be limited. Yet, it was reliable enough to communicate with Digger.

She stood in the doorway, organizing her rant. She watched him shovelling food from his plate straight into his mouth, oblivious to how much turmoil that same mouth just created. Instead, she sat down at the kitchen table, hands burying her face. She crossed her arms on the table, then rested her forehead on them and closed her eyes, hoping to calm her thoughts.

"*Wheel of Fortune* is on," Digger reminded her as his socked feet padded across the kitchen floor to wash his plate and fork.

"Thanks." She stifled her anger. "I'll just rest my eyes a bit." Before returning to his chair, he checked outside the door, hoping Useless was hovering nearby. Disappointed, he returned to his chair. Reba texted Sonnet instead.

"Checking in. Are you OK?" A pause.

"Yes."

"I don't have any leftovers to bring you."

"Thank you. I'm OK."

"Need anything?"

"No."

"Mind if I come over?" There was a long gap before Sonnet responded.

"I'm in my bed clothes."

"Me too." Another pause. "And I'm not getting changed."

"I'll put the kettle on."

"Need anything?"

"Still no."

Sonnet made no effort to tidy up, other than to hide her pills, set two mugs out and warm the teapot. Reba arrived at her door, an unzipped jacket and boots covering her pajama-clad figure, holding a small takeout container of butter tarts. Sonnet let her in and Reba hung her coat on the doorknob, not bothering to straighten her boots when she kicked them off her socked feet. Rufus sauntered out of Sonnet's room to investigate.

"Ah, so that's where he's hiding," Reba said, letting him outside without asking Sonnet if she minded.

"He's starting to think he lives here."

"Digger wishes he'd live at our house. Between you, me, and what's-his-name next door, he's well looked after."

"He must be a stray."

"He is. Cousin Al told me one day at the diner that he's a descendant of the lighthouse keeper's dog."

"Who's Cousin Al?"

"Oh, he's the old guy that used to look after all three properties here, and keep the overgrowth off the road. You've never met him?" Reba asked as she sat down at the table.

"Never. Maybe he came around when I was working."

"Maybe, but he still came and cut the brush back from the land after our property owners stopped paying him. Can't really blame the guy. I only know what he tells me when he comes in for breakfast."

Sonnet scratched her head. "So, how is he connected to the dog?"

"Cousin Al knew the old lighthouse keeper. The name might have been Anderson. Apparently, his dog knocked up one of the labs living here during summer. The marina people fed the stray pup, who got left behind in the fall. When the summer folks came back, two dogs made more puppies, just like the other summer romances that have been going on here for decades."

Sonnet hadn't expected the folklore, but it was better than being questioned about self-harm. She poured tea and, in keeping with pajama etiquette, set the milk carton on the table instead of using a creamer. The sugar bowl could also have used a wipe, but she didn't bother with that either. Sonnet sat across from Reba, hoping she wouldn't stay beyond one cup, and hurried the conversation along.

"Did you come over just to check on me?"

"Yes and no."

"Well, now you know the 'yes' part."

Reba felt less welcome. She set her tea down. They both waited, and then waited some more.

"I'm mad at Digger."

"I have no parenting skills to offer you."

"I know that. I just thought checking in on you would be better than yelling at him."

"You probably want to tell me why you're mad at him." Sonnet wasn't interested in knowing, but hoped that the quicker Reba vented, the sooner she'd leave.

"It's a long story ... and you're in it." Sonnet silently cringed, then eyed her suspiciously.

"I barely know you."

"Well, that's partially why I'm mad at Digger."

"And I barely know your son."

"I know that, too, but here's what happened." Reba swished her cup and finished her tea. "Remember the storm?"

"Which one?"

"The first one. Remember when we were stranded at the diner, and I told you that those three men were some of the people who spent the night?"

"I do." Reba topped up her tea; Sonnet covered her cup with her hand when Reba offered her more.

"Well, the guy I call Montana spent the night on the floor beside me."

Sonnet straightened up, ready to silence Reba if she intended to share any intimate details. Reba read her face.

"There was no sex," she said, and Sonnet's shoulders relaxed. "But I'd been having these spells that no one knew about but me, and when I was having them, I didn't realize what was happening, so I just kept on doing whatever I was doing."

Sonnet frowned. "I'm confused. Spells, as in seizures?"

"Well, yes, but I didn't know what they were until almost a week ago."

"So, what does that have to do with me?"

"Well, on the day we took you to the hospital, we hung around the waiting room a bit to see if you were okay or needed a ride home. While we were in the waiting room, I had another spell. I hardly slept the night before, and there was way too much commotion in the Emergency Department. Montana wanted me to stay and see a doctor, because we were already at the hospital. But I got scared and said no."

"Hmmm."

"Exactly. But it happened again five or so days ago, and Montana insisted I see a doctor. He even took me."

"He's a smart man."

Reba looked down, rotating the sugar bowl between her hands. "The doctor did tests, figuring I was having seizures, and put me on medication."

"Antiseizure medication?"

"Yup. So now I take it every day, and hooray, no more seizures."

"That's wonderful."

"I agree. So, today I started to drive again, but Digger said I'm not supposed to."

"He's right."

"But I feel fine." The sugar bowl spun faster.

"It takes time for the medication to become fully effective."

"But I haven't had any more seizures."

"But you shouldn't drive until you're medically cleared."

"But Montana's gone home and Digger and I have to get to work."

"Isn't Digger old enough to drive?"

"He is, but it'll take months for him to get his license, and that's if he even decides to learn. I can't afford to rely on others, whether I pay them or not. It's not fair when I can drive myself."

"But what if you get caught?"

"I won't."

"And what if you have another seizure?"

"I won't. I can't."

"But what if you did, and smashed up the car with your son in it? Would you be able to forgive yourself?" Reba stood up abruptly, then set the sugar bowl down; it smacked against the wooden table. Both women gasped loudly.

"I'm so sorry. I didn't mean to do that."

Sonnet ignored her comment.

"You see, if you were driving, and I was in the car, and you killed me, it wouldn't matter, because I have no one. Death is trivial to me. But … what if you lost Digger, or worse, if he lost you?"

"I have to go now." Reba couldn't pull her boots on fast enough.

"No, you don't. If you think you can run and hide from the inevitable, one way or another, you will get caught."

"You're not going to call the cops, are you?"

"I have nothing to lose, whether I do or don't. I might be dead tomorrow." Reba's eyes grew wide, and her mouth dropped.

"You can't do that."

"Why not?"

Reba's heart pounded hard and fast. Her phone buzzed in her pocket. Certain it was Digger, she ignored it. It was not his nature to go looking for her.

"Look, Reba. Why don't we make an agreement?"

"I don't think I like the sound of this."

"That's fine, then. Good night." Sonnet went to open the door.

"What kind of an agreement?"

"Something we'll both benefit from."

"I don't understand."

"You will. Are you in, or not?"

"I don't even know what I'm agreeing to."

"I just raised the bar. Now, are you in, or out?"

"I'm in," she said, sighing loudly.

"That's good, because now I want you to go home and offer your son driving lessons for Christmas." Reba pursed her lips in defiance.

"And what do I get in return?"

"A neighbour who will stay alive."

"That's blackmail." She instantly recalled accusing Montana of the same thing when he took her to the hospital.

"It's being proactive, rather than reactive, but call it what you wish. Kind of like living and dying. Now it's time for you to go."

"Huh?"

"Time for you to leave. I'll wait for your text to confirm that you've asked him, and what his answer is."

"Like tonight?"

Sonnet stood close enough to Reba to catch the scent of bacon in her hair, pointed at the blue numbers on her microwave clock.

"You have one hour to text me his answer." Reba shook her head as she zipped up her jacket.

"How did I get myself into this mess?"

"You started this mess when you invited yourself over."

Reba mumbled a thank you for the tea and was out the door. Sonnet caught sight of Rufus walking up the lane from what she assumed was the Adlers' bunkie. She couldn't help but smile when she saw him ignore Reba, just as Reba ignored him. But when he spotted Sonnet, he ran the rest of the way to her, tail high in the air, and paws barely touching the ground.

6:55 PM
(Almost an hour later)

"Digger said he wants to take driving lessons."

"That's good news. Are you both working tomorrow?"

"Yes."

"What time am I picking you up?"

"OMG !!! Thank you!!! 7:30 AM."

"You're welcome. I would prefer you not use the Lord's name in vain."

"So sorry. Thank you again. And Digger thanks you, too."

"And did you tell your son that you loved him?"

> "I did. Twice. Good night, and thank you again."

It wasn't until just before Reba texted Sonnet that she saw that it was Montana's call she missed when she was at Sonnet's house. As much as she wanted to ignore Digger's chatter and call him back, she listened patiently for fifty very long minutes while he vented his worries, then excitement about driving.

When she called Montana back, not once but twice, his voice mail was full.

DECEMBER 22ND

7:20 AM

The Adlers were dressed, fed and at Sonnet's dark house ten minutes earlier than she had expected. They knocked impatiently on her door, Digger fretting about an unfamiliar driver while Reba fretted, first about whether Sonnet kept her commitment to keep living and then about getting them to work.

Sonnet hurried from the bathroom to her bedroom to finish dressing, hoping the Adlers hadn't seen her half-naked. She finally opened the door, tugging a comb through her matted, grey hair while trying to put on her coat.

"We're early."

"You are. The car's unlocked."

Digger hustled over to Sonnet's SUV and exhaled enough forceful breaths to blow the light dusting of snow off her windows. He climbed into the front passenger seat to familiarize himself with Sonnet's dashboard and compare her driving skills to his mother's. Reba took the seat behind Sonnet to watch her in the rearview mirror.

All but Sonnet's face was covered in winter wear. She slid behind the wheel, started the car and clicked the defroster up a few notches. Acutely aware of Digger scrutinizing her every move, she spoke once they were on the main road.

"How am I doing?"

"Good. Really good."

"I'm sure you'll do well once you get your learner's permit."

"I hope so."

Reba was distracted. She was silent during the drive, like the radio. Digger filled his cheeks with air and then made soft rhythmic sounds, similar to dripping water hitting a metal surface. Sonnet dropped him off first, and after a cordial thank you, he closed the door so hard that both women jumped.

"He's used to my car. You really have to slam it."

"I see."

The rest of the ride was silent until Sonnet pulled into the front entrance.

"Thank you. And I, I mean it, we really appreciate this."

"You're welcome."

"If we can't find a ride home, I'll call a taxi," she said.

"Maybe text me before you pay someone? No promises."

"That would be amazing. Thank you. And Sonnet?"

"Yes?"

"I'm glad you got up this morning."

Reba cautiously closed the door after a subtle wave and before entering the diner. Sonnet considered her words; it was enough of a reason to live another day.

7:22 AM

Fletcher hadn't gone to sleep yet and saw Sonnet drive off with the Adlers at the same time they usually left every workday. That left him alone on the lane for the next thirty minutes; enough time to enter at least one, if not both homes.

He approached Sonnet's house, unlocked her door and removed his boots. He allotted five minutes for a walkabout, including a few seconds to pilfer five antidepressants from Sonnet's prescription bottle in her cupboard before retracing his steps, retrieving a fragment of a brittle oak leaf from her doormat, and locking the door behind him.

From her house, he walked straight to the Adlers'. Entering their house took some fidgeting, and just as the key clicked to unlock their door, he heard a car engine. He wiggled the key out and headed into the woods, away from the bunkies.

7:55 AM

Reba was already pouring coffee refills, and Digger was unpacking cases of baked beans at work when Sonnet arrived home and found the ten-dollar bill Digger left on his seat. She wondered if he'd lost it or left it to pay for her fuel. She half-expected to find Rufus waiting for her. There were wet spots on her deck, but no wind to displace sparse clusters of leaves scattered across it; she told herself everything was fine. She tested her doorknob before unlocking it, then walked in, hung her coat and put the kettle on. Reaching into the cupboard for her mug, she immediately noticed that the pharmacy label on one of her two pill bottles was facing the back of the cupboard. A time-saving habit adopted from years of doing medication counts, she still positioned labels towards the inventory taker. Sonnet doubted she'd taken her antidepressant just before the Adlers arrived – or perhaps, she had. She tried not to let it bother her, made tea, but went back to her medication bottle. She checked the dispensing date, calculating that against when she actually started taking it. She peered into the bottle, stopping short of pouring the pills out to count them. She froze when she heard shuffling outside her door and was relieved to hear Rufus's tail hitting the door in perfect intervals, waiting impatiently for breakfast.

After gulping down his kibble, Rufus polished off her oatmeal. With more thoughts and energy than she could muster on most mornings, she bundled up for a short walk to the dead end of the lane and back. The dog waited patiently for her to put warm boots on; there was almost no snow, but she hated cold feet. Out they went, his head within petting reach of her hand, frequently glancing up as if to check on her. When they passed the Adler's house, Rufus headed across their deck and, after an overabundance of sniffing and tail-wagging, he bounded down the steps and into the woods.

"Tucker!"

She turned in the direction from which the voice came, thinking it was Fletcher. Rustling leaf sounds faded into the woods, then returned. Alone and weak, she hurried across the lane, away from the bunkies and hid behind a dense thicket opposite the Adlers' bunkie. She saw Rufus reappear and follow Fletcher up the Adlers' deck steps, then dig into his pocket, open the screen and main door while Rufus waited, pacing across the deck. She breathed deeply to calm herself, hoping Rufus would not catch her scent. She stood, paralyzed for the five minutes he was inside, then watched him lock up and leave their property, the dog at his heels. Only once did Rufus hesitate, nose high in the air and front paw raised, then look her way. When Fletcher entered his own unlocked door, she waited five more long and tense minutes before taking laboured steps through the dense, wooded side of the lane. Once she felt she was out of Fletcher's sight, she crossed the lane to her bunkie and locked herself inside.

Boots and coat still on, she emptied the prescription bottle onto her kitchen table, scattering the pills like tiny breath mints. Using a pen, she isolated them into two piles of ten and one pile of three. She counted and recounted them, adamant that there should be five more pills than what lay in front of her.

5:00 PM

As arranged, Sonnet picked up Digger before Reba. He was happy to assume the front seat and felt comfortable beside her.

"Do you like your job?" she asked.

"I don't mind it. I like things organized, and Joe lets me do it my way."

"That's good."

"Did you like your nursing job?"

"For the most part, I did."

"Then why aren't you working anymore?"

"That's a complicated question. The short answer is that I didn't think I was a good nurse anymore."

"Oh. And is the long answer really, really long?" Sonnet hesitated before answering.

"It's longer than the drive to pick up your mom."

"Then you can tell me another day."

"Good idea," she said, pulling the folded bill from her pocket. "You left this on my seat this morning."

"That's for taking us to work." She wavered about accepting it, sliding it partway into the CD holder.

Reba was in a foul mood when Sonnet picked her up, the scent of fried food overriding the aroma of the lasagna in the box that was on Digger's lap. There was no conversation until Sonnet noticed that Reba and Digger were exchanging a silent dialogue.

"I already did," he finally said to Reba.

"Digger offered to pay for gas, but I won't accept it," Sonnet offered.

"Why not? We've inconvenienced you, and gas isn't cheap."

"You helped me, and I'm reciprocating."

Reba huffed a few times before responding. "Under one condition. Or maybe we should call it an agreement." She poked her head up to see more of Sonnet's face in the rear-view mirror.

"And what might that be?"

"That you come for dinner on Christmas Day. It won't be anything fancy."

Digger's eyes grew wide at his mother's unexpected offer; he turned sideways to watch the interaction.

For decades, Sonnet never celebrated Christmas beyond attending Mass. She always worked, often double shifts, to allow the others to be home with their loved ones. Work gave her a reason, and an excuse, not to get absorbed in anything more than the spiritual dates on her calendar. She hadn't thought about the gift baskets that filled the unit's kitchen counter and nursing station, or overhearing her coworkers' happy stories.

"Hmmm, I'm not …"

"You don't need to hang around just to make us feel better. You can just eat and run. No strings attached."

"Thank you, that would be nice."

"And about that 'nothing fancy' part, it includes your clothes." Reba saw Sonnet in the mirror, sure that her grey eyes were a little glassy.

"What can I bring?"

"Right now, just yourself, but if I think of something, I'll let you know."

Sonnet turned to Digger, who looked neither pleased nor displeased, but the orange gadget he'd been spinning lay still in his hand. She turned into the Adlers' driveway, and when they left her vehicle, she eased away ever so slowly to watch them unlock their locked door and then enter their home as if nothing was amiss.

DECEMBER 24TH

8:45 AM

Sonnet was up early and, for a change, with plans. She drove the Adlers to work, her gram's faded recipe card for Irish meringues tucked into her pocket. She hadn't baked since she moved to Polly Lane, but Reba's unexpected dinner invite deserved a contribution. She drove into the grocery store parking lot after delivering Reba and Digger and then waited for the store to open. She bought more eggs, cream of tartar, and pecans and was on her way, unnoticed by Digger.

Home within the hour, Rufus was waiting to accompany her at breakfast. He stayed close while she mixed the meringue ingredients and spooned out even dollops onto a foil-covered pan – she hadn't thought to buy parchment paper. She felt a pleasant apprehension as she slid the pan onto the rack in the preheated oven and made a sign of the cross for good measure, just as her gram had done. She set the microwave timer, impatient for the ding so she could sample the confectionery clouds from her past.

Rufus went for a nap while she rummaged through an old stationery box, disappointed to find only one blank Christmas card; she had hoped for two. She carefully thought out how to best script her message, scribbling her ballpoint pen tip across a crumpled receipt, hoping that no blobs of ink would smear her card. She carefully wrote and addressed the note to whom it was intended. Coat and boots on, she tiptoed across her deck, down the lane and slid the envelope securely between her neighbour's wooden and screen doors.

She hurried back home, unnoticed again, and plugged the kettle in, startled when the timer dinged; the meringues were baked. She pulled the pan out, insulating her hand with a folded tea towel, and admired her effort; they looked perfect. She felt nostalgia more than depression, but just for that moment.

11:45 AM

The luxury black rental, resembling a presidential motorcade vehicle, barreled down Polly's Lane, screeching to a crawl only after hitting the first big pothole. The driver manoeuvred around the rest of them before arriving at the Hope bunkie.

"Cousin Al should have filled these in before we came," Mrs. Hope complained.

"Cousin Al doesn't work for us, or any of the residents anymore," an already exasperated Mr. Hope explained, pulling into Fletcher's driveway. "This place looks like a dump. I wonder what he's been doing, or not doing, around here."

"Honey, don't be so hard on him. It's Christmas, so give him a break."

"I've been giving him a break for twenty years."

"Please. You might be miserable, but don't ruin it for the rest of us."

The Hopes both exited the car at the same time. Mrs. Hope's sparkly heels lost their sparkle in the muddy gravel before she even got to the deck.

"I'll check the main house while you get Fletcher. He's probably still in bed," Mr. Hope grumbled, then disappeared around the bunkie, cursing his son, whom he felt sure had disappointed him again. Most of the manor's veranda had not been boarded up for the winter, and whatever was stored on the porch had been rearranged by the wind.

Mrs. Hope found a card, addressed to "The Hope Family". Pleased, thinking that one of the summer residents remembered them, she tucked it in her purse and knocked on Fletcher's door. Barefoot, he opened it on the second round of knocks, a luxurious towel wrapped around his waist.

"Come in, Mom, I'm just deciding what to wear." Fletcher pecked her on the cheek and disappeared into his bedroom. She gave the place a once-over, then started quickly transferring dirty dishes from wherever her son had laid them into the sink, then tidying up what else she could before her husband walked in, and Fletcher came out. She also wiped the Korean delivery girl's stray black hair strands out of the bathroom sink, gathered the garbage liner full of used condom wrappers from the bathroom, knotted the bag and dumped it in the kitchen trash, just as father and son converged there.

"Dad, so good to see you." Fletcher's hand was received with a limp response.

"Merry Christmas, son. All set?"

"I'll be just a minute – my overnight bag is packed." Fletcher picked up the box of gifts his bed partner had wrapped for him before joining her multigenerational family to celebrate Christmas, all that happening between meal deliveries. Both she and Fletcher agreed that their relationship would remain as it was, mostly about sleepovers and minimally about commitment. He only needed to spend a minute watching the nonverbal interaction between his parents to know he did not want what they had. He handed the box over to his father, who clicked the remote in his hand to open the car trunk and headed out the door. Within five minutes, Fletcher followed, suit bag looped over one shoulder, overnight bag over the other. He locked and deadbolted the door behind him and waited, with more patience than his father had, as his mother walked awkwardly, trying to salvage her red-soled shoes.

3:00 PM

Reba hurried the last customer through their order and out the diner door, flipped the sign to CLOSED, and placed the wilted poinsettia in a box along with her belongings. Once Ziggy locked up, she reluctantly hoisted herself up into his pickup truck, the box serving as an effective barrier between them. Ziggy delivered Reba to the grocery store, and then, as prearranged, Joe would drive the Adlers home. Grouchy as she was to be in such close proximity to her boss, the ride gave Reba extra time to make a list of what she needed to make a decent Christmas dinner.

When Ziggy dropped her off at the grocery store, she offered as sweet a thank you as she could manage for the ride and his regifted bottle of wine. She set the box in her grocery cart, then wandered through the store, lingering around the kitchen gadgets while Joe gently herded the customers to the checkout lines. Throwing a new potato peeler into her cart, she spotted Digger at the reduced-produce rack. He handed her several marked-down items, including a large turkey breast and all the vegetables they needed.

Joe's wife, Tekla, scanned in the groceries at the checkout station; Joe had already dismissed his regular cashiers. She eyed the turkey breast label suspiciously after reading the 'best before' date.

"Wow. Fifty percent off, and still so fresh?" Tekla said in a strong Polish accent, without looking at the purchasers.

"Just ring it in," said Joe from the next checkout aisle, switching his smock for his coat.

"Okay, doc," Tekla chirped, and it wasn't until then that both she and Reba realized he had intentionally marked down the price.

"Thank you. Thank you both so much." Reba, humbled, shook both their hands.

"Digger told me you're having company for Christmas dinner," Joe said.

"Yup. The nurse that lives two doors over."

"Then it'll be a nicer day for all of you." Reba knew he was sincere and gave Joe a prolonged hug, her substantial cleavage tight enough against him to fluster both him and Tekla. "Okay, everybody, it's time to go home," he said, as Digger packed their groceries, unfazed by his mother's show of appreciation.

The ride to the Adlers' passed quickly while they talked about Polish and Maritime holiday traditions. Arriving at the bunkie, the Adlers unloaded their bags, then each put one down on the deck long enough to wave to Joe and his wife.

Digger headed for the shower while Reba unpacked groceries. When her phone rang, she fumbled through her pockets to retrieve it. She answered it on the fourth ring.

"Are you cooking dinner yet?" His voice made her heart sing.

"Dinner's not 'til tomorrow. Are you coming?"

"I wish I could. Just you and Digger?" Montana asked.

"And the nurse."

"That's nice."

"What about you? Got the whole gang together?"

"Yup, and one more than I expected."

"Is that good or bad?"

"Not sure yet. We're at my son's house, and he decided to invite his mother. She had no place to go."

"Huh." She sank into a kitchen chair.

"It's only one evening, so hopefully everyone will be civil."

"She better behave, because it's Christmas and you're the one she dumped."

He didn't comment, switching subjects and hopefully Reba's attitude. "So, you probably noticed that I tried calling you a few times."

"I did. And when I called you back, your voicemail was full."

"Lots of buddies calling, but I'm glad we connected. Snowing pretty hard here. And in New Abino?"

"It's beautiful here."

"Nice."

"I kinda miss you."

"Me too."

"Any word on when you're coming back?"

"According to the boss, he says it'll be at least a month. As I said before, other tradesmen are using the trailer at the building site, and the permit only allows one trailer on site, but apparently, there are new plans to have a small cabin built for a maintenance person the author plans to hire. So, for sure, the boss says we're coming back. Probably more than once."

"I sure hope so."

"Digger's good?"

"Really good. He's mentioned you a few times."

"And hopefully in a good way."

"Always in a good way."

"I'm coming!" He yelled, not to Reba, but someone in the distance. "Hey, listen. I gotta go carve the elk."

"Elk?"

"Yes, ma'am. Shot a big one, so we're having that instead of turkey. Maybe I can call you in a few days?"

"Sure."

"Merry Christmas, Reba, and the same to Digger."

"Merry Christmas."

She paused before tapping her screen to end the call, overhearing his hearty laugh, which was intended for someone near him. Four minutes, exactly four minutes, was the duration of their call. At least he called, she consoled herself, and four hurried minutes were better than none.

6:00 PM

Sonnet was overcome with regret. *What have I done? What if Fletcher retaliates?* Rufus followed her with inquisitive eyes; normally, he'd ignore her and make himself at home on her blanket. She texted Reba.

> "Hi. I saw a minivan drive your way and back a few hours ago. Are you home now?"
> "Yup. Digger's boss drove us home. U OK?"
> "Yes."
> "Want company for a bit?" Sonnet considered Reba's offer for a few moments.
> "Sure."
> "Give me an hour."
> "Okay."

Within that hour, Reba lathered and rinsed every remnant of her job away, passively wondering if there might be room for two adults in her shower. That is, if she and Montana were ever in a situation to be creative there, she thought, while she dried her hair. As she left the bathroom, Digger was pulling his dinner out of the microwave.

"Do you want me to heat yours up, Mom?"

"Maybe later. I'm going to run over to Sonnet's for a cup of tea."

"Will you be home for *Wheel of Fortune*?"

"I'll try, but more likely for *Jeopardy*."

Dressed to go, Reba took her phone and a small appetizer tray she bought on sale at the grocery store to Sonnet's bunkie. As Sonnet let Rufus out, Reba texted Digger to call the dog, now a regular visitor. Sonnet welcomed Reba, but her frown concerned Reba.

"Oh no. Did I do something wrong?"

"Heavens, no."

"Well, you sure look like you've got a pickle stuck where it shouldn't be."

"I've not heard that before."

Reba laughed nervously as she unpacked brie cheese, crackers and a fancy little jar of pepper jelly from the gift tray and set it on the table, reminding herself that Sonnet would not know the crude phrases that floated around the diner. Sonnet's small plate of meringues was already on the table with steaming mugs of tea, the offerings momentarily distracting the women from what was really on their minds.

"Hmmm... you'd think it was Christmas or something," Reba said, biting into a meringue. "This is delicious."

"I baked them for dessert tomorrow."

"There's nothing better than homemade cookies. Digger will be thrilled."

Sonnet smiled. Rarely was her baking complimented because she rarely baked.

"What time is dinner?"

"When the turkey comes out, but why don't you come around four?"

"Four it will be," Sonnet said, layering a bit of jelly over the brie-covered cracker.

"Is this your dinner?" Reba asked.

"Well, in fact, it is."

"Mine too. Nothing like dessert for dinner," she giggled, selecting a second cookie. "You look a little, ah, less sick today."

"I'll take that as a compliment." Sonnet noticed a bit of jelly on her finger and licked it off.

"Are you taking those happy pills?" Sonnet, taken off guard, looked down but didn't respond, so Reba carried on. "I took those once. White and green capsules, just like the ones you have ... and let me tell you, they worked like a charm." A hint of a smile from Sonnet, but no confirmation. "I gained a few pounds and did some pretty stupid things while taking them, but when I stopped being so miserable, the doctor took me off of them."

"Ah."

"Ah, what?" Reba asked.

"It's nothing."

"It must be something, 'cause you wouldn't have said 'Ah'." Elbows on the table, Sonnet lifted her hands to her cheeks, staring pensively at the clock until Reba interrupted her. "I can just tell that something's bothering you. It's written all over your face."

Sonnet shifted her gaze to Reba, who looked away, then back to Sonnet and watched her carefully as she spoke.

"I have to tell you something that I should have told you earlier, and I've also done something I regret."

"Now you've got me going. What is it?" Reba asked, propping her elbows up on the table, one hand on her mug and an open hand leaning against the side of her face.

"Have you or Digger noticed anything missing in your house?"

Reba sat up straight and put her mug down. Sonnet moved the sugar bowl to her side of the table.

"No, but I haven't looked. Why?"

"I saw Fletcher unlock your door and walk into your house."

"No shit! When was that?"

"Two days ago."

"And you're just telling me now?" Reba, slightly agitated, leaned closer to Sonnet.

"I'm sorry. I've not been thinking straight."

"I'm going to blast that creep."

"He's been inside my house, too. At least twice."

"Holy shit! How the hell did he get in?"

"Somehow, he has our keys."

Reba instantly stood up and patted her pockets. "Mine are at home."

Sonnet pulled her keys off the hook by the outside door and handed them to Reba, who turned them over and repeatedly inspected them. "They look the same as mine, but we should check both. Mine are also old and worn."

"And," Sonnet continued, "I've also done something that I would never normally do."

"And what's that?"

"I wrote a Christmas card to Fletcher's parents."

"Well, that's nice. Nothing wrong with that," Reba said, just as Sonnet shook her head.

"In the card, I told his parents that I knew he was breaking into our houses because I saw him come into yours and mine."

"You didn't!"

"I did. And I deeply regret it."

"Why?"

"Why? Reba, what if he comes back and hurts us?"

"Ooooh… that's not good," Reba answered, thinking more of Digger's safety than her own, even though he had eighty pounds of strength, height and muscle over her.

"I have no idea what made me do that," Sonnet said, taking a deep swallow of her tea.

"Maybe your pills?" Sonnet sat up straight and raised her eyebrows. Reba placed her hand on Sonnet's arm. "Hey, it's all right."

"But it's not."

"Just because you're a nurse doesn't mean you're not like the rest of us. Hmmm… that didn't sound so good. But maybe if I told you about all of the messes that I've gotten myself into, pills or no pills, you wouldn't let me in here. We're all human. We make mistakes. Most of us get over it—and trust me, you can too."

"Thank you."

"We'll just have to get the locks changed on our doors. I wish Montana were here."

"Who's he again?"

"He's the guy who took you to the hospital, pulled your car out, was kind to my kid, drove us to work, and, oh yeah, had sex with me in his pickup truck by the marina, then skipped out of town."

"That's too much information." Sonnet put her hands over her ears and scrunched her face up, making Reba grin.

"So, you think telling Fletcher's filthy rich parents that their son is breaking into houses because he has nothing better to do is a problem? I think sleeping with yet another guy I might never see again is a bigger problem. But you know what my biggest problem is?"

"I'm afraid to ask." Sonnet was focusing on her regrets, while Reba was focusing on Montana.

"I like this guy. He's fought many of his own battles, but, you know, there's just something about him. He's not like the other guys I've been with," she rambled on while Sonnet was thinking about locks.

"Does your door have a deadbolt?" she asked Reba, who immediately looked at Sonnet's door.

"Nope. Our door looks just like yours."

"Well, I doubt I'm going to sleep much until we at least get these locks changed."

"I've got it! I'll text Cousin Al because I think Fletcher's parents should not only pay for new locks but also hire Cousin Al to install them. Their son's most of the problem, but we can also blame the owners for not changing the locks years ago." Sonnet nodded. Finally, they were both trying to remedy the same problem. Reba searched her pockets until she found her phone, then clicked rapidly on the screen. "There. Done!" Sonnet heard her own phone ping in the living room, puzzled because she rarely received messages.

"Thank you."

"I've included you in the text to Cousin Al. Now he's got your phone number as well." Sonnet gasped; her eyes were wild with fear. Reba felt defensive. "What? What did I do wrong?"

"That's my private number."

"Are you afraid of Cousin Al having it? He's harmless," Reba answered, realizing she hit a nerve, then started tapping the keyboard again, unsettling Sonnet even more.

"I'm sure he is, but it's just that I'm very cautious about anyone knowing my phone number or where I live," Sonnet explained she was a private person, but didn't divulge her fear of Stan finding her. When her phone pinged again, she shuddered.

"Done," said Reba. "I've asked him not to share your number. Sonnet, I trust Cousin Al more than anyone, except Digger." Sonnet felt marginally better.

Reba stood up and got dressed for the walk back home.

"Thank you for coming, Reba."

"Me too. Fletcher said he was away with his parents for a few days, so no need to worry. See you tomorrow at four-ish?" She eyed the table.

"Four o'clock it is."

"Hey, I'll make you a deal."

"Oh no."

"If I take two meringues so Digger will know what's for dessert, you can keep the cheese and crackers."

"That's a deal."

"And I'll send Useless, I mean Rufus, back to protect you."

Reba was out the door and home within minutes, laying one cookie in front of Digger just as *Jeopardy* was starting, having finished the other cookie while walking home. Sonnet waited for Rufus, hoping he would leave the Adlers and come right over. When she opened her door, he was crossing Fletcher's yard and running towards her, as relieved to see her as she was to see the Hope bunkie, unlit and as black as the sky above it.

7:00 PM

Shortly after Mrs. Hope sat down to dinner with her family at a prestigious casino restaurant, she quietly opened the Christmas card she had taken from between Fletcher's doors. While the others were preoccupied comparing appetizers, she quickly read it to herself, just before her plan to share it with her family, but then, just as quickly, she slid it back into her purse. After discreetly dabbing tears from her cosmetically adjusted face, she carried on with the evening as if nothing in her life had changed.

Christmas Day

11:00 AM

Reba and Digger both slept in and enjoyed coffee and chocolate croissants as they opened their gifts. Digger unwrapped a new green shirt, an updated version of the three he already owned, with a card tucked into the breast pocket. In it, Reba neatly printed 'January 2nd' inside the outline of a car she had sketched. When she confirmed that he would start driving lessons on that date, he leaped from his chair and hugged her. She cried, knowing that the bond that kept them so connected might loosen, and more independence made him vulnerable to exploitation. Reba opened a pretty salad bowl and the January edition of a year's subscription to *People* magazine. She reciprocated the hug and headed to the kitchen to start worrying about dinner.

Montana woke up to the happy banter of his children and grandchildren in the room adjacent to where he slept. He knew he would be rewarded someday for driving his ex-wife home the evening before. This avoided any chance of the weather forcing her to spend the night in the room designated for him and being demoted to the couch where three rambunctious toddlers were now bellowing "Three little monkeys jumping on the bed, one fell off and broke his head..."

Sonnet went to Mass at the Cathedral, asking God again to keep Mary safe and to forgive both Francis and herself for breaking their vows of chastity. As the congregation funnelled out and the choir hallelujahed their final chorus, Sonnet carefully took in her surroundings. It might be the last time she would pray in this hallowed place of worship.

The Hope family woke at scattered intervals that morning. Fletcher had managed to sneak the Korean delivery girl in and out of his hotel room unnoticed. He then met his family, including his sister Faith and her pretty friend, for brunch, both of whom were confused about why Fletcher's mother changed her mind about playing matchmaker.

An hour earlier, Mrs. Hope had thrown the anonymous, unsigned Christmas card away. It was the same card she opened at the restaurant, the one accusing Fletcher of unlawfully entering his neighbour's homes and stealing prescription drugs. It also included some remedial options, including notifying the police. She parked herself in the atrium to people-watch and procrastinate about what to do about her miserable secret.

Mr. Hope ate brunch with his family before they dispersed. With no other plan than reconnecting for dinner, he bided his time at the slot machines until he could get back home to the business of making money, instead of wasting it.

4:00 PM

As Sonnet walked to the Adlers', enough snow had fallen to call it a white Christmas. She avoided walking across the Hope property as if setting foot on it would bring more bad luck. She was welcomed by Reba with a red-eyed hug, followed by an awkward one from Digger. Sonnet slid into her worn slippers and was complimented on her baggy Christmas sweater, one that fit better when she carried a healthier weight.

Digger had already set the table with a plastic floral tablecloth and festive serviettes that were marked down to half-price at the grocery store, and to add to the Christmas display, he transferred the poinsettia Reba was working to revive to the centre of the table. He placed wine glasses exactly above the knives, oblivious to the chaos of colours and patterns in front of him.

Sonnet presented Digger with a shortbread tin full of meringues. He opened it and helped himself to one before replacing the lid and passing it to Reba. Sonnet pulled a washed carrot from her pocket and gave it to him.

"Digger, this is for the table."

"But carrots are stored in the fridge."

"In Ireland, one stays on the Christmas table as a midnight snack for Rudolf."

"Then on the table, it should go," Reba insisted, opening the oven to a blast of heat and delicious aromas. She scooped mashed potatoes and veggies into serving bowls and sliced the turkey breast onto a small platter that she couldn't remember using before. The trio assembled at the small table, which Digger had moved away from the wall to accommodate their guest.

"Sonnet, can you bless this food? And, fair warning, we're, ah, a little rusty with the praying stuff." Sonnet smiled at the Adlers, both feeling awkward about Sonnet's spirituality.

"Usually only a priest does that, but instead, we'll pray and ask God to bless this beautiful meal."

Awkwardly, the Adlers followed Sonnet's lead, bowing heads and joining hands. Sonnet's prayer was heartfelt and touching, the women's past memories stirring different emotions. After a long pause, Reba picked up a set of tongs.

"That was super holy, Sonnet. Now let's eat." A frenzy of moving dishes and serving utensils followed until there was food on their plates.

"Oh! I forgot the wine!" Reba popped out of her chair and peeled some used tape away from the bottle Ziggy re-gifted to her. She unscrewed the bottle, stopped, and then looked sheepishly at Sonnet. "Ah, are you okay if we have a little of this with dinner, cause if you're, ah, abstaining, we can skip the booze."

It took Sonnet a moment to interpret what Reba was thinking when she spoke: the empty whiskey bottle in Sonnet's sink and Reba's reminder of what she knew.

"It was a momentary lapse in judgment. I rarely drink liquor, but will take a bit of wine with company."

"That's exactly what I was hoping to hear," Reba said, quick to pour from the bottle. They toasted their good food, health, and happiness. Digger dove his fork into his heaping plate, while Reba's heart swelled watching Sonnet eat a little bit of everything she'd prepared.

Rufus remained under the table and within inches of Digger, who snuck him everything edible for the entire duration of their simple, yet perfect Christmas meal.

5:00 PM

As much as Gracie loved her job at the library, she appreciated her time away from it. Mason hoped for the week off from his busy practice, but was still interrupted by calls. The pair had Christmas lunch with Winnie Firestone and Gracie's daughter, Tess, at Gracie's condo. Because Winnie and Gracie lived on the same floor, it was a very convenient arrangement. The Firestones and Mason's parents enjoyed many Christmas lunches together, so it only seemed fitting to carry on the tradition after everyone except Winnie had passed away.

Tess bonded with her mother as they cleaned up, while Winnie and Mason slept off their meals on opposite ends of Gracie's sofa. Upon waking, Winnie headed home to wait for her family to call with a new round of excuses explaining why they weren't spending Christmas with her.

6:00 PM

Bellies full at the Adlers', the two-legged and four-legged males relocated to the living room, while the women rested their slippered feet on Digger's kitchen chair. Neither felt the urgency to move or clean up. Sonnet listened as Reba shared her sins and finished the wine.

Mellowed and marinated, she felt bold enough to delve into Sonnet's mysterious past. She got up and patted her palm across the dusty fridge top until she located a yellowed envelope. She wiped her hand on her apron, then placed the envelope within Sonnet's reach.

"I keep them up there, in case the lake floods over. They're the only ones I have."

Sonnet slid out some pictures of Digger in his early years, flipping them over to read the notes. There was only one professional portrait, a photographer's proof.

"I couldn't afford twenty bucks for the whole package. I gave him a dollar for the proof and left. It was the only one in the batch where he was looking at the camera. He always stared away from people's faces, so I should have clued in then that he was different."

"He was a beautiful baby. And such a fine young man now."

Reba poked through the pictures and slid over a picture of her entire family, pointing to some members. "Look at the pile of them. This one and, oh yeah, that one and his wife call me every so often, but the rest of them couldn't be bothered with us. Once I left town, it was like the black sheep was not only out of sight but out of mind."

"I'm sorry," Sonnet said, thinking of her two brothers, something she rarely did. Like Sonnet, they kept mostly to themselves and their devotion to their faith.

"Did your daughter have a name?" Reba thought it was a safe question.

"Mary."

"Pretty. Easy to spell."

"They were all Marys." Reba hid her confusion by draining the last of her wine, while Sonnet did the same with the half-cup she was served, blaming it on loosening her thoughts and her tongue.

"All Marys? You said you had just one." Reba leaned closer to Sonnet. "I wish I had more wine."

"I did. And I've had more than enough wine."

"So, who were all these Marys?"

"If I tell you, you must keep it to yourself."

"Of course."

By the look Sonnet gave her new confidante, Reba sensed she had no choice. She loaded four meringues onto Digger's soiled serviette and delivered them to him, then resumed her seat, brushing her feet against Sonnet's on the chair.

Sonnet began by unravelling her years in the convent, then moved on to the homes for unwed girls, how all girls were christened Mary until most received new names when they were adopted out.

"Jeez Louise, no wonder there were so many of them. Fifteen minutes of pleasure for the guy, and he carries on. Fifteen minutes, not always pleasant, and it changes a girl's life forever."

"It wasn't like that. He wasn't a one-night stand." A mix of emotions flooded Sonnet. She buried her head in her hands, still needing to defend herself. "It was a relationship that lasted two years."

"Two years until you got pregnant? And no birth control? I think you set a record. Did he at least offer to marry you?" Sonnet shook her head slowly, still cradling it in her hands.

"It was a hopeless situation. He was a priest. Worshipped and adored by many. Any way you look at it, for me, for him, for the church and community, it would have been a scandal."

"But what about the baby? Where is your Mary?"

Sonnet looked up, imprints from her nails marking her forehead, her grey hair dishevelled around her face.

"No longer my Mary. I've asked myself that question a thousand times."

"Half of her comes from you. Aren't you curious to find her?"

"That would be next to impossible."

"I beg to differ, with all this new technology stuff."

"She doesn't even know my name, not that it matters. I'm listed as deceased on the birth certificate, and her father is marked as unknown. There's no record that we conceived her."

"But there are DNA tests. And social media."

Sonnet raised her eyebrows at Reba and shook her head.

"I know nothing about social media. And there is no way on God's green earth that I would ask my doctor to do a DNA test."

"Sonnet. Listen."

"I don't want to do this."

"We can Google her up, and Digger can order the kit, and then you can do the test …"

"Oh no. And please leave Digger out of this."

"Fair enough. But listen, if maybe, just maybe, someone connected to her is out there, the DNA company will send you a hint."

"But I don't even know where she is, or if she's alive."

"You'll never know unless you try." Reba stood up, held up the folded ten-dollar bill that Sonnet wouldn't accept from Digger and took her phone off the counter. She tapped away, then turned the screen to Sonnet. "Here's one of the websites. If we can't do this, which I'm sure we can, Kat at the diner will help us. She doesn't know you, and I'll tell her it's for me. Then you submit your mouth swab directly to the DNA company."

The thought of an unknown person becoming involved in Sonnet's personal life made her even more uncomfortable than Reba's offering. She looked at the time on the clock – three hours flew by like one. She stood up. "I'll need to think about this."

"Don't think too long, because there's a Boxing Day sale that ends in two days."

"I'll let you know."

"Digger, come say goodbye to Mrs. O'Brien."

"It's actually Miss O'Brien."

"Gotcha."

Digger reported to the kitchen, with Rufus at his heels, who whimpered when Sonnet put her boots and coat on.

"He doesn't want you to leave," Digger said. She and the dog looked deeply into each other's eyes.

"I think you've got a decision to make," she said to Rufus. She buttoned her coat as Reba portioned a second meal into a container and passed it to her. Rufus stood beside her, his nose as close to Sonnet's leftovers as she would allow.

"Thank you for such a nice Christmas," she said.

"It was for us, too. And don't forget to think about what we talked about," winked Reba, then shut the door after Sonnet and Rufus left.

"What did you talk about?"

"How gorgeous you were as a baby. Now, do you think *Wheel of Fortune* is on, or shall we do the dishes?" she asked as Digger went to check the programs.

Rufus's nose stayed close to Sonnet's gloved hand as they walked home, and it wasn't the hand that was empty.

7:00 PM

After Gracie's daughter Tess was loaded up with gifts, leftovers and lots of hugs, she went home. Gracie and Mason decided on a scenic walk along the Niagara River to the illuminated Falls. Mason laced his first boot up as Gracie chose her warm parka. A paper fell out of her pocket and landed beside Mason's other boot.

"Need this?" He passed it to Gracie, immediately seeing her demeanour change. "You're upset. What is it?"

"You don't want to know."

"Will it upset me as much as it's upsetting you?"

"More."

"Well, what is it?"

"Mason, it's Christmas, let's just enjoy the rest of the day."

"Does it involve me?"

"No, not at all. Let's go for a long walk."

It was indeed a long walk, but not the peaceful one both hoped for, even though the snow on the sidewalk sparkled in the streetlights. Gracie kept her hands in her pockets instead of looping her arm through Mason's. By the time they were at the majestic Falls, they had stopped conversing. Silently, a few feet apart, they faced the thundering waters. Mason scanned the view behind him, then walked to a two-sided bench anchored on an ornate concrete base. His gloved hand cleared a wide spot of snow from both sides of the bench, and he sat down, his back to the Falls. The wooden slats creaked as Gracie took the spot facing the water.

"What just happened that made you so upset? We were having such a perfect day, and now it's like there's something terrible written on that paper." She placed her hands deep in her pockets and stared at the Falls, mist moistening their faces. "Look, it can't be that bad. I'm a lawyer, for God's sake. I'm sure I've witnessed, heard, and read much worse." She didn't move or speak. He stood up and walked back to the Falls, where the wet snow began to freeze. He turned and called to her, the deafening water making it all but impossible for her to hear. He came back to her.

"It's getting icy. Let's go home."

Gracie rose and walked beside him on the grassy edge of the sidewalk, neither of them speaking for most of the walk home. Slipping on a small patch of ice, she gasped as she regained her footing. He extended his arm - this time, she took it. Slowly and silently, they returned to her condo. Mason kept his coat on, indicative of his ambivalence about spending the night. Just as he leaned forward to offer her a kiss, she pulled the folded slip of paper from her pocket and slid it into his.

"Please don't read it until you get home." And that was all Gracie said before they shared an uncomfortable pause. No kiss, no hug, just a whispered "Merry Christmas," after which she slowly closed the door behind him.

8:00 PM

Mrs. Hope had arranged for Christmas dinner to be served in a private dining room at their upscale hotel. The room and table were too large for the four Hopes and Faith's friend Jessica. The extra space between guests suited everyone, especially Jessica and Fletcher, who had no interest in each other.

"Well, tomorrow comes early for us old folks, so I'm heading up to our room," Frederick said after a second cup of decaf coffee. Mrs. Hope pecked him on the cheek, and he disappeared, while the remaining four staked out their Boxing Day shopping agenda for the next day.

8:30 PM

In less than twenty minutes, Mason had driven home, changed into his pyjamas and robe and poured himself a nightcap. He emptied his pocket of his phone, the slip of paper from Gracie and the boxed engagement ring he had intended to offer her. He settled into his favourite leather recliner, aware of the gap between his and his deceased wife's chair, the space where he'd removed her knitting basket earlier that day. He opened the tiny blue box holding the new engagement ring, its rainbow of colours sparkling as he rotated it in the glow of his reading lamp. Tucked back in its velvet box, he laid it down, then retrieved the piece of paper resting under his phone. He took a long pull of his drink, unfolded the paper and read it.

My Last Wishes:

- *<u>No</u> funeral, but please request a Mass be said in my memory at the Cathedral*
- *Please donate the Bible lying on or beside me to Trinity College Library in Dublin, Ireland (to be dispersed as the library sees fit)*
- *Contact the Reese family, who own the place I rent, to see what furnishings belong to them*
- *Please donate all my clothes and other possessions, labelled and packed in boxes in the adjacent room to the women's shelter*

A small sticky note included the final request: *Ask Grace Sheehan to forward this to the secretary at the Cathedral.* He flipped the sticky note over, seeing Sonnet O'Brien's name neatly printed on the back.

He read the note again, defeated by the romantic intentions he had meticulously planned and then abandoned. Instead, he texted Gracie, certain she'd still be wide awake.

"I read the note. Who was this person?"

"Is, not was. She's the one who wanted books about medically assisted death."

"And you were so upset because?"

"It's not a topic we agree upon."

"And?"

"You saw the sticky note with my name."

"And?"

"She left this in a library book."

His screen lit up with Gracie's call.

"Hi."

"Mason, I'm so upset because I have no idea if she's dead or alive."

"So that's what's bothering you."

"Yes."

"Then let me predict what you're thinking. You're thinking that because you've delivered books to her, you know where she lives."

"I do."

"Grace, you're not driving there tonight."

"I won't sleep."

"Then it's a good thing you're off tomorrow. You can sleep all day."

"She seemed so down. And Mason, she looked so sick when she returned the books."

"Then she should see her doctor."

"She did."

"Grace, listen. This is not your problem."

"I have her phone number. Maybe I can call her."

"Bad idea. Especially on Christmas Day. Then … does that also mean she has your phone number?"

"Not my number, but the library's mobile number because she's part of the outreach program. If I call from my phone, she won't know that it's me calling."

"I understand that you want to call her, and when she answers, you'll know she's alive, and then you're going to do what, hang up? Or wish her Merry Christmas and then hang up?"

"I don't know what to do. I just would prefer to know that she's okay."

"I get that. So, you know what the right thing to do is?"

"Call the police."

"Exactly. You can call them now, or you can call them tomorrow, or not at all." There was a long, tense pause. "When did you find her note?" Another long moment passed before she responded.

"Four days ago." The next gap was even longer.

"Grace. There is nothing you can do now if she's–" he stopped mid-sentence.

"If she's dead? But Mason, what if she's still alive?"

"What difference would it make right now? If you must know, call the police, let them look into it and call you back."

"Okay."

"Do you want me to come over?"

"No, I'll be fine."

"Tomorrow's a whole new day, Grace. Then we can talk more about this when we're not so tired."

"Okay."

"Are you going to be all right?"

"I think so."

"Have a hot bath, climb into bed and imagine me beside you giving you good advice."

"Consider it done."

"That's good because I'm ready to do the same."

"Good night, Mason. I love you."

"And I love you too," he said, slowly circling the perimeter of the ring box with his finger.

Their call ended, Mason finished his drink and headed to bed, hoping Gracie did the same.

8:45 PM

Gracie sat in her favourite chair near her condo's huge arched windows, taking in the night sky. A new book lay unopened on her lap; it was one of the novels that the library chose for its book clubs, and in her experience, books often inspired conversations that grew friendships. Sonnet was not her friend, but thinking about her brought back memories of days Gracie spent with her close friend Livy, whose life was cut short by chance, not choice.

Gracie couldn't concentrate on the words of the novel title in front of her, and despite her busy day, sleep was far away. She ruminated about Sonnet's note, permanently imprinted in her mind. Every word, and especially the last sentence. She looked at the screenshot she had taken of it, the sticky note, and Sonnet's phone number, taken from the library's phone screen. She checked the time - too late to call an unwell person, and as Mason advised her, it was inappropriate for her to be calling a library patron from her personal phone. But then, what would any of this matter if Sonnet weren't alive?

Mason always gave sound advice. Gracie envisioned the police arriving at Sonnet's door to check on her well-being, then being advised that it was Gracie who called the police. No, she did not feel comfortable doing that. She couldn't read, she didn't want to watch TV; the only thing rolling through her mind, over and over again, was Sonnet.

A far cry from the new nightie Mason would have taken pleasure in removing, Gracie looked at her favourite sleepwear. Warm flannels and the bulky, knitted grey woollen socks she had inherited from a friend's grandmother. She removed her jewelry and set it on her night table, with the exception of Livy's platinum and diamond band. Very different than the socks, but both inherited and dear to her. She twirled Livy's ring as she considered her options.

No, she could not just sit there and wait. Thirty minutes to drive there, then back; she had nothing to lose. She walked to the window and looked at the street below. The roads were clear, and Mason was safe at home. And probably fast asleep.

Her slippers were quickly replaced by boots, and her parka was still warm on the inside. With keys, purse, phone, and gloved hands holding them, Gracie left her condo, walked quietly past the other residents' doors, including Winnie's, and out of the building to her car. Scraping the thin crust of frozen snow off her windows while it heated up, she was on her way within minutes. The city streets were barren, as was the lightly populated highway, until she turned onto the New Abino exit. These roads had not been salted or sanded, and with light snow falling, she slowed to a more cautious speed. One large pickup truck approached from behind and roared past her, red tail lights vanishing into the night. The farther she drove away from the highway, the more anxious and aware she became of her main intention, just to see some sign of life at Sonnet's address, and return home. Nothing else.

High beams on, she slowed down further as the main, unlit rural road narrowed. Houses became spaced farther apart. A pair of deer mingling on the roadside forced her to brake quickly. Already on edge, she waited until the large creatures gracefully sauntered away.

Exhaling loudly as she approached Polly's Lane, she carefully turned off the main road, skidding a few times as she navigated down the sloped, slippery entrance. There was no evidence of another vehicle's tires preceding her path.

Ever so slowly, she forged on. Her old Volvo groaned loudly as its undercarriage scraped a deep pothole, forcing her to slow down to a snail's pace.

Sonnet heard the vehicle approaching before she saw it, instantly panicking. Was it a stranger lost, or looking for something they were not going to find on the lane, or had Stan finally tracked her down? Or maybe, and most likely, she tried to convince herself that it was Fletcher's family bringing him home. Her heart pounded so hard, stabbing her with violent flashbacks of her past, that it was hard to exhale. One lit lamp in her living room allowed her to read, but turning it off would tell the vehicle occupants, passing much too slowly, that someone was in the house. Grateful that her living room curtains were closed, Sonnet rose on shaky legs and walked into the blackened kitchen. She gently pulled back an inch of the curtain covering the door's small window, catching the taillights of the car as it rolled by Fletcher's bunkie towards the Adlers.

After Gracie passed the reflective green marker, labelled Lot 1, she thought she saw a sliver of light along the outer edge of the living room curtain, but was more focused on avoiding another pothole than looking for signs of life there. She passed the second bunkie marker and driveway, then spotted the black and yellow checkered dead-end sign at the end of the lane. Several rooms were lit in the last residence. She briefly considered stopping to inquire if someone living there knew Sonnet, then immediately dismissed the thought. Safety first, she rationalized, circling the dead end until she faced the opposite direction. She saw a very tall shadow visible in the third bunkie window, then observed a smaller shadow moving closer to the tall one, moving what Gracie realized was an illuminated phone. She shuddered, thinking they might be filming her.

Reba texted Sonnet.

> "Are you still awake? Did you see the car passing your driveway?"

Gracie kept driving with her hands locked on the steering wheel. She passed the middle bunkie and the blackness behind it, her car crawling past Sonnet's house again. Yes! A light was indeed on at the bunkie marked Lot 1. She felt hopeful, thinking that if she just stopped for one minute, something or someone would show signs of a human presence. She knew Sonnet lived alone and recognized her parked vehicle.

Reba texted Sonnet again.

> "Are you awake? Do you want us to come over? I think we should call the police. We see the taillights of a car stopped in front of your house."

Sonnet watched the vehicle, her body stiff and cold as marble. Her phone, sitting on the couch beside her book, was lighting up and dinging at the exact time as the strange car stood in front of her house. *For the love of God,* she thought, *who would watch and text me at the same time - and on such a holy day as this?* She remained there, too petrified to see the source of the text.

As the clock on her car dashboard switched to display the next minute, Gracie's wish came true. The curtains in Sonnet's living room moved, not once, but twice. And yes, when they moved a third time, she gently put her foot on the gas, skidding here and there on the slippery incline. Rather than risk sliding sideways, or worse, off the lane, she backed up as far as Fletcher's driveway, then stepped hard on the gas, tires spinning in the dirt until she was successful in getting her car and her courage back onto the main road.

Rufus, awakened by Sonnet's phone pinging and a car motor running, rose up, stretched, then manoeuvred his way between Sonnet's living room curtain and the window. He sat down and moved the curtain so he could watch the vehicle do what it did until it drove away.

He walked to the kitchen and leaned against a frazzled Sonnet's thigh, hoping she could sense that he wanted a treat. Unsuccessful, even with a few more nudges to make his point, he followed her back to the sofa.

After a few mindful breaths and self-reassurance, Sonnet read Reba's text, and then responded.

> "Hi Reba. Whoever it was just left. Thank you for worrying about me."
> "Do you want us to come over?"
> "No. I'll be fine."
> "You sure? Maybe we should call the police."
> "And tell them a car drove up and down our lane, and nothing happened?"
> "OK. You're right. But we were worried."
> "As was I. Thank you for your kindness."
> "Merry Christmas, Sonnet."
> "Merry Christmas, Reba. And Digger, too."

10:55 PM

Gracie sped back to Niagara Falls and stopped at a service station on a main street. She examined her car, heavily splattered with dirt from the rural roads, dirt she'd have difficulty explaining. The young, male gas bar attendant, half asleep, switched the green OPEN neon sign to CLOSED. He was not happy to see Gracie approach him.

"Sorry, lady, but I've shut off the gas tanks. You'll have to go to the station down the road. It's open all night."

"I don't need gas. I just want to drive through the car wash."

"Sorry, but that's closed too."

"But can't you turn it on for just five minutes? I'll be quick."

"Nope. It's eleven. We're closed." He pointed at his watch to emphasize his point.

"Wait! Please wait!"

Gracie held up her index finger, then ran the ten steps back to her car, returning with her wallet.

"Cash register and machines are down too, ma'am."

Ignoring his words, she fished out the crisp one-hundred-dollar bill her neighbour Winnie gave her for Christmas. She held it close enough for the attendant to read the denomination.

"Please," she pleaded.

"I can't change that."

"Look. Because it's Christmas, you can have it all. Please take it. My son needs my car to propose to his girlfriend tomorrow, and I can't lend it to him when it's covered in all this dirt. I'm sure you can understand," she lied, as convincingly as she could.

It worked.

He shuffled over to the car wash, unlocked a small panel door and flicked whatever switches he needed to activate the system, then pointed to his watch and held up five fingers.

Gracie navigated her car into the car wash enclosure and watched while a large mechanical arm sprayed a multicoloured foaming detergent, washed and rinsed her vehicle. She didn't bother with the air-dry cycle, speeding off just as all the service station lights went black.

Relieved to be back home, she put her coat and boots away. Never having changed out of her pyjamas and favourite woollen socks, she served herself a generous helping of leftover pumpkin pie and watched the rest of *Miracle on Thirty-Fourth Street* on TV. By the time the pie disappeared, she had calmed down. She lay her head against a pillow, her eyelids growing heavy. She fell asleep, promising herself not to divulge to anyone, especially Mason, where she had spent her last waking hour of Christmas.

December 26th

9:30 AM

The Hope family gathered for breakfast at the hotel buffet after Mr. Hope had a very early phone consultation with his lawyer. He had no idea what her billing hours were costing him, but it was better than waking up beside a miserable wife. They'd been up late arguing, then after a few unexpected texts, agreed with something Mrs. Hope would soon realize was only part of the plan, providing his lawyer agreed as well.

Fletcher's sister and her friend were more interested in heading to the outlet mall than spending time at the buffet and, with Mr. Hope's nod, excused themselves, blew big kisses to the parents and hurried off to shop.

This left Fletcher and his parents facing each other at opposite ends of a table for six. Mrs. Hope summoned the server and asked to be relocated to a smaller booth in a quiet section of the restaurant. Enticed with a generous tip, the server guided them to a booth with a stunning view of the Falls.

"I'll take this seat," Mr. Hope said gruffly, granting himself the most picturesque view. Fletcher had no option but to sit between his parents, facing other diners.

"Fletcher, honey," Mrs. Hope started, placing her diamond-laden fingers over her son's. "We've been thinking …"

Fletcher was immediately reminded of the previous times his mother initiated her conversation using that phrase – it did not usually end in his favour. Fletcher looked towards his father, who, by his smirk, gave Fletcher the impression that this little meeting was initiated by his mother. Mr. Hope stood up, adjusted his belt, and pointed to his seat.

"I need to use the restroom, and when I come back, this seat is still mine," he warned, then sauntered off.

Her fingers still on Fletcher's hand, Mrs. Hope pinched the skin on the back of his hand once, then harder the second time.

"Ouch! That hurts."

"Then listen to me, quickly, and listen to me carefully," she said. "What you felt is nothing compared to what you're going to feel if you end up back in jail."

"Jail? For what?" His voice was louder than his mother approved of. She shushed him, then opened the screenshot of Sonnet's card.

"For this! Look at it very carefully," she hissed, shoving her phone screen in his face, which flushed as he read the inside note. "Now, read it again."

"I don't have to. Who gave you that?"

"How the hell would I know? There's no signature, but here's the deal. Your father has no idea that this card even exists, and last night I talked him into bringing you back with us."

Fletcher knew he now had two problems: the card's author and the fact that he was in Canada through a deportation order.

"But I thought I couldn't go home."

"Dad talked to the lawyer this morning, and I think she's going to make a case that you were unjustly deported and, that being separated from your family has caused us all undue hardship. Fletcher, he knows absolutely nothing about this card," she said, keeping the screen inches from his face, "but he made something clear to me many times and again last night. If you commit another offence and humiliate him, he'll not only disown you but cut you off from your inheritance." His mother's last words were all Fletcher needed to hear to make him fully cooperate. She didn't let up.

"While your father is making history in the world of big business, your contribution has been one notch above nothing. So, if whoever wrote this goes to the police, we're screwed. No. You're screwed. No more money, no more family, no more anything. Do. You. Understand? You have no choice but to come home with us."

"But where will I go?"

"I don't know – hopefully back to Georgia. We'll set you up in an apartment, but only if you keep your mouth shut and your nose clean. I think Dad will somehow help get you a job. Got it? Oh, no, here comes your father. Remember, if he finds out about this card, he'd call the police himself."

Mrs. Hope waved the server over to top up their coffees, just as Mr. Hope slid back into his seat. Fletcher's head was spinning.

"What did I miss?" Mr. Hope tapped his hand against his pants, double-checking that the zipper was up.

"Not much. But I did tell Fletcher how much we missed him, and that, with your permission and our lawyer's approval, we'll bring him home."

"Your mother worries about you more than I do," he said. "Leaving here was all her idea."

"And I'm very grateful for it," Fletcher said, looking at the pinch marks on his hand as he held his coffee cup to be refilled.

"I checked the main house while you were packing your bag. You didn't board up much of the veranda."

"The weather's been terrible, Dad, and we've had power outages."

"The screw drill works on batteries."

"It needed charging."

"Nevertheless, I've decided, we're never there, so there's no value in keeping the place."

Both Fletcher's and Mrs. Hope's mouths sagged at the same time.

"Fred, you never mentioned that to me," Mrs. Hope whined.

"Well, like what you sprung on me last night, life is full of surprises."

"But, Dad ..."

"You, Fletcher, have no say in this. I've decided to put it on the market. I spoke with Scott Reese, and he's also going to list his place. Can't afford the repairs, and I don't like the tariffs. Ours looks like a dump now, but it's in much better shape than his. We'll use the same real estate agent, and he's agreed to lower the commission fee."

"But Fred, it's our summer home."

"What about our villa in Portugal, the cottage in Germany, and don't forget Hilton Head? Unlike him," he said, pointing to Fletcher, "Somebody maintains the villa and the condo. Much nicer, and we won't need to cross this border."

"But …"

"But what, son? You're costing me thousands of dollars a month, and I'm getting nothing in return but Korean food delivery receipts."

"You see those?" Fletcher straightened up, as did his mother.

"I see and know everything. My auditor even tells me when you need more toilet paper. I know everything you spend my money on. Just like he will when you fly out of this country. Today." Fletcher felt like he was literally and figuratively suffocating in the booth. His mother's phone pinged.

"Check-out is soon. Fred, honey, what time does the pilot want us there?"

Mr. Hope checked his expensive watch.

"In four hours." He looked at his wife. "Can you arrange a late check-out? I'll stay at the hotel and work, while you go back and help Fletcher pack up his things." He turned to his son. "You've got a max weight of a hundred pounds to bring back on our plane. We'll arrange to have the rest of your stuff shipped back."

"But if I fly back with you, I can't come back here to finish packing up my stuff," Fletcher whined, more interested in finishing up with the Korean delivery girl than packing.

"Not my problem, so you damn well better get cracking." Mr. Hope checked his watch again. "You've got exactly three hours to get there, pack up, and be back here for the airport driver," he barked, handing his wife the keys to the oversized black rental vehicle. "And don't be late."

"Yes, sir," Fletcher replied, knowing not to argue with his father, who took his paper and headed off alone.

10:00 AM

Gracie woke up to the chime of her alarm, then showered and readied herself for Mason to arrive. They had already planned to walk down the street and have breakfast before inviting Winnie back to her condo for leftovers later that day. She decided that if Mason didn't mention Sonnet's note outlining her last wishes, then neither would she. And if he did, she'd be cautious with her words.

After a long shower and some strong coffee, Mason drove his black Cadillac over to Gracie's condo and parked beside her old white Volvo. He usually paid little attention to her car but noticed it was clean, thinking she had taken the initiative to make it look more presentable at Christmas. He decided that if Gracie didn't mention the last wishes note from the woman on her book route, neither would he. Sonnet's note was back in his pocket, but the little blue box was not; Mason had a premonition that if they got sidetracked, today might not be the best day to discuss their future.

10:05 AM

Reba texted her neighbour.

> "Good morning, Sonnet."
> "Hi Reba."
> "Did you sleep?"
> "Yes, but poorly."
> "Feel like having a cup of tea?"
> "No thank you. I'm going back to bed."
> "Is the dog still with you?"
> "Yes."
> "Do you mind letting him out? Digger was whistling for him but he didn't come."
> "I'll let him out now."
> "Great. Digger's already back on the deck, waiting to call him."
> "The dog's outside."
> "Thanks. Sleep well & feel better."
> "Thank you."

10:10 AM

Fletcher pointed to the potholes as Mrs. Hope slowly navigated the large vehicle around them on Polly's Lane. They pulled into their driveway and got out, this time both in sensible footwear. Their discussion during the drive from the hotel was tense; Mrs. Hope asked her son which of his neighbours he thought wrote the note. He lied, saying he didn't know his neighbour, only the dog and the delivery drivers who came down the lane.

She pulled into the Hope bunkie driveway and locked the big SUV, humouring Fletcher because there was no one around to steal it. She turned around, walking back up the lane.

"Mom, where are you going?" She motioned him over.

"Not me. You and I, as in '*we*', are going next door."

"Why?"

"Because you're going to apologize for breaking into that house."

"I never broke in. Her door was unlocked, and I went to check up on her, being the good guy that I am." He didn't see his mother raise her micro-needled eyebrows. "As if it matters, I locked it on the way out," he said, holding up his key. She stopped abruptly and faced him.

"Your, I mean, our key fits her door?"

Fletcher didn't answer, both realizing his stupid mistake. She continued walking, her son lagging three feet behind, hoping at least the dog would come to his rescue.

"Mom, I already apologized." Furious, she stopped and turned around again.

"Then you'll apologize again." She put her hands on her hips. "So, if our key unlocks her door, does it also work in the other bunkie?" Fletcher didn't answer. "I thought so. Now, get over here," she ordered as she stepped onto Sonnet's deck and knocked slightly harder on the door than she meant to.

(At the same time)

"Mom, there's a huge limo truck next door," Digger said, petting Rufus. Reba ran to the living room window to check it out, but needed a better look. They both walked out onto the deck, Reba rubbing her upper arms for warmth.

"Huh. You're right. Black, kind of like a hearse."

"More like the police commissioner's limo on *Blue Bloods*."

"It's not the one that came last night. That one was smaller."

"And a light colour. Different tail lights," he mused.

"I'm going for a little walk to take a picture of the license plate. Coming?"

"No, but be careful, Mom." Reba put her coat on and called the dog to accompany her, Rufus being unaware she needed him as her security detail. Digger changed his mind and decided to follow.

(Seconds later)

Mrs. Hope waited after the first knock on Sonnet's door, banging twice more before seeing the living room curtains move. She crossed the deck and banged her fist against the glass.

Sonnet, petrified, did not respond but texted Reba.

> "There's someone outside, banging on my window."
> "Hang on. I'm already heading your way."

> "Thank God."
> "Just passing what's-his-name's house. Big SUV there. Got a shot of the license plate number."

"Miss O'Brien! It's Fletcher from next door," Fletcher opened the screen door and yelled into the small space between her main door and its frame. Sonnet hurried to the bathroom, suddenly needing to empty her bowels.

The well-dressed couple on Sonnet's deck didn't intimidate Reba as she came closer and called to them. Not used to seeing Fletcher in his dress clothes, she gave him a once-over before recognizing him, still feeling the urge to yell at them.

"Heh!"

Both Hopes looked towards her.

"Tucker!" Fletcher called for the dog, his tail wagging as he ran toward Fletcher. Mrs. Hope, more accustomed to pampered lap dogs, became frightened by Rufus's size and started shrieking, which startled everyone, including the dog, who barked defensively at Mrs. Hope.

"Mom! Stop! He's harmless," Fletcher yelled. Whimpering, the dog poked his nose against the screen door Fletcher held open and hoped, like the others, that Sonnet would let him in.

Reba texted Sonnet again, smelling wealth on the well-assembled woman standing before her.

> "Sonnet, open the door. I'm outside with Fletcher & maybe his mom. It's okay."

"Is this your son?" Reba motioned toward Fletcher just as Sonnet, pyjamas shielded by her winter coat, opened the door a fraction. Rufus forced his way in, relieved to get away from the commotion on the porch. Mrs. Hope got right down to business.

"Are you the lady who wrote the Christmas card?" Mrs. Hope questioned Sonnet, distracted by her purple cast. Sonnet's jaundiced face showed only terror.

"Not just her. There were three of us who wrote it," Reba interjected. "Her, me, and my kid, who's got six inches of height and sixty more pounds of muscle on yours," she boasted, pointing her thumb up at Digger while his hands fidgeted in his pockets.

"Fletcher?" Mrs. Hope glared at her son, waiting for him to apologize.

"What?" Five adults stood frozen until Fletcher processed his mother's message. "Oh, yeah. I'm sorry for opening your doors. I was just looking for Tucker."

"That's bullshit!" Reba responded. "You were snooping around! That's what you were doing. Not sure what you were expecting to find, 'cause we're squeaking by on pennies, while you're farting gold nuggets out your ..." She stopped mid-sentence.

"Well, it's never going to happen again," Mrs. Hope said.

"And how are you so sure? How are you gonna prove that?"

"Because my parents want me back in Georgia with them," Fletcher said.

"Whoo hoo!" Reba squealed. "And when might that happen?"

"Today," Fletcher said, starting down the deck steps and gesturing for his mother to follow.

"Now, just hold on a minute, here," Reba continued. "How are we gonna know the next person moving in isn't going to break in?"

"Now you're being unreasonable," Mrs. Hope said.

"Like Hell we're not, because we already figured out that our keys are all the same," Reba said as she stepped closer to Mrs. Hope. "And… how many years have you owned this place?"

Fletcher answered instead, instantly recalling celebrating his tenth birthday there. "Thirty."

"So, for thirty years, these locks have never been changed?" She held a set of keys up and jingled them. "We'll consider your son's apology, but only if you change the locks. All of them. Otherwise, we have no option but to call the cops."

Mrs. Hope and Fletcher glared at Reba, Mrs. Hope speaking first.

"That's not fair. I didn't know that until now, and we don't even own the two cabins you're living in."

"We don't care." Reba, chin held high in defiance. She moved beside Sonnet to support her emotionally, looping her arm through hers for physical assistance and solidarity.

"But I don't even have money on me."

"Shucks. We all have our rigours and hardships," Reba quoted Montana yet again, then lifted her index finger and pointed it back and forth between the Hopes. "So, here's the deal. You buy the locks, pay Cousin Al to pick them up and install them, and we won't report him," Reba said, pointing an accusatory index finger at Fletcher. The

Hopes looked at each other in disbelief. "And ... that's non-negotiable. I see Cousin Al all the time, so you can bet your fancy pants that I'll be asking him if you paid him fairly. If he's not happy, the police call still stands."

The Hopes shook their heads in disgust.

"That sounds like blackmail," Mrs. Hope complained.

"Blackmail, coercion, persuasion, you can call it whatever you want," Reba taunted, searching her phone for Cousin Al's number. She turned the screen toward Mrs. Hope.

"Here's his number."

"Fletcher, I haven't got my glasses. Can you put this in my phone?" She passed it to him. He took it, tapped in the numbers, and returned it to his mother. Reba lifted her hands in the air.

"Not so fast - I don't trust you. Repeat his number back to me, and it better be right." Fletcher took the phone back and recited it correctly. Reba looked at the time on her screen." It's almost eleven o'clock. Now, you've got exactly twenty-four hours to get those locks and transfer Cousin Al enough money for his labour so that he'll be skipping right over here to make us safe. Got it?" Reba's message couldn't be clearer.

"Yes, we do."

"And make sure our locks have deadbolts," Reba added after a gentle nudge from Sonnet, both women feeling vindicated.

The Hopes were outside and at the bottom of the two-deck steps before Fletcher turned around and looked at Sonnet, her shaky hand resting on Rufus's head.

"I hope you feel better," he said softly. "Bye, Tucker."

Finally, Sonnet sensed some remorse in his voice and, in her heart, forgave him. Rufus didn't and stuck like glue to Sonnet's side.

11:00 AM

Fletcher and his mother ordered three new industrial door locks. With deadbolts. Fletcher stayed inside the bunkie, haphazardly throwing clothes into the empty box that the new generator came in. Mrs. Hope went onto the deck and called Cousin Al, offering to generously compensate him for the time-sensitive favour of improving the safety and security of Polly's Lane. She also asked him to lend a hand, if needed, to the real estate agent for showings. While he paused for a moment to process the potential change of ownership, she upped the ante, adding another hundred dollars for his inconvenience. While he again tried to make sense of her generous compensation, she told him to take whatever tools he wanted from their garage, without thinking to consult with her husband.

She went inside, cleaned out the contents of the kitchen pantry and fridge and left everything in disorganized heaps on Fletcher's deck, while Fletcher filled three more suitcases with useless things, which his mother then forced him to put back with a promise to replace them when they arrived back in Georgia. He snuck into the bathroom, flushed Sonnet's antidepressants down the toilet, and quickly texted the Korean delivery girl, telling her he was going on an extended vacation and would call her soon.

12:30 PM

Digger texted his mother.

> "Mom, can you ask Miss O'Brien if I can have Useless back?"

Reba was still in Sonnet's kitchen when the big black SUV passed her bunkie and roared up the lane.

"Hasta la vista," Reba said to Sonnet, sharing a gentle hug to celebrate Fletcher's departure before texting Digger back.

> "Whistle for him. I'm just letting him out and onto her deck."

"Do you truly believe that he's gone?" Sonnet asked Reba, handing her the second-last meringue as she closed the door after letting the dog out.

"Well, if his key fits our door locks, it should be easy enough to find out."

"I do not want to go anywhere near that property."

> "Mom! Come outside!"

Reba, still in socked feet, ran outside and onto Sonnet's deck.

> "What's wrong, Digger?"

When Digger didn't respond, Reba put her shoes and coat on and ran out to the lane. That's when she spotted

Digger running towards Fletcher's deck. By then, Rufus was helping himself to whatever he determined was easily accessible and consumable. Reba raced to the middle bunkie, arriving about the same time as her son, both working to shoo the dog away from his good fortune.

"Take Useless home, keep him inside, then bring some boxes here. We'll give Miss O'Brien first choice, then keep the rest. What we won't eat, Rufus certainly will."

Digger obeyed, as did the dog, smacking his jowls as he was reluctantly led back to the Adlers'. Digger returned to Fletcher's house and helped his mother fill two boxes and take them to Sonnet, who stood at the door, her housecoat covering her pyjamas.

"Alms for the poor?" was all Sonnet could think of, glancing over the high-priced groceries.

"You take whatever you want, and we'll take whatever you don't," Reba offered.

"We don't sell most of this at the store," Digger added. Sonnet studied the items, then pulled her housecoat tighter.

"Thank you, but there is nothing that I need."

"Surely you'll need some flour and sugar. And the eggs, at least take the eggs," Reba pleaded. Sonnet shook her head each time Reba lifted an offering out of the box. "Here. Take these, and there is no negotiating," Reba argued, handing over a few boxes of imported cookies that she hoped would put a little weight on Sonnet.

"That's more than enough, thank you."

"One more," Reba insisted and placed a box of crackers on the cookies. "Now I hope you get some rest, 'cause you don't look so good today."

"Thank you. I will."

Reba shifted the weight of the box so that it leaned against her abdomen, straightened up, and walked back to the Hope bunkie. Putting the box down, both Reba and Digger peeked through the living room window, where the curtains were parted a few inches.

"Huh. Furniture looks like it came from a mansion," Reba mumbled, imagining herself cuddling up on the leather sofa with Montana.

"I didn't like Fletcher, and I don't like anything of his stuff. Except for the food. Let's go, Mom."

It took the Adlers two trips to bring the rest of Fletcher's discards home, as excited to fill their pantry as Rufus was to eat an extra serving of the gourmet dog food Digger unpacked. Pleased with their accomplishments, they decided to snack all day long and do nothing but watch holiday reruns.

Sonnet put the unopened packages on her kitchen counter and, beyond exhaustion, crawled back into bed.

1:15 PM

Mr. Hope's pilot summoned him after the rest of his passengers had boarded and were choosing which wine to have with lunch. The pilot explained that, by adding Fletcher and all of his extra baggage, Mr. Hope's private aircraft would need to top up the fuel tank when the plane landed at the Newark, New Jersey airport for the one-hour layover Mr. Hope had hastily arranged before flying on to the Atlanta airport. Mr. Hope directed the pilot to arrange for refuelling; he was not concerned about the delay, as he had already booked an urgent meeting with an international business partner.

The plane took off with nary a wobble, soon cruising through clear skies as the Hopes feasted on chicken cordon bleu and imported wines.

2:45 PM

Fifteen minutes before their plane landed in Newark, and while the family finished their wine and coffee, Frederick Hope dropped his bomb.

"Fletcher, when we land in Newark, you and your luggage will be transferred to a different plane."

"What? But why, honey? And what possessed you to schedule a meeting in New Jersey on Boxing Day? This is such an inconvenience." As he often did when Mrs. Hope whined, Frederick ignored his wife, directing his attention back to Fletcher.

"Like I started to say, Fletcher, you will be disembarking here and boarding another plane. The pilot also needs to refuel this plane."

"But why? Should we have packed a little lighter for Fletcher?" Again, Mr. Hope ignored his wife, eyes riveted on his son. Fletcher, by now, sensed by his father's mood that he should pay attention rather than empty the last of the last bottle of wine; Mr. Hope removed it from Fletcher's reach and rested its base on his own thigh, waiting for their attention.

"Finally. Now listen up, because I'm only saying this one more time. Fletcher, you will be getting off when we land." The looks of confusion were evident, except, of course, on Mr. Hope's face. "You messed up your life in Georgia and were deported back to Canada."

"But," Mrs. Hope interrupted.

"Shut. Up." Mr. Hope snarled through clenched teeth. Mrs. Hope, never having heard her husband direct those words to her, did exactly that.

"Fletcher, you fucked up at home, and you fucked up in Canada," Mr. Hope said, alternating livid glares between his wife and son. "And, if you two think I don't know about your trespassing and snooping through the other bunkies on Polly Lane, let alone scaring the hell out of the neighbours, then you're both fools." Mrs. Hope's chin quivered; she had never been called a fool by her husband, especially in front of others. "And how did I know? Because Cousin Al had a question, then fed me answers to questions I didn't even have to ask. So, now, with our president back in office again, you know that you're not coming back to Georgia with your criminal record. And you're certainly not returning to New Abino."

"So where am I going?" Beads of anxious sweat formed across Fletcher's furrowed brows.

"Germany."

"Germany?" gasped Mrs. Hope, her mouth gaping. Fletcher's sister and her friend leaned in to listen better, just as the pilot activated the plane's landing gear.

"Germany?!? Why Germany?" Fletcher asked, bewildered.

"Three good reasons. Actually, four. We have business dealings near Berlin, and we also have that little cottage in the village nearby where you will stay. You'll be out of sight and out of my mind and, finally, if you so much as even think about doing something illegal, the German police will haul your lazy ass off to jail and, it will be weeks before we even find out you're in there."

"But Frederick…" Mrs. Hope pleaded.

"Too late to negotiate," Mr. Hope said, palms raised to create a barrier between himself and his family. "End of our discussion," he said, shaking his head slowly from side to side, as the plane's engines roared out any opportunity for more conversation.

The Hope's small jet touched the runway with the ease of a bird, screeched to a crawl, and then taxied directly to another identical private plane waiting in the wings. The Hope family farewells were hasty, and despite her sobs, Mrs. Hope was secretly relieved when Fletcher and his worldly possessions were transferred from one aircraft to the next, and their son was back in the air before anyone could change their mind.

December 28th

9:00 AM

Sonnet woke up, even sicker than when she went to bed. She vomited whatever bits of food she'd consumed the day before, didn't make it to the bathroom in the middle of the night, and exhausted what little energy she had cleaning up after herself. When her phone, plugged into its charger in the kitchen, rang and rang, she didn't have the stamina to get up and answer it. She lay in bed, reflecting on the milestones of her first fifteen years, including her mother's suicide, and despite not knowing how, her father's desperation to make all things normal for his children. So many unanswered questions and no mother to ask, then raised and nurtured by brothers, who thankfully knew never to touch her despite the urges they felt. Her only lover had unknowingly entered into her life and was rapidly removed, neither of them having the courage to reach out to find the other. She rolled over and fell back asleep, as if she had not even seen the night.

Dr. Torres called Sonnet, not once, but four times in the same number of days, and each time her voicemail was full. Her arm needed another X-ray. She needed bloodwork, and he hoped to persuade her again to agree to an oncology referral, and maybe even a psychiatry referral. He needed to lay eyes on her and would offer to make a house call and tell her that, if she was still interested in medical assistance in dying, he had names of other provision providers to offer. It was the least he could do, but each time he was unable to reach her, he worried even more.

Reba finished her second coffee and most of the *People* magazine Digger bought her for Christmas. Joe had picked up Digger for work long ago, so the rumbling of an engine coming down the lane was unexpected. Dressed in an oversized, stained sweatshirt and leggings tucked into old socks, she listened. It sounded like a truck.

She opened the curtains wide, then stepped outside onto the deck. Yes, it was a truck coming, and it was white, just like Montana's crew drove. She instantly felt lightheaded, coffee churning in her stomach. She ran her fingers repeatedly through her mess of hair and secured it up with the scrunchie she removed from her wrist. The truck circled the dead end, and her heart pounded with happiness as it slowed when it approached her driveway. When she realized it was not his truck, and not Montana, she wanted to sob. The unknown driver waved and drove on, stopping near the other bunkies. Quickly donning her winter coat and sneakers, she headed over to investigate.

The driver left his door ajar, opened the tailgate and pulled something bulky out. Rufus left Sonnet's deck to see what the commotion was about. The driver, needing strange dogs to be his friend, bent over and spoke to Rufus in a calm manner. Not only was he generous in winning the dog over, but this well-prepared man also brought treats.

Reba greeted the driver with cautious curiosity and got her answers without asking. He pounded one 'For Sale' sign in a metal frame into the frozen ground in front of the Hope bunkie and a second one near their shore, facing the lake. Rufus trailed him there and back. Reba frowned, scratching her head when the man returned and posted an identical sign in front of Sonnet's bunkie, and then another one by the lake.

"Huh. That sign shouldn't be over this far," she told him, pointing to a short wooden stake in the ground, the top half painted red. "Look, here's the property line." The man, wearing a lime green reflective vest over his parka, returned to his truck and retrieved a clipboard.

"My work order says that both properties are listed for sale as of today. Same company, same agent." He double-checked his instructions to ensure they matched.

"But nobody told us, and we live here," she protested, speaking on behalf of her and Sonnet.

"Hey, I'm just doing my job. I put these signs up according to the order," he smiled with polite determination, feeding Rufus another treat while Reba snapped a picture of the sign. "If you call the number, the agent can give you more details." He gave Rufus a third treat, quite pleased that yet another dog didn't bite the hand that fed him, hopped back in his truck and then drove away.

Reba doubted that these expensive but tired vacation properties would sell quickly, especially in the middle of winter. The Hope buildings were also better maintained and therefore more marketable than the Reese's; nonetheless, she decided to update Sonnet first.

> "Hi. Look outside your window, then text me. I don't want to come over in case you're still in bed."

1:00 PM

Sonnet woke up and made tea to wash down her dry toast. She felt marginally stronger but stiff from sleeping so long. She read Reba's text, looked at the signs, and then texted her back, asking for a bit of time to make herself presentable. Not feeling well enough to stand in the shower, she bathed carefully and washed her hair. She rummaged through her clothes to find a pair of leggings that would not fall off her, then layered one cable-knit sweater over another.

She heard a vehicle, recognizing the logo and yellow flashing light on the roof of Marty's mail vehicle. He backed into Sonnet's driveway, left his vehicle running and knocked firmly on her door. When she opened it, Marty's face dropped.

"Oh! Miss O'Brien," was all he could muster.

"I know. I've been sick." She raised her hands and attempted to fluff up her wet hair.

"No wonder I haven't seen you when I visit my mom at the hospital. Speaking of which, I've got your mail. This one needs a signature," he added, handing her an envelope that she recognized came from her employer. She signed for it before he passed her a small box.

"Thank you," she said and closed the door before he could wish her well or ask any questions. She sat down at the table, checked the time and poured some weak tea.

She opened the first package, which, as before, was a registered letter and forms from the hospital advising her she needed to provide updated medical information to continue receiving sick benefits. She looked at the questions on the forms, one for her and one for Dr. Torres to complete. She had no intention of answering her questions or burdening him with more paperwork. She looked at the date on which the forms needed to be returned. What difference would this make now, she questioned herself, throwing the forms in the garbage, just as Reba knocked on her door, accompanied by Rufus. She let them in and balanced against the counter as she filled the dog's bowls.

"Oh, you got it!" Reba said, picking up the small box from the table and holding it up to her. It was then that she noticed the change in her neighbour. "Wow, no disrespect, but you look like … you look terrible – like yellowy. Did you even sleep last night?" Sonnet thought before she answered.

"Not much," was all she was willing to offer as Reba passed her the box.

"Open it."

And Sonnet did. Not surprising to Reba, it was an ancestry DNA kit. Sonnet set it down on the table and slid it back to Reba.

"Thank you, but no thank you."

"But this is a present for you, for driving us to work. And, so that you can find your Mary – if she hasn't already tried to find you. See, you just take this …"

"I said, no thank you." Sonnet stood up, leaning heavily against the table as she did.

"Don't you want to find out where she is? And maybe even her father?" Mentioning Francis upset Sonnet even more.

"No. No. No."

"Okay then. I guess that's a no."

"Now what about the sign?"

"I know it's not in front of my house, but I was wondering if you knew this place was going up for sale."

"I didn't."

"I'm planning on calling and asking the real estate agent, but thought if you had some questions, I could ask them all at once." Sonnet could barely think straight, wanting nothing more than for Reba to leave.

"Maybe you can ask about the closing date." She hoped this would send Reba out the door sooner.

"Good idea. I'll ask about both places," Reba said, sensing by Sonnet's wilting appearance that she should go. "You look like you could use another nap. Why don't I come back tomorrow?"

"Maybe in two or three days? I'm feeling terrible, and I don't want you to catch what I have."

"Good thinking. But do you want me to make you some chicken soup? I can drop it off after Digger gets home."

"No, thank you. I had some toast, so maybe that will help."

"Okay, then." Reba stood up and headed for the door. When Sonnet moved closer to her, Reba inhaled as deeply as she could, then exhaled. "Hope you feel better, my friend, and make sure you call if you need anything."

"I will. Fair warning, I'm silencing my phone so I can sleep," she added.

"Good idea, too. But I'll text you tomorrow to see how you're feeling."

"Maybe wait a day?"

Reba nodded, closed the door and heard the click of Sonnet's lock behind her, glad that at least the dog would keep her company. She remembered her grandfather's skin gradually turning yellow from too many years of drinking, but Sonnet only smelled like booze once, when she was found unresponsive. Not any other day, including the good whiff Reba took of her rancid breath today.

5:00 PM

The real estate agent returned Reba's voicemail. Once he discredited her as a prospective buyer, he confirmed in an encouraging voice that both properties had negotiable closing dates, and the rental agreements would continue until the owners decided otherwise.

Reba could barely contain her excitement when she texted Montana.

> "Hey there. Finished work yet?"
> "Just dropped the crew off. Still in my truck."
> "Any updates about when you're coming back?"
> "Still about a month away, and when we get access to the trailer."
> "Lots of work back home?"

"Yup, but should finish up in a few weeks."

"Big job?"

"Yup. A high, hot and heavy one."

"I like that. And then?"

"We take a break, then head back to the author's place near you."

"Nice. FYI, the jerk next door moved out."

"Really?"

"Yup. It's vacant, furnished & up for rent!"

"How many bedrooms?"

"Two."

"Where would I sleep?"

"That's negotiable."

"I like that."

"I miss you."

"Me too."

"Wanna come check it out?"

"If it's next to yours, it's perfect."

"Sure hope so."

"Boss might send me up early. And…"

"And what?"

"The author is building a cabin for a property manager."

"Nice."

"What if I took the property and maintenance job?"

"Are you teasing me?"

"Nope."

"Maybe I could be your maintenance guy, too."

"Don't mess with me."

"I'm not. But we could mess around again when I come back?"
"Really?"
"Only if you can wait."
"I can wait."
"Not much choice."
"I'll wait. As long as it takes."
"Miss you."
"Miss you too. So does Digger."
"Me too. Say hi."
"Will do."
"Gotta go. Keep smiling."

The last text from Montana was a pink emoji heart. Reba sent two back. She also texted Montana the Hope and Reese families' real estate agent details. And, he might even consider offering to do some electrical upgrades for a reduction in his rent. She hung up, wondered if she overstepped her boundaries, and then dismissed it. Any pitch to have Montana closer was worth it. She heard a vehicle approaching, came to the door and watched Joe drop Digger off, waved him goodbye, then brought Digger in to tell him the hopeful news.

8:00 PM

Sonnet didn't eat lunch, and she didn't eat dinner. There was no point. She sat on the sofa to rest some more; the only sounds were from her labouring lungs and Rufus's gentle snore beside her.

Carrying forward her thoughts from the night before, she thought about her life's work, first as a nun, and then as a nurse. She thought about the love she received from Francis and the mistake she made with her marriage to Stan. On the cancer floor, she had many gentle conversations with her patients, and those who loved them, about the stages of grief in dying: denial, anger, bargaining, depression and finally acceptance. She acknowledged to herself that she had moved through each of them, alone, having accepted that fate long ago.

She had initially considered taking a drive to the lighthouse, but changed her mind, fearful that she wouldn't have enough strength to carry out her plan. Instead, she filled Rufus's dishes again and set them outside on the deck. She kissed the soft fur on his forehead and let him go. He watched her with sad eyes as she closed the door. *He knows,* she thought. *He knows.* She changed into her newest flannel nightgown and took some sips of tea to moisten her throat. She slid twenty-three antidepressants into her hand and swallowed them all with the rest of her tea.

Picking a pen from the kitchen table, she wrote two sentences on a blank piece of paper. The first was the name of one of her brothers and his phone number, hoping it was still current. On the second line, she printed Gracie Sheehan's name and phone number and asked that she be contacted.

Sonnet went to her bedroom and set the note beside her bed. She tucked herself under her blankets, reached into her drawer and pulled out her Bible. She ran her fingers across the navy cover, worn with age and use, like her. She opened it and placed her hand over Francis' name. It felt warm and secure, as if his hand was enveloping hers, but much lighter now. Just like her soul.

Slowly and quietly, she began to whisper her favourite poem, aptly named *Sonnet 43*, and written long, long ago by Elizabeth Barrett Browning:

> *How do I love thee? Let me count the ways.*
> *I love thee to the depth and breadth and height*
> *My soul can reach, when feeling out of sight*
> *For the ends of being and ideal grace.*
> *I love thee to the level of every day's*
> *Most quiet need, by sun and candlelight.*
> *I love thee freely, as men strive for right.*
> *I love thee purely, as they turn from praise.*
> *I love thee with the passion put to use*
> *In my old griefs, and in my childhood's faith.*
> *I love thee with a love I seemed to lose*
> *With my lost saints. I love thee with the breath,*
> *Smiles, tears, of all my life, and if God choose,*
> *I shall but love thee better after death.*

Sonnet O'Brien kept whispering the poem, softly to Francis and then herself, over and over again, until finally, her heart grew still forever.

10:00 PM

Reba approached her son, sitting in his favourite chair. She kissed his forehead, then scratched behind Rufus's ears, snoring contentedly beside Digger. She headed for bed, mentally checking that she had all the ingredients to make some soup and bring it to Sonnet in the morning. Reba would then tell her about their potential new neighbour, temporary to begin with, but who knows what their future would bring? Her phone pinged on her bedside table, just after she turned out the lights; the words were brightly illuminated on her screen.

> "Just spoke with my boss. Is that place next door to you still available?"
> "Yes!"
> "Want a new neighbour?"
> "Yes!"
> "And company to ring in the New Year?"
> "Yes!"

Reba tucked herself under her blankets, feeling warm and secure, imagining Montana's crooked fingers looping through hers.

~ The End ~

NOTES

Worry monks still exist. These miniature wooden sculptures, each created with unique characteristics, were inspired by stone carvings in Ireland. The intent of rotating them round and round in one's hand was to soothe the worrier, following the historical tradition of worry stones, worry beads and worry dolls. Today, these have been replaced by more sophisticated sensory tools such as fidget spinners, rings, and other options, including medication.

In 2024, I retired from nursing for the third time, after a long and storied journey. As mentioned in the beginning, this novel is dedicated to the incredible healthcare providers who understood the intrinsic and extrinsic needs of their patients and gave until there was nothing left. Recent (2025) registration data for the province of Ontario, Canada, showed that for every ten nurses who enter the workforce, six leave. The alarming rates of workplace stress and injury, witnessing patient suffering and death, trigger PTSD in twenty-three percent of health care professionals. This is not caused by a character flaw or a weak personality, but repeated traumatic exposures. In Montana's words, most of us survive the 'rigours and hardships' that infiltrate our profession. Sadly, some don't.

If you work or have worked in health care, I thank you. Many people thank you. If you, or someone you care about, is struggling, the Canadian Mental Health

Association is one of many non-urgent and crisis resources available – please check what is offered near you.

Instead of stigmatizing mental illness, we should acknowledge it and the courage it takes to get help.

Acknowledgments

There are many more people to thank, some of whom I may have inadvertently missed. Thank you to all the 'Rebas' of the world, parents of adult children with special qualities and abilities. You taught me to appreciate that life can be all well and good, despite our differences.

Thank you, Bernie Coyne, for breaking your wrists when I was imagining an event to hospitalize Sonnet. Although very inconvenient for you, they happened at perfect intervals of my writing and revising this novel. I'm so happy you fully recovered and still make the best jam.

My sincerest thanks to Michael Glueckert, who happened to be in the wrong place at the right time when I was developing the character Montana. When I saw you hopping back and forth over that private stone fence in Coco, I thought you were an inconvenience until a few days later, when you became a gold mine of inspiration.

Thank you to the Canadian Authors Association (Niagara Branch) novel writers' group, especially James Bryan Simpson, for your very insightful critiques and for pointing out the trees, especially when I couldn't see the forest. Big hugs to Bernie, Laurie, Janice, Barbara, Lydia and Cathy's book club for the same.

Thank you to the real Rufus who lives in Costa Rica, and the dogs in our neighbourhood who I meet, dog-mother and love in return for slobbery hugs and longing looks of affection.

Lee and Mélanie, Alexa and Max, and of course, Craig, you make my life whole. Thank you for being the wonderful people that you are. It is a gift to be able to love, laugh and write.

And finally, John, thank you for, among many other things, building the most beautiful, peaceful retreat for me to write, and vacuuming only when I'm not there. You are the best. All the time.

About the Author

Yvonne's love of words began in childhood. As a nurse, her writing skills earned her acclaim in many clinical settings and professional publications; however, she never lost her desire to write literary fiction. She has authored three contemporary fiction novels about human adversity and is writing her fourth, about four mothers and the people attached to them, whether they like each other or not.

Yvonne is a past member of the Canadian Authors Association and a four-time reviewer for the Whistler Independent Book Awards. She facilitates programs for aspiring writers, including a writers' group at her local library, and is lucky enough to interview best-selling authors for the Lincoln Pelham Public Library's *Books on the Bench* events. In 2024, she was honoured with the Lincoln Pelham Public Library's Volunteer Peer Award.

She attended McMaster and Brock University, as well as Mohawk and Niagara College.

Yvonne lives in Pelham with her husband John and would love to hear from you via her email address: yvonneloveslibraries@gmail.com.